Wanted:

One Ghost

Believe In Fate!

Loni Lynne

Loni Lynne

www.crescentmoonpress.com

Wanted: One Ghost
Loni Lynne

ISBN: 978-1-939173-35-5
E-ISBN: 978-1-939173-36-2

Cover Art: Taria Reed
Editor: Judy Roth
Layout/Typesetting: jimandzetta.com

Crescent Moon Press
1385 Highway 35
Box 269
Middletown, NJ 07748

Crescent Moon Press electronic publication/print publication: June 2013 www.crescentmoonpress.com

To my family, thank you for your love and support. To all my friends, thanks for listening and sharing in my excitement.

To fate, I'm still holding on tight.

Chapter One

"This is where James Addison's execution took place," the college student explained with a hint of boredom, despite the gruesome account. With a practiced flourish of his colonial cape, he turned and pointed at the huge elm tree in the center of Kings Mill, Maryland's city park. "Rumor has it he was drawn and quartered in public as a traitor to the Crown. The colonial rebellion was on the rise, and King George III was serious about punishing those caught for treason."

Yawning in boredom, James leaned against a gaslight post. He wasn't worried anyone would witness such a breach of etiquette. He was a ghost after all. The dialogue sounded practiced and boring as it had every Friday and Saturday since the season began. This was Tony's second year now giving the tour. From September until the end of November, he'd repeated the same quotes every weekend night, just a bit of information and then he would move on to the next 'haunted spot' of Kings Mill.

Dressed in colonial period costume and carrying a tin lantern, Tony tried to look authentic and make the story eerily dramatic for his guests, but to James the tour was plain tedious. Why, he could give the presentation himself, if he weren't a ghost. He chuckled to himself.

"Excuse me," someone from the group piped up, stopping the flow of the tour. "What had James Addison done to be accused of treason? Was he one of the Sons of Liberty as some of the books claim? As the son of a British earl, I can't imagine him part of such a group."

Curious about the identity of the person who knew so much about him, James pushed off the lamppost and strolled toward the group. The people suddenly parted revealing a tiny figure in leggings and woolens. A tilt of the waif's head

~ ☾ ~

let slip a long, feminine braid of reddish-brown hair.

What had I done to be accused of treason? He'd suffered
the same question for over two hundred and thirty years, but
until now, he'd never heard anyone ask it aloud. At least not
that he knew of. Those damn Sons of Liberty had made life
difficult for many loyal to the crown.

They had been the cause of the skirmishes during his last
few years of life in the colonies. Why, he remembered Boston
having lost a shipment of tea and then another similar
catastrophe happened aboard the *Peggy Stewart* in
Annapolis Harbor. Those rascals had deliberately tossed
crates of his precious English tea overboard in the name of
liberty.

He'd begun to hoard each shipment, in case there was a
run on it. But it wasn't just the tea. The colonists were
refusing to uphold the tax England had put on the stamps to
authenticate documentation. He'd heard some of the stamp
officers had been run out of town or tarred and feathered just
for doing their jobs. It was downright scandalous!

James leaned casually against the hanging elm tree, tilted
his tricorne down over his eyes, and settled in to hear what
the tour guide had to say for himself.

The lad stopped, and for the first time this season,
deviated from his normal, routine script. James could tell he
was a little unprepared as he struggled to answer.

"Why was James Addison chosen for execution? A good
question." He cleared his throat nervously, swinging the
lantern lightly at his side. "I think it's because Henry Samuel,
the county land commissioner, demanded Addison's
execution. He'd had an affair with Henry Samuel's wife. "

So *that* was why he was murdered? Henry thought he'd
had an affair with Catherine? Did the man ever confront him,
ask him face to face, and call him out? No—not once! *Rot and
nonsense!* Disgusted, he turned to walk away.

The woman burst forth again. "Was he given a trial?"

James stopped in his tracks, circled around the tree to get
a closer peek at the young woman. No one had ever asked
whether he'd been given a trail before. Was this woman
curious about his innocence? He'd hoped, over the years,

~ ☾ ~

someone would give him the answer to why he hadn't been afforded a trial two hundred and thirty-eight years ago. No one had cared to ask. Until now.

The boy shrugged. "There wasn't any record of a trial. Maybe Henry Samuel wanted to get rid of his wife's lover and receive accolades from England. It would make him look good in the king's eyes if he'd found a rebel-traitor and executed him." James rolled his eyes and jammed his hands into his pockets. What rubbish!

The young lad waited only a brief amount of time before rounding up his group and herding them off to the next ghost house.

Shuffling along, James managed to kick up a few stones in disgust. Well at least he'd learned something tonight even though it didn't help much. Not a damn thing he could do about it in this ethereal form of hell.

James watched sadly as the group drifted further down the street, on to the next haunted spot, the Old Town Tavern. Supposedly it was haunted by Millie Taylor who'd been accidentally killed in a brawl. Damn shame, too. She'd been a lusty wench! He fondly remembered a few stolen moments nestled against her ample breasts. And then there was the night he'd bedded her and the other tavern maid to solve a dispute between the two women. It was just one of the stories that now labeled him for his sexual pursuits.

He'd always been considered a lady's man and enjoyed the attention it aroused, but hearing about his past and being remembered for nothing but his dalliances had become a bit tiring. Now, he was known as the town character, a joke, a folly. No one seemed to care about his true part in making Kings Mill what it had been.

He was so tired of it all. There had to be some reason he was still here beyond the jokes and his infamous dalliances. The monotony of whatever existence he was in had worn him down. After two-hundred and thirty-eight years, his spirit remained bound to the last place he'd breathed life on earth, unable to move on to the afterlife. He wasn't sure why he was still here. Maybe he was waiting for someone to care enough and find out the truth behind his death. Listening to the ghost

~ ☾ ~

tours over the years, he wondered if maybe his lack of knowledge about his execution might be the key to what was holding him here. All he knew was Henry Samuel had given the order for his execution. Did he need to find out why before the powers-that-be let him move on? *Damn you, Henry!* Ranting loudly at the man, he raised his fist to the heavens, though if he really thought about it, the man would be in a much hotter place.

James stopped in his tracks and turned around, sensing he wasn't alone. One guest remained behind. The young woman dressed in the leggings and woolens, her small, flat hat cocked jauntily over her eyes stood there, smiling at him.

Was she really smiling at him or just in his general direction? The empty spot where his heart should have been, leaped. Could she see him or was she looking at something behind him?

No. Impossible! No one could see him. After all these years of yearning for someone to hear him, he was fooling himself, no doubt.

When she moved on to the tree and looked up into the branches, her braid flopped over her shoulder. He wanted to tug on the glorious rope.

She was rather pretty, a pert nose, high, rounded cheeks. When she closed her eyes, long lashes feathered against those rosy cheeks. Her long braid swished from left to right against her shoulder blades as she tilted her head and breathed in the late October air. That same magical smile surfaced again, and she went from pretty to beautiful.

Opening her eyes, she examined the damn tree.

"Did you ever wonder what trees would tell us if they could talk?" She glanced towards him again. "Do you think James Addison was really hanged from these branches?" A hint of melancholy tinged her voice like such an event saddened her.

James looked to the right of him, to the left. No one was there. Who was she talking to, the blasted tree? The wind picked up and tugged a strand of her hair loose from under her cap.

She rooted around in the satchel she carried and dug out a small box shaped instrument he'd seen so many people use

~ ☾ ~

over the years. He'd always wondered what they were for. As he watched curiously, she took aim, pushed down on the button and a flash went off. The tilt of her face as she looked up at the branches exposed the angle of her jaw and gave him a sudden urge to kiss her along the tender line right below her ear. The woman closed her eyes again, breathing in the night once more. Her gloved hand caressed the raspy bark of the tree.

"I wonder why he was never given a trial. Wasn't the Treason Act of 1695 enacted at the time? James Addison should have been provided a counsel and jury for his crimes." She turned towards him again. "Was he really executed for treason?"

"*Was he really executed for treason?*" James said, mimicking her feminine voice with his own British brogue, as he walked toward the odd girl, wanting to shout in her face at the idiocy of her questioning the bloody tree. Didn't she know how foolish she looked? "No, he wasn't executed for treason. He was beaten to a bloody pulp and murdered!"

With eyes gone wide, the girl stared up at him, her fixed attention giving him a moment's pause. And so it should. Nobody had noticed him, much less held him in thrall for over two centuries.

"Murdered?" she asked back. "Are you sure?"

James stiffened. Dear God in heaven! Was she actually talking to him? He looked behind him to see if she might be addressing someone else. No one was there. Gathering his wits, he studied her closely. Could this girl hear him, see him?

"Yes," he said curtly, a bit stunned. He waited with baited breath for her reply.

Her gaze never left him. "Yes, you're sure he was murdered?" she questioned him intently. "Where did you obtain your information?"

James paced from side to side and did a little jig, to see if she could follow his movements. She did. She even laughed at his dance and gave him an odd look. Bloody Hell! She could see and hear him! She was smiling and didn't seem frightened in the least.

"So what do you think really happened to James Addison?"

~ ☾ ~

With one boot crossed over the other, the young woman leaned saucily against the tree as if settling in for a story. Openly admiring her slender limbs encased in leggings beneath the hem of her woolen coat, James lost his train of thought.

She, on the other hand, didn't appear shocked at his appearance. But then he supposed he resembled the tour guide, dressed in colonial garb, his tricorne hat and manor coat nothing out of the ordinary.

Wanting to be able to talk with someone again, he moved cautiously towards her. He would do well to remember to play along as a ghost-guide and not give himself away.

"To answer your earlier question, there wasn't any trial. He was hung, pure and simple. Neither judge nor jury ever convicted him.

"Addison was kidnapped on his way home from the local tavern, tied and trussed up like a Michaelmas goose. He woke up with a knot on his noggin' and shackled in the gaol. No one came to speak on his behalf. The next day he was brought, hooded and bound, before the people at this very tree to be made an 'example of for treason,'" he relayed with a hint of disgust. Let her take his anger for what it was. He didn't care. He was finally able to tell someone his side of the story—as he'd lived it.

He looked up at the tree and his body shuddered, remembering the night of his death. His fists clenched to his sides at the thought of the injustice. There had been no one to voice his side of the story to. No one to listen. *She* was listening now, though. *She* could hear him!

And listen she did. Her eyes never left him, her interest fixed on what he said.

A sense of awareness surrounded him for the first time in so long. She gave him a sense of hope. If she could see him and hear him, could she help him find out the truth about his death so he could move on?

"Do you believe my story?" he asked.

She shrugged and tugged the tiny brim of her hat. "Not necessarily. Why should your tale be any more truthful than your co-worker's? Besides, ghost tours are supposed to be for

~ ☾ ~

fun, not fact. You're meant to scare and intrigue with tales of paranormal activities mixed with local lore and a touch of history to make it seem real."

James tried hard not to laugh. "So you don't believe in spirits?" If she only knew, would she be so comfortable standing there talking with him?

"I'm not discounting the possibility of ghosts or even your story. Anything is possible, I suppose."

Even in the darkness with the false gaslights and partial moon shining down on them, her eyes twinkled like the stars he enjoyed gazing upon at night. With such a genuine and infectious smile, he couldn't help but return her grin.

He nodded toward the group who had made their way up the street to the next location of ghostly activity. "You're missing the rest of the tour over at the Old Town Tavern and a fascinating tale about Millie the Tavern maid."

"Ah, yes, one of James Addison's regular 'lady friends.' I've read about his escapades with some of the women of colonial Kings Mill." She bit her lip. An innocent smile teased her charming face. "Let's see, if I remember correctly, it had to do with a rather public dispute between Millie and another tavern maid as to whom James Addison preferred in his bed. To settle the cat-fight, James Addison drunkenly proposed a ménage a trio to appease them."

Sheepishly, James rocked back and forth on his heels. "Yes, that is the tale."

She looked him over with interest. "One of only a few hundred bawdy stories on the local legend I'm afraid. There really isn't much factual information to be found on James Addison. I'm surprised you know as much as you do." She crossed her arms over her chest, wrenching the coat around her. "Where did you find your knowledge about his past? I've never heard the theory of him being murdered or the details you provided about his death."

James studied her, trying to find out how to proceed without causing her distress or her asking more questions than he was comfortable answering. If she didn't know he was a ghost, he would have to tread lightly not to scare her off.

~ ☾ ~

"A bit of personal research." He shrugged. "I'm quite fond of the man." He accompanied his statement with a lopsided grin.

She nodded. "History has made him out to be a very colorful character. He was an astute businessman, founding father, and lady's man."

He couldn't help but preen and wondered what she would do if she knew she was talking with *the* James Addison.

"What do *you* find so fascinating about him?" he asked.

She looked around, taking in her surroundings. "The mystery behind him, I suppose. There are no real facts about the man. Only history and mystery," she rhymed teasingly. "Two of the reasons I offer myself to research historical data, to dig up the past, so to speak. I want to right the wrongs of the history books, or at least provide as much truth to them as possible."

"How do you know so much about a time you've never lived?" he asked.

"I studied early American History under Dr. Robert Moreland at the College of William and Mary, one of the foremost colleges specializing in American History," she explained proudly as she extended her gloved hand. "I'm Dr. April Branford."

A doctor? She didn't look like any doctor he'd ever met. He looked warily down at her hand. He couldn't take hold of it. His hand would shimmer right through hers. He was in no hurry to send the poor girl screaming into the night upon her discovery.

Seeming a bit embarrassed, she slowly lowered her arm, but hid it by focusing her interest on the old courthouse building and aiming the thin, square box at the old structure. James blinked as the quick flash of light illuminated the night.

"I've been hired by Kenneth Miles to research as much as I can on James Addison and the Kings Mill gristmill business he started. It's more of a temporary job while I'm waiting to hear about a few teaching positions I applied to for the spring semester." She stopped talking, turned back to him, giving him a perplexed stare. "You know, Kenneth Miles, the British

~ ☾ ~

billionaire?" She sighed when he still didn't comment.

He had no idea who she was speaking of, and realized a bit too late, maybe he should. "Oh, yes Kenneth Miles...really?" he said, feigning interest.

"He recently discovered he's a distant relative of James Addison and has a fascination for the man, too. He's looking into proving James Addison owned the land and gristmill in which Kings Mill is named for."

James frowned. "What's to prove? Everyone knows he was the proprietor."

"That's one belief. There are those who say Henry Samuel owned it. But no one has been able to find documentation to prove it one way or the other." Dr. Branford shrugged. "Mr. Miles hired me to unearth historical documentation proving Addison owned it."

Of course he owned the mill and the land! He bought the land for 500 British pounds and signed the deed with Henry Samuel, the louse. How the fop had managed to become the land commissioner for the western Maryland colony he had no idea. Even Lord Calvert thought the man was a bit of a horse's arse.

But this was a turn of events for him. Here was someone with an actual curiosity about his past. Would she be able to help him find out the truth about his death? James's hopes lifted, and then dropped as quickly. *Good luck.* The mystery of his death was still unsolved. Someone would have surely pieced it together by now if there were any clues to be found.

Dr. April Branford eyed him with a shy grin, biting her lower lip, an innocent yet provocative gesture. How long had she been staring at him? He wasn't sure, lost as he'd been in his thoughts. But he was intrigued. Nice to know he could still hold the interest of the fairer sex.

Hell's bells. Unused to having an actual person he could talk to, he'd drifted off. If he wanted answers, he would need to remain focused on her.

"Is something the matter?" he asked.

"We seem to have a common interest in James Addison and Kings Mill's history. I was wondering if you could show me around. Give me a private tour? You have a much better

~ ☾ ~

flair for telling a tale than your co-worker. Perhaps give me your opinions on James Addison, who you think he really was, over a cup of coffee?"

She was a bold minx, asking a man to accompany her, and without a chaperone!

Was the girl being coy with him? Her lashes lowered and she turned her face away momentarily. When she looked back she was grinning shyly, her teeth planted in her luscious bottom lip again.

By George! She was flirting with him! He could almost feel his non-existent heart beating in his hollow chest. He wouldn't be able to touch her but the company of the comely lass, after all this time, was definitely something he didn't want to pass up.

"I would be delighted, Dr. Branford." He doffed his hat and bowed low over his extended leg in true gentlemanly fashion. This could be the start to something wonderful!

Or perhaps you'll end up scaring the bloody hell out of the poor girl.

~ ☾ ~

Chapter Two

April couldn't believe her good fortune as she walked beside her tour guide. He provided a highly detailed account of the small Maryland town of Kings Mill, formerly known as Kings Land, before the arrival of James Addison and his productive gristmill. The mill had produced a great deal of grain and flour for the colonies and England.

He talked briefly of various punitive acts by King George III and, looking properly offended, discussed the radical Sons of Liberty who seemed to pop up everywhere in the colonies. With his yummy British accent, he played the part of a pre-Revolutionary War colonist to the hilt. Honestly, the man was wasted as a tour guide. He should be treading the boards as a Thespian.

The fact he was easy on the eyes didn't hurt either. His angular jaw with a light touch of shadowed scruff gave him a ruggedly handsome appeal. His black hair was tied back in a colonial style queue. A feminine urge to untie it and run her fingers through its length hit her with amazing force.

While she fought to focus on his words and not the man himself, she soaked up the atmosphere surrounding them, inhaling the essence of the bygone era in the small reminders around her. Replicas of old gaslights illuminating the brick paved sidewalks, Georgian-style townhomes with carriage lights hanging at their door, and single artificial candles placed in multi-paned windows hinted at the cozy warmth of what America had been in its youth. Still, something toyed with her ability to sense the historical aura of the colonial town. What could it be?

Her guide stopped in front of the house where she was staying. The brick colonial home, established in 1760, sat majestically on the street facing the backside of the

~ ☾ ~

courthouse. A plaque by the front door named the manor a
Maryland Historical Site.

Renovated many times over the years, the house still
maintained the original décor. April loved the red brick
exterior walls with the haze of white wash owners had applied
over time. The black shutters, contrasting against the colonial
paned windows, highlighted the glow of the candlelight. Even
though it was nearly November, wooden rocking chairs and a
small wicker table still resided on the front porch, hinting at
summertime when folks sat on their porches and observed
their neighbors parading by.

"This house belonged to Henry Samuel, the first land
commissioner to Kings Land," her guide indicated with a
condescending snort.

"I know. This is my aunt's house. Actually, she's my great-
aunt...on my mother's side. I'm staying here while I'm
working on my research," she rambled.

His brows arched and he tilted his head, looking her over,
making her feel the intensity of his eyes from under the
shadowed light of his tricorne. He appeared a bit perturbed.

"Interesting. Are you a distant relation to Henry Samuel?"

"No relation. After my uncle passed away six years ago, my
aunt bought the house. She wanted to get away to the country
after living in Baltimore most of her life.

"I see." He stared attentively at her, studying her again
with those deep, dark eyes.

Heat scorched along her neck and up to her cheeks under
his intent scrutiny. She was a historian for God's sake, not
some tourist with a crush on a historical re-enactor. Perhaps
her hormones were finally kicking in. God knows they hadn't
while she'd been focused on her studies!

Whatever her sudden condition, every time she looked
into this man's eyes she lost her place in the conversation and
began to perspire. She shivered, averting her glance from his
intensity, and turned her attention on anything but her
handsome guide.

Perhaps it was her natural gift of psychometry kicking in. It
had a tendency to appear when she was in places of historical
importance. Her volunteer dig at Jamestown two summers ago

~ ☾ ~

nearly hospitalized her with the intensity. She suffered fevers, hallucinations, even allergy like symptoms, probably because of all the dirt and dust surrounding the artifacts and digging sites.

She'd always known she was different, but it wasn't until her professor, Dr. Moreland had noticed her gift that she learned to harness her ability and use it in her historical research. He had the ability, too. But it wasn't as prominent as hers. At times, she had no control. Touching objects alone brought forth empathic images and emotions of previous owners, making her feel like she was a part of them.

Her Aunt Vickie said it was a strong part of her natural aura. It would hit her and she would find herself sensing pieces of time from the past, represented in the object of a certain time period. Going into museums was a nightmare. Any artifacts not under glass would set off her senses to their history, and she'd lose herself in another time. Her ability made for great details on historical papers and theses but gave her such a pinch physically.

Kings Mill dated back to 1740, a time prior to the American Revolution. Many of these houses and streets, the very air of the town, maintained the atoms and molecules making up its history. The lingering energy of the past surrounded her, attaching to her skin, so she'd soaked the essence of every sensory object she experienced. Scents, sights, but mostly touch affected her power. Possessing the gift of psychometry made her impulsive sometimes. Like now, she wanted to reach out and touch the man's costume because of its authenticity.

Oh hell, April, who are you kidding? You want to touch the man. She shoved her hands deeper into her coat pockets to keep her itchy fingers at bay.

Her guide had stopped talking and was staring at her. Chagrined, she realized once again, she had no clue what he'd said. She shook herself, releasing the empathic connection with him.

"Are you well? My apologies for rambling on. I don't often have the opportunity to converse, or have a captive audience. You must think me a bore. You came for a ghost tour and here I am giving you a lecture."

~ ☾ ~

"Oh, please." She batted her hand in the air. "I'm a historian, remember? Lectures and tours of historical pasts is what I live and breathe." April laughed self-consciously.

He was the first guy in quite a while to impress her with knowledge, not just his looks. "I find it refreshing to hear someone as excited about history as I am. My ex-boyfriend, Jason, was the only one who understood my love of history. One of the things we shared an interest in was a love for the past. We were both history geeks." She stiffened with embarrassment after relaying such information to a complete stranger.

He doesn't care about your love life or lack thereof, she berated herself.

But he belied her observation when her colonial guide grinned at her with amused fascination. "Really...history *geeks*?"

Noticing the familiar sign down the street on the main corner of town, she tilted her head in the direction of the café. Hopefully she could make up for her blundering, social-idiot appearance.

"The coffee shop is still open. Would you care for the cup I promised earlier? We can continue our conversation inside, with a latte or cappuccino."

An awkward moment of silence followed. The bells in the Episcopal Church toned quarter to the hour. Her guide went completely still and stared at her with those intense eyes. His lips quirked in an odd half smile again, setting her heart to race. He looked towards the church further down the street.

"I appreciate the offer, but I will have to decline. I cannot stay much longer."

"Oh. I'm sorry. I didn't mean to take up your time. I'm sure you have to report back to the store before heading home."

She held out her gloved hand again. He didn't respond and only looked down on her hand with a sense of sadness. What was wrong with this guy? Why didn't he want to touch her? She didn't have the mange.

Tucking both hands back into her coat pockets, April blushed.

~ ☾ ~

"You didn't take up my time, Dr. Branford. I'm delighted to talk with you but I must take my leave. Perhaps we'll meet another time." He touched the brim of his hat in salute and turned, walking away from her.

April wanted to capture his entire look—for historical purposes, of course. "Wait! Can I take a picture of you? I love your authenticity. Not many people can pull it off so well."

He turned around as he crossed to the other side of the street. "A...picture?"

"Yes." She looked around trying to find the perfect setting for him. She caught his shrug of indifference. "Stand over by the lamp post. Do you mind?" She crossed the cobbled road to get a better angle as her subject stood in front of the light she'd pointed to. She quickly shot the picture and looked up at him.

He touched the side of his hat again in salute and sauntered away, his manor coat billowing behind him like a great raven's wing. Damn, but he was a fine looking man!

It's the costume. He's an ordinary guy, April. You've always been attracted to history—he reeks of history, right down to his colonial style, buckled shoes.

Shaking her head she turned off the power to her camera. Dropping it into her hobo bag, she sighed heavily. Darn, she hadn't even gotten his name!

***

"So, did you have a good time?" Victoria Snyder asked when April walked in from the grand foyer.

"Hello, Aunt Vickie. I didn't expect to see you awake." April hung her purse, coat, hat, and scarf on the coat tree and joined her aunt in the parlor.

"Just doing a Sudoku puzzle and having a cup of tea before Leno." The woman placed her puzzle book on the small Victorian side table next to her chair. "So, tell me everything!"

A warm fire blazed in the antique hearth, and small bowls of pumpkin spiced potpourri filled the air with delicious fragrance, lending an air of coziness to the parlor. She loved visiting her aunt. Vickie had a way of adding just the right touch to any atmosphere. Unfortunately, April hadn't been able to visit her since she'd moved to Kings Mill because of

~ ☾ ~

her studies and life in Williamsburg. She had missed the long talks with the woman.

But now she was a bit apprehensive. She could almost sense what Aunt Vickie wanted to converse about—and it wasn't as simple as a 'ghost tour.'

April shrugged. "It was a ghost tour." She would keep the conversation light and simple.

Vickie nodded her head toward the kitchen. "There's still some hot water for tea on the stove. Get yourself a cup. I want to hear all about it."

April made herself a cup of tea and reluctantly returned to the front room. No use postponing the inevitable. If she didn't tell her aunt about the ghost tour tonight, she'd have to do so in the morning.

Her relative leaned forward in her chair, anxious as a school girl to hear juicy details of a friend's date. "So, did you see anything?"

Bingo! There it was. The family lecture of ghosts and metaphysics. Her aunt had insisted on the tour, going so far as to purchase the ticket when April called to ask if she could stay with her during her research project. Aunt Vickie thought a ghost tour would be a good place to start, for more than practical reasons, April was sure.

"No. I didn't see anything." April sighed, knowing it would be useless to stave off the unavoidable interrogation. She leaned against the open archway, letting her aunt know she wasn't settling in for a long talk. "I wish you and Grams would give up. Maybe I'm not meant to have the gift of paranormal sight the rest of the Wilton women possess. Wouldn't I have already experienced it by now if I did? Perhaps I'm more like the Branford side and received the more 'logical' bones."

Each woman on her mother's side of the family was blessed, or cursed, with the ability to intermingle with the paranormal. Aunt Vickie could sense people's auras, living or dead, and foretold futures based on the workings of fate. Her ability to pick up on psychic energy was pretty amazing, though she only used her gifts when she thought it was necessary, which to April was quite often. Her grandmother,

~ ☾ ~

Dorothea, could sense ghosts in various realms, and often see them, depending on the realm they were in.

Over the years Grandma Dottie and Aunt Vickie had studied metaphysics. They were well known among their circle of friends who believed in spirits and hauntings. Ghost hunters and parapsychologists called upon their talents to help rid families of ghosts from their homes or give lectures at workshops.

April didn't doubt any of their gifts. Parapsychology was a strong art within her family, and with her natural penchant for psychometry, she supposed anything could be possible. She just hadn't encountered it herself.

"You are a Wilton woman! God is waiting for the right time. You'll know when it happens. Or is this more about how Jason called you a fraud in front of the crew you were volunteering with at the Jamestown expedition?"

April groaned, pinching the bridge of her nose. "Oh please, I don't want to discuss this. Jason and I are history—"

"—and good riddance I say." She shook her bony finger at April. "I told you when you introduced him to me that your auras and bio-rhythms were not compatible." Victoria Snyder puffed up her chest proudly. "You need to move away from his negative energies and accept your gift, learn from it, and see where it wants to take you. Our gifts and fate guide us to where we need to be. We Wilton women value the gifts we have, you should too."

"Except my mother," April whispered, looking down at her hands. Her mother's gift had caused her parents' divorce when she was a young teenager. She didn't like to bring it up but this was one of those times. Maybe her mom was right to be afraid of her gift.

Aunt Vickie let out her breath wearily. "Yes well, your mother hasn't found how to work with her gift for clairaudience. She can't control the voices of the ghosts who come to her for help and they frighten her. And what's worse, she refuses to even try. That's why she has those damn headaches."

"Can we stop talking about this?" April asked.

"Fine." Her aunt sat back, apparently giving up badgering

~ ☾ ~

her for now. "Tell me all about the tour. I felt a strong presence when I went, especially around the old hanging tree. I believe there is some unresolved, live energy residing there. But truthfully, I think the tour is mostly historical legend and entertainment."

"Ghost tours are just forms of entertainment for tourists and ghost aficionados," April agreed. Her thoughts focused on her tour guide and their brief walk, and her lips molded into a smile over the rim of her tea cup. "But I did happen to meet a nice re-enactor. He seemed to know quite a bit about Kings Mill's history and James Addison."

"You met a nice man? Did you ask him out to dinner?"

Aunt Vickie was her champion when it came to her love life. Yes, she agreed she should have listened to Aunt Vickie about Jason's lack of a true aura. It would have saved her a lot of heartache.

"Of course I didn't ask him out to dinner!" She sipped her tea and gave her aunt a cheeky grin. "I did ask him to join me for a cup of coffee, but he refused." She shrugged as if it didn't matter.

April put down her cup and saucer on the small Victorian tea table beside her and went for her purse. "He let me take a picture of him though. I have it here somewhere." She grinned, thinking about her personal tour guide and what her aunt would think of him when she saw him. They both shared a preference for tall, dark haired men.

"You sly girl, you!" Aunt Vickie beamed proudly. "I'll make a Wilton woman out of you yet."

April's digital camera came to life and she switched the setting to playback, scrolling through the photos. She'd taken a bevy of pictures, ones of the hanging tree, some of the colonial storefronts and historical houses, the front and back of the courthouse. She came across the last picture, the one she'd taken right outside, and then it went back to her older photos. Everything was there but the picture of her guide. She gasped and thumbed frantically through the pictures again.

"What's wrong, April dear?" Her aunt got up from the chair and came over to her, bringing her cup of tea with her.

"It was here...I mean, the picture is here but he isn't." The

~ ☾ ~

photo showed part of the brick cobbled street, a corner of courthouse, and the lamp post she'd had her guide stand in front of. There was a bright, fuzzy ball of light obscuring part of the gaslight. Could it be a possible reflection off the light and her flash? She'd captured him in the frame, she was positive!

Her aunt looked over her arm at the frame revealing the street along with the courthouse. April didn't like the knowing smile and twinkle to her aunt's eye. "Oh, he's there," she said, peering up from over her tea cup.

"What do you mean?" She was almost afraid to ask.

"You've managed to capture what we call residual paranormal energy. See the spot of fuzzy light in the middle of the picture? You've captured an image of a paranormal orb. Welcome to the family, April. You've seen your first ghost."

~ ☾ ~

Chapter Three

The tinkling of old fashioned cowbells over the gift shop's door startled April. Catching her breath she looked around, hoping no one had seen her jump. The store was quiet. Not many people out and about at eleven o'clock in the morning on a Sunday in downtown Kings Mill. Most were still at church. She had to wait until the store opened though to set the record straight from last night.

Despite her family gift, she refused to believe the man she'd spent over an hour with was a ghost. She didn't discount the possibility of live energy or life after death, but too many variables remained where paranormal activity could be debunked. Abnormal energy levels could cause hallucinations, specks of dust and moisture on a camera lens could be misconstrued as ghostly orbs, and drops in temperature could be low-lying areas of land near a marshy field or a drafty old house. Everything could be explained away and she would debunk her aunt's theory for her own peace of mind.

Damn! Now she sounded like Jason. But what happened to her was different. The man she'd talked to was real, not some shimmering apparition. She'd posed questions and he'd replied. She would find out about her ghost tour guide and finally put to rest the troubling notion that kept her up most of the night.

Admiring the odds and ends in the small, Georgian-styled townhouse-turned store, April thumbed through a few books on the local history of Kings Mill while she waited patiently for the college girl behind the counter to finish her phone call.

She spotted a book about the excavations of the old mill ruins back in the late 1980s written by the local historian and director of Kings Mill's Historical Society, Dr. Elizabeth

~ ☾ ~

"Beth" Freelane—the woman she would be meeting tomorrow. Dr. Moreland had scheduled an appointment for April to meet with her to get some pointers on James Addison and the mill. The woman was the foremost authority on the local history since taking over the historical society in 1986.

Thinking it would give her a sense of who the woman was and her take on the history of Kings Mill's local legend, before they actually met face to face, April picked up the book. Maybe it would reveal a bit more about James Addison. For being such a legend around here, there really was very little information on the man.

Moving towards the counter where the girl was still talking on the phone, April paused to admire the turn-about display of kitschy magnets. A cartoon figure of a gravedigger reading; *I Dig Dead People,* made her laugh. Cute. And then the ever popular; *Ghosts Are People, Too* and one her Grams or Aunt Vickie might say to her; *Just because you can't see it doesn't mean it's not there.* But one in particular caught her eye. *Believe in Fate.* The phrase called to her as if daring her to follow through.

April scoffed. She knew her aunt would argue the point, but fate didn't make things happen. People *made* things happen. April picked it up along with the other three. They would make a nice addition to her eclectic magnet collection.

The clerk hung up the phone. Taking her items up to the counter, April noticed the clerk wore the sweatshirt with the *Ghosts Are People Too* emblazoned across the front.

"Hello. Can I help you?" she asked.

"Yes, I need to know some information about the ghost tour last night."

"You took the tour? How did you like it?"

"Very informative." April nodded in what she hoped was an enthusiastic response.

"We're having another tour on Wednesday night, Halloween, if you're interested."

"Thank you. I'll think about it." She waited for the girl to finish her promotional speech so she could ask her question.

"Tickets are limited. We only have a few left for our last tour at ten o'clock. We're actually going into Lilac Grove

~ ☾ ~

Cemetery for the tour and taking in Henry Samuel's grave and some of the local legends buried there," she gushed in a bubbly-cute voice.

April's professional and metaphysical interest merged with excitement. One thing she loved was old cemeteries. They were filled with historical wonder, from the weathered tombstones and creative epitaphs, to the interest of old architectural family crypts. She'd written her first term paper in college on old cemeteries. She'd found a peculiar hobby of taking etchings of unique engravings.

"Would the tour include James Addison's grave?"

The clerk shook her head after a thoughtful moment. "He doesn't have one. Or at least, no one knows its whereabouts. There's no record of his burial according to the historical documents." She rolled her eyes. "Trust me, my boss would have found it and used it in the tour by now."

A Halloween cemetery tour! What a fun way to spend one of her favorite holidays. "Sure, put me down for a ticket."

"Just one?"

She thought about her Aunt Vickie. No, she was joining a group of her friends for *Sangrias and Séances* to celebrate Samhain. "Yes, just one."

The girl rang up her order as April looked at the scrapbook of pictures from the ghost tours given in the past. She was hoping to see her guide among the many pictures of the blond guy who'd led their tour, but no such luck.

"You don't have pictures of the dark haired tour guide?" April asked.

"Dark haired tour guide?" The girl shook her head, her brow curled. "We don't have anyone with dark hair, just Tony. We barely get enough interest for one tour guide, much less any others."

"Is this Tony?" She pointed to the picture of the guy she started her tour with last night.

The girl behind the counter nodded. "Yeah, he's my boyfriend. We've been dating since senior year in high school," she explained.

"There were two tour guides last night dressed in almost identical, period costumes so I assumed they were working

~ ☾ ~

together." If Tony was the only one, who had she been with? Her brow furrowed and her heartbeat quickened. No, she wasn't going to believe—

"This man had dark hair, stood about six foot. I never got his name," April replied anxiously, trailing off as the clerk kept shaking her head slowly. She had to make the girl understand. There *had* been another guide. She'd talked to him.

"Weird." The girl leaned over the counter. "Are you saying someone else was giving the tour, too?"

"Yes. He was dressed in the same costume."

She shrugged. "Maybe he was some guy dressed up from a weekend Halloween party. Everyone had a costume party this weekend since the thirty-first falls on a Wednesday this year." The girl finished processing her order and handed her the bag of items, including the ticket for the Halloween/Cemetery tour.

Taking her purchase with a slight smile, April nodded. "Sure, that's probably who I saw." She said good-bye, wishing the young woman a good day and quickly headed out. She felt better now. Of course, Halloween party! Why hadn't she thought of that?

***

Sitting in the café, lazily stirring the foam into her latte, April mulled the possibility of truly having seen a ghost. Just because the girl had said they didn't have any dark-haired tour guides didn't mean he wasn't some random guy in a costume. As close as it was to Halloween, he might have been coming back from a weekend party or something.

But according to her aunt, the evidence of his ghostly apparition was there in her camera. She looked warily down at her purse nestled between her feet. She wasn't going to look at the picture again. Having gone over it a hundred times last night, one more peek wouldn't erase the orb from the view finder.

April didn't want to delete the photo, either. Confused and bothered by the possibility of almost believing the odd form could be a ghost, she put the idea away, back to the farthest reaches of her mind. She was too practical to think a simple

~ ☾ ~

speck of dust on her lens could be misconstrued as a ghost. Besides, she had research to do. Since she had some books to work with now she might find something of interest. A lead of some sort she could report to Kenneth Miles tomorrow when he called for an update.

Settling in with her latte and the excavation of the mill site book, April tried to put last night's events behind her. When her cell phone vibrated in her jeans pocket, she noted the caller ID, and her heart gave a little jolt. Why was Kenneth Miles calling her on a Sunday? She took a deep breath and plastered on her most professional smile.

"Hello, Mr. Miles," she greeted in her most professional voice.

A voice on the other end crackled with static. "Is this Dr. Branford?"

"Yes it is. What may I do for you?"

Thank God she was sitting down. This was actually Kenneth Miles, the man she was working for. She could try to deny the fact he was 'the most financially influential man in the world' and try to look at him as a 'normal man' but having him on the phone made her palms sweat.

"What's your progress with the documents? I'm meeting with my share holders tomorrow and need to be able to give them something positive. This land purchase is my foremost priority. I need to know if James Addison owned the property before he died. "

"As a matter of fact, I'm researching the legend of your ancestor as we speak. I have to say there's not much here. I'll have more information Monday when I have a chance to go through the records at the Historical Society." A lull in conversation had April thinking of a moment of calm before the storm.

"Legend! I don't want bedtime stories, d*octor*. I need evidence and cold hard facts. No one is going to accept a legend in a business venture."

April felt her ire rise. She didn't care if he was one of the richest men in the world, Mr. Miles needed to have some woman pinch him hard.

"I understand your concern, Mr. Miles. I'm doing the best

~ ☾ ~

I can with the information available. There hasn't been enough factual history since most of the history connected with James Addison is based on stories and legends. Once we can separate the truth from fiction, I'll have more to go on."

"I'm sorry for my loss of temper, doctor, but I don't like excuses. Robert Moreland insisted I was getting the best person for the job. I want an expert on this case and I'm counting on you to find the documents to James's claim on the land." A healthy pause followed. "Money is no object. Do what you must to get the job done," he barked out.

April wasn't sure if he was complimenting her or questioning her abilities. Still, if Dr. Moreland had sung her praises, she needed to make her mentor proud. And if she could pull off this investigation by solving the historical equation of the mysterious James Addison and his untimely demise, what a feather it would be in her cap! Such a triumph could clinch her career.

"I want you to keep me abreast of your progress on a daily basis. I will be arriving in Kings Mill for the festivities in a few weeks and hope to have the information and historical record of deed found by then. As I said, if you find you need anything to move the process along, don't hesitate to contact me. I want the document, Dr. Branford. Don't fail me."

She closed her eyes and let her breath out slowly so he couldn't hear it over the line. "Of course sir, I will do everything in my power to get my hands on it."

"Still, I want daily reports sent to my email. As soon as you find something of importance, I expect immediate details. I look forward to meeting with you in a few weeks, doctor."

"I look forward to meeting you too, Mr. Miles." Without saying so much as goodbye, he rang off.

The image of a gruff, balding man came to mind when she thought of Kenneth Miles and all of his billions. He kept out of the media limelight so no one knew much about him. Paparazzi had tried to get photos of him for years, but the man was as elusive as the Loch Ness Monster. Some tabloids even stated he was as fictitious as Betty Crocker. A label made up by an internationally successful corporation to appease an audience of investors.

~ ☾ ~

But she would be meeting the real man face to face in less than a month for the annual James Addison/Kings Mill Day festivities. Would the press get wind of his appearance and try to take over the town? Having Kenneth here would be great publicity for the small town, but she secretly thought it might diminish the memory of James Addison in all the attention and hoopla. The situation didn't sit well with her. April didn't care how wealthy Kenneth Miles was.

***

April tried to settle in to read the hardback book she'd purchased. The excavation of Kings Mill should be fascinating. But twenty minutes of mind numbing legal crap on procuring excavation rights led to her thumbing through the black and white photos in the middle pages that were mostly group photos of the digging team and volunteer archeologists. A picture of a silver chatelaine unearthed in the manor house cellar popped up as she rifled through the pages. April sat up and examined the photo.

A chatelaine was a very important implement to a lady of the house, much like a smart phone with all of its apps. It contained everything a woman needed to run a household. Each chain was attached to items such as door keys, keys to china hutches and secretary desks. Dainty scissors, needle holders, and writing tools were also favorite items to be found on one.

This one was a silver brooch in a fleur-de-lis design. Three chains still hung from it containing two skeleton keys, one larger than the other. What could the priceless artifact reveal to her if she could ever get her hands on it? Something as intimate and personal as a woman's chatelaine would still contain the owner's memories and emotional details. Just thinking about it made her fingers itch.

She spied a picture of her aunt's house as it had been in 1987. Underneath the photo, the caption explained it had been Henry Samuels's residence before his death in December 1774. Some historians believed Henry was the owner of the mill instead of James Addison, but no formal deed had ever been found. Besides, this didn't help her. April needed proof of James Addison owning the mill, not Henry

~ ☾ ~

Samuel. A small portrait of the stout, middle aged man with great jowls wearing a small periwig was on the following page. The picture depicted what she thought a colonial land commissioner would look like. Even his beady little eyes screamed of political power.

She turned the page. The last glossy insert stopped her heart cold. James Edward Addison, second son of the Earl of Sunderbury, stared back at her, the image a copy of a painting from a personal collection from England. He'd been twenty-one at the time of the sitting, just shy of taking leave for the Maryland colony. The man had a high brow, firm jaw line, and an aristocratic bearing for one so youthful. The picture portrayed only his torso but he had nice broad shoulders and his dark hair wasn't covered with a powdered wig like Henry. His white linen shirt contrasted with his dark, scruffy jaw line.

Enthralled by it, she peered closer at the picture. Those eyes! They mesmerized her. Even from the pages of the book, the look in his eyes spoke volumes as if he were trying to communicate with her. The black and white picture didn't reveal their color, but James's passion resonated, sending chills up her spine.

But the most amazing thing was, for all intense purposes, James Addison bore a striking resemblance to her guide.

No. It couldn't be. No...no!

April slammed shut the book and shook her head, refusing to believe for one minute—

"May I borrow this seat?"

A clutch of women settled around the table next to hers. While she'd immersed herself in research, the cafe had become more crowded and seating was at a premium. She noted the time on her watch. The twenty minutes had moved into forty-five while she'd obsessed over the middle of the book.

"Of course, I'm finished anyway." She tried to smile at the group. Once she gathered her wits and her belongings, she stood and threw her bag over her shoulder.

Afternoon sunshine hit her as she emerged from the coffee house. But even the bright rays didn't stop her from shivering

~ ☾ ~

at the realization she had possibly seen a ghost. April found herself right back in her dilemma. Doggedly determined not to believe such bull, she crossed the street with a no nonsense gait, as if trying to outrun her over active imagination. No way in hell was she going to believe her guide was a ghost, and definitely not the ghost of James Addison!

Upon crossing the street she stopped mid stride. But what if it was true? She was a member of the Wilton clan and a woman. She was born into the trait. It was a very real possibility. She didn't need to experience the family curse. Not now when she was about to prove herself in her field.

She did not see ghosts, she told herself. She had her gift of psychometry. That was enough. April needed to focus on her research and get a handle on the past because the present was too confusing. She had no desire to go back to Aunt Vickie's and have her try to reason with her about her ghostly heritage. She needed to do something to keep her mind focused on her task. She was a historian. She needed to research her subject. The book in her hands called her name. That settled it! She would drive out to the old mill site and see what she could find.

***

The drive was further than April anticipated. The outskirts of Kings Mill gave way to large, stately mansions littered along the rolling hillsides below the Appalachian mountain ridge. She passed a few subdivisions, the little villages filled with cookie-cutter single-family homes. The parcel of land for which the town was named was outside the actual city limits, far from the downtown area.

Pulling off the road, April got out and locked the doors. Tucking a stray piece of hair under her cap, she walked around the car, looking out onto the field in front of her. A roadside, historical plaque caught her attention.

Kings Mill
One of the early gristmills in the area operated by James Addison, until his death in 1774. The nearby town of Kings Mill was named in honor of the famous mill which produced most of the grain flour for the area for many years until a

~ ☾ ~

fire in December 1774 destroyed both the mill and manor house.

April shivered. Even though she'd bundled in her woolen pea coat, hat and scarf, she was still chilled. Reading the commemorative inscription again, she noted the sign said, 'operated' not 'owned.' There was the source of her angst. Had James Addison only operated the mill? Was the mill owned by Henry Samuel, instead of James as some of the local history proclaimed?

Psychic energy dominated this place. She didn't need artifacts to get a reading of the history throbbing around her. Her psychometry picked up on it, feeding off of the historical essence still living within the site. Something as simple as closing her eyes and inhaling the air around her brought on a sense of déjà vu. History haunted her, not ghosts, as Aunt Vickie always hoped.

Just because you can't see it, doesn't mean it's not there.

The quote seemed to float on the sudden burst of a breeze, as if whispered to her by an ethereal presence—or her Aunt Vickie. April sighed and rolled her eyes. Parting the weeds and brambles, she crossed the shallow ditch and stepped forward into a large, barren field. Naked trees stood in the foreground against a back drop of the grey Appalachian mountain range.

She stooped to pick up a field rock and held it in her hand, looking around at the peaceful scene. The wind picked up a bit again, rustling the tall grasses against her legs. April closed her eyes and inhaled the late autumn air.

Suddenly, the air turned heavy and pungent. Thick smoke strangled her airways, burning and seizing her chest as she fought to take a breath. Coughing and gasping, the scent became stronger the more she tried to breath. Her eyes flew open and she looked around—nothing. She dropped the rock back to the ground. Tears blurred her vision.

Damn! Were her allergies flaring up again? Of course, all the pollen and dry weeds around here were enough to make anyone's sinuses irritated. She wiped her eyes with the back of her hand.

~ ☾ ~

The wind stopped. Nothing moved. Not even the grass. Apprehension prickled her spine. A sane woman would have left. Not April, she was used to this sensation. It was history beckoning to her. She walked further away from the safety of her car and headed towards the barren fields beyond the slight ridge.

She stopped at a partial stone foundation buried into the ground a couple of feet deep. Weeds, bramble bushes, and saplings laid down their homestead within the rocky structure, but she could still see the outline of the old building. April assumed it was the remains of the manor house. It had to be the house because there were no indications of a creek or damned up pond to show this was the remains of the water powered mill.

Lowering herself down into what was left of the foundation, she hoped to get a sense of time and place to help her distinguish the truth behind the object of her interest. Scorch marks were evident on some of the stones where the elements hadn't touched them, but moss and lichen had taken over much of the remainder. Black soot smudged the base of the far wall and drew her toward the anomaly. Time and elements should have worn away any markings by now. Why were they still here? Frowning, April brushed the stone to see if she could remove the black ash.

Fire scorched her hand. She tried to pull back from the stone wall but her hand was locked onto it as if magnetized. No matter how much she tried to dislodge herself, April couldn't release her palm. Panic set in as she desperately pulled at her arm.

A strong smell of burning wood filled her nostrils. Muffled screams startled her and she turned abruptly to see the manor house burning around her. Licks of flame fanned her body. Terrified, April screamed only to realize the scene was images from the past. She stood in the middle of the flames, and yet nothing around her was real. There was no heat, no real fire.

April heard a muffled noise and saw movement just beyond her vision of flames. She had to squint to see through the shimmering heat waves. A woman struggled, bound and

~ ☾ ~

gagged, and next to her was the unconscious body of a young man.

She watched in horror as the flames caught on the hem of the girl's dress and inched up in slow motion. April couldn't move, couldn't breathe. Standing encased in time and space, she could only watch helplessly as the woman pleaded, looking at her with large round eyes above the gag. The woman's voice squealed, muffled against the cloth, as the fire engulfed her.

The sound of splintering wood overhead caused April to crouch low against her captive wall. She cried out, knowing she could very well be taking her last breath. The creaking and snapping of the timbers holding the house in place caved in on them in an orange-red, hellish inferno.

***

Moments passed as she sat crouched low against the wall to protect herself from the ceiling coming down on her. When she dared to look, April removed her free arm from over her head. Everything she'd witnessed was a hallucination.

The stone wall released her from its captive grip. Her hand fell to her side, limp and trembling. Her throat was raw from screaming. Had she screamed? She must have. Maybe it was her own voice she'd heard in her head, not the young woman she thought she'd seen. Dazed, she scanned the space where she'd seen the girl tied up. On trembling legs she inched towards the spot. Dropping to her knees she inspected the ground. Nothing was there, not even a sense of time.

What had just happened to her? She blamed it on her psychometry, but her gift had never been this intense. She'd felt as if she'd actually been transported back in time. Had she witnessed the mill fire back in 1774? If so, who were the two people she'd seen burn to death?

April studied the stone wall which had held her captive. There was nothing out of the ordinary about it. It was only a wall. Her fingers tingled. She rubbed her hands together to try to dispel the effect. Dear God, her hand itched to touch the wall again! The one touch had changed her reality. Part of her wanted to test the theory but fear took hold. She couldn't—she didn't want to go back there and view the scene

~ ☾ ~

again. She needed to get out of here.

Rising from the ruins, she struggled to pull herself together. She was in shock. Her numb body tingled. Her jaw ached from clenching it to keep her teeth from rattling. It popped painfully when a sneezing fit took hold. Her throat burned and the canals along her Eustachian tubes itched annoyingly. Her seasonal allergies had grabbed her with a vengeance!

She ran back towards her car, up the ridge past the fields of wheat and workers. She stopped. Workers? People were out in the fields who hadn't been there before! The lands were no longer barren. Field hands worked the crop. Stumbling under the weight of her disbelief, she tried to get her brain to deny what it was seeing.

She turned around looking behind her towards the ruins. There stood a large, colonial manor house in its glory, no longer on fire. How could that be when only moments before she'd been held hostage to its unique historical powers, as if she'd been part of its history as it burned to ash in another dimension of time.

This. Could not. Be happening. This was un-freakin' believable!

With her heart racing she slowly turned back to view the fields and sneezed loudly. Eyes from the past looked up from their work and stopped their toiling. They were as shocked to see her standing there on top of the knoll as she was to see them.

She had to get out of here. This was too much for a sane mind to fathom. But her mind refused to obey her command. She stood there in shock and awe.

The figure of a man appeared, his broad shoulders and lean hips encased in tight fitting beige breeches and a linen shirt. His dark hair was tied back in a queue. He stood between her and the fields perusing his workers, but as if he too sensed her presence, he turned around.

April's breath caught in her throat as they stared at each other across time and space. His quizzical interest turned to one of possible recognition, his lips quirked into a smile, and he touched two fingers to his forehead in salute. It was James

~ ☾ ~

Addison, the man she'd met last night, the one in the portrait, the legend she'd been assigned to research. As soon as she made the mental connection, the images around her shivered into nothing but mist, and then disappeared altogether.

~ ☾ ~

Chapter Four

The atmosphere in the cemetery hung thick and damp and a cold wind whistled eerily around the barren trees as the small group of people made their way deep into the grounds. The old, white marble obelisks and arched stones, large crypts, and wrought iron fences were natural decorations for this night. Even the misty fog rolling along the hallowed grounds couldn't have been improved upon by a Hollywood studio special effects department.

April found the scene beautiful in a surreal way. The pungent aroma of wood smoke from the festive bonfires in the streets and surrounding chimneys mingled with the damp smell of foliage. She sneezed into her wad of tissues and blew her nose. A couple in the tour group 'blessed' her under their whispered breath as Tony began the tour talk.

"We've been given the run of the cemetery so it is just us tonight and possibly a few ghosts," Tony joked as he led the group of thirty people into Lilac Grove, Kings Mill's oldest cemetery. "Stay close, the one touching you may or may not be of this world. If anyone gets too spooked, you are free to leave but please, let me know so I don't assume you are trapped in some crypt or have been turned into a zombie."

Stunted laughter and attempts at ghoulish jokes to lighten the eerie mood made April snort in amusement. This was a cemetery. Nothing here at night that wasn't here during the day. Not even on All Hallows Eve. Only overactive imaginations roamed along the shadowed paths. Tony swung his replica tin lantern around, whether to ward off the dark shadows or because he was scared as hell, April wasn't sure. But tonight, her mystery guide was nowhere to be seen.

She'd come to the conclusion her Sunday afternoon fright at the old mill ruins was her own case of overactive

~ ☾ ~

imagination and intense sinus related conditions. An incident while she'd been volunteering at the Jamestown excavation site had given her the same kind of experience of two distinct eras in history appearing to overlap each other. She'd relayed her findings to her group of friends she'd been working with.

The same day she'd come down with bronchitis and a high fever.

No one had believed her bizarre stories, including Jason. He'd told her the fever had caused her to hallucinate. He'd taken it upon himself to announce her illogical findings as part of her illness. When she found out he'd discredited her among their peers, it had been the beginning of the end of their two-year relationship. It had only gone downhill from there.

And true to past history, by the time she returned to Aunt Vickie's after the mill site visit, she'd suffered from a full-blown sinus infection. Not even her aunt's herbal teas and home remedies fixed her. So Monday morning she'd postponed her meeting with Beth Freelane to go to the walk-in clinic where she waited three hours to see a doctor for antibiotics and decongestants.

She supposed it was for the best. Beth was dealing with electricians and painters at the new historical society site for the next few days and wouldn't be available to meet with her until after Halloween. Beth couldn't even offer her the crates of documents because they were being carted from various buildings in town to the new site. Until she could sort them out, she had no idea what they contained. April sighed. Another roadblock for her in this unsolvable mystery. She dreaded emailing Kenneth Miles about her lack of progress. So she'd put off her correspondence to him and decided to enjoy the festive cemetery ghost tour tonight instead.

The group's path wove through the divided plots of new and old headstones. They stopped every few feet and looked around as Tony weaved stories about former citizens of Kings Mill who were now interred in the various graves.

Restlessly, she glanced around. Although she hadn't fully recovered from the sniffles, her senses were as active as ever. The fact she was in a cemetery filled with natural historical

~ ☾ ~

energy didn't stop her from enjoying the tour. She trailed the
rest of the group, kind of the odd man out, taking in her
surroundings at her own pace.

"This is the grave site of Henry Samuel, Kings Land's first
land commissioner. His grave is the tall pointy thing you see
up on the hill." Tony pointed to a historical nameplate
attached to a pole squeaking with an eerie, metallic rasp.
"Rumor has it Henry owned the mill site. I know most of you
think James Addison owned the mill, but there isn't any
documentation to prove it, which would mean it could have
still been in the land commissioner's possession."

April peered up the small hill to see the stark white obelisk
standing very pronounced against the black, moonless sky. At
the moment, it seemed to be the focal point in the cemetery.
Even from here she could see the intricate designs etched into
the old marble. She would love to get a rubbing of it perhaps
before they left. Besides, Henry Samuel's grave was the
closest thing to her research she had to go on right now. His
reference to a connection with James Addison was all she
had—that and she was staying in his historical home.

"Tony," she spoke up, making her voice sound weak and
stuffy. "I think I'm going to head out. My allergies are really
kicking my butt, and I'm all congested."

"Are you sure? We're just about done, only a few more
graves to see."

"Yes, I'm sure. Thanks for the tour and Happy Halloween
everyone." She began to walk backwards away from the group
as they waved good-bye.

She stayed in the shadows and watched the rest of the
group move on, until they rounded the bend of the path. Once
she was out of their sight, she reached into her large bag,
retrieved her small sketchbook, pencil, and mini flashlight.
Double checking to make sure the coast was clear, she made
her way up the small dirt path to Henry Samuels's monument.

The roots of the firs were tangled and exposed in areas,
moss and lichen grew around the bottom of the obelisk grave
marker, a layer of dead branches and fan-like fir needles
surrounded the base. She could read the month and year of
his death but the date was a bit obscure.

~ ☾ ~

She buried her nose into a fresh tissue as she held back a sneeze so she didn't alert the rest of the group of her whereabouts.

Wiping her nose she knelt in front of the tombstone and placed the end of the flashlight between her teeth to give her direct light on what she was doing. The soggy ground soaked into the knees of her jeans. She could hear the faint voices of the group from just over the rise, yet she felt a prickling of unease. Glancing around, she didn't see anything.

She wiped moisture from the front of the headstone with her scarf, revealing the blackened embossing on the aged marble. Angling the paper over part of the intricate design, she fumbled with the pencil in her gloved hand. The cumbersome gloves had to go. Removing the offending obstacles and tossing them to the side, April rubbed her pencil over the markings, steadying herself against the marble with her other hand.

A jolt of heat coursed from her palm to her shoulder and she jerked back. Falling onto her bottom, she dropped the pencil and paper. Nearly choking on the flashlight, she threw the light to the side and fought to catch her breath. Still tingling from the shock, she shook her arm to relieve the pain.

She picked up the flashlight again and slowly approached the gravestone. Her heart thudded in her ears. Reaching out for the paper and pencil she had dropped, she kept her eye on the stone as if waiting for it to move. Cautiously, she leaned forward and touched it. The marble was as cold and even-surfaced as an old tombstone in late October should be.

Confused, she inched away on her knees, backing away from the headstone, a frightening wariness settling over her as she slowly stood up and continued moving cautiously away from the monument.

"Henry Samuel is not worthy of your fascination, Dr. Branford."

April gasped and whirled, shining the flashlight into the night. There, mere inches in front of her, stood her mysterious tour guide. A moment of relief caused her to catch her breath before the toe of her boot caught on a loose tree

~ ☾ ~

root, sending her falling through a chilly mist of air. She landed on her hands and knees.

Quickly, she turned over and stared up at her re-enactor, who stood between her and Henry Samuel's grave. So close she should have fallen into him. And then the truth of the situation hit her. She crab crawled away from him and the tombstone, her eyes wide with horror.

She couldn't think. "Oh my God! Oh my God!" Her voice shook with the only words she could say.

He smiled down at her, tilting his tricorne back on his head, revealing those damn hypnotic eyes.

"I haven't heard a lady say that to me for some time. Nice to know I haven't lost my touch," he preened.

"You're...not...real," April gasped, holding her chest as she tried desperately to find her footing. "You're...a...ghost. You really are a ghost!"

He shrugged. "I suppose so. No one has told me any differently. But then no one has been able to talk to me in two hundred and thirty-eight years. You're the first." With an elegant flourish, he bowed to her.

"Oh my God!" She was shaking so badly she couldn't move. Her muscles had frozen. The seat of her jeans was wet but she wasn't sure if she had peed herself or the damp ground had soaked into them.

He extended his hand in a gentlemanly fashion to help her up, but she only stared at the proffered limb. He sighed.

"Of course. It would do me no good to try and help you up since I'm..."

"...not real. You're not real. This isn't happening to me." April closed her eyes and tried to repeat the mantra over and over again, hoping her mental state would finally sort out the situation and thrust her back into reality. She opened her eyes. He was still there, his infuriatingly charming smile, just short of a laugh, etched into one devilishly handsome face.

Scrambling for purchase she grabbed her articles, keeping a close eye on her specter and quickly walked backwards down the knoll until she was on the cobblestone path. She had to get out of here. *Where was the damn exit!*

***

~ ☾ ~

James turned frantic. April Branford was walking, no—
running away from him. He'd feared this would happen, but
he didn't wish for her to leave. He needed her. Giving her a
bit of room, he kept pace while he reasoned with her.

"I wanted to tell you when we met. But I figured my
presence would be frightening if you knew you could see me."
She didn't slow a bit, if anything her pace hastened. "I hoped
you might fall for me. I didn't expect you to fall into me," he
explained, waiting for her response to his intentional attempt
at humor. She didn't give him one.

He couldn't blame her. How would he have reacted if he
had been approached by a ghost in his day?

She cursed in a very unladylike fashion, then laughed
hysterically, and cursed again. Both died to an almost gut-
wrenching sob and a brief prayer asking God, 'why now?' She
seemed to be ignoring everything he was saying to her. James
wasn't sure if he was supposed to do anything.

He tried a different tactic. "Why were you weeping over
Henry Samuel's grave? Did you find something about the fop
deserving of your attention?" James asked.

"I wasn't weeping over his grave," April informed him. "I
was taking a headstone rubbing when you approached and
just about scared the piss out of me."

"I am truly sorry." He didn't intend to cause her distress.
"I thought you were in Kings Mill to find out the truth about
James Addison?"

She stopped, looked around, nibbling her lip, before
turning her wide-eyed attention back to him. "Who are you?"

The questioning look of fear in her eyes was plain and
simple. She was afraid of him. She had every right to be
scared of a specter, but he didn't want her to fear him. He'd
waited for years for someone to come along and see him,
sense him—talk to him. He couldn't let her run away from
him now.

"You already know the answer, Dr. Branford. You saw me
out at the mill the other day."

Her eyes widened. He could see her chest rising rapidly
within the confines of her woolen coat as she shook her head
in denial. "You're...James Addison."

~ ☾ ~

The quietly spoken words weren't a question or a doubt, she knew, but whether or not she accepted the knowledge was yet to be seen.

"Really, I did want to tell you the truth about me, but I couldn't. Not knowing how you would react, I couldn't take the chance of having you run away from me. I don't want you to fear me, or what I am. You're the only person who has ever been able to see me in this form. But more importantly, you're the only person who's cared."

She stopped and turned. "I can see you. But you're not real...I don't know..."

"You make me feel real again," he said softly, his voice wavering with emotion.

She shook her head and muttered profanities under her breath to her Aunt Vickie and someone named Wilton. "I don't have time for ghosts. I've a case to solve. Go back to wherever it is you came from." April waved him off, holding her forehead as if warding off a headache.

"I can't. This is where I am. Right here, right now. There is no place for me to go back to." He would hold her in his arms if only he could touch her. James knew this couldn't be easy for her to understand. "Perhaps I could be of assistance to you, since you know who I am."

"You're a ghost. I need tangible evidence of James Addison's life. I'll be a laughing stock to my employer if I try to tell him my research is based on facts from a ghost. I need proof. Besides, how do I know you really are James Addison?"

"You don't," he agreed. "But what would it take to prove to you I am?"

"Tell me where he is buried," she challenged.

James shrugged. "Easy enough, but I would prefer to show you." He began to lead the way, deeper into the cemetery grounds.

"I call bullshit. There is no record of his burial, I've researched his information. If he was executed, his body parts could be anywhere." She scoffed heavily and turned away, moving toward the front of the cemetery, back to the entrance from where she'd started with the rest of the tour group.

~ ☾ ~

She was leaving, not only the cemetery, but him. He couldn't have her walk away from this moment, from him. Somehow he knew he needed to be with April Branford no matter what.

"Of course there are no records. My remains were buried in a pauper's grave after having been displayed publicly to warn others who might wish to commit treason." He scoffed. "Each night I return to my gravestone only to wake in the past, savoring the life I knew at the mill, like you witnessed the other day. Then I'm transported here into the present and walk the streets of Kings Mill, searching for someone to see me, help me, or perhaps guide me to move on. I can't prove anything. I'm hoping you might believe in me, if only a little."

Biting her lip, she stopped walking. James noticed she nibbled the luscious bit of flesh when she seemed uncertain or nervous. With tentative steps she approached, daring to get closer to him. Those sparkling eyes narrowed speculatively as she reached out to touch him and of course—went right through his ethereal body. Closing her eyes, she shook her head skeptically. His soul ached wanting to dispel all of her fears as she struggled to come to terms with what he was. Spooking her was the last thing he wanted to do.

When her gaze met his again, he knew, deep in whatever he was made of, April Branford was his destiny. If only he knew how to convince her to feel the same way. He needed her to trust him. But how did a ghost coerce a practical woman to accept who he was and believe in him?

Moments ticked by. Finally, her rigid stance lessened on a deep sigh and she gave him a curt nod.

He smiled, touched his tricorne in salute, and led her deeper into the cemetery.

They stopped short of the linked fence surrounding Lilac Grove. Stately oaks, bare of leaves, towered overhead, but the wind whispered through them as if in greeting. Other than the grounds keeper, no one viewed this area much. Not even flowers or flags marked the passing of time.

He peered down on the woman. She hadn't said a word, just followed him blindly. She was still shaking. James occasionally caught her looking at him, and then she'd move

~ ☾ ~

away. It didn't seem to be in repulsion. Perhaps it was in confusion.

She stiffened her body and forced her arms to her sides by shoving her hands deep into her coat pockets. She was as tightly wound as the eight day clock he had purchased for his mantle years ago. He didn't want to see her springs explode from the tension she held.

"Are you warm enough in your woolen coat?" he asked, hoping casual conversation might help her relax.

"I'm fine..." She stopped talking and stared wide-eyed into his eyes again.

He wished he could soothe her wariness. Perhaps if he could kiss her it might erase all her fears. He'd been known to make a woman forget her troubles a time or two in the past. A kiss from her would definitely do something for him.

She looked around, frowning.

"Where are we?"

"The least visited area of the cemetery," James replied, knowing without taking his eyes from her, exactly where they were.

April viewed the solemn rows of tiny marbled bricks sticking out of the ground. "The paupers' graves."

James nodded.

The only indications of the graves were a series of numbers imprinted onto the tops of the most identifiable bricks. Some were so cracked and decayed from time and the overgrowth of roots they weren't recognizable. Others were barely visible, eaten up by the shifting of the earth beneath them. One stone seemed generally intact, the number ten barely visible, etched on the top. April stepped closer to inspect it more thoroughly.

She knelt down. Removing her gloves, she brushed a bit of leaves and debris off of the grayed marble, then respectfully caressed the stone.

"James Addison's grave."

He hadn't needed to tell her. She knew as if drawn to it. Her reverent touch across the old marble pierced his soul, as if it'd been caressed by her fingers.

She looked up at him. "Odd, how would I know that?" She

~ ☾ ~

returned her interest to the stone marker. "It's as if..."

April Branford cried out. Her hand began to glow where it lay on the stone. The stone took on an illumination, radiating from within her, outward like a candle's dancing flame, only brighter.

Before James could answer or help her, the light fragmented and penetrated him like a sword. He was thrown backwards. Pressure and pain ripped into his chest, intensifying as it spread outward through his extremities. This wasn't gentle. His immortal soul was being pierced, ripped asunder by an invisible hand.

Stumbling, James gasped, clutching his chest where he knew his heart would have been, if he had one. What was happening? The marble brick beneath April's hands continued to radiate an inferno of orange light. Even though she cried out for him to help her, she kept her hands stationary against the glowing marble, her face contorting as she squeezed her eyes shut against her shock and pain. He could feel it. What she felt echoed in his senses, reverberating between them as if they were mirrored objects catching the same reflection. The glow of light illuminated her, cascading through her and blasting him with its brilliance.

Bloody Hell! The pain drove him to his knees.

"Stop!" he choked out, gasping from the ache.

James shielded his eyes from the bright intensity. A prickling of awareness crept into him. Peering down at his hands he realized he glowed with the same unearthly light as did she and the stone. His soul stretched and ached to fill with solid mass. Agony and pain wrenched through him, making him wither on the ground, until the pain lessened to a dull, quivering twinge. Then he heard it, for the first time in over two hundred years, the mortal thumping of his heart.

Lifting his head he searched April out across the small space between them. Her body was lying across his gravestone, her eyes wide with shock. Her lips moved, speaking to him, but he couldn't hear her through the intense ringing and cacophony of sounds blaring in his ears. The pain slowly ebbed. Gingerly, James breathed. Sharp, icy shards filled his lungs, like a babe sucking in new life. His bare

~ ☾ ~

fingers dug into the rich earth. Wet leaves and soil feathered from between digits of flesh and bone. Inhaling the fragrant scents of dead foliage beneath his nose, a thousand sensations bore down upon him, overwhelming his mind. He was alive!

Unable to speak because of the emotion clogging his throat, he gave silent thanks to the woman. Whatever power she possessed, she was the answer to his prayers.

He noticed April had not risen from his grave. With her eyes closed tightly, she struggled for release from his stone, but it held her fast. She groaned and sobbed before the illumination around her dimmed and darkness surrounded them. She lay exhausted and weak across his meager tombstone. Opening her eyes, she was able to slowly remove her hand and reach out to him, seeking his help.

His body struggled to rise, but he was too weak to support the new mass of weight. Exhausted, he slumped back to the ground, vividly shaking as tremors rocked through him.

"It's you. You really are James Addison," she gasped in between breaths.

Her voice shook. She lay there, quivering in the aftermath of what they had witnessed together. Raising her hands in front of her face, as if she were uncertain who they belonged to, she turned them over, studying them.

Slowly, painfully, he inched his way across the few feet that separated them. Reaching her side, James held out his hand, spanning the ground between them. His hand shook, partially with fear but mostly with wonder. Would she be able to take hold and actually sense his touch now?

Her sobs were muffled, but she slowly rolled over, reaching out for his hand in return. Her eyes roamed in a quick beat from his hand to his face, checking for permission to touch him. The smooth, warm silkiness of her palm encompassed in his set his body on fire, in a good way. No woman had made him feel this alive, even when he lived centuries ago. What power did this woman have to make him feel whole again?

"Dear God, you are alive! *What have I done?*"

~ ☾ ~

Chapter Five

April felt Aunt Vickie's eyes bore into her from across the parlor without even glancing towards the woman. Minutes ticked by on the mantle clock, the Westminster Chimes still echoing the quarter hour. James Addison walked about the room, touching everything, marveling at his re-born senses. They hadn't spoken directly to each other since the gravesite. Still shaking inside, April was relieved she was sitting down. Her brain had disconnected somewhere between feeling James's hand touching hers and arriving back at the house. She didn't even remember dialing Aunt Vickie's number much less how she'd managed to get back to the entrance of the cemetery.

Vickie had arrived within moments, annoyed for having been taken out of her Sangria and Séances party, until April explained the man's presence. The shock and uncertainty echoing in her aunt's eyes proved to April what happened wasn't normal by any means—even to a woman who dealt with the paranormal on a daily basis.

Barely recovered from the fright of meeting her first ghost, April was thrown into the unknown of how she brought a ghost back from the grave. Over and over again she muttered, 'What have I done?' First to James and then to her aunt.

What bothered her, though, was her aunt couldn't even answer her question. Aunt Vickie stared at her as if she were the anomaly and not James.

"What did you do, April?" Vickie asked, her eyes narrowing.

"I don't know. I was hoping you would be able to answer the question. You are, after all, the expert."

"There are those of us who can talk, see, and sometimes communicate in their realm but never have I heard of

~ ☾ ~

someone being able to revive the dead." The older woman shook her head in befuddlement. "I don't even know where to begin. What did you do?"

"I don't know!" April stood up abruptly, and then realized she wasn't quite ready to stand. Her legs shook. She grasped the doorway arch and pressed her forehead against the smooth, polished woodwork. "One minute I was removing leaves from the stone and the next my hands were plastered to it like magnets. I saw James glowing and writhing in pain. I couldn't pull away no matter how hard I tried, and then..." She trailed off as James stared at her.

The look in his eyes stole her breath. What did this man want of her? He had said he needed her, and she was the only one who had ever seen him, been able to talk to him. She'd known it was him. He bore all the characteristics of the portrait she'd seen in the book. Why didn't she connect the two? Oh, who was she kidding? She had. Everything in her mind had screamed for her to accept the fact. From the moment her aunt told her about the orb she should have known. Only she wasn't willing to accept the truth.

"How do you feel?" Aunt Vickie asked James as he walked around the chairs and sat down.

James Addison cut an elegant figure of man. Maneuvering around the closed confines of the parlor as if made for the room, April saw the regal bearing in his stance. His demeanor spoke of charm and grace even for a man as tall and broad of shoulder as he was. She couldn't help but admire the pull of his breeches across his thighs and hips as he sat carefully on the settee, his arm stretched out along the back of the cushion.

"I feel alive, thanks to the good doctor." He smiled, picking a piece of lint from his sleeve. His stomach rumbled, echoing in the room. "And perhaps a bit famished," he added.

"I should think so. It's been awhile since you've eaten," Aunt Vickie replied, getting up from her seat. She turned to April. "Sitting here with a slack jaw isn't going to solve anything, dear. Here's your chance for actual historical knowledge, in the flesh. Why not make the most of the opportunity you're given and collect as much information as

~ ☾ ~

you can? But I think some food and perhaps taking him shopping for some proper clothes might be beneficial first."

"It's nearly midnight."

"There's a SuperMart and a diner nearby that are open twenty-four hours. Take him to get something to eat and then fit him with some clothing and articles he may need to see him through for awhile." Waving a hand as if warding off a pesky fly, her aunt rose from the chair and approached the stairs.

April panicked. She couldn't be alone with James Addison. Not yet. She needed her aunt to answer more questions. "Where are you going?"

Vickie stopped and looked at James first, and then back to April. "To prepare a room for our guest. Then I'm calling your mother and grandmother. I have a feeling we're going to need all the paranormal help we can get." Her aunt pointed a finger at her. "*You* are going to take Mr. Addison out for a bite to eat. Go easy though, we want to introduce food to him slowly. He's your responsibility, April."

***

Half an hour later, sitting across from James in the diner, April still couldn't believe the man she'd known only a few days was really James Addison. She looked up from her menu. *What did you talk about with someone you just brought to life?*

What had she done to cause him to re-materialize into a flesh and blood being? What power did she have connecting her with other realms? Being able to see or hear dead people was fine. Bringing them to life, not so much! Did it have something to do with James Addison in particular, or with her unique ability?

She needed guidance. If Aunt Vickie couldn't tell her anything useful, what good would it do to have her grandmother and mother here? Contacting her mother would be a lost cause. The woman struggled with her own ghostly abilities. Knowing her daughter could reincarnate the dead? The situation would throw Virginia Branford over the edge. She would lose her mind. April didn't want the guilt of having put her mother in a straight-jacket.

~ ☾ ~

"What do you recommend? What is a ham-bur-ger?" James Addison frowned, looking over his menu and sounding out the word.

She could still hear the excessive rumblings of his bicentennial empty stomach. He was out of his element with modern day cuisine. Williamsburg taverns and restaurants would have been more adaptable to his time frame but this wasn't Williamsburg.

"A hamburger is ground beef cooked in a patty and placed between two rolls or buns. You can get it cooked to your liking and they top it with all sorts of fixings."

"How do you prefer your hamburger?"

"I like mine medium-rare with mayonnaise, lettuce and tomato and the fries are actually strips of potatoes fried in oil. They're very good."

"Then I shall have one with fries!" he announced slapping the menu closed. "Do they serve ale?"

"No. Not here. Try the cola, it's really good, especially with hamburgers and fries."

The buxom-blonde waitress took their order, smiling and flirting shamelessly with James. The woman couldn't take her eyes off him.

April had never been the jealous type but suddenly, the little green monster in her came to life.

James seemed to be enjoying every moment of banter. He was, after all, James Addison. If he was anything like the books said, between his charm and womanizing ways, she would have her hands full keeping history from repeating itself.

"The serving wench is nothing I expected," James noted in a whisper when their server left.

"She's not a 'serving wench.' They are referred to as waitresses or servers. Wench is a derogatory term now."

He shrugged. "It wasn't much different in my time. But it was acceptable in certain circles."

April watched him touch everything around them as they waited for their food. The napkin holder fascinated him. He pulled napkin after napkin out, examining each piece of paper, making a mess as he tore the pieces to shreds. She let

~ ☾ ~

him. The man hadn't been able to touch anything in so long. April would gladly plant a few trees to cover the ones sacrificing themselves for his curiosity.

"I've seen progress evolve over the years. But I never thought I would be more than a spectator."

He fingered the glass ketchup bottle, nearly knocking it over. The little packets of sugar and artificial sweeteners were next. He tasted each one, preferring the real sugar over the rest. A pile of yellow, pink, blue, and white paper packets littered the table, mingling with the shredded paper napkins. Finally she had to stop him. People from the other booths were beginning to stare. He was like an obsessed, hyperactive child who couldn't keep his hands still. He finished pouring the sugar from the last white sugar packet into his mouth. Great! More sugar to hype him up.

"It's amazing to see sugar in such abundance. A cone of sugar was an expensive item only the wealthy were able to afford. Even then, we used nippers to pinch off pieces for our tea to make it last longer. Now it comes in so many packages."

"Cost of production is not as expensive. We process it here in the states. It's transported in from other parts of the country." All the things he didn't know! April wasn't sure exactly where to start.

When their food arrived he dove into the burger with a vengeance.

She grabbed his hand, marveling at its warmth and solid form for a moment before remembering why she wanted to stop him. "Take it easy. I'm not sure how your stomach will handle food yet."

James nodded and slowed down, savoring each bite. She offered a bite of her turkey melt. His eyebrows raised in delight over the mixture of meat and cheese on toasted sourdough. Dredging a fry in ketchup, April held it out for him to try. He nibbled the crispy potato from her fingers. Soft, masculine lips nipped the tip of her finger causing a fluttering of butterfly wings low in her belly. The shivery sensation made her squirm in the vinyl booth.

"What do you think?"

~ ☾ ~

"Delicious." His eyes darkened, dangerously so. "The crispy potato was, too."

"You're impossible." Heat radiated up from her collar. His silver eyes were bluer than the luminous gray she was used to. Did his eye color change have anything to do with his mortality? What was the state of his mortality? Was this permanent or would they wake up tomorrow to find him a ghost again?

James took a large gulp of cola, only to immediately cough and sputter. April reached for a napkin and handed it to him. Okay, carbonation was new to him.

"It's a bit fizzy. Try sipping it." On the verge of bursting into a full-fledged giggle, April bit back a smile. "Here, try it with a straw. Take small sips." This whole situation was too much to take in. Here she was with a two hundred plus year old man trying to teach him the things she'd always taken for granted. Wow! Wait until he got a load of a television or her laptop.

***

James noticed people coming and going while they ate. A couple of young men walked in the diner wearing pants hanging off of their hips, sporting caps worn backwards and big holes in their ears. He shivered at the idea of wearing such things.

He was comfortable in his attire and didn't think he would be able to wear the clothing he saw. Why some even looked like rags the way they were tattered in the knees. Not very many people wore his clothing—except for the ghost tour guide on the weekends, so he would have to adapt.

His brow wrinkled. He hadn't realized the situation until the waitress returned and asked if he wished for another refill on his cola, but he had drunk a few glasses of the dark brew and found himself in need of relief. Dear Lord! He hadn't had a need to drink or eat in so long, he'd wondered if all of his internals worked.

"I'm afraid I might need use of a..." How did one broach the delicate subject in this day and age? He looked around, unsure of what to do or where he needed to go.

"Oh, a restroom?" April asked.

"Well, I won't be resting, no, I need to--"

~ ☾ ~

"It's called a restroom. See where the man went?" She motioned with a nod of her head to a man in a red hat. He'd walked through a door off to the side of the diner. "There's two doors, one for women, one for men."

"I shall return momentarily."

The room was well lit with a row of three basins along the wall and stalls painted red along another. The man with the red cap stood at one of the two troughs against the other wall opposite the basins, relieving himself. This was all new to him. He walked up to the other trough and proceeded to remove himself from his breeches as the man looked at him with oddity.

Relieving himself, James watched from the corner of his eye as the man finished his business and pushed down on a little silver handle sending a rush of water into the trough.

"Well, isn't that just dandy?" James exclaimed aloud, awed by the contraption.

The man gave him another odd look and backed away as he left the washroom.

A whoosh of sound from one of the stalls startled him, and a big man walked out and stopped to wash at another basin. James watched as he turned on the silver knobs, wet his hands, and then put them under a contraption on the wall that released a foamy substance. Shaking his head, James went to the basins and turned on the knobs. Water flowed, and a small sign above the sinks near the mirrors showed hands lathered in bubbles. He put his hands under the water. It was warm! How delightful!

The man turned to another machine on the wall and rubbed his hands under the blast of air. The man watched him with keen interest and gave him a half smile before leaving. James peered at himself in the mirror. Yes, he would need a change of clothing. Perhaps he was the peculiar character. No wonder they had looked at him funny.

They ended their meal. He'd finished off the hamburger and fries with a piece of pumpkin pie that he devoured with the sweet cream topping. He was accustomed to paying with coins if he didn't have a tab at his local tavern, but now his pockets were empty.

~ ☾ ~

"I would like to establish a tab here," he told the waitress who'd served them when they approached the cash register.

"Um, we don't set up tabs here. Cash or credit cards only." She looked to Dr. Branford who handed her a small card. The waitress swiped it against a box with buttons. The box made a slight whirring sound and spit out a piece of paper. She ripped it off the box and gave it to April to sign with a writing instrument.

He watched her scrawl her name on the piece of paper. She was scribbling! Wasn't she a doctor? She should know how to write properly.

"Your penmanship is atrocious! I can barely decipher the difference between your 'A' and your 'B.' Did you not have proper tutoring?"

"My handwriting is fine. We don't use penmanship very often. We have computers to do much of our writing," she commented when they were out of earshot of the customers lingering about.

"That is no excuse for lack of a proper, formal signature."

After she'd opened his door, he sat in the car. It was low to the ground but comfortable. She'd adjusted the seat for his long legs. Still, he wasn't quite sure about the experience. He'd held on for dear life as she had driven them here to the diner. The quick pace of the machine in such close proximity to others instilled a sense of unease in him. He'd seen cars in the streets of Kings Mill over the decades but he'd never been able to ride in one.

He liked the idea of the harness strap that crossed his body. He'd been amazed when April had first introduced him to it before driving to the diner. She'd insisted he had to wear one because it was the law.

"You need to buckle up your seat belt."

"My what?"

"The strap across your chest...like before."

He must have given her a curious look because she reached across him to grab a strap of material near the door. James inhaled the freshness of her unique scent. Heather and lavender fields came to mind with a bit of something sweet, vanilla perhaps? Her hand rested on his thigh for balance,

~ ☾ ~

mere inches from his groin. He watched her push the metal
clasp into an apparatus which seemed to be its mate. A piece
of her dark, auburn hair came loose from her braid and
drifted against her cheek.

James took the opportunity to touch it. Her hair had been
a source of fascination for him since they met. Smooth, like
the finest silks shipped in from the Orient. Caressing the
strand between his thumb and finger, he delighted in the
texture. The curl mesmerized him for moments, until he
noticed the wary look in April's eyes.

"I've wanted to touch your hair since the first time I saw
you, dreamed of how soft it might be."

His fingers continued their intimate caress of her hair. She
was so close to him, her scent enveloped him. She backed
away, her eyes alive with wonder. He couldn't stop looking
into them, reading what he hoped was a mutual attraction.
After a moment he found his bearings and focused on what
needed to be done. His arousal by having her so close to him
couldn't be a good thing. Dr. Branford was not a woman to
use lightly.

Nothing had prepared him for being able to touch and
interact with April Branford. This was a different time and
era. She was a modern woman and he was a much older man.
He had nothing to give her but his undying gratitude. He
would need to be cautious of his ardor for fear of scaring her
away.

April drove him to the outskirts of his normal domain and
he thrilled at finally being able to go beyond his usual
confines. Kings Mill had spread out from the small village
he'd known in his day. Marveling at the sites, they passed the
cemetery and drove on past stores larger than his family
estate in England. April tried to engage him in conversation
but he was mesmerized by everything around him while they
drove. He could do nothing but gape.

"I had no idea! This is quite extraordinary!" he managed to
say as April drove past each building or object along their
way.

He found everything fascinating. His brow furrowed when
she turned to stare briefly at him.

~ ☾ ~

"What? For the past two hundred thirty-eight years, I haven't stepped outside of the confines of Kings Mill."

April appeared a bit confused. "You mean from the historical district?"

"In my day, the boundaries of the village stopped at the Episcopal Church and its graveyard."

"But I saw you out at the mill site. How is it possible?"

He shook his head, wondering. "I live there. It's my home. Though I'm still confused as how you were able to be in my time frame the other day when you showed up."

"What do you mean?"

He watched as she guided the car behind another at a red signal light. He'd figured out over the years the red light caused people and these unique carriages to stop and the green ones to move forward. Signals were a right bloody good idea, seeing some of these damned horseless contraptions going so fast at times.

"Nothing like it has ever happened before. I've been able to move between times somehow but never realized someone else could, too."

"I think it might have something to do with my gift."

"Gift?"

April sighed. "I have the ability to touch objects or be in a surrounding of historical importance and somehow connect to the past. It's referred to as *archeological psychometry*."

"Is that how you could see me?"

"I'm not sure. The maternal side of my family has the ability to communicate with ghosts." She paused. "I've never had the ability, until now."

"Perhaps it's fate. We don't control our own destiny. If we did, I would never have been murdered by Henry Samuel."

As they stopped at a red light, April turned away from her task to stare at him briefly. She nibbled on her lower lip and turned back to the road ahead when the light changed to green. The car lurched forward, and he clutched the side of the door as they traveled faster than any horse had taken him.

Within moments they were in a paved field of other automobiles in front of a large building with a grand

~ ☾ ~

entrance. He stayed in the seat, still unsure how to work the restraining harness across his body. April walked around to the passenger side and opened his door.

"Are you getting out?"

"I seem to be at a loss as how to unlatch my seat belt."

She sighed as she reached across his lap again, like she had done to buckle him in, and pushed the small red button to release the silver clip. Their eyes held and James noted the catch in her breathing. She was just as affected by their closeness as he was—which was a good sign. He enjoyed having her stretched across his lap. He would have to remember to feign helplessness more often, if it meant having her in such close proximity.

***

April grabbed a shopping cart and walked into the SuperMart with her colonial dressed man parading behind her in a stupor. It was Halloween, well technically according to her watch it was now the first of November. Still, she could use Halloween to her advantage for at least a few more hours.

She hurried him through the store, taking him by the arm to keep him from stopping and ogling. He was too busy gawking at all the items to be paying attention to where he needed to be. The smattering of early morning shoppers stared at him as he touched and fondled everything he came across. He didn't seem to find their looks daunting at all. He stopped from time to time, doffing his tricorne and greeting people as they stared at his costume.

"What size do you wear?" April asked as she took in the shelves of jeans.

"Size? I had my clothing tailored to fit." Shrugging, James went back to touching the material of a half-zippered fleece pullover. "Soft. This would be warm."

"Do you like it?" Smiling she held up a pair of jeans to his waist, measuring length and width. He took the pants from her hands and examined them.

"These are like the ones you wear."

"Kind of. They're called blue jeans. They were created back in the late 1800's by a man known as Levi Strauss. He made them for the men out in the western states during the gold

~ ☾ ~

rush." She trailed off in her explanation when James studied her with interest as if one of her students settling in for a history lesson. His cocky grin left her feeling flushed. She didn't want to feel like a history teacher right now. "I'll explain later. They're comfortable and modern. They can also be used for casual dress or more semi-formal. I think a pair of jeans or two and a pair of black dress slacks will suffice for now."

She found a couple of pairs for him to try on in close sizes and pushed him in the direction of the dressing rooms, along with a couple of dress shirts and sport shirts.

He stopped short as he held out the jeans, pointing to the zigzagged enclosure down the middle. "What is this?"

Oops, she forgot. They didn't have zippers in his day. "It's a zipper. It's used as an enclosure for clothing. You pull up on the little copper tab after you put the pants on." April bit her lip. "Be sure you have everything out of the way first." She cleared her throat nervously.

She never thought something as mundane as a zipper could make her uncomfortable but thinking of where the zipper would be touching left her fantasizing about the man history had insisted was a 'ladies man.' What was it about him boasted the image, other than his dark good looks and charm?

James's brow quirked but he smiled teasingly as he disappeared into the dressing room.

Yeah, just don't zip your dick up. I hear its hell bringing it back down. And I'm not going to be the one to do it.

A few minutes later, James modeled the clothing for her. "How do the jeans feel?"

"It would seem they are a bit uncomfortable if they constantly rub against me. Wouldn't I break out in a rash?"

Didn't he wear linen drawers?

"I prefer to be au naturel," he remarked as if sensing her confusion. "It's easier for the ladies..."

"Here." She cut him off, tossing a package of cotton briefs to him. "Try these. I would hate to have you chafe." And no, she didn't want to hear why it had been easier for the ladies! The grin on his face told her he was one big tease. Should she

~ ☾ ~

expect anything less from *the* James Addison? She tossed a couple more packages of briefs into their shopping cart.

With a full wardrobe of pants and shirts for any occasion, and even a winter coat, James was set for however long he might be staying. They purchased enough toiletries to get him through for a while and went to check out. Anything else, they could figure out and come back later. April realized what time it was and how exhausted she should be.

James pointed to the advertisement of a young boy enjoying a soft-serve ice cream cone as they passed the small ice cream store inside the Super Mart. "What is that?"

"Ice cream," April replied. She could eat ice cream any time of the year. "Frozen milk or cream, served in a crunchy, cake-like shell. Would you like to try one?"

She didn't wait for his response but ordered two vanilla cones, plain, no sprinkles. She would let him elaborate once he tasted the treat as it was. She handed him his, wrapped in a paper napkin. He stared at it, unsure what to make of the creamy substance.

"Is there no utensil? How does one eat ice cream in a cone?"

"With your mouth, like this...let me show you."

Taking her ice cream cone April licked around the base to catch the drips and continued up the creamy concoction until she formed a smooth point. Finishing, she wrapped her mouth around the tip of the vanilla cream and bit off the top with her lips. James sat on the bench, staring silently while his ice cream began to run in rivulets over his hand.

"Your ice cream is melting, James. You need to eat it quickly!" April laughed, unsure why he stared at her with such intent. But when his blue eyes darkened to the color of midnight sky and mimicked her earlier instructions—exaggerating every sip, lick and dip of his tongue against the smooth cream, and then licking any melted drips from the inside rim of the cone—she understood completely, and had never envied an ice cream cone more than she did right then. Her heart thudded in her chest and echoed its throbbing pulse lower in her body, sending thrilling arcs of heat coursing through her.

~ ☾ ~

"I think I like ice cream...very much," James whispered as he used a napkin to finish cleaning his fingers and lips. "I think you do, too, April Branford."

~ ☾ ~

Chapter Six

James scowled at the clothes he dumped on the bed. *Gifts from a woman!* He should be grateful—he was alive. April gave him life again, a chance to redeem himself, to find the truth of his past. How many others in his situation ever received a second chance?

Still, having no job or possible source of income bothered him. He felt kept, like a mistress. He would need to find a job. Perhaps his mill was still in operation, he could work there. But how long was he here for, a day, a week, a fort night...forever?

No matter! A man needed a source of income to support himself and his lady. Was April his lady? She had money to pay for things. She had a job, a life of her own. But he would be damned if he would let her support him! He had to find income so he could pay her back. Living off of a woman was unheard of. His father would have boxed his ears at such a thought.

He stared at the items as if they offended him. He didn't have much of a choice right now. The clothing would have to suffice, but he would pay April back as soon as he could.

Putting the clothes away in his bureau, James heard a soft knock. He crossed the room to open the door.

"Hi," April said a bit nervously, holding a bag from the drug store.

Glittery gems outlined the word 'Angel' on her black shirt that matched long black pants dwarfing her slender figure. Her hair was still secured in the long rope but her face shone of freshly washed skin, making her green eyes even brighter without all the black eye kohl she normally wore to outline them. Yes, she was his *angel*. How else could he describe anyone with the ability to bring him to life?

~ ☾ ~

"I wanted to bring you the rest of your stuff."

She shifted from one foot to the other. James glanced down to see fluffy baby lambs on her feet. Here was this sexy, mysterious woman who held his life in her very capable hands—wearing sheep on her feet.

"They were a gift from my mother. They keep my feet warm," she explained with a bit of annoyance in her voice as she looked up at him again.

"You're adorable—like a kitten my sister Elsbeth used to have," he said. April Branford appeared so soft and delicate, he wanted to cuddle her.

"Yes well, thank you." She frowned, pushing a dangling curl behind her ear.

She should let her hair fall free so he could run his fingers through it, or wrap the damn braid around his fist as he took her against the wall. He felt his body tighten at the thought. No, now was not the time to be thinking these thoughts.

"I wanted to see if there might be anything you needed before I turned in for the night."

You, Dr. Branford. I need you.

"Well, now that you mention it..." James couldn't help but lead her on a bit. The way her pupils dilated and color raced to her cheeks he had no doubt she knew what he was thinking. The way she'd tempted him while they'd enjoyed their ice cream cones was an innocent gesture on her part, but it had left him hard and eager to have her mouth on him.

He knew she hadn't realized what provocative thoughts the simple use of her tongue did to him, until he turned the tables on her. The excitement in her eyes and hitch in her breathing told him everything he needed to know. Would she taste as creamy and sweet?

"I would like water brought up for a bath in the morning. It's been awhile."

She cleared her throat, her fingers brushing a stray curl out of her face. Was embarrassment flushing her cheeks? "I forgot you're not used to our modern facilities." She stepped across his bedroom threshold before stopping and taking a step back. "May I come in?"

"Of course." He ushered her in with a flourish of his hand.

~ ☾ ~

Anytime, my dear.

She led him to the door which opened into the wash closet. He had yet to explore the smaller room filled with odd contraptions. Looking around he wasn't sure what to make of some of the items.

Once she explained in thorough detail how everything worked, much like the knobs and levers in the men's room at the diner, James couldn't wait to try out the 'shower.' The idea of warm water cascading over him—with the little vibrating thingy sounded wonderfully relaxing. He wished he'd thought of such a unique device especially after days of working in the fields.

She walked back to his bed and retrieved the bag she'd brought over as he reveled in the delight of the pulsing water hitting his hand. April removed a green bottle from the bag.

"This is shower gel. It's like soap and you use it with this pouf." She showed him a black netted ball on a string. "Here, smell. I love the scent of this brand. I use it sometimes, even though it's more of a guy's fragrance."

She pulled out another bottle. "Here is a two-in-one shampoo and conditioner for your hair." She placed the shower gel and shampoo on the wire shelf hanging from the shower head. "And here is your razor and shaving gel. The razor has three blades for close, comfortable shaving so there are fewer nicks and cuts. You use the foam to lather your face and then shave. I'm sure you know how to do that. It's easier now, though."

He took the razor from her fingers, admiring the design. James didn't know what to make of all the wonderful items. This razor alone would have saved him so much trouble in his time.

'There! You're all set." She paused and her cheeks turned pink. "By the way, these days, people tend to take showers on a daily basis."

Daily? He prided himself on always being clean. He'd always had someone heat a copper hip tub of water once a week for him. Not many of his time did. Some in his era found bathing a cumbersome event. He enjoyed a tub for many things—including indulging in a bit of 'clean fun' now

~ ☾ ~

and again for him and his current lady friend. But daily?
Well, if it was the normal thing to do, he would have to fit in.
"I look forward to enjoying such luxuries. But I might need
a bit of help. What shall I do for washing my back?"
April's eyes lit with a knowing gleam. "I'm sure we could
figure out a solution, if it becomes an issue."
James drew a seductive smile. "I'm almost positive it *will*
become an issue."
The slow pull of her bottom lip between her teeth brought
James's smile up a bit. Dear God, she was actually
considering his offer! His attention immediately went to
peruse her body. Her nipples were prominent points against
the linen of her top. She couldn't deny her attraction to him,
even though their banter was mostly in jest.
He pointed to her shirt. "Are you chilled?"
She looked down in confusion. Her eyes went round, her
cheeks flushed with color. She quickly crossed her arms over
her chest, and making a hasty retreat for her chambers, called
'good night' as she stormed across the open hallway. He had
to laugh or take their mutual interest a step further.
Yes, James had noticed the vividly embossed points
pressing outward from her shirt. If bantering with him
caused April to become aroused, he wondered what the actual
act of making love would do to her. He was beyond primed to
show the good doctor how aroused he could make her.

***

He thought she was 'adorable' like a kitten! She didn't
want to be adorable, she wanted to be sexy! Studying herself
in the full length mirror she realized 'adorable' was the most
charming word he could probably have come up with. Sexy
was not in her repertoire of characteristics, never had been
really.
No, she was more the academic geeky girl. In her mind,
she was still a pre-pubescent school girl at a slumber party
from Hell. Hair pulled back in a severe braid, no make-up, a
long, shapeless t-shirt top and lounge pants, with fuzzy lamb
slippers. Nope, nothing sexy there. All she needed to
complete the look was her braces from her teenage years.
Why did she even care what he thought of her? James

~ ☾ ~

Addison was the ghost of her research project. She might have brought him to life, but technically he was still a ghost. A man who was long since dead, whether he'd been executed or not. He would be what, two hundred and seventy by now? How could she find him even remotely attractive? Okay, so he didn't look a day over thirty-three and with the stigma of being noted as a ladies' man—she was curious. What made him so popular with the ladies of his time? Was it his charm, his smile? April bit her lip in deep thought. Or possibly something more unique?

Her interest was purely for research. It wasn't every day a historian got up close and personal with their historical subject. What constituted a 'ladies man' back in his day? The stories of his ménage a trios with the tavern wenches were interesting but was he good at pleasing a woman or just a rumor of historical escapades? April's face flamed at the thought of possibly finding out. Would she offer herself in the name of research to appease her curiosity?

You're supposed to be professional! You aren't a woman on the make. You have work to do, Dr. April Branford, and so far you have done a piss-poor job!

She needed to focus on her job if she was serious about her career. Ten years of school attested to her seriousness. Her connection to James Addison should be professional only. She shouldn't care what he thought of her looks. She was only attracted to him because he spoke her language, history. His attraction was because she'd brought him to life. She was the only person, and a woman, who he'd been able to interact with in over two hundred years. If she wanted to work on impressing James Addison it needed to be strictly on a professional level. Besides, as a man, James Addison was way out of her league.

Getting into bed she reached over to turn off the bedside lamp. *Oh, hell! Who are you kidding, April?* She paused. *Sexy, huh?* Throwing back the covers she proceeded to wiggle out of her lounge pants and top, leaving her naked except for her panties. She felt uncomfortably naked. She was going a bit off the deep end. Putting her top back on, April left the lounge pants off. The whole 'sexy' thing would have to be gradual.

~ ☾ ~

***

April stared around the darkened room, trying to let her pupils dilate enough to see. Why was she awake? The blue digital numbers on her travel alarm clock read 3:45 a.m. She hadn't fallen asleep until nearly two-thirty since she couldn't get James Addison out of her thoughts.

She'd even gotten up and sent an email to Kenneth Miles on her lack of progress. Technically her progress had exceeded her expectations, having been the only person in known history to have located James Addison's remains. But she couldn't brag. Telling Kenneth, James Addison led her to his own grave might have the man questioning her sanity.

He was arriving in a few weeks. Great! Would James still be around? What would Kenneth think if confronted with his two hundred seventy year old ancestor?

It would be ironic. The reality of working for a descendant of James Addison and turning the actual legend to life seemed more than a bit coincidental. It was as if it were preordained by fa...no, she wasn't going to say the "f" word.

A faint sound coming from the bedroom on the other side of the wall had her stopping and turning around. Muffled through the plaster, it sounded like a woman's sob. Who was sleeping in the other room? Her aunt's room was downstairs at the back of the house. Had her aunt invited a friend over while they had been out?

April couldn't go back to sleep knowing someone was crying in the next room. She flipped on her bedside lamp and slipping into her robe and lamb booties, tip-toed out into the darkened hallway.

The door of the room next to hers was slightly ajar. Listening at the opening she couldn't hear anything. She accidentally nudged the door a bit with her head, causing it to squeak open on its rusty hinges.

"Hello?" April called out. She peeked around the solid wood door and pressed the old button style light switch illuminating the room. The antique switch worried her. How many times had she told her aunt to get the electric re-wired in this house?

No one occupied the room. The white, shabby-chic vintage

~ ☾ ~

room was perfectly neat and tidy, the petal pink Chenille
bedspread and shams all in place. Even though April knew it
would be a waste of time, she checked the door to the
adjoining bathroom. The muffled sobs she'd heard couldn't
have been this far from her own wall. The bathroom was
empty. Walking back into the bedroom she noticed a strong
smell of lilac that hadn't been there before.

She followed the fragrance to an antique secretary desk in
the corner of the room, surrounded by a chill in the air. The
strong scent seemed to emanate from here. She checked the
window and noticed a draft coming from around the casing,
accounting for the drop in temperature.

She waited for the sound of the weeping woman but didn't
hear it anymore. Her arms prickled with goose bumps as her
heart began to race and yet, she didn't move. The flowery
scent now overwhelmed her.

Cold drafts, phantom odors, unexplained weeping, what
was happening to her? Was this another situation with her
heightened sense of psychometry? Her whole body shook, her
teeth chattered as she wrapped her arms around herself to
keep from falling apart. She reached for the antique desk to
anchor herself to something solid.

Run! Her mind screamed. But her body refused to move.
She felt weighted down as if someone or something had a
hold of her, not wanting her to leave.

Stay...Help me, please.

Had a woman just spoken to her? Her eyes went wide,
taking in her surroundings. The desk, she was touching the
desk! Damn it! She let go of the solid piece of furniture and
inched away from the inner room. A sense of helplessness
and confusion meshed with the fear inside of her. Spurts of
adrenaline raced through her blood stream.

What was happening to her? Bringing ghosts to life,
stepping into scenes from history, and now this? Could this
be more than her gift working with her? Psychometry was a
powerful, metaphysical talent, but what if it went beyond the
simple act of getting a minor reading—what if she had the
ability to interact with the realms of the afterlife? Maybe what
happened to her at the mill site was real. It wasn't just her

~ ☾ ~

allergies and sinus infection. She'd actually stepped into another realm. James had said as much. He'd seen her from his past. Was this all happening because of her psychometry? Or was there something more? But she couldn't face another ghost now. She was too tired, physically and emotionally.

"This is not happening," she told herself out loud. She looked around the room as if to see a specter floating by. "Go away, now!"

She closed her eyes tightly, and when she blinked them open again a sense of calm settled over her. She needed her gardenia oil. With all the emotional struggles from today, she needed something soothing to help her fight these strange occurrences. No. What she needed to do was stop touching the damned antiques! She would be fine as long as she kept her hands to herself from now on. Did it mean she shouldn't touch James? *Yeah, when donkeys fly!*

~ ☾ ~

Chapter Seven

April reached for her coat and accessories as she walked into the grand entrance and saw her aunt at the dining room table eating breakfast. "Is James up? I wanted to head out to meet with Dr. Freelane as soon as possible this morning."

"Slow down, April, you haven't even had breakfast." Aunt Vickie poured orange juice into the elegant, depression era glass. "Sit. We need to talk. Besides, James is still here. You can't just leave him alone. I have my water aerobics class this morning."

April sighed and slipped into the chair with defeat. The whole day seemed a waste now. Her main objective was to meet with Dr. Freelane and go over records, documents, facts...anything she could find on James Addison and Kings Mill.

Her aunt studied her intently. "Are you wearing your hair differently this morning, my dear? I must say it's very becoming pulled back."

Reaching up she patted the quick twist she'd secured loosely at the nape of her neck. "Yes, well I thought a change might be nice," April explained herself but stopped when her aunt gave her the knowing look. "You said we needed to talk?"

"I've given your situation with James a lot of thought. I even contacted a few people in my paranormal society to give me their take on what could have happened," Aunt Vickie said, turning her focus to the subject at hand.

"You've let others know what I did?" Great! That was all she needed. To be hounded by entertainment rags and groupies of ghost hunters wanting to see if her James Addison was the real thing.

"Nobody I can't trust with the secret. We need to

~ ☾ ~

make this a national spectacle," her aunt replied as if she assumed April would make it one. "But everyone seems to be in concurrence on your problem. Your psychometry is enhancing the paranormal energies around you. The stronger the energy, the more it is brought to light. I noticed a strong aura surrounding both you and James—the colors are so closely linked."

"I might believe it if he were still a ghost, Aunt Vickie." She stopped and listened. The water running above them told her James was awake and enjoying his first shower ever. "But he's a real man. How do you explain that?"

"You were both in close proximity to James's remains. You were touching his tombstone. It's an artifact of his remains dating back to his burial, and it was All Hallows Eve. You know as well as I, Halloween is the time when the spiritual realm is in closest proximity to ours. Something tells me James was already close enough to our realm of time. Your gift and the timing brought him the rest of the way." Vickie leaned forward, placing her elbows on the table. "I'm going to go out on a limb and say the connection between your energies, auras, and psychometry all mirrored the effects of each other until..."

"Until his soul and his body merged to life again."

"Exactly my dear!" Aunt Vickie leaned back, sipping her tea and looking pleased with April's acceptance.

April rubbed her face in aggravation. "I don't believe this." She picked up her muffin, cut it in half and began buttering it with the sweet honey whipped butter her aunt liked.

"You doubt what your own eyes and heart tell you are true? Stop being so damn pessimistic and cynical, April. Start feeling and trusting with your heart. Fate has a way of leading us where we need to be for a reason."

"Fate? Fate!" Throwing her untouched muffin half to her plate, she took her napkin and wiped her lips and fingers and prepared to leave. "God, if I hear one more reference to fate, I swear I will scream."

"Watch your language, April Branford, don't you dare take His name in vain."

For all of her aunt's belief's in the supernatural and the

~ ☾ ~

deities of old, she still practiced her beliefs in Christianity. April sighed and sat back down. "Sorry."

Her aunt shrugged. April felt bad for raising her voice to her aunt. One thing her family prided themselves on was their ability to know when something was meant to be.

"Knowing how everything went yesterday, did you sleep last night?" Her aunt changed the subject.

"I finally went to sleep about two, until I thought I heard a woman weeping in the other room next to mine. It was only the wind. You need to get the windows caulked, there is a draft up there." Picking up her muffin half she took a bite.

"Was she there?"

April stopped chewing, watching her aunt. "Was who there?"

"The weeping woman," Vickie sighed as if she were answering an idiot. "I've sensed her presence since I moved in six years ago. She's been known to visit a time or two, usually around November or December. But she's more of a residual essence to me, not an active one." Vickie stared thoughtfully towards the upper floor of the house. "Poor thing, she seems to be distraught, and a bit fearful. The room belonged to her, so I always keep it tidy."

Distraught, fearful? Crap! Yeah, those were the feelings she'd gotten last night, too. "You're saying there is a woman staying in the room?" April turned in her seat to face her aunt.

"Not a real woman—oh, I'm sure she was at one point. Most residual haunts need to be released before they can move on." She shrugged. "I suppose that's why this time of year she seems to emerge. Perhaps something drastic happened to her around now and this point brings her into focus."

"I didn't see a weeping woman. Just heard the draft from the old window making it sound like someone crying." April didn't want to admit to her possible connection. She had enough to deal with right now. One ghost was more than she could handle.

"If you say so," Aunt Vickie sighed. "I know she's there. Maybe she called out to you last night for help. You have it in

~ ☾ ~

you to give peace and solve mysteries left unanswered. The spirits just want to move on—yet they can't always reach out to those who can help them."

"And what am I supposed to do? Bring them to life so they can relive their time on Earth and solve their deaths so they can move on?"

"I'm saying you may be the connection between the present and the past they need to touch." Vickie sat forward and reached for April's hand, holding it reverently. "Your touch and ability to understand history is their only hope in telling their stories, and setting the records straight. Without the truth, ghosts flounder aimlessly until someone comes along to set them free. You are their only hope."

***

Initially, James wasn't sure if he could sleep. He hadn't in so long. Afraid he might not wake up if he did fall asleep, he'd tossed and turned for a good hour or two. But once sleep hit him it was deep and blissful. He woke up refreshed and ready for the first full day of the rest of his life, however long that might be. The clock at his bedside table illuminated oddly disjointed numbers, eight o'clock in the morning. Would April be awake? James listened intently for any sounds of movement from across the hall, but heard none.

Cold air touched his naked skin. He could feel hot and cold as if he were truly alive again. He wasn't as prepared for the cool air as he assumed he'd be. He should've worn the lounge pants, as April had called them, but it wasn't his style. Now he stared down at the gooseflesh dotting his naked form. Sighing, he was glad April Branford wasn't around to witness his chill. The temperature did nothing to show his attributes. She might wonder why the history books had proclaimed him to be such a 'ladies man' when his family jewels appeared less than favorable.

Looking forward to experiencing a shower, James had toyed with the idea of taking one last night, but he didn't want to have to go through the trouble of heating water twice, especially if he was only going to sleep afterward. No, starting his new life fresh would be preferable. He couldn't wait to enjoy hot and cold running water. No more having to lug the

~ ☾ ~

hip tub up to his room or wait for pails of water to be heated for him.

Stepping into the shower he was hit full force with a warm, needle-like spray. He marveled at the true miracle of water cascading over his hand as he leaned against the solid, tiled wall. Moments spent warming his body under the fountain, letting his skin soak in moisture felt like the Heaven he'd waited forever for. He touched his face, feeling the raspy growth of whiskers. Flexing his fingers he pinched himself, reveling in the senses of actual contact. Hair plastered against his head, he let the water, running in rivulets down his face, mix with unabashed tears of being alive again. He wasn't an emotional man, but someone thought him worthy enough to be given a second chance. Should a man cry from such a simple pleasure of life?

***

It had taken him a few tries with the oddly shaped razor but after nicking his throat a few times he realized he didn't have to use so much pressure to wield the contraption. He did come to the conclusion he was alive, or at least had blood running through his veins. He combed his hair back after a ridiculous amount of time of washing it. The directions on the green bottle said to 'wash, rinse and repeat.' How many times was he supposed to? It didn't give any indication, and he figured it had been a long while so he continued at least six times. He had to agree with April, he did enjoy the fragrance of the body wash. It reminded him of the heather fields and evergreens back home in England.

When he went downstairs, he found April sitting at the dining room table, finishing up breaking her fast with her Aunt Vickie.

"Good morrow dear gentle ladies."

Both looked at him simultaneously. Their raised eyebrows had him checking himself for possible faux pas in modern attire.

He turned himself inside out trying to see what wrong he'd committed. "Is there something amiss? Did I not dress properly?"

"No...I mean yes, you're fine," April stammered, before taking a sip from her cup.

~ ☾ ~

"Wow! What an understatement," Aunt Vickie mumbled under her breath as she stood to take her leave.

"Please, don't leave on my account, Miss Snyder."

She waved him off. "I have my water aerobics class this morning, I should be going." She looked him over and glanced towards April who was focused on stirring cream into her cup.

"Forgive me," he began. "Have I interrupted anything?"

"No. Nothing at all." Vickie Snyder patted his freshly shaven cheek. "Sit down and have some breakfast. April will get you a plate from the kitchen and some tea."

"If it's not too much trouble—"

"No trouble at all, James." April rose from her seat and exchanged a look with her aunt he couldn't quite read, before she headed into the kitchen.

"How are you feeling this morning, Mr. Addison?" Aunt Vickie caught his attention again.

"Alive and quite well, Miss Snyder," he returned jovially, taking her hand and placing a brief kiss to the woman's fingers. "And you?"

"Wishing I were forty years younger or born in the 1740's. Take your pick."

James cocked his eyebrow and studied the woman inquisitively. It finally dawned on him. "Why, Miss Snyder, I do believe you are flirting with me."

"I would have to be blind in both eyes and without any senses not to," the old woman's smile was charming and infectious. "And stop calling me Miss Snyder. You make me sound like some school marm. Please, call me Vickie."

"Very well, Vickie." He rubbed his fingers lightly over the woman's knuckles before delicately dropping her hand. "If you address me as James."

April returned with a tray of a steaming plate of food and a delicate china teapot and set it on the table.

"Oh, by the way." Vickie went to retrieve her coat from the coat tree. James helped her put it on when he saw her struggle. "Thank you. I wanted to let you know you have the house to yourselves tonight. I have tickets to the Baltimore Symphony Orchestra with my friend, Abby. I won't be home

~ ☾ ~

until late so don't wait up for me."

James found her announcement confusing. She was leaving April alone with...him? "You would leave your niece without a chaperone while there is a man about? Should I find another form of residence?"

"We don't stand on such formality anymore, James. Besides, it might be you in need of the chaperone."

April jumped in clearing her throat. "Don't you have your water aerobics class to attend, Aunt Vickie?"

James didn't miss the heated stare aimed at the older woman from his delightful angel.

"Matter of fact I do." She grabbed her bag near the door and waved with her fingers, laughing as she headed out the door.

"You'll have to excuse my Aunt Vickie. She's rather odd at times," April said as he sat down in front of the plate of fluffy eggs, crispy bacon, and what looked like a soft scone.

James unfolded his napkin and placed it in his lap. "On the contrary, I find her quite charming. She's a woman who's experienced life and is not afraid to speak her mind."

"Yes, well she sometimes speaks her mind too frankly, I'm afraid."

"I've learned speaking one's mind is of great advantage. It doesn't leave anything up for questioning." He poked his fork into the fluffy eggs, sampling to see if his taste buds still worked this morning. "Did you and your ex-boyfriend speak openly to one another?"

"Jason?"

"Yes, you spoke of him the other day, when we met. Perhaps you shared a lack of communication causing you to drift apart." He was so intent on eating he didn't realize the awkward silence until he looked up to see sadness in April's eyes. "I'm sorry. Did I say something I ought not to have?"

"No," she whispered. "We just had different values."

"Such as?"

"He didn't believe in my gift." Her heavy sigh spoke of the heartache she must have witnessed. "He thought my psychometry was a hoax, some idiocy I had made up to make myself important, or rather 'odd,' to him and our mutual

~ ☾ ~

friends." She shrugged as if it didn't matter. "He even questioned my paper on the Salem Witch Trials, making fun of me and asking if I was there at the time."

"The bastard!" James sat forward, wondering how she could have endured such a sniveling louse. "Did he not see your talents? Could he not honestly sense your true ability to connect on some level with the past?"

April smiled. "I appreciate your support, James, but you weren't there."

"I've seen what you can do. I'm living proof." He munched viciously on a piece of bacon. "Well, good riddance, I say. You're much too intelligent and kind to be shackled to a man who can't find it in his heart to honor a woman such as you." He stopped chewing. "Are there more idiots in this world who think such thoughts?"

"Unfortunately, yes. Intelligence is subjective."

"Well, I hope you can keep me away from these short-sighted imbeciles, like your Jason."

"He's not my Jason anymore," April said as she leaned on her hand contemplatively. "I hope I've learned to move on."

"—and accept your talent for what it is?" James reached across the table to take her free hand, giving it a gentle, affectionate squeeze. "Never doubt what you've done to me, for me, April Branford. You are an amazing woman."

~ ☾ ~

Chapter Eight

"So what are we to do today?" James asked as they walked down the street bordering the old courthouse.

"I need to meet with Dr. Freelane. I called her a little bit ago to make sure she was available. She is the foremost historian on Kings Mill history. She runs the historical society. Unfortunately, she's the only full time employee and she's swamped with moving into a new building the city received a grant for last year."

"How is it unfortunate? I would think a new building would provide a great opportunity." James stopped to look in one of the law office windows as they passed by.

It didn't occur to her he'd stopped abruptly until he wasn't there to catch her response to his question. She turned around to see him staring oddly at the lead glass.

Going back the few steps she touched his arm, bringing him out of his stupor. "What's wrong?"

He nodded his head at the window. "Henry's office."

"Really? I didn't know."

"The last time I was here I had purchased a piece of land to expand to the north of my immediate property." His voice was low and sad. "It was less than a fortnight before my death."

"I'm sorry, James." April looked up at the door sign for a local law firm. The front window was a large plate glass, still reminiscent of the antiquity needed to maintain historical status for Kings Mill. No one was in the lobby but she could see the receptionist peaking up over her desk watching them warily. "Do you want to go inside?"

James seemed to break out of his spell and looked at her with an odd frown. "Why would I want to go in? Henry is no longer there. Trust me, if he was I would gladly give him a thrashing."

~ ☾ ~

"Wouldn't you want to ask him why he had you killed?"

He looked at her as if she was daft. "Well, of course I would!"

"Would that be before or after you thrashed him?"

"Before I thrashed him. The man wouldn't be able to speak after I got done with him." James growled menacingly.

April took him by the arm. She needed to get this man away from his need for revenge against someone no longer alive. "Come on. We have a lot to do today and I hope you can help me sort through all the documents I might be able to get my hands on."

***

They had walked to the present historical society office, a small Victorian townhouse with the main floor used as a small museum and visitor center. The door was locked and a small note telling them to meet Dr. Freelane at the new location two blocks down was taped to the door.

Proceeding to the new building, they encountered a flurry of activity going on with contractors, engineers, and various other construction employees swarming in and out of the airy wood and glass office. April and James walked in to the smell of epoxy and fresh paints. They side stepped the whir of electrical drills and nail guns to approach a woman in her mid to late fifties with a severe, grayish-silver bun knotted at the back of her head. She was busy dealing with a construction foreman, arguing over where electrical outlets were supposed to go. The woman glanced up, holding up her finger for them to wait just a moment as she finished her discussion with the man in the white hard hat.

April looked around at the sparse area. The beige walls matched the neutral tones of the commercial grade carpet. Large wooden beams crossed the cathedral-style ceiling full of recessed lighting. It appeared almost too modern to be a historical society. But it was esthetically pleasing to most people. Truthfully, she preferred the musty smells of old buildings to modern facilities.

"Dr. Branford?"

April turned when she was addressed. "Dr. Freelane, it's a pleasure to finally meet you."

~ ☾ ~

"Please, call me Beth." They shook hands. "Dr. Moreland has told me so much about you. I feel I know you already."

"Should I be worried?"

"Not at all. He speaks highly of you." She turned to James. "Are you two together?"

"Ah, yes..." April hadn't really figured out how she was going to address James but they'd agreed to use an alias for him while dealing with outsiders. "This is my good friend, Jim Adams, from England."

"Oh. I didn't know you were bringing a friend with you."

"I'm helping Dr. Branford out with some of her research. I have a bit of insight into James Addison."

Beth Freelane's historical interest perked up. "Really? How so? There isn't a whole lot of information gathered on the man."

"I'm familiar with his English background, not too much with his life in the colonies. I was hoping you and Dr. Branford might help me."

Beth gasped and placed a hand to her chest. "Well, by all means this is a delightful situation. I might be able to piece more about our local legend together with some of your knowledge. Will you be staying long?"

"For now. I'm not sure how long though."

Damn if that wasn't the understatement of all time, April thought as she let James handle himself with Beth Freelane. So far they'd managed to avoid any questions or incidents to put up red flags.

"I would be delighted to chat with you about what you know of James Addison." Beth glowed but April wasn't sure if it was with feminine interest or purely historical.

James took Beth's hand, and as he had done with her Aunt Vickie, placed a subtle brush of his lips against her slender fingers. The woman blushed down to her gray roots.

She bore no wedding ring and looked like a throw-back to a Math teacher April had in high school who'd been teaching since before the Abacus. The only thing missing from Beth Freelane were the black, horn-rimmed glasses of the 1950's.

Beth showed them to the back room where empty filing drawers were lined against the wall like armored knights of

~ ☾ ~

old awaiting their turn in battle. In between the rows of filing cabinets were totes, plastic milk crates, and moving boxes filled with old ledgers, wrapped accordion file folders, and random stacks of papers bundled together with twine and old rubber bands.

"Welcome to my Hell." Beth waved her hand over the miscellaneous collection. "We've never had the room to house all of the historical documents over the centuries or the manpower to record them for posterity. I've put in for funding to have one of the students from Towson University come work with me next summer. Until then, I'm surrounded with mountains of files, overseeing the new building project, and of course, working with the Friends of Kings Mill Historical Society for the festivities this next month."

"My great-aunt is on the committee, Victoria Snyder," April explained her connection.

"You're Vickie's niece? Really! So you must be staying at the Samuel house." Beth's voice trailed off as if distracted.

"Yes. It's convenient and I get to visit with my aunt," April said bringing the woman back to the present. She looked around at the chaos Beth spoke of. "Are these the documents you agreed to let me search through?"

Nodding, the woman closed her eyes and sighed. "Be my guest. There is no rhyme or reason to them. Some came to me from city hall, some from the courthouse, and others have been brought in from law offices and other historical buildings in the area—family heirlooms, birth certificates, death notices—God only knows what you'll find."

"I'll see what I can do to help you out a bit while I'm searching for the documents I need." April turned to James who was standing by, dumbfounded by the mess taking up the large back room. "You in on this with me, Ja...Jim?" She caught herself at the last minute.

He shrugged. "In for a hay-penny, in for a pound as my father used to say."

***

They stopped long enough to take a stroll for an afternoon spot of tea and warm scones at the local café. James gritted his teeth as April paid for his cup of Earl Grey and sweet. It

~ ☾ ~

galled him to have her spend another hard earned coin on him. A man had his pride in any century! At least he hoped a man still thought that way. Seeing the population of men over the centuries, he wondered if they hadn't lost a bit of their masculinity. Why from the looks of some lately, they didn't even have the decency to pull up their breeches in a lady's presence. It was appalling. Their sires should have taken a strap to them!

"One would think we would have made some headway in all those files today," April said as they headed back to her aunt's house later that evening.

"There definitely is quite a number to search through." He turned to her. "Do you think we'll find what you're looking for?"

"I don't know. It would be sad if we didn't. Not just for our sake but history's sake in general."

They walked solemnly into the empty house and removed their outer layers of winter clothing, hanging them up on the clothes tree. April touched her hair. The bulbous mass she'd pinned up had become unraveled over the day.

He enjoyed her braid and wondered at her change in style. He'd noticed Dr. Freelane sporting a similar style, but much more severe. Most women walking the streets wore their hair unbound. It would have been considered scandalous by the women in his day. But truthfully, if April didn't care to wear her braid or bun, he would like very much to see it down, loose around her shoulders.

"I suppose I'll go upstairs and get ready for dinner. I also want to check in with Kenneth Miles and let him know about today's progress." She started up the stairs. "Let's say we meet back down here in thirty minutes?"

James looked to the clock on the mantle. "Very well. I too shall freshen up."

A half an hour later, James awaited April's appearance. He began to pace. It was good to know some things never changed. Women still liked to keep a man waiting.

He'd changed into the dark slacks and a linen shirt she'd purchased for him. It seemed a bit formal for what he'd witnessed at the diner last night. Perhaps he was overdressed

~ ☾ ~

for an evening out? He was perspiring, anticipating the inevitable and feeling lower and lower. It would be humiliating to know she was paying for another meal for him. He paced the confines of the dining room, waiting. He fingered his collar away from his throat. Was the collar of his shirt too tight?

He didn't feel comfortable going out and taking advantage of April. She'd done so much for him already. There had to be some way he could contribute and not feel like such a cad. James looked around the dining room. He would starve before she would pay for his meal again tonight. He didn't give a damn if it was common for a woman to foot the bill once in awhile!

His eyes lit on the table near the front window in the parlor. It was small with a lace runner accompanied by a candlestick ensconced in a hurricane glass globe. Two side chairs sat at either end. It was a cozy setting for two people to enjoy tea or...dinner.

An idea started to form in his head. It was silly, frivolous, and she might not even approve. But damn it, he just might be able to make it work.

***

Silence met her on the other end of the phone. April waited for whatever Kenneth Miles would throw at her verbally after she'd told him she had nothing new to reveal. Biting her lip she held her breath for the string of profanities to follow. But nothing came. She slowly exhaled.

"Mr. Miles?" she asked gently for fear of retribution.

"I'm here, Dr. Branford— disappointed is all, and a bit tired."

She could hear him sighing from thousands of miles away. It was nearly midnight in England so yes he would be tired.

"I understand, sir. I'm sorry I don't have more for you at this moment. I don't know what else to do right now. I'm afraid I'm at a stand-still." Should she tell him about James Addison? How could she without him thinking her a loon?

"I need you to keep looking. I'm counting on you. I've been able to extend the hearings for a few weeks, but I intend to be in Kings Mill for the celebration. I want to be there to show

~ ☾ ~

my support since I've learned about James Addison and Kings Mill."

April couldn't agree more. "Perhaps together we might be able to honor James's memory. I look forward to paying my respects to the man. The more I've gotten to know him, the more I feel he wasn't given justice."

"And you know this how? He was accused of crimes against the crown. Is there documentation proving his innocence?"

"No. If I'd found any, I would have informed you, Mr. Miles." April tried to back track. She was treading on thin ice by opening her heart and her mouth at the same time. "It's just a feeling I have. I can't explain it."

"I know of those feelings, Dr. Branford. One of the reasons why I'm so good with investing is having those feelings of being in the right place at the right time. My own intuition plays a big part in my business dealings. Right now, something is telling me the Kings Mill site is an investment of a lifetime. All I know is its imperative for me to be able to find those documents and have access to the land."

April couldn't help but smile. Kenneth Miles was as infatuated with this whole James Addison case as she was, but for different reasons. She almost thought they might be kindred spirits.

She needed to get to the bottom of James's case before Mr. Miles showed up. Her future depended on finding out the truth. Besides, how could she introduce both men without being thoroughly questioned? How did you introduce a long deceased relative to their kin? She hadn't been tutored in that kind of protocol. There was no way to explain it really.

Speaking of her ghost, James was waiting for her. Every moment without him could be precious time she may never have again. Looking at her mousy appearance in the vanity mirror she wasn't going anywhere. She didn't have time for a shower. Her hair had all but fallen down around her throughout the day. If they were going to go out she needed to look a bit better, even touching up her simple make-up would help take the dark shadows of the past few nights of restlessness from under her eyes.

~ ☾ ~

Changing into her black dress slacks and wrinkle free
white blouse she always packed for possible dinner functions
while on business, made her feel better. She looked more
professional and less like a college student. She took down
her hair and brushed it out, twisting it back up and securing
it with her clip again.

Wearing it down wasn't an option, not with James. Very
few women wore their hair down in his day, unless they were
in bed. She didn't need to project wanting to be considered a
trollop or easy, though thinking about it she wouldn't mind
finding out about the legendary side to the man. He was a
gentleman, handsome, charming and ...not of this time
frame.

Looking at herself in the mirror of the Chippendale vanity,
she realized she hadn't looked this put together for Jason—
ever. She wanted a different look from the studious, college
girl but didn't want to look like the studious, stuffy professor
either. She turned to view herself from every angle. This
would work, she liked it. She finished herself off with light
sprits of perfume and a swipe of clear gloss to her lips.
Grabbing her small purse instead of her large hobo bag she
would keep it simple yet elegant tonight and take him out for
steak and seafood at one of the nearby colonial taverns.

James's bedroom door had been left open. His room was
dark. Looking at her watch she realized she was a bit later
than she had intended to be. He must be waiting for her
down stairs. Soft light met her as she descended the wide
staircase.

"James?"

James stepped from the shadows and looked up at her
from the base of the stairs. April nearly lost her footing in her
sling-back, kitten heels. If ever a man could make her turn
into a puddle of goo on the floor he would be the one to do so.
His hair was slicked back and tied in a queue with the bit of
leather strap he wore. The day's worth of dark scruff lined his
jaw and upper lip. God help her, she loved the natural male
image it gave him.

"You look beautiful, Dr. Branford."

How many women in his day had swooned when they

~ ☾ ~

heard the husky timbre of his voice? Men like James Addison might have been the reason fainting couches and smelling salts were needed.

April's cheeks warmed at the compliment. "Thank you. So do you. What I mean to say is—you look very nice." Flustered, like some shy adolescent, could she be any more of an idiot. But he only smiled his warm, sexy smile and held out his hand for her to take.

She placed her hand in his. It was amazing to think she couldn't touch him only a few days ago. Now he was real. His hand enveloped hers and he raised her hand to his lips and gently kissed her knuckles, making her feel feminine and delicate.

His eyes never left hers. Her heart hammered wildly beneath her rib cage as a river of fire flowed through her blood stream. Was she going to combust? Have a heart attack? Or perhaps both? Could a woman die from wanting a man so badly?

James placed her hand on the crook of his arm and escorted her to the table. "Oh wow! It's wonderful," April gasped.

There before her was a table set for two. Candlelight flickered behind the hurricane globe, casting prisms of light off of the wine goblets near a setting of her Aunt Vickie's fine china. On a small serving table, James had arranged a virtual smorgasbord of sliced fruits, vegetables, cheeses, cold meats, and her aunt's date bread with tiny dishes of her honey whipped butter.

He'd planned this intimate display in less time than it took her to dress and prepare herself. No one had ever made her feel more like a queen.

"Do you like it? You're not offended because I did this instead of going out to dinner?" James asked.

"Not at all, James. This really is wonderful."

Only a bit of light glowed from a small fire in the grate of the parlor fireplace. A few strategically placed candles around the room and one in the window added to the romantic ambiance.

"I wanted to properly show you my appreciation. I feel as

~ ☾ ~

if I am taking advantage of you and have no way of repaying your kindness. You're a woman who should dine on the finest fare and have the rarest of gems bestowed upon her. And yet I cannot gift you with any of those items. It makes a man feel less than he's worth."

He laid a hand on her back as he guided her into her chair. His touch sent tiny electrical impulses coursing through her.

"I don't look at it that way. A woman can take care of herself and help a friend out in need. Besides, you're worth it. It's not every day a historian can actually sit and chat with someone from the past. Can you imagine how many professors and scientists would love to meet you?" She tried to keep the situation light, business-like by making him see the situation from her perspective. She could deal with the professional side of their encounter.

"I do see your point, though. Just because times have changed, doesn't mean your social graces have. I suppose it is difficult for you to accept." April let him slide her chair up to the table for her. "I do appreciate the thought. It's wonderful. I've never had a man make a romantic dinner for me. Thank you, James."

He smiled slightly as he poured her a glass of wine from a bottle chilling in a wine bucket. His eyes danced merrily from his attention to the glass, back to her. "The men in this time must be daft not to have the good sense to show such a beautiful woman as you, her true worth. I must right this wrong, immediately. Let me lavish you with the affection you deserve."

God, he was romantic. She didn't know if he was teasing or if this was the James Addison the history books had commented about. Whatever he was, she was delighted to be with him and hoped to find out everything about the infamous 'ladies man.' But more importantly, she wished to be the only lady he desired in this time. She took in the whole scene. This was like something out of a colonial period setting. The only thing missing were the strolling minstrels. But then, having James to herself was even better.

"I don't think I've ever seen a more perfect setting for a meal. It's simple, yet as elegant as any five star restaurants. It's absolutely beautiful."

~ ☾ ~

"I'm delighted you are pleased." James sat down, seeming to relax a bit more. "I would like to make a toast." He raised his glass of wine, staring at her across the candlelit table. "To your kindness, beauty, and your unique gift, Dr. Branford. You've given me back my life after so many years. I can never repay you for such generosity."

The soft clink of his glass against hers made her realize how real all of this was. As she watched him take a healthy sip, everything she worried about seemed to go out the window with his smoldering gaze. This is how a man should make a woman feel.

Damn! He was good. She had to keep reminding herself this was James Addison—he was used to seducing women. But she wanted to be counted among his conquests and right now. The way her body responded to every nuance he sent her way, she could care less about right or wrong.

Dinner was amazing. The man apologized for not knowing how to cook and yet he had sliced up such a wonderful, appetizing array of delectable nibbles. She was full by the time she finished her second wedge of her aunt's date bread. James made himself comfortable by leaning casually in his chair and feeding on a small bunch of grapes.

"Tell me about your time here in Kings Mill. I want to know everything the books didn't say." April leaned on her elbow, gazing at him across the candle lit table. The two glasses of wine and cozy atmosphere had mellowed her, ever so slightly.

"Not much to tell, really. I arrived here the spring of 1763. I was but twenty and two, eager to take on the new world, make something of myself. I knew I would never possess anything of my own in England. My brother Andrew inherited the lands and title. In June I purchased the land the manor and mill sit on. The man I hired, Daniel Smith, arrived from the Chesapeake area mills shortly thereafter. Together, with a few other indentured servants, we constructed the two buildings, a barracks to house my workers and planted our first crop."

James's eyes lit up while he talked. She knew he was remembering good times.

~ ☾ ~

He talked of building his fortune with the mill. How he hired on some of the most devoted workers and enjoyed working beside them in the fields when needed. He spoke fondly of his foreman, Daniel, of the two of them overseeing most of the work. The young man had stayed on after his servitude and wanted James to help him build his house.

Although most men of his noble standing would have balked at performing such a task, James seemed to be pleased to have been asked by a former servant.

"You helped him build his house? Really?" she asked, pulling the rind from her orange wedge. Putting the orange down, she leaned forward as her professional mind broke through her wine induced mellowness. "If you bought other land, there should be records of those purchases. There should be records of servitude filed also."

"And records of those released from servitude. I know I filed them within the system. Daniel's paperwork should be somewhere if you need proof," James added. "I also made sure a deed of my property was left to Daniel in case anything was to happen.

"The rise of the colonial rebellion had many loyal to the Crown securing their lands to those they could trust. I sent my attorney in London and also the one here in town, Peter Hyman, documents to secure my holdings under Daniel's name for such an occasion. If I had to pick up arms for my King and Country, I needed to make sure the mill continued to thrive."

April was excited about the news. "So there are other places to look possibly? Peter Hyman and even in London? I'll let Kenneth know as soon as possible. Maybe he can set his people to find something there," she sighed.

"Who is this Kenneth Miles you seem to agonize about?" James twirled his remaining wine in his goblet.

"He's your distant relative from your sister, Elsbeth's side, if what he's told Dr. Moreland is true. Something like your fifth great nephew. Anyway, he happens to be a British billionaire with his fingers in everything from foreign trade to magazine production. He started out in construction until he developed his empire."

~ ☾ ~

"I have wealthy kin in England? What would he want here in the colonies?"

"In the United States you mean?" April laughed.

James waved his mistake off. "Well then, what would this man want to accomplish by your findings?"

"He wants entitlement to the Kings Mill site, if I can find proof of your ownership." April shook her head.

"Do you want him to have the land?" James asked.

"I don't know. This job has me at odds with myself. I was hired to do a job but I hate to see historical lands and resources used for anything but history. Kings Mill site would be a beneficial historical landmark. I'm not sure it should be used for another housing or business development. The meaning of the area would lose something in translation.

"But he's also able to bring employment into the county. With the economy in a slump lately, it would be a good venture for the job market. That's a risk. I'm unsure which way it should go. In the meantime, I'm doing the job I was hired to do or trying to."

By the third glass of wine April wasn't sure if it was the atmosphere or the wine making her warm and content. The warmth from the fire behind them could be part of it but she was positive it had more to do with James. They lulled into a comfortable silence as the last of the food and wine were consumed. She didn't want to move and lose this moment in time. Sitting with James was a dream, one she didn't want to wake up from. If a man could be perfect, this would be him.

"What are you thinking, Dr. April Branford?" His smile and deep tenor hit her sensual mode.

"I'm thinking how I wish you would call me just plain April."

"You wish me to speak with you on intimate terms?"

"This is 2012, James. We don't stand on formality as you did back in the 1700's."

Watching him slowly swallow the last sip of his wine, his throat worked reflexively against the collar of his shirt, sending liquid heat to pool in her core. All she could think of was him sipping on her. How could something as simple as watching him drink be so seductive?

~ ☾ ~

James was bold, dark masculinity. He worked the land and managed field hands, yet here he sat, larger than life, holding a crystal goblet so delicately in his hand. She envied the bowl of the glass, wishing it were her breast being gently cupped in the large, warm hand.

"Perhaps it is better to keep formal. You do realize it has been over two centuries since I've been intimate with a woman?"

"I'm well aware of the separation of time, James." Her voice sounded like a husky echo in her head. She was playing with fire. She was on fire.

"And you think I'm immune to your charms? Do not think for one moment your beauty and sensual appeal are not affecting me, April Branford. Your eyes tell me far too much."

Grinning into her hand she rested her chin on the table. "Well, it's a start. I guess April Branford is better than Dr. Branford." She laughed.

Neither one had time to commit to a relationship. Hell, she didn't even know how long James had on Earth. She was still so clueless about her natural abilities and what kind of power it held. Perhaps she was moving too fast. Maybe it was the wine and candlelight making her giddy and warm in places not warmed before.

April needed a distraction to separate herself from the atmosphere to find out. She could do so by clearing the dishes. Standing, her legs wobbled as she went to remove his plate. The wine had made her body soft and distorted her equilibrium. Beginning to fall, James quickly stood and caught her in his arms.

Warm breath laced with sweet wine cascaded over her jaw. He was so close. His hands came up, cupping her chin and jaw with the touch of an intimate lover. James's brow furrowed as he studied her lips before dipping in to place a soft simple kiss. Just a touch, but it wasn't enough for her. She needed all of him.

~ ☾ ~

Chapter Nine

This was supposed to be a simple kiss to see if her lips were as soft and sweet as they looked. Hadn't he just told her it had been two centuries since his last contact with a woman? Did she think he could resist her? He needed to kiss her like he needed his next breath and God help him—it had been a long time since breathing or kissing.

But the simple kiss never came. At first touch, her lips opened in a gasp and he was lost to her taste and the life she gave to his dead senses. Like the day she brought him physically to life, his body ached as need pierced needles of pleasure through him. With one hand, she tugged lightly at his hair as her other caressed his jaw. She gave herself to his kiss like no woman ever had.

She was a feast to a famished man. The minx gave her all and when her tongue darted past his lips to joust with his, the shock of such an intimate tryst nearly brought him to his knees. He cupped her head in his hand, feeling the soft silk of her curls surrounding his fingers as he tasted the wine on her tongue. Her body pressed intimately against him and he knew then, if he hadn't before, every part of his body was alive.

James let the fight of good intentions go to hell. She was soft and pliant to his hard, aching desire. He forgot everything except for the feel of this 'life-giving' woman pressed against him as she gave her heat, surrounding him in her essence.

The buttons on his collar slowly slipped from their holes. April's fingers released the tight constricting material until his entire chest was bare to the cool air. Her hands skimmed over his skin, and as she nibbled at his lower lip, he sucked in his breath. The warmth of her hands sent shivers coursing

~ ☾ ~

through to his soul. Her lips left his to trail heated kisses over his jaw, his throat and down to his collar bones. All James could do was hold on for dear life. Good intentions were pushed to the furthest recesses of his brain. When her fingers slid around his ribs to caress the naked skin of his back, James stopped thinking. He needed this woman!

The only thought he had was to undress her. His heart said to go slowly, like savoring a wrapped gift, peeking at every detail. But his libido demanded fast and furious. The two warred with each other, fighting for dominance. Groaning, he settled for taking it slow and letting her set the pace. His hands unclasped her hair clip and let her hair fall. He gathered it up in his hands, let it cascade over his fingers. God, he'd wanted to do this since their first meeting.

He tugged her hair back, just a brief pull to test the waters. Did she want slow and easy or wild, uncontrolled passion? Her head came up under the pressure of his fingers, fire smoldering in her eyes like green flame. The passionate fire was what he'd craved to see. Her soft gasp told him one thing, she wanted this as much as he did. Wildness hid under the timid, scholarly woman, and he wanted to see her in all her glory. Before he could take the lead, her mouth joined his again with a ferocity setting his heart to knock in his chest.

Was someone at the door? He didn't want to stop. He wanted to carry this woman to the nearest bed and make love to her so passionately neither would be able to move for days.

No, it's only my heart beating against my rib cage. Don't stop.

But the beating became louder and it wasn't the same sound he heard in his chest. Someone was knocking on the door. Parting from their heated embrace, he groaned. Catching his breath was difficult.

"Someone is at the door."

April stepped out of his arms and tucking her hair behind her ears, gave him a quick, sad smile for having their moment interrupted. She looked ravished. Her hair and clothes were disheveled. Was she as unsteady as he was? Silently he damned whoever was at the door. Perhaps whoever it was would get the hint with their wild appearance and move on

~ ☾ ~

quickly. Nothing would please him more than to enjoy this woman thoroughly from head to toe. The knocking became more intense and was followed by a rapid series of shrill ringing from the old fashioned door bell. "Coming! Who is it?" April called out.

James righted himself and tucked his shirt back into his slacks. He saw a worried, almost apologetic look pass over her features as she opened the door. Immediately April was embraced by an elderly woman in a bright orange outfit.

"Oh, sweetie, I knew you had it in you! Didn't I tell you, Virginia? It was just a matter of time before our April would show her true talents."

April gave a small smile. "Hello, Grams. Hello, Mom."

Another woman, one younger who looked a bit like April, gave her a brief hug. But this woman was more reserved and didn't seem as flamboyant as the older one.

"So, is this your ghost?"

James wasn't sure what to do as April's mother circled him taking him in as if he were on display. Her eyes were accessing and skeptical, not only of him though. April was being equally scrutinized by her mother. James stood staunchly by April's side, almost defying her mother to say anything derogatory against their appearance.

"Oh dear, Ginny," April's grandmother giggled, after a quick perusal of their appearance. "I think we interrupted April's paranormal investigation."

James took a few moments to clear his conscience. The women's arrival couldn't have been timed better. If it wasn't for them he would no doubt be ravishing April on the hard wood floor. He wasn't sure what he should do now.

April had nervously introduced him to her grandmother, Dorothea, or Grandma Dottie as April called her, who seemed delighted with their indelicate tryst. Her mother, Virginia, well, he'd seen over-protective fathers with kinder eyes. She'd critically assessed, not saying anything. She was much too quiet for his likes. He could deal with a woman's ranting but not her silence. He quietly slipped away to the kitchen to prepare another tray of food for the new arrivals. He couldn't

~ ☾ ~

fault April's mother, the woman was right to question his motives—hell, he wasn't even sure what his motives were.

Taking a deep breath, he made his way back to the parlor. "...You don't know anything about this man. You've only known him for a few days and he's a ghost to boot, and here you are sleeping with him!"

Well, April's mother hadn't remained silent for long. James placed the tray in front of their guests. Virginia Branford stopped talking immediately as they all looked up at him. April appeared a bit out of sorts. He easily made his decision and sat in the empty chair facing the women. A gentleman wouldn't leave an innocent to handle a social injustice by his hand. April didn't deserve the implications her mother laid on her shoulders.

"Mrs. Branford, I must intervene. Your daughter knows me more than anyone else has ever cared to know me in over two-hundred years, possibly before then. I may have been a ghost a few days ago, but your daughter brought me to life. I think God has a reason for it, but as of yet we aren't quite sure what His plans are. As for our sleeping arrangements, I can assure you, until I ask her father's permission for her hand in marriage, her virtue will remain intact."

Grandma Dottie coughed slightly into her hand as she raised a questioning eyebrow at her granddaughter. Virginia Branford snorted, taking the glass of milk he offered.

April deserved no less. As he said the words aloud, he realized he meant them. She wasn't a trollop to be dallied with when his needs required fulfilling. She was a woman a man made a future with. Until he knew how much time he had in this realm, he couldn't offer her more than his gratitude. What happened between them earlier would never be able to go any further.

Color heightened in April's cheeks as she glared at him. "I don't need you to fight my battles, James. I'm old enough to do as I please without asking permission from my family."

"You are a young woman without the guidance and protection of a man. Your reputation is at stake." Did she not realize as wonderful and odd as this situation was between them, she was still a single woman in the company of a

~ ☾ ~

historically known rake? Having her name bandied about in public gatherings because of their living arrangements could be misconstrued and harmful to her ethical and professional life.

"This happens to be 2012, James. Your archaic ideals went out when my grandmother burned her bra at Woodstock in the 1960's!"

Dottie cleared her throat. "Actually, I burned my bra at a sit-in while I was protesting in Washington D.C., dear. Woodstock was a music fest. Your uncle was conceived there. For the record, I wasn't wearing a bra."

James turned his attention to Dottie, whose casual smile intrigued him. The older woman seemed quite forward and didn't have any qualms about how she spoke.

April's distress was vivid. With her face buried in her hands, she mumbled something about, "this is not the time, Grams".

Virginia stood abruptly. "Can we just get to the bottom of what is happening? I'm not pleased with this one bit and you know it, Mother! I've dreaded the day April would find her gift. Contrary to popular belief, Dorothea Evans, not all of us wish this atrocity on our off-spring. This is not a rite of passage like adolescence..."

"If I remember correctly, Ginny, you botched that up for the poor girl, too. A bottle of Midol, a health center book, *You and Your Body,* and your copy of, *Are You There God, It's Me Margaret,* does not prepare a young girl for womanhood! I ended up being the one to show her how to dress a cucumber!"

April stood to leave. "I don't have to sit here and listen to this."

Confused, James looked from one woman to another. He noticed a shade of color highlighting April's cheeks and throat in embarrassment. Dressing a cucumber? What did preparing vegetables have to do with womanhood? Was it a delicacy of sorts a woman ate to bring her fertility?

"Where are you going, young lady?" her mother addressed her.

"Anywhere but here!" April turned back to her mother,

~ ☾ ~

annoyance written in her face. She picked up her dirty dishes. "When you and Grams are ready to stop talking about my sex life, then I might consider discussing things." She put the dishes back down carefully. "I managed to bring a ghost to life and all you two can do is argue and degrade each other. *I need answers!*

"I don't even know why Aunt Vickie called you. You two are always bickering about your gifts. I've dreaded the day my gift arrived because of this very reason! Maybe I hoped things would change if I really needed your guidance...like now."

The room fell silent. James remained where he sat, uncertain how to respond. The air was filled with heavy emotion. He assumed April was embarrassed by the debacle between the women in her family and their rituals for preparing for womanhood. Her dire need to get answers from the women she loved and respected showed in her stress. The reality dawned on him right then, she really didn't know how she brought him to life or the consequences of her actions.

"Oh, dear. I suppose this is a bit over-board for you, April," her grandmother soothed. "Virginia, we are being a bit much. And James doesn't need to see our dirty laundry being aired. Let's all take a cleansing breath and clear our minds so we can focus on what's important."

James took a deep breath as did Dottie, but the other two women rolled their eyes and sighed with acceptance.

"Now, can I explain what's happened? I need your help and guidance on what I did and what I need to do. But under no circumstances will there be any more bickering or references to my sex life...or yours, Grams. Understood?"

***

"So tell us what happened when you resurrected James?" Her grandmother asked, reaching for the last piece of date bread on the tray.

April tried to explain everything that had happened between her and James since they'd met. The details to the ghostly encounter at Henry's tombstone were a bit convoluted as she'd been mostly in shock. Even her explanation of what happened when she'd gone to James's grave wasn't clear.

~ ☾ ~

Her grandmother listened intently. "So you didn't realize, even when Vickie told you you'd taken a picture of James—that you'd been talking to a ghost?" She sighed as she rolled her eyes towards her daughter. "She's more like you than I wanted her to be, Virginia."

"He didn't seem 'ghostly.' He was more solid than a wispy apparition in an old haunted house, kind of ghost," April defended herself.

Her mother sat quietly in the chair. Her pale features were pinched in concentration as her fingers probed along her temples.

"Are you all right, Virginia?" Grandma Dottie asked.

"I'm fine, Mom, just give me a minute," she exhaled deeply, clearly trying to dispel the pain.

Reaching for her purse, her mother took out a vial of pain relief, shook out a couple, and downed them with the rest of her milk. April knew she was in the beginnings of one of her migraines. The symptoms were common now. Was being around James causing her to suffer?

Her mother waved her grandmother on. "Go ahead with the questions, Mother. I'll be fine in a few moments when the meds kick in. We need to find out what we can to help, April."

Grandma Dottie nodded slowly, keeping a trained eye on April's mother before turning back to the interrogation. April looked to James for guidance. So much of yesterday afternoon was like a weird dream. She explained the incident, what she could remember, as her grandmother pondered the situation. She revealed the sights, sounds, smells, everything in essence to what her grandmother might need as evidence in her metaphysical inquiries.

Grandma Dottie wrinkled her brow, deep in concentration. She turned to James. "What about you, James? What do you remember?"

"Pain. For the first time in over two-hundred-thirty years, I felt pain, heat. A warm rush of water filled me while my muscles cramped and seized. Then scents and sounds engulfed my senses." He laughed. "I wonder if it was anything similar to how Adam felt when God created him from the Earth."

~ ☾ ~

April cursed herself. She hadn't asked him what he'd gone through. They hadn't really talked about the situation after it happened. She had been too shocked.

She nibbled nervously on her bottom lip. "What did I do, Grams?"

"You did what you were meant to do. It's not for us to question." Grandma Dottie smiled and reached over to pat her hand. "All I can think of is your acute sense of psychometry has manifested with your joined spiritual essence. We are all made up of energy. It never leaves us—even in death. When two forces of equal levels of live energy interact, the connection is complete. It's probably a one in a billion chance—or as your Aunt Vickie would say, 'fate.'"

Sighing, April slumped back in the chair, defeated. "Aunt Vickie said the same thing this morning when we talked." Was this as simple as the combination of energy, metaphysics, and fate? Could she accept it as gospel? She turned to the only other woman who might be able to help her. "Mom?"

Sweat beaded her mother's brow. Her eyes closed tightly as if shielding her from pain.

Going to her side, April leaned over and checked her forehead. "Are you okay, Mom?"

The pinched expression hadn't left her mother's face. The migraine was getting worse if her color and the spring of tears sliding from behind her closed eyes were any indication. She stood up on shaky legs as she held her head in pain.

"I need to go outside. The voices are hurting my head. There is so much anger and fear..." her mother's voice trailed off as she paced frantically, clutching at the sides of her head as if trying to keep it together.

"I've got her, April." Grandma Dottie took her daughter by the elbow and guided her towards the front door. "I need you to find my vial of gardenia essence in my tote bag. Bring it to me, and then fix a cup of chamomile and mint tea. Let it steep," she instructed as she grabbed their jackets on the way out the door.

James appeared concerned. "Is your mother going to be all right?" he asked softly as they began to clear the tea dishes.

~ ☾ ~

"My mother can hear ghosts. Aunt Vickie seems to think a woman's ghost still resides in the room upstairs next to mine, but I wonder if there are others, too." April busied herself with rummaging through her grandmother's tapestry tote bag where she kept all her herbal remedies. "Can you sense them or see them?"

She noted he was looking around as if he could possibly see one floating nearby. "No. I never saw one when I was a ghost. Why would I be able to see one now?"

"I don't know." She shrugged. "I guess I just assumed you could."

His other hand came up to caress her cheek. "I'm sorry for taking advantage of you earlier. If it wasn't for your family's arrival, I don't know what I would have done. Can you ever forgive me?" April's insides shivered with the friction. Such a simple gesture but she felt it all the way to her toes.

Damn, he was apologizing for kissing her when all she could think of was taking it to the next level. "There is nothing to forgive. I don't remember telling you to stop."

His smile was kind but his eyes bore a troubled sadness.

"Your eyes are saying way too much, Dr. Branford. You haven't the experience to deal with a libertine like me. I'm used to loose women, a quick tumble with no commitments. You are innocent and young. If I were any less of a man I would take you up on your unspoken offer. You tempt me as no other woman has. But I am a gentleman, first and foremost. I won't slake my lust on your innocence and kindness. You mean more to me than a quick tumble in the sheets."

He was back to calling her by her professional name. Damn him! His touch drifted away from her cheek and he nodded towards the vial in her hand. Right, she needed to get this to her grandmother.

"Let me get the water for tea. Your mother needs your help right now."

She nodded in agreement and went to deliver the vial of gardenia essence to her grandmother. Of course her mother needed her help. Her ghost-man was probably causing her headaches.

~ ☾ ~

James Addison thought she was innocent and young? Did he not realize how old she was? In his time she would be considered an old maid by now. And what did her innocence mean in his standards? Innocent as in virgin or innocent as in unknowing what she was up against with a man of his breeding? She wasn't a virgin in the physical sense. But she had a feeling she'd never experienced a man like James Addison, either. Making love with him would probably be equivalent to a first time experience. He was high potency absinthe to the simple beers and occasional pitcher of margaritas with friends. One sip of him would either put her under the table or make her an addict. She wasn't sure she was ready for either but wondered what it would be like to try.

***

April woke up to find herself mummy-wrapped in her sheets. She disengaged herself from the linen shroud and grumbled. Why couldn't she have made love to James last night? Would she be waking up entangled around his body instead of the sheets if her mother and grandmother hadn't shown up when they did? This was the infamous scoundrel and seducer James Addison. Well the history books were wrong—he wasn't a scoundrel, he was an honest man. Here she was expecting God only knows what but *nooo*, she went and fell in love with an honorable ghost. Great! Just effin' great!

April stopped herself. Had she fallen in love with James Addison? Was it even possible? She'd only known him for a few days, as her mother stated so vehemently last night. Dear God her head hurt. For being a practical professor of history, she had acquired some fantastical, personal issues to work out.

She'd dressed casually and met her grandmother in the hallway.

"Good morning, dear." The old woman's voice was low and quiet.

"'Morning, Grams." April watched her grandmother walk around the landing and hallway with her crystal dangling on its leather lanyard. It remained motionless until she neared

~ ☽ ~

the steps and then it spun in perfectly concentric circles. The older woman nodded, sighed, and then smiled thoughtfully.

"So, how did last night go?" A knowing twinkle lit up her grandmother's eyes.

She could play coy and dumb or just get it over with. There was no fooling Dottie Evans. "It didn't. He's honorable and didn't wish to dishonor me with my family present."

"Oh dear, I am sorry. I just figured with the way he kept looking at you all through our little snack he was ready to devour you body and soul, family be damned. And since his appearance when we arrived was a bit, shall we say—rumpled, I assumed some positive return of affections. Ghost or no ghost, I have a feeling making love with him would be a total mind rush."

April couldn't believe this conversation with her sixty-seven year old grandmother. The only thing April wished to discuss with her grandmother was paranormal activities. She'd learned not to discuss her sex life with the members of the Wilton women clan. They could take an idea and run wild with it. Knowing James and his history, they might be pretty accurate with their assumptions, and she really didn't want to think about their reaction. "Your mother is up and ready to go. Rough night for her last night, but she woke up hungry this morning. I'm famished. James is famished. Vickie is taking us all out to the diner for breakfast, and we have tons of things we need to do, discuss, and figure out."

Grandma Dottie stopped and looked behind her. "There's something unsettling here, Vickie mentioned it last night, but I sense it too—so it must be strong. We need to help these poor people. They're caught in a residual time loop within their worst moments and because of it, they can't move on."

"I can't worry about the other ghosts. I need your help with James, Grams. He's what I'm focused on." April knew any paranormal experience would be an issue to her family, especially if there was unrest among lost souls. But her issue with James was paramount. Everything else could wait.

Aunt Vickie slowly made it up the stairs, joining them in time to overhear their conversation. Shaking her head, she looked around at the emptiness surrounding them and then

~ ☾ ~

closed her eyes. "No. There is a message here. Something combined with you, James, and these entities."

"This place is really haunted? Is it the woman you say haunts the bedroom?" April asked.

"There are two, I think. One is a man and the other a woman. I don't know the specifics."

April watched her aunt walk around the landing hallway with her eyes closed. She walked close to the stairs and stopped.

"Dottie, I need you and Virginia to work on finding who we are dealing with. I haven't had any one on one interaction with them. I just feel the connection." Aunt Vickie came out of her trance and shivered. This was a sign April knew her aunt used to shake off negative energies. April hugged her arms feeling a chill coursing through her. Had Aunt Vickie transferred the negative energy to her before heading back downstairs?

"Don't fret, April. We have time," Grandma Dottie soothed, placing a hand to her brow. Her grandmother's touch gave her a sense of calm. More than any salve could do. "I'm not worried. The spirits will be here until their souls can be cleansed. As I said, we have much to do. A good breakfast should help us get going. We need to find out what abilities your gift has so we can learn to control its power."

"I need to check my email messages before I leave in case Mr. Miles has sent me anything."

"We'll be downstairs."

***

The room felt chillier than it had when she'd left it a few moments ago but she'd just taken a hot shower. The humidity had probably dissipated in the time she'd been talking with her grandmother and aunt. She went to her laptop and powered it up, knocking over some research books along with the bag from the gift store. The book on the excavation site opened up to James's picture. How could she not have seen the resemblance between the two?

This was the same man she'd brought to life. She should have known her tour guide had been *the* James Addison. She'd had all the facts given to her by her aunt, the photo

~ ☾ ~

she'd taken, even the image of him at the mill site. This picture was him to a 'T'. There was the look she'd fallen for the first night she met him. What had he been thinking when the portrait was painted? She smiled and placed the book on the bed. She picked up the package from the gift store again. The magnet, *'Believe in Fate'* fell out.

"Okay, Aunt Vickie, I get the hint." She wasn't talking to the woman but she might as well have been. She re-packaged the magnet and stuffed the brown paper bag into her duffle. There! The damn thing wouldn't fall out again to be a constant reminder of things she didn't want to acknowledge.

Kenneth hadn't left her any messages. She did send him one, telling him about James having sent copies of documents for Daniel to his attorney in London and the fact she would check into finding Peter Hyman's records here in Kings Mill. She didn't have a whole lot to report.

April sighed and logged off of her laptop, watching the small icon lights on the machine fade off as it powered down. Gathering her notebook she turned to leave and slammed into an immovable energy field. Like a mime stuck in a box, she literally found the whole area around her blocked. An invisible barricade held her back, forcing her into a corner.

Panic set in as she pushed against the indiscernible wall with her shoulder, only to have it push back until she was pressed up against the interior corner of her room. She tried to scream for help, but her throat constricted painfully, as if someone was choking her. A vise-like pain pressed against her jaw and her senses became overwhelmed with a fetid stench. If this were a man on the street she would knee him in the groin, but she wasn't sure what she was dealing with.

Still, she brought her knee up hard as if it was a man attacking her, and the force receded instantly. She wasn't sure if it was because of her actions or the presence of her mother in the doorway calling her name.

"Did you not hear me? We've been waiting for you for ten minutes now. Come on, I'm starved. Bad enough you kept us up late and then slept in until nine-thirty."

Shaking, chills coursed through her body. April looked around, rubbing her jaw which still ached. She didn't want to

~ ☾ ~

frighten her mother. Whatever happened was gone now. She was fine. Taking the time to register her mother's ranting, she realized what she was saying. Ten minutes hadn't passed. No way! She'd only been on the laptop for a few minutes at most.

Her mother came into the room and held a hand to her face. "Are you all right, April? You look a bit pale." She stopped, looked around, as if listening for something.

"I'm fine, Mom, I just—" Her mother held a finger to her lips and she stopped talking. With Virginia guiding her by the hand they quickly left the room, shutting the door behind them.

Not a word was spoken. Her mother silently moved her down the grand staircase and out of the house. James trailed after them with their coats from the foyer coat tree. Grandma Dottie and Aunt Vickie were waiting outside, sitting in the wicker chairs conversing. They stopped talking as her mother hurried them out of the house and down the porch steps.

Aunt Vickie went back to the door, stopped, looked up at the house and quickly locked the door. Puzzled, she hurried down the front steps, waiting for her mother to explain. Grandma Dottie followed behind knowing something was up. Both women looked to her for an explanation. Seeing the eager retreat of her mother's pace, April knew this wasn't the time or place for discussion. James looked at her confused and slightly angry that something had happened to affect both her and her mother so severely. "What's wrong?" He turned to the other women. "What's going on?"

Aunt Vickie raised her eyebrow questioningly at him, a hint of a smile forming. "That's what we would like to know."

~ ☾ ~

Chapter Ten

Not sure if she should talk yet, April kept in stride with her mother as they led the way down the street and around the corner to the Town Diner. Her mother's quiet demeanor and quick pace worried her. April glanced back briefly every few minutes. Still, no one said a word.

The proprietor greeted Aunt Vickie who happily introduced everyone in the party. After greeting several of the locals her aunt knew, they retreated to a private room. The casual, happy attitudes of her aunt, grandmother, and mother evaporated when the waitress left to retrieve their drinks.

"What happened in your bedroom?" her mother leaned over the table. The tension in her voice brooked no argument.

Appalled, her grandmother glared at her daughter. "None of your damn business, Virginia! What happened between April and James last night is between them. They're both consenting adults."

"What did you two do last night?" Aunt Vickie asked April as she leaned over the table, smiling, eager for details. James coughed at her aunt's brassiness.

April sighed. "It wasn't James. Would you all stop with the sexual innuendos? Your embarrassing me and making James feel uncomfortable." April looked at her mother. "I'm not sure what happened this morning, Mom."

"Something happened? When?" Grandma Dottie's attention moved from her mother to her and back.

James's glare landed on her as did everyone else's attention. They all wanted to know what happened this morning. April hated being grilled.

"I'd just checked my emails when I was forced up against the wall. I didn't see anything but couldn't move. Then I sensed pain shooting up my neck and jaw as if someone was

~ ☽ ~

trying to choke me. I tried to scream for help but I couldn't speak. So I instinctively brought my knee up. If it was a man I think I nailed him good. He let go but then you showed up, Mom."

"You were attacked in your bedroom?" James's eyes rounded on her.

"A man attacked you in my house?!" Aunt Vickie blanched, placing her hand on her own throat. "Oh, dear Lord!"

"That's it! We need a thorough cleansing of the house!" Grandma Dottie slammed her menu down.

Her mother nodded in agreement. "I heard it, April. There was a presence in the room with you. And not very friendly."

"Who did this to you?" James demanded. His jaw tightened with the same rage April saw in his eyes.

"I don't know. I couldn't see anything." She didn't want to get him all riled up. Besides, how could anyone fight an invisible entity?

"You will not be alone in the house any more. I will be at your side at all times." His fingers clenched into fists, turning the knuckles white. "I will set up a cot in your room to make sure you are safe at night."

"You'll do no such thing. This is ridiculous, James." April rolled her eyes, trying to make light of the situation.

"Yes. Why set up a cot? You could just share the bed. It's big enough," Grandma Dottie smirked with a knowing look in her eyes.

"Mother!" Her mom gasped, peeking up from behind the large menu.

"Oh please, Virginia. She's nearly thirty years old and I'm not getting any younger. I would like to see a great-grandchild someday before I move on. She's definitely not a virgin anymore. Besides, no one her age is." Dottie turned to James to explain the sexual relationships now.

April wanted the floor to open up and swallow her whole. She hid behind the menu, pretending deep interest in her choices of food as her grandmother gave her research subject details about sex after the age of the 'sexual revolution.' Even another ghostly encounter would be welcomed over her grandmother discussing sex with James Addison.

~ ☾ ~

"I see. Well, things have changed a bit," she could hear James say to her grandmother. *Dear God, let the topic go away!*

Thankfully God answered her prayers by sending the waitress back right then with their drinks. Unfortunately, James picked back up on the topic when the waitress left.

"This Jason person never asked for your hand in marriage though he took your innocence? Did your father not call him out?" James interrogated. He'd turned his body towards her, leaning casually on his elbow, with eyebrows raised as if he were a trial lawyer, and she was the nervous witness on the stand.

"Oh, Jason wasn't her first," Aunt Vickie added ever so helpfully. "Didn't you and Scott Barnes take a trip up to the family cabin in Deep Creek Lake your freshman year at Frostburg?"

"Not now, Aunt Vickie," April groaned, placing her head on the table and covering her ears as the two elderly sisters discussed her past sexual relationships as if she wasn't even there.

Lifting her head from the Formica table top, April glared from her grandmother to her aunt. "Can we possibly talk about something else, like what we need to do now?"

James's lips thinned into a grim line. Was he appalled by her past relationships? Did he think poorly of her now? Was he one of those types who held double-standards when it came to men and women and their sexual escapades? But then, it shouldn't bother her. The more information he had, the more he could understand she wasn't an innocent and could handle anything he might dish out when it came to sex.

The waitress blessedly broke the tension when she placed a basket of jams, margarine, and syrup in the middle of the table and took their order.

"Okay, back to the topic at hand," her mother said, fixing her coffee. "We need to figure out what happened in the time frame April was up in her room."

"I wasn't up there for long, Mom, a couple of minutes at most." April took a sip of her orange juice. "Just long enough to check my emails."

~ ☾ ~

Her grandmother shook her head cautiously. "No dear, you were up there much longer. From the time I told you to meet us downstairs to when your mother went up to get you—we'd been waiting for nearly fifteen minutes."

Looking around the table and seeing the nods from the others she shook her head in denial. "Fifteen minutes, no. That's impossible."

"Did you notice anything at all? Could you see a different reality or sense a change in your surroundings?" Aunt Vickie asked.

"No, just the invisible box I seemed to be in and the sense of someone's hands on my throat. I smelled rot and decay but, I don't know, it could have been my imagination."

Aunt Vickie nodded. "I say there was a warp in the realms."

"You're jumping to conclusions, Victoria, realms can't manipulate time," Grandma Dottie scoffed.

"No, but strong energy levels can," April's mother piped up.

All the other women looked to her as if she'd lost her mind. This wasn't something Virginia Branford would offer up. She tended to avoid all talk of the paranormal.

"You two have told me for years how strong levels of spiritual energy can manifest into different realms from a ghostly perspective. Who's to say April can't do the same from this realm into the next?"

James snapped his fingers. "Perhaps this is what happened to you Sunday when you came out to the mill site, why my workers and I could see you in our past realm."

"Excuse me?" April's mother looked up from her coffee cup at James and then at April. "What is he talking about?" She looked for answers from the other two women yet they showed the same perplexed, inquisitive, what-didn't-you-tell-us look in their eyes. "April May Branford—" her mother's warning threatened to explode.

She hated it when her mother used her full name! It was never a good thing, and she was beyond getting caught with her hand in the cookie jar, especially in front of James.

Now she had four sets of eyes trained on her, waiting for her answer.

~ ☾ ~

April sighed. "It was a fluke. I was exploring the property and had some allergy issues causing me to hallucinate—like I did that time in Jamestown," she explained. "I got scared and as I was leaving witnessed a scene from James's time. I didn't think anything of it until he mentioned having been able to see me that day." She wasn't going to tell them about what she'd witnessed at the manor house ruins. They would go ballistic on her! Like they were about to go ballistic on her now.

"And when did you tell me about this?" Aunt Vickie asked with slight irritation. "I asked you to tell me everything, April. Everything is important in order to find out what your true gift is. You can't discount anything, not a single iota of information."

"I didn't think it was really important at the time." She looked up with remorse, knowing now what affect it might have. "I didn't want you to think I was crazy or..."

"...or suffering from the family curse?" her mother added. The other two women sighed with a hint of frustration.

"Well, I think we need to check out this mill site. I would like to get some readings on it, personally," Aunt Vickie said to change the delicate subject.

Turning to James, April touched his hand. "Are you okay with going back there, James? I know it's going to be different now the mill is no longer there."

"It's no longer there?" He looked around the table. "What happened to it?"

The women all looked to one another. "You don't know?" Vickie asked.

He shook his head slowly, looking towards April. She pinched the bridge of her nose and closed her eyes. She really didn't want to reveal the truth to him, but someone had to. "James, it burned down in a fire only a few weeks after your death. Everything was destroyed. No one knows how or why."

He shook his head. "No. Daniel wouldn't have let anything happen to the mill."

Vickie reached over and patted his hand. "I know this is difficult for you to take in, James. Records show it happened during Sunday mass while everyone from the mill was in

~ ☾ ~

church...everyone except Daniel Smith. But he was never found in order to be brought in for questioning."

"Ridiculous! Are you assuming Daniel had something to do—? No, not Daniel. I could imagine anyone but Daniel." James's finger punctuated his statement on the tabletop. "Daniel loved the mill as much as I did, even more at times."

"There is no record stating who was accused of the crime. We can't jump to conclusions, Aunt Vickie, anymore than to say James committed treason. Its hearsay and legend until all the facts are in place."

James's hand tightened around her fingers. She looked worriedly into his eyes.

"I need to go there, April. I need to see what is left of my land now."

***

The trip back to the manor ruins seemed quicker this time. Grandma Dottie walked over and read the marker. April knelt down to remove debris from the plaque. Looking up from her task, she noticed Aunt Vickie meditating. The older woman closed her eyes and placed her crystal to her brow, one of the most common chakra centers in the body in psychometry. She turned three-hundred and sixty degrees and began to walk trance-like into the overgrowth of field beyond. Not knowing what to do, never experiencing her aunt's ability, April looked to her grandmother for guidance. A subtle nod told her to go ahead. Throwing the dead foliage to the side, she followed her aunt.

Watching her walk around with her eyes closed scared April. The woman could fall and break her hip or something. Her aunt didn't seem at all bothered by her lack of sight and made her way through the tall grasses and weeds on her own as well as or better than most with their eyes opened. She was used to using all five physical senses; sight, touch, hearing, smell, and taste all working in conjunction with each other— or separately if needed. April tried to catch some essence of the spiritual world surrounding Vickie but gave up as she realized this wasn't her gift. Instead, she quietly followed.

She didn't want to speak and pull Aunt Vickie out of whatever hold possessed her, but she motioned for the others

~ ☾ ~

to follow. Her aunt walked uninhibited into the middle of the great field. Peace and contentment lined her face like a child enjoying the warmth of the sun bearing down on her. Then she stumbled, falling to her knees and clutching her head momentarily, in concentration. April wanted to help her but her grandmother stopped her with her hand, letting the moment pass.

"What did you see?" April asked looking around at their surroundings, hoping to see something to bring everything into perspective.

Her aunt looked up at her with a wan smile. "I don't see anything, honey. You should know that."

"What did you sense, Vickie?" Grandma asked, correcting the difference of Vickie's gift.

"Calm, tranquility. And then—" She stopped speaking, her brow furrowed. Vickie rose to her feet and walked silently, without answering, to where James stood along the top of the knoll over-looking the rest of his fields. Side by side they let their eyes roam over the emptiness. April and the rest of the women followed, confused.

"What do you see?" April whispered as she touched James's arm,

He looked down at her, a small frown knotting his brow. "Nothing anymore. Just barren fields."

"You don't see them?"

"You don't hear them?"

Her mother and grandmother spoke at the same time.

Dottie gasped, "Why, there are people out there working the fields!" She laughed with surprise.

"And they're singing!" Her mother actually appeared delighted.

April had never seen such joy on her mother's face at witnessing her gift. Most of the time when her mother experienced the slightest paranormal condition, she left the scene or went into immediate panic, knowing the migraines would follow. This time she stood there, on the knoll, listening with great pleasure. Her eyes were closed, and her face tipped contentedly towards the field. "Well yes, they did sing a good deal. It helped to pass the time." James shrugged.

~ ☾ ~

"What do you see or feel, April?" he asked, gazing down at her.

"Nothing." She shook her head sadly, wishing she could participate and listen to their songs.

"Don't feel bad, dear," Aunt Vickie patted her hand. "I'm sensing this isn't where you need to be. You're needed...elsewhere..." she trailed off. Vickie turned towards the northeast and nodded. "Come with me."

Being gently pulled by her aunt in the direction of the manor house ruins, April followed. She didn't want to go back there but without a great deal of explanation she didn't have much choice. Panic set in. Would it happen again? Would she feel the heat of the stone foundation? Part of her wanted to see if she did. Would she see the same scene?

"There's something here. I feel a strong entity. More than one. I'm getting a sense of urgency, frantic. There are three souls involved in a chaotic event."

She didn't remember anything of the sort. There had been only two entities, a woman and a man but if someone else was there, she hadn't picked up on them.

"I smell smoke...a fire perhaps." Vickie walked closer to the foundation. She stopped at the edge. "I sense someone needing your help."

Aunt Vickie closed her eyes momentarily and when she opened them she looked to April almost accusingly. "You know what you need to do. I sense you've already been here, come to your true gift—they need you. It's up to you whether you want to help them or cause them to forever linger in their eternal nightmare."

If this had been last week, April would think her aunt crazy. Now, she knew what the woman was telling her. She'd been through too much not to know.

Trembling on the edge of uncertainty April looked from the foundation ruins to her aunt. The older woman stared at her with sad acceptance. April knew she had to make the right choice. She hoped she was strong enough to make it.

Was she more her mother's child? Afraid of her gift, whatever it was supposed to be? She needed to accept it. If not for herself, then for James or the two images she

~ ☾ ~

witnessed. Were they not flesh and blood people at one time? Didn't they still have an emotional conscious?

But she didn't want to go through the agony of what transpired the other day. Seeing those two people burn and not being able to do anything to save them...how could she help them now?

April found herself nodding to her aunt and lowered herself back down into the stone foundation. Sweat prickled her palms. Her heart throbbed erratically within the confines of her ribs. Nausea rose to her throat but she moved on, trying to locate the area of the wall she touched before. Would it matter?

Aunt Vickie nodded down at her. Okay, she would hold out her hand and see what happened. Maybe this time she would get lucky and nothing would.

Touching the stone, the heat hit her full force. This wasn't the gradual heat exchange like before. Her hand stayed there. April expected to see the scene exactly as she remembered. Instead a fight was in progress. A burley man, dressed in clothes of a colonial dandy, materialized swinging a spade at a younger man dressed in simple working linens. The young man moved out of the way just as the shovel swiped where his head had been only seconds before.

The larger man, angered at the miss, threw the shovel to the side and took a dive at the smaller man, straight into his solar plexus. The two men fell against the wall. The big brute grabbed the other man's throat with his hands and pounded his head into the stone foundation. April flinched and squinted against the gruesome vision.

Out of the edges of the scene a young woman leaped onto the older man's back, beating him with her tiny fists. Determined to do harm, the woman continued to pummel him with everything she possessed. Her hair flew about her in wild disarray as the man tried to shake her off, like a wet dog shedding water. Looking from them to the other man, April could see he was unconscious—was he dead? She couldn't tell. She couldn't remove her hand from the wall to get a closer look.

Her thoughts of saving the man were interrupted when the

~ ☾ ~

woman ended up tossed near her feet. A strong scent of lilac filled April's senses. The man approached them in a menacing stance, his mouth opened in a yell, but no sound came out. It was as if April were watching a movie on mute. Subtle movement from the prone man's body caught the looming brute's attention.

The distraction was enough to let the woman glance at her. *She could see her!* Her ghostly fingers worked frantically, toying with the trinkets pinned to her apron pocket, trying to communicate as if April were a part of the scene. The woman held the intricately carved piece of jewelry out to her, showing her the detailed design. It was difficult to make out. What was it? Could it possibly be a chatelaine? What did she want her to do with it? What could she do?

Sighing, the woman stopped and waited, turning her head and closing her eyes tightly from the scene happening behind her. April looked up to see the wild man pick up the spade, and with sickening accuracy, bring it down upon the other man's unsuspecting head. There would have been no way to survive such cruelty.

The lilac scent was so strong now. The woman knelt before her. She opened her eyes, pleading with her, as tears streamed down her cheeks. Did the woman know what was going to happen? Was that why she was trying to communicate with her? This wasn't a residual haunting then. Dear God was she actually an active participant in another realm of history?

April's stomach knotted. She turned her attention to the woman who in a last ditch effort, yanked the delicate chain from her apron, and threw it towards her. Instinctively, April held out her free hand to catch it, but there was nothing but air. This was only an image, nothing tangible. The woman closed her eyes again in defeat, buried her face in her hands, and waited as if she knew what was to come.

The man approached them. Anger poured off of him like sweat. His meaty hands grabbed the woman, but his eyes strayed towards April. A brief moment of shock when he noticed her presence crossed his features before giving in to a foul sneer. His beady-eyed stare never left April as he forced

~ ☾ ~

the blonde woman over to the opposite wall.

Crying out, April tried with all her might to pull away from whatever held her against the stone wall. She knew what was going to happen. She'd seen it the other day. But how could she help an image of history long since past? She couldn't stop the inevitable from taking place. But she didn't want to witness the horrible scene again.

"Damn it, Aunt Vickie! Bring her back!" Her mother yelled in what sounded like a pool of deep water.

"Be gone!" Her aunt's voice echoed in the far recesses of her mind.

~ ☾ ~

Chapter Eleven

Trembling violently, like the weeds and brush around her, April sat crouched against the remaining foundation. Tears streaked down her cheeks as the scene replayed in her head. Her grandmother's arms enclosed her, pulling her into her embrace. Small touches and gentle kisses covered her hair and face.

The scuffle of feet on gravel and dirt brought her head up from Dottie's bosom to see James jump into the foundation pit. He looked as if he just ran a marathon. His eyes wild and skin covered in sweat, he glanced around at each woman before squatting down and brushing away a tear from her cheek.

"What the hell happened?" James once again looked to Dottie for an explanation.

Her grandmother only shook her head. "She phased. One minute she was here and the next her body just shimmered into…" Dottie looked to Vickie for a possible answer.

Vickie stood by, her brow furrowed with confusion as she waved her hands in an ancient, ritualistic manner over the area where she'd sensed the spirits. Her mother sat on the edge of the foundation cellar pit, staring down at her. An odd look of understanding and horror mixed into her normal business-like expression. April shuddered. Pure adrenaline and shock racked her body.

"Sweetie, I need to help Vickie." Her grandma kissed her forehead and nodded to James, releasing her to his care while she went to converse quietly with her aunt.

James's arms settled around her as he sat against the rock foundation and lifted her onto his lap. His security and strength was a balm to her shattered soul. His hand lightly pressed her head into his chest where the rhythmic

~ ☾ ~

thrumming of his heart lulled her gently back into a more controlled state. His lips brushed the crown of her head as his strong hands roamed over her back with reassuring strokes.

April wasn't an emotional weakling and never allowed herself to cling to anyone. For the first time since becoming a woman, she never wanted this moment in James's arms to end. She barely knew the man—she wasn't even sure if he was real and yet here he was. Her rock.

"We need to get her out of here and back home," her mother spoke up finally as she stood, brushing dirt from her pants, and offered Aunt Vickie her hand to help her out of the ruins. Aunt Vickie nodded her agreement as she was pulled up from inside the wall.

"Is the house any safer for her right now?" James asked.

Her grandmother pondered momentarily, looking to Vickie for guidance. "No. You're absolutely right, James. The entity is probably still there, waiting to harm her." She motioned for her daughter and Aunt Vickie to help her out of the shallow pit. "We have work to do before April can return to the house." Raising her hand up to the others so they could give her a hand out of the foundation, grandma pulled herself up over the wall.

"What happened just now?" James asked. The hollow echo of his voice rumbled in his chest against April's ear. "You said she phased..."

"I'm...I'm sorry," April stuttered as the shock began to wear off. "I hadn't expected it to be so...The last time I did it, I was caught in the image of a fire. I was unable to move as a beam fell and the house collapsed on us."

"Us who?" James asked with confusion, putting her away from him so he could see her face. "What are you talking about?"

Shaking, April looked around at the barren ruins. "The young woman was tied up. Alive and struggling while the fire raged around us. The man was lying next to her unconscious or dead, I'm not sure which. I couldn't move away from the wall. I could only watch. It was horrible." April shuddered. She glanced up at the women she'd trusted since birth,

~ ☾ ~

searching for answers in their eyes. "Did everything I witness really happen?"

"What are you talking about, dear?" her grandmother asked gently. She turned to her sister. "Vickie, what is she talking about?"

Her aunt didn't answer. She was busy concentrating on the area around them. April was able to get her bearings, thanks to the sturdy, solid strength of James. With a bit of assistance from both her mother and James, she raised herself out of the cellar foundation to stand beside the others. James followed, maneuvering his long legs up the field stone wall and grabbing at a protruding root. She looked at the four people standing around her. This was it.

"Lately, my gift of psychometry has taken on more than normal activity. I thought it had to do with my allergies, but I think it's really happening. I sometimes don't even have to touch an object—just be near an active haunting or a site of great historical importance." She turned to her mother. "The longer I'm connected, the more intense everything becomes. I can see images, residuals of a specific past and they interact with me," April confessed as she tried to stem her tears of confusion. The worried expressions on the other women's faces didn't help. They only intensified her fears. For the first time in her life April was scared of her abilities.

Aunt Vickie stepped forward taking her hand. April let her aunt's fingers trace the lines in her palms, studying the natural etchings represented there. Giving it a reassuring squeeze, her aunt looked from her to James and back. A moment of interest crossed her face, giving way to a sad smile. "You did more than see them sweetie, you phased. Somehow you can step into their realm, like James stepped into yours."

***

Aunt Vickie and Grandma Dottie returned to the house to cleanse the malevolent spirit while they sent James and her mother to help April shop for groceries. Still, something kept April from feeling right about her surroundings when they got home. The prickling of sensations, like being around a highly-charged electrical

~ ☾ ~

atmosphere, kept her rubbing the chills from her arms. When she asked if the area was clear both women appeared doubtful. They only shrugged. *Great, no one in her family knew.* They were the only people in her world she could rely on for metaphysical or paranormal situations and they couldn't help her.

As she lay across her bed, trying to focus on her research books, James busied himself with pecking questions into the internet about anything he wanted to find out. She'd spent a good hour showing him how to use the keyboard and mouse. Then she'd given him a list of historical eras he might find fascinating since his death. So far, he'd managed to keep himself amused.

April's mind wandered. What did her aunt mean when she said, she phased? Her mother hadn't wanted to talk about what happened at the mill site after they'd left. But she needed answers. Had she actually 'stepped' into another realm from the past? Was there a reason she could witness what she had?

She needed to bury herself back into her research. Besides, if she concentrated on her job, she wouldn't think about her connection to the ghosts and it wouldn't affect her. *Yeah and the National Deficit would go away overnight, too.* She didn't need to get behind on her original purpose for being in Kings Mill though.

Again, she feared the task was hopeless. When James took a break from surfing the net, she'd taken a moment to check her messages. Kenneth's reply from her earlier email had come through. He was ecstatic about her revelation of documents being transferred to lawyers and he would look into it from his end. But he was curious to know where she'd found the information. She hadn't thought about that. Could she pretend ignorance and say she never got his email?

Two hours later, April hadn't found anything more to go on. This was ridiculous! Researching through information was better done with a peaceful atmosphere. She couldn't concentrate at all. A part of her wanted time to be alone and think clearly. The other part of her didn't want to be left alone after what had happened in her ghostly attack.

~ ☾ ~

April closed her eyes and pressed her fingers to her lids, rubbing the tension away before opening them to a blurry view. Frustration and pent up energy had finally won out over her focus and intelligence. She closed her books, marking the pages with her various notes. Gathering them up, she placed them on the bedside table and began to pace.

"Are you all right?" James asked, looking up from the lap top.

She ran her fingers through her hair, untying her braid and letting it loose. "Am I all right?" She snorted. "I've managed to change the laws of nature by bringing a dead man to life. I touch ruins and see ghosts who are suffering intolerable fates. What's even more troubling is they see me and think I can help them. I can't! And you ask me if I'm all right?" Walking to the edge of the room, April lightly banged her forehead against the papered wall in frustration.

Gentle hands enclosed her shoulders, turning her around to face a solid chest. Warm lips brushed her bangs, the edge of her temple.

"I can't shake the images, James. They were so real."

He stroked her back, lovingly. "It was real. You were there, according to your grandmother and aunt. I know what you went through. I've experienced it for over two hundred years."

"You've seen it? You've seen the manor house like I did?" April looked up into smoky gray eyes. She loved how James's eyes changed with his moods. Right now they were a soft, wispy color but the other night, while sharing his embrace, they were steel blue.

"No. Not the manor house. I see the fields and the workers—just as I did when I was alive. I've even witnessed my execution. The first time it happened I was in the same state of shock you are in and knew I couldn't do anything to change it."

"Do you interact with the others in your realm?"

"There are no others. I can see them but they don't know I'm there."

"Then why is the young woman in my sightings trying to talk to me?" April asked more to herself than James.

~ ☾ ~

"Is it because of your gift? Perhaps she's asking for help, somehow sensing you have the ability to help her. I guess we just need to find out how to help her. Who is she?"

"I don't know. I've seen her twice in the manor cellar. Once when she was tied up and the house was on fire and then today when she was trying to protect the young man from the other man's beating."

"I didn't have any women in the manor. A few of the men working my lands were married, but women never came out to the house...except..."

His brow creased. "Describe these people you saw."

April hesitated. What if he knew these people who'd died? What would he think? It really didn't matter anymore. They would all be long gone, even if they had lived full lives. "The young woman was a bit shorter than me, with dainty features and blonde hair. I would venture to guess she was somewhere in her late teens, early twenties."

April gave as much detail as she could remember about the three people. The young woman who interacted with her and the villainous man were easy to describe. But she hadn't gotten a good look at the younger man other than to know he was younger and probably died from the knock to his head before the fire could claim his life.

She didn't have a lot to go on and watched James's brow crinkle as he tried to remember faces, the people from so many centuries ago. His face cleared and his eyes opened wide. "I know who your woman is. There is only one woman I would know by that description. Your ghost is Catherine Samuel, Henry's wife." His brow crinkled in confusion. "But what in bloody hell would she be doing in my cellar?"

***

The soft sound of April's deep, even breaths alerted James she'd finally drifted off to sleep. He kept to his word and wasn't leaving her side. The day's activities had left her exhausted. His eyes adjusted to the night. He hoped to spot some clue that might tell him who or what dared to bother her. But he was met with only darkness.

Her soft hand rested on his chest. A sigh of contentment escaped her lips but damned if he could sleep with this

~ ☾ ~

woman so close to him. April insisted he sleep in the bed with her and not on a pile of blankets on the hard floor. How ironic she would choose a simple linen shift to wear as her night clothing. Did she think such an unbecoming piece of fabric would deter him from wanting her? Hardly! She could wear a grain sack and he would still want her.

Fully clothed in the jeans and a shirt he'd worn all day, he wasn't comfortable. James slept *au naturel* when he was alive but would be damned if he did so now with April lying there, tempting him. She wasn't one of his tarts from the local pub, nor a widowed matron looking for a reminder of sexual fulfillment. April was much more to him.

Was it because he'd been alone for so long? No, it was something deeper he couldn't put a finger on. Was it sexual? Two hundred thirty-eight years of celibacy prompted him to say 'yes.' But if that were the case, he would have taken her up on her offer last night. In his past, he wouldn't have hesitated.

You're losing your touch, James Addison.

April shifted and sighed. She flipped over onto her stomach and snuggled into her pillow. Taking a deep breath, James groaned inwardly. Having her in such close proximity made things hard. He glanced down at the lower half of his body. He didn't need to visualize his state of discomfort to know it was there. It ached and throbbed against the stiff material of the pants.

Think about something else.

Closing his eyes, he tried to envision the characters April described to him. The only young, blonde woman he knew was Catherine. She fit the description. But he still couldn't figure out what she would have been doing in the cellar. Had she been lured down there by the man who'd killed her? Who was the man? Could it have been one of his field hands looking to attack her? Had chaos ensued at the mill once he was executed?

Where was Daniel during this time? Daniel would have escorted Catherine safely about the manor, like always. He wouldn't have let danger befall her. Could the young man who'd been bludgeoned been Daniel? God, he hoped not! It was bad enough to imagine Catherine being burned alive, but

~ ☾ ~

not Daniel, too. James shuddered at the thought.

Who would have wanted to hurt Catherine? She was a saint. She came to the mill with her maid to purchase her flour and grains directly from him once every other week. In return, she brought her delicious, freshly baked scones, cream, and jams to share. James looked forward to those visits. Catherine's scones and her sweet, timid disposition reminded him a bit of home and his little sister, Elsbeth. James always made sure Daniel escorted her and her maid safely back home after each visit.

Catherine being Henry's bride didn't sit well with James—never had. Henry Samuel was one lucky bastard to have acquired such a sweet girl. Rumors swirled of Henry having won Catherine's indenture in a card game from a plantation owner along the Chesapeake. Henry was much older than Catherine. His tastes in sexual activities were questionable. Many a night in the taverns, Henry would boast of his pursuits. He spoke of various mistresses on the side. James thought the stories just ramblings of an inebriated sot. But many of James's women mentioned hearing of the man's harsh treatment of their friends.

One never questioned another man's relationship with his wife. Besides, his association with Henry was pure commerce. They rarely conversed outside of business and casual pleasantries.

April gave a startled jolt, bringing him out of his musings. She didn't wake but flipped over again, tossing her head frantically from side to side as if in the midst of a bad dream. Propping himself up on an elbow, James reached over to soothe her. A chilly spot of air met his hand as he went to touch her, but it dissipated as he caressed her arm.

Her brow arched and relaxed in slumber as her breathing returned to normal. Perhaps she caught a chill from the sudden breeze. Moving the pillow she'd thrown to the side in her tossing, he gave in and wrapped her in his embrace. This was strictly for medicinal purposes—he was keeping her warm with his natural body heat. Good thing Mr. Levi Strauss made a strong material for his trousers. It was going to be a long, *hard* night.

~ ☾ ~

***

James must have dozed off. April shook him awake. She leaned over him, her eyes wide.

"Did you hear that?" she asked, biting her bottom lip.

James rubbed the sleep from his eyes. "What?"

"The woman crying. It must be the ghost Aunt Vickie told us about."

"I don't hear anything. Are you sure?" *Of course she was sure, you imbecile! She comes from a long line of ghost enchantresses and brought your sorry arse to life.* He strained his hearing to catch on to what she heard but he heard nothing, only the quiet emptiness of the room.

She reached over and turned on the bedside lamp. He blinked his eyes to adjust to the brightness. Throwing her covers off, April scurried quickly around the room until she located her lamb booties and slipped them on her feet.

"Where are you going?" He asked, forcing himself awake.

"I want to see who she is. And see if there is anything my family can do to help her. I'm surprised Aunt Vickie hasn't tried since she's lived here." She threw her robe around her and pulled her long, amber hair out from under the collar. Tilting her head in the direction of the other room, her eyes widened. "She's sobbing hysterically now." April studied him with curiosity. "You don't hear that at all?"

"April, you shouldn't do this. You should wait for your mother..."

"My mother can't handle ghosts. I don't want to stress her out any more than she is. Just being in this house is giving her migraines."

"What about your grandmother. We can wake her up," James offered. He really didn't want April dealing with a possible ghost on her own—not after what had happened to her so far. Could she bring other ghosts back to life if she didn't know any better, like she'd done with him?

"Fine. Wake Grams up if you feel the need to. I'm going to check on our crying woman."

James hoped Dottie was a light sleeper. April was getting in way over her head.

~ ☾ ~

Chapter Twelve

The hallway was empty. Goosebumps dotted April's arms as she neared the bedroom door. Should she knock? What was the protocol for barging in on a ghost?

A sudden creaking of the door on its hinge made April wince. Well, if she wanted to approach the weeping woman with stealth, the plan just went to Hell. Peeking around the door, with one eye closed, she was greeted by the vision of a startled woman. The young woman maneuvered quickly from her sitting position at the large secretary desk in the corner of the room, to stand defiantly in front of it. Was she trying to hide something? The ghostly vision looked directly at her.

April would never forget the woman's face. Though her hair was modestly styled up in a lady-like fashion of colonial times, her frantic features would haunt her forever. Tears streaked down her cheeks. Anguish and fear were etched even deeper. April was positive this was the same woman from the manor house.

Unbelievable!

Moments passed as they stared at each other. April's ghostly friend seemed to relax a bit as she slowly made her way a bit farther into the room. Again, the scent of lilac permeated the room. It was the ghost's scent, her fragrance.

"Who...are you?" April asked, her voice trembling a bit.

The young woman's gaze darted around the room in anxiousness. She wiped at her cheeks with the back of her hand and focused on April again.

"Can you see me?" April asked.

A subtle, unsure nod of the ghost's head caused April to relax a bit, but then relaxing while viewing a ghost didn't make sense to her.

An idea came to her mind. If this woman was dressed in

~ ☾ ~

colonial period and the house had belonged to Henry Samuel, could this be his wife? James seemed to think the woman she'd witnessed in his cellar had been her. "Are you Catherine Samuel?"

The ghost nodded.

Excited she finally had a few answers to go on, April continued. "What is it you need? I want to help you."

The ghostly figure's shoulders slumped with relief. Her hands flew wildly with emphasis as she began to move her lips. As fast as she was talking there would have been no way a lip-reader could keep up. Confused, April tried to get her to slow down.

"I can't hear you. Why can't I hear you now when I could hear you crying a few minutes ago? What are you trying to tell me?"

Her ghost stopped and sighed. Turning away in silent defeat she fumbled with her trinkets hanging from her apron and approached the writing desk where she had been. *Those trinkets, she had thrown them at April in the mill site scene.*

The shimmery image unlocked a drawer, and secreting something from the drop down desktop, put it in the small drawer underneath. She turned back and a look of pure terror marred her delicate features.

The door flew open, slamming hard against the wall as a fierce breeze blew into the room from the hallway. April watched in fascination as a haze of dust and air formed a solid entity. It was the man from the manor house ruins—the burly man, except this time he was still wearing a formal day suit. A periwig sat haphazardly on his balding head. Even with the wig, the ruddy jowls were all she needed to identify him. Bitter, beady eyes full of dark anger trained on the woman at the desk. Catherine cringed into her small corner as if expecting the worst. But he stopped when he saw April standing in her robe near the door.

The man's momentary shock was replaced by a sickening sneer of delight. Did he know her? He had seen her in the manor house. Did he remember? Who was this man? His attention diverted back to the woman at the desk, her hands frantically fingering the chains and various lockets tied to her

~ ☾ ~

apron front. She stopped playing with the bobbles instantly at his glare. Was she trying to get April to notice them? He looked from one to the other as if trying to guess what kind of game they were playing.

April felt the terrible friction of being entrapped, like earlier. With one menacing step toward her she instantly knew his intent and began backing away toward the door to safety. She never made it.

Trapped between the wall and his body, the situation was exactly like this morning's incident in her room. Though he wasn't corporeal, she felt the pressure as if he were a solid man. Fear escalated through her. His beefy hand grabbed her hair, forcing her head backwards. A foul stench of putrid body odor and rotting teeth made her gag.

He sneered as his face drew ever closer to hers. "*You have no clue what you have done.*"

What did she do? How could she hear him when she couldn't hear Catherine? What did this all mean? April fought his hold on her, forcing her face away from his fetid stench and thin lips. She screamed, long and shrill. Where were James and her grandmother? They should be here by now.

Bright light flooded the room. She squealed and turned away, covering her eyes from the sudden sensitivity.

"What the hell is going on?" James bellowed, coming into the opened room.

James and Grandma Dottie stood in the doorway. Her grandmother's features pinched as she stumbled backwards, away from the room as if being bowled over by someone leaving in a hurry. Aunt Vickie and her mother rushed in, wrapping their bathrobes around them. April felt the security of James's arms around her as she rocked back and forth from the frightful incident. She could still see the man's face, feel his rank breath on her face, hear his grating voice echoing in her ears. What had she done? Who was he? What did he want from her? Voices of those she loved were whispering around her, but all she could hear was *his* voice.

"Get her out, James," her mother said, finally stepping forward, surveying the now empty room. April hazarded a

~ ☾ ~

glance around as James gathered her up in his arms and pulled her from the scene, and her mother ventured forth, listening to her surroundings.

"What is it, Virginia? What do you hear?" her grandmother asked.

"Nothing now. But I hear echoes of voices; angry, scared...I don't know." Her mother shook her head.

Out in the hallway, Aunt Vickie patted James's shoulder. "We'll handle it from here, James. You take care of April. She's going to need your strength. Give us a moment."

April felt the shift of her body being carried in James's strong arms. Once placed on her bed, she curled into the fetal position and prayed for God to be merciful and take away her family curse. *At least give me a clue as to what the hell I did wrong!*

***

Carrying April back into her suite at her aunt's instruction, James laid her gently on the bed, wrapping the counterpane around her.

"Where were you? What took you so long to bring Grams?" April asked, her body still shaking.

"I'd just left you. I hadn't been gone more than a minute or two. By the time we got to the room the door had slammed shut and we couldn't get in. Didn't you hear us banging on the door?"

"No."

Her voice was so small and quiet as she physically retreated, wrapping herself into a ball.

"April?" He touched her gently, brushing back a wayward curl of hair and tucking it behind her ear.

"It seemed like forever. Catherine was sitting there at the desk crying when I peeked in. I startled her. She was trying to tell me something but I couldn't hear her. Then she was pleading with me. That's when he came in."

"Who was he?"

"Evil. He was dressed in gentleman's clothing and a periwig. Catherine was frightened of him. She had every right to be." She turned to him, her face pale but blotchy as color seeped back into her skin. "I think it was the man in the

~ ☾ ~

cellar. He looked like him in the face and body. Like an old English bulldog, only rabid."

James's lip curled in disgust. "Henry Samuel."

April scurried off of his lap and reached for a book on the table. Flipping through pages she came upon the black and white photos. "It's him!" She shoved the book at him and paced.

"Why didn't I make the connection? This is the man I just saw. I should have known. I should've remembered seeing him in this book."

"You weren't expecting him. Don't be so hard on yourself."

But James didn't feel comfortable knowing Henry's ghost was the culprit in both life and death. He was torturing April. Why? Did the ghost know he was around? What would Henry do if he found out the man he'd executed was alive and well? Maybe he knew and he was trying to get to James through tormenting April? Damn! He wished he could see the ghost like the women of this house did. He would demand satisfaction for the man's evil actions. But how could he fight something not there?

"I don't know what to do." April sat back down on the bed. She wrung her hands frantically in her lap. Looking up at him, her eyes filled with wariness. "He had you executed. He killed Catherine and the other man. What kind of man are we dealing with?"

"I don't know. I wish I'd known Henry better back in the day—but I didn't." James took her hands and rubbed his finger over the back of her knuckles, feeling the slight shaking in her hands. He put his free arm around her, pulling her up onto his lap. She felt good there, snuggled under his chin, her head resting against his heart.

"I will promise you this, April, I'll do everything in my power, alive or dead, to keep you safe from Henry Samuel. You have to trust me."

"I...I...do trust you, James. I'm just...scared. Hold me," April managed to murmur in between stuttering breaths.

"I am holding you, sweet lass," James whispered against her ear, kissing the dangling end of the strand of hair he'd placed against the delicate pink shell.

~ ☾ ~

"Closer."

April turned into him, moving her shift so her bare leg could wrap around his hips and thighs. James's heartbeat struggled to remain steady. She burrowed her head into his chest, literally trying her damndest to crawl into his skin.

"If I were any closer, I dare say we would be inside one another." James tried for a bit of humor, letting the rumble of his laughter echo in his chest. Her face tilted up. God help him, he was lost to the need he saw reflected in her eyes.

"Would that be a bad thing?" April asked with innocent wonder.

Yes...no...Hell, this was a heck of a bloody time to go noble! He ached to accommodate her, but he would rather die again than take her while she was so vulnerable.

"You've had a fright. I would be a bloody bastard to use your weakness for my own gain." He did tuck her closer to him and rubbed the chills from her arms, letting her body relax against him even though he was as wound up as his pocket watch.

Aunt Vickie knocked and stepped in to check on them briefly. James jumped, ready to defend April's honor. But Vickie only nodded, gave him the thumbs up and a sly-wink before closing the door. These modern women were an odd-lot. In his day, he would have been run out of town, tarred and feathered for the intimate position they shared.

April hadn't moved in quite awhile, but her breathing had relaxed and the tremors had subsided as he continued to methodically stroke her hair, back and shoulders, easing the tension from her body. Assuming she was asleep, he stopped his ministrations to let her rest peacefully.

"Don't stop," she said, her voice muffled against his shirt. "Your touch feels good."

So much for thinking she was asleep. "You're tired. You've been through quite a bit lately. You need to rest."

April rose up, her knees on either side of his lap, her hands on his shoulders. She glared down at him. "Don't tell me what I need. I know what I need. I need you," she fumed. "Why won't you make love to me? I'm more than willing. What is so different about me than the other women you bedded? Are

~ ☾ ~

you afraid because of my gift? Do you see me as a freak?"

She thought he didn't want to make love to her? Where the hell did she come up with such an imbecilic notion? Did she not understand what kind of torture it was for him to be this close to her and not assuage his physical cravings? He was fighting a damn battle to keep her safe from him. Neither one had any idea how much time they would have together. He couldn't offer anything to her without knowing if he was alive or just another form of ghostly material she needed to fear.

"You have it all wrong, April Branford. I want you so very much, and I'm not to be confused with your past lover. I'm not Jason. He was a weak imbecile who couldn't accept how wonderful and gifted you are. If it wasn't for everything you are, I wouldn't be alive right now."

In one fluid movement, April stripped off her chemise and settled herself closer to him. "Then prove it. If you are *the* James Addison, the rakish scoundrel I've read about, prove it to me. If you want me so much, take what I'm offering, for however long we have."

Bloody hell! For the first time in his randy, demented life, James Addison didn't know what to do with a naked woman sitting atop of him. April sat there like a knight going into battle. Her armor was soft pale skin shining in the lamp light. Her hair tumbled gloriously over her shoulders in a wild mane. She was naked and beautiful and a goddess meant to be worshiped. His hands itched to touch her and yet all he could do was stare, taking her beauty in, and praying to God he still remembered how to pleasure a woman.

***

April sat astride James's lap. Was this familiar to him? Did women take the lead in his time? Then she didn't care, he was here with her now. She didn't worry about right or wrong, and time, no one knew how much time they had on Earth. James's frail existence showed her as much. She was grabbing time while she had time to grab. Her craving for this man, since the day she'd met him, won out over propriety and worrying about tomorrow. They were both consenting adults and she'd be damned if he waited to ask for her parent's permission.

~ ☾ ~

Not sure what to expect, she hadn't been ready for James Addison's assault on her. His hardness rasped against her naked, feminine core. The material of his jeans touched off jolts of electricity as she rubbed wantonly across his erection. She moaned at the feel. Silver-gray eyes glowed in the dim light. She could tell he was hesitant and knew he was trying to be noble. Damn him! She didn't want noble, she wanted him! Now!

"You can touch me. I promise I won't break," she teased as she brought his hand up to her breast.

It was a perfect fit. As big as his hands were, she was adequate in size. The darker coloring and crisp black hairs were a stark contrast against her pale skin. He was callused and rough, the texture sending triggers of delight coursing through her. The rasp of his thumb over her sensitive nipple made her ache with raw hunger.

Leaning back a bit she moved against his manhood, rubbing herself over the rough material of his jeans, imitating what she hoped to do when she had him naked. She could feel the hardened length but wanted all of him.

She looked up from under her lashes to gauge his reaction. His deep inhales filled with unleashed tension rained hot over her face. He was holding back but only by a thread. The evidence of his need shimmered in his stormy grey eyes. She moved sinfully, rubbing her breasts against him as she rode his lap.

"April," James's voice came out like a ragged warning.

She'd played it safe for too long. She'd never wanted to go crazy on a man before. But James brought out the wild in her. The denim material was a damn nuisance. Reaching down between them she pushed the copper button through the hole on his fly and grazed his erection through the rough material. He gasped but she continued to free him. Pulling the zipper down slowly, she felt his natural heat radiate from him.

Cupping him gently she removed him from his constraints to the sound of his stuttered groan. He was hot silk wrapped around hard steel. April reveled in being the first woman to touch him in centuries. She wanted to bring every part of him to life with her hands, her body, and her mouth.

~ ☾ ~

She slid off his lap and pushed him back on the bed, stripping him of the infuriating jeans and briefs. She wanted to see all of James Addison. The man in all his glory.

"April...dear God!" James gasped.

She touched him, marveling at the mystery behind the man. She treated him as gently as she would a freshly found artifact with light delicate touches and a sense of wonder.

"You don't know what you do, angel," James's voice sounded hoarse to her ears.

She let him go. Her feminine power took over. She liked this new side to her—daring and bold. "Oh, I think I do."

She returned to straddle him in his prone position. Finding his hand, she again placed it on her breast. His fingers brushed over the sensitive skin as lightly as she'd touched him and then he tweaked her nipple, just a light pinch setting off a chain reaction throughout her nerves to make her throb. She pressed wantonly against him, feeling his heat and hardness. Her head lowered to meet his. Their sexual tension was palpable in their ragged breathing. Perspiration dotted his brow. He was fighting it.

"Please James..."

Her soft plea was all he'd needed to lose his control. She was lifted off of his lap, and he left her side only to remove his shirt before placing his body atop hers, resting his weight on his muscular arms as his lips crashed down on hers with such intensity she thought he was going to swallow her whole.

The kiss gentled as her hands stroked the corded muscles of his back and shoulders, and then he began exploring more than her mouth. His lips trailed over her cheeks, her jaw, nipping their way down the column of her throat.

April arched her back as his mouth found her breasts and tormented them with alternating kisses, nibbles, and gentle suckling. She gasped at the intensity and the thoroughness of his exploration. He maneuvered them both so he could touch her with his hands as well as his lips.

She jumped and giggled lightly as his mouth found the sensitive spot on her belly. He growled low in his throat and continued his exploration. His teeth nipped her hip and she gasped but then his hand found its own center of

~ ☾ ~

attention and she nearly came off the bed.

All of her moisture had pooled from just wanting him, long before he'd begun to touch her. She closed her eyes. Now she was just a ball of aching need. But he took his time, igniting her passions even further with his touch, finding all the sensitive areas and some she didn't even know existed, until she was a wiggling mass of pent up frustration waiting to be unleashed.

She opened her eyes and saw James in all his masculine glory. This was the man the history books wrote about. He sat poised between her thighs, readying himself. Her body throbbed, her heart ached to bursting. This man was all hers—for now.

James leaned over her, touching her womanhood lightly, making sure she was ready too. "April, my heart...are you sure?"

She reached up and brushed her hand over his. "I've never been more so in my life, James."

"It's been so long. Let me know if I hurt you."

She wanted to weep. He was thinking of her, not wanting to hurt her. Were her eyes glowing as brightly as his? He parted her legs gently and entered her in one swift move of his hips.

April couldn't help but arch up into him. She closed her eyes and bit her lip to keep from crying out at the welcomed intrusion. James didn't move. Stretching her, he let her adjust to his size.

They moved together, their bodies in tune, giving and receiving. April wrapped her legs around his hips, bringing him closer. His body strained to hold back. She was on the precipice waiting for him to take the leap with her. Tender nerves ignited within her and she dug her fingers into his shoulders as she arched and leaped. She pulled him along as she felt his body stiffen inside of her before he pumped deeper, burying his face into the hollow of her throat to stifle the deep moan of release.

April couldn't help but grin into the darkened room as the legendary rake, James Addison lay heavily upon her, sated but exhausted. *So ghosts really do moan.*

~ ☾ ~

Chapter Thirteen

James woke early. His body was well-rested, sated and naked, lying next to an equally naked April. He ached, but it was a good ache, physically. He threw an arm over his eyes and groaned inwardly. Last night had happened so fast. One minute he'd been consoling a frightened woman, and then she'd tempted him to take actions he hadn't intended. But she'd felt so damn good, and it had been so long since he'd enjoyed the pleasures a woman could give. He'd tried to remember if it had ever been that good. All he knew was he never wanted it to end.

Now in the light of day, realizing he'd gone over the edge and done something he'd had no intention of doing, he was at a loss. He'd lost control last night, if he ever really had it. April could be carrying his child, and there would be nothing he could do if his time on Earth were to end as suddenly as it began.

The thought of conceiving a wee one didn't chill him the way it once had. Was it because he knew how precious life was? Was he possibly being given the chance to create a life from his death? He looked over at his angel-woman who'd brought life to his body and heart.

The morning light sprinkling in through the lacy sheers colored her hair with kisses of flame. Her cheek nested in the riot of fire, so peaceful, her lips slightly parted and moist. She was beautiful. The image of her rounded with his child toyed at the fore front of his thoughts. His cock twitched at the possibility of seeing her in such a maternal state, knowing it was his babe. A ghost of a man only days ago and now dreaming of a future with a woman he barely knew. Could fate be any kinder or crueler? Was he here permanently or only for a brief time until they could solve the real reason for his death?

Quietly, without waking his sleeping beauty, he slipped

~ ☾ ~

from their bed and dressed in the pants she'd tossed to the floor. He only had the shirt from last night as he had yet to retrieve his clothing from the other room. It would have to do. He'd done with less in his life. How many nights had he run from a ladies room, so not to get caught and forced to wed? Now, he was seriously thinking of settling down with one woman, and no one was even forcing his hand. He was losing his touch.

She stirred in her sleep, snuggling into the pillows he'd just left. Her deep inhale made her smile and she continued to dream peacefully. Yes, April Branford was unique. She was the first woman to tug at his heart strings just by being in her presence. His smile faded as he realized he had no right to feel this way. There could be nothing between them until he knew for sure whether or not he would still be around for them to have a future. In the meantime, he needed to take responsibility for his actions, make a future available to them for whatever time they had. He needed a job, a home for them, and a minister to bless their union before there *was* a babe to consider.

***

April stood up and began to pace. "I can't sit here any longer while you're all sipping your coffee and eating glazed donuts as if this is an everyday occurrence. There is too much at stake and my time is dwindling. I need to find some way to contact Catherine Samuel. If I can't find the documents, I need to do something. If she needs my help then I need to find a way to help her. Grams, Aunt Vickie, are you with me on this?"

James had finished his last glazed donut, a delicacy for certain, and wiped his lips. She was on edge and he wondered what had brought the condition on, besides what she'd just said. Yes, the ghostly encounter last night was surely on her mind, but he'd hoped their intimacy might have eased a bit of it. Was she upset over what had happened? Was she having second thoughts about him? It had been awhile. Maybe he didn't live up to expectations or was too old fashioned for the rituals of pleasures now. He remained quiet. They needed to talk, but he wished to get her alone first.

~ ☾ ~

Aunt Vickie began cleaning up the breakfast dishes. "I know you're frustrated, but honey, let me know what you need me to do. We'll work it out."

"Thanks. I just feel so helpless." April tried to smile, but it came out a bit weak.

"I know, dear. It's never easy to accept our gifts. Take it one day at a time. Something has got to give and when it does, open yourself to it. Don't be afraid." Vickie looked to her sister, still sitting, as she continued to drink from an empty cup. "Stop dawdling, Dottie, I could use some help with dishes in the kitchen."

"But we only used the cups, everything else was paper. Surely you don't need my help with just a couple of cups..." her voice trailed off as Vickie jerked her head in April and James's direction. "Oh, well yes—I suppose I could dry the cups for you."

James watched as April's grandmother and aunt left the room. It was just the two of them, the atmosphere thick with uncertainty. James sat forward in his chair, his hands clasped together tightly between his wide spread legs. The fingers gripped each other so firmly their knuckles were white. Now would be as good a time as ever to broach the subject they needed to discuss.

James cleared his throat, rubbing the back of his neck nervously. "I stopped by and talked to the reverend from the Episcopal Church this morning."

April gave him a queer look. Where was the woman he'd watch sleep so peacefully this morning? Now she looked troubled and uncertain. Did she regret last night?

"Really," she said with cool indifference, her mind clearly elsewhere.

"He said he would be more than willing to officiate our wedding."

She looked around her, and then back at him. Her brows knotted in confusion.

"Excuse me? What wedding?"

James stood up quickly. Now it was his turn to pace. He stopped. "I intend to do right by you."

He wasn't sure what he expected but the rolling of her eyes

~ ☾ ~

as she wiped a hand over her face wasn't it. A woman in his day would be honored for a man who'd taken advantage of her to ask for her hand in marriage.

"James, this is 2012. You don't need to propose marriage just because we made love. It was wonderful, don't get me wrong, but I don't expect you to marry me because of it." She sighed. "I'm just not ready for this…there are too many unknown factors at stake. Let's just take it one day at a time."

James's jaw tightened as he considered her words. Her indifference to his proposal had him feeling like a fool. He didn't give a damn about what was or wasn't expected in 2012! A knife to his heart couldn't have hurt worse than what she'd said, or maybe it was how she'd said it.

"I see." Walking over to the mantle he pretended to study a simple picture on the small shelf. He wanted to regain his composure. She was probably right. There were too many issues they needed to work out. Still, it didn't make his pride smart any less.

"What if there is a babe?" He turned to her. She was fidgeting. Could she be as nervous as he? "I have to admit, I didn't take the precautions I am used to taking with a woman. I was caught up in the moment." A small smile played on his lips to soothe the distress and unease he saw in her face.

A glimmer of hope touched his heart as her hands unconsciously fluttered over her stomach as if the idea of carrying his child excited her somehow.

"We'll deal with the situation if it comes up. Right now, I'm more concerned with other issues we have at hand, not 'what ifs.'" She dismissed the idea but couldn't meet his eyes.

She was hiding from him. Perhaps last night didn't mean as much to her as it did to him. Was it only her curiosity that drove her to make love to him? His reputation as a great lover of women was well known in the history books. He should be delighted to have such an interesting title. But it didn't mean anything to him now. In fact the title bothered him a bit. He didn't want her to think of him as randy, hopping from one woman's bed to another. He wanted her and her alone. If she'd been his back in the 1770's he would never have needed to search further.

~ ☾ ~

"What situation are you two talking about?"

April looked up guiltily as her mother walked into the room, slowly sipping a cup of herbal tea. James noticed Virginia Branford looked deathly pale and weak. "What situation?" she repeated looking from him to April for some sort of answer.

"Our future, Mrs. Branford." James sat down in the chair.

She slumped onto the settee, took another sip of her tea and held her head. "So what were you discussing about your future? Are you even sure you're really alive?" She addressed him with the dressing down of a protective parent. "I don't see how you can be. Whatever my daughter did to bring you to life I'm sure can be undone."

She turned her attention towards April. "And just because you jump into the sack doesn't mean he'll stick around for the long run. Use your head, April May Branford."

Virginia's words came out in an angry snarl. April's jaw tightened and her fists clenched at her sides. When she turned to him, he saw the regret and uncertainty she felt about them and what they had done.

"Mom, that is your migraine talking. I can't believe you could be so obtuse. I'm a consenting adult, and you have no right to question my private life."

"No," James replied quietly. Bowing his head he let his hands drop between his knees in defeat. "I suppose you are right, Virginia. I don't know for sure." James looked up warily at April, her eyes fuming with pent up anger at her mother. "You're mother is only looking out for your best interests...as am I. But yes, I should have thought more clearly on our delicate situation. I should have never let things go so far last night."

He stood and walked out of the room. He didn't want mother and daughter to fight about him. April's mother was right in her way. His future was uncertain.

His ego lay in tatters. Worse, it felt as if his heart had been ripped out again. First her rejection of his proposal, and now her mother's refusal to accept him as a human being in this realm. He didn't stand a chance in hell of winning their favor.

"I love you, but you can be such a bitch at times, Mother,"

~ ☾ ~

he heard April seethe in his defense. He smiled briefly but it was short lived and not worthy of a victory. Not if he couldn't convince her of his intentions.

***

James stood on the back porch, the brisk November air biting into his skin. He couldn't promise April anything permanent. No matter how alive she made him feel, he was still a ghost, some sort of phenomenal being brought to life for a brief moment in time. He wasn't supposed to be alive and how long he would remain in this form, no one was sure. But he would fight like hell to try and stay alive if it meant having April in his future.

The cold wind mocked him with its icy chill. How ironic! God must be laughing at him. He'd spent his life forming relationships with women based on appeasing his sexual wants, never settling for any one woman. Now he'd finally found the one woman who could tempt him beyond all others, and he couldn't have her.

"You're going to catch a cold out here," April murmured from behind him.

She placed his jacket over his shoulders and wrapped her arms around him. This felt right; her holding him like this, molding her body to his. April shifted into his arms and burrowed into his chest.

"This is my fault. I should've never come to Kings Mill. You would still be where you were."

"You're right, I would be." He tilted her face up and saw the concern cross her brow. "I would still be alone in my haze of time, slipping between witnessing my execution, walking aimlessly in the present, and viewing the ghosts of my past life—replaying them over and over until they became so much of me, I knew nothing else."

"You were in a residual time loop."

"Until you came along and noticed me under the tree. You set me free."

"The tree," she said with a harsh snort.

James laughed. "I thought you were talking to the tree when I saw you. I didn't realize at the time you could see me. When you responded to my mocking you, I didn't know what

~ ☾ ~

to think. I remember I did a little dance to see if you could follow my movements."

Touching her cheek the connection between them flourished, and the uncomfortable awkwardness of their earlier discussion melted away. "You have no idea what you did to me. I'll never be able to explain what I felt." Placing her hand against his chest, he held it there, gazing into her eyes, trying to tell her how he felt about her, about them and how right they were together.

She lowered her face into his coat. Her giggle was muffled, but he felt it against his heart. "You thought I was talking to the tree? All I thought was how I could strike up a conversation with a hot looking tour guide."

"Little did you know you were talking to a ghost. Might as well have been talking to a tree," James replied, poking her small nose playfully.

"If trees could talk, yeah right," April scoffed. She looked up at him. Her eyes lit up like live embers, sparking and glowing. "That's it! If trees could talk!" April gasped, repeating it as if it were a mantra. The embers in her eyes suddenly burst into flame. He could actually see her mind working its excited mischief on an enlightening thought.

This did not bode well for him.

***

"I forbid it!" James bellowed as he rose from his seat at the dining room table where he was going over the classified ads. He walked up to April and glared down at her.

"You can't forbid me from doing anything. Besides, I have to," she replied with more bravado then she felt. Was she sure she was ready to take on such an enormous task? She was thinking about doing something no one had any proof of actually doing—phasing into another time realm. She knew she could do it. She'd been doing it without conscious thought. This time she would be in control.

She looked to her family for support. "Come on Aunt Vickie, you said it was my time to find my purpose. Well, this is my purpose—to step between the realms and find the truth to the unsolved mysteries of time."

Vickie looked uneasily to Dottie. April turned her attention

~ ☾ ~

on her. "Grams, you of all people know the importance of helping set lost souls free. You've begged Mom to accept it. What is so different from what you all do to help the souls then what I'm proposing?"

"We understand the simplicity of our gifts, April dear, yours—well, it's something we can't quite comprehend. Physically phasing into realms of time is just not easy to grasp." Aunt Vickie reached over and patted her hand. "We can't help with what we don't understand. The risk to you might be greater than we can manage."

"As I said, you are not going to do so, April!" James demanded. "Damn my past! My past is not worth your life. I've been dead for over two hundred years. Execution or no execution, I should still be dead. What do you propose to find if you were to go back in time?"

"The truth!" April jumped up, tired of being hounded and questioned. "I'll be able to set the history books to right."

James leaped up from his seat and rounded on her. "And you'll have proof? How?" A vein throbbed in his forehead, the corded tendons in his neck and throat standing out prominently as his face mottled with fury.

"All you will see is my execution. Strong women have fainted from the shock, never to fully recover from such a gruesome public display. And you're willing to step back in time and witness it. For what, your own satisfaction? Because there is no evidence you could possibly find to bring back and set any history books to right."

They stood toe to toe, neither one willing to budge as they glared at one another. James's breath sighed out against her forehead as he took her face in his hands. "April, love, don't do this. Please. I could never forgive myself if anything...*anything* happened to you." His eyes went all dark with emotion. "I would rather die a thousand deaths at my executioner's hand than have you suffer one moment of my traumatic experience."

April closed her eyes, afraid of the fervor reeling within her from James's impassioned plea. Didn't he realize she was doing this for him? To set him free so he could be released from his past anguish? This was the whole 'setting lost souls

~ ☾ ~

free' to move on. But did she want him to 'move on' and where did one's spirit actually move on to?

The sound of muffled sniffles from the table had her glancing towards Aunt Vickie and her grandmother who were holding hands and looking on with misty eyes and smiling like a couple of women immersed in their 'shows.'

"Well, it's about time someone in this house had some sense in them. It's just a shame it has to be a ghost."

James dropped his hands from her face. April turned around to see her mother leaning casually in the archway to the dining room where they were seated. She'd gone upstairs to shower and freshen herself after berating James for his proposal earlier, and now she was back to add fuel to the fire.

"Virginia, that's enough." Grandma Dottie stood up, and wiping the moisture from her cheeks, turned a stern-lipped frown on her mother. "We don't need any more of your negative energy. Frankly, I've had about all I can take of your attitude."

"Dottie," Aunt Vickie cautioned, "don't add to it." She expelled a heavy breath. "I think we are all overcome emotionally right now. We need to meditate and focus our positive energies elsewhere. I for one have a book to read before my next book club meeting."

"I agree, Vickie. I'm going to go work on the afghan I've been trying to finish up for the church Christmas bazaar next month." Grandma Dottie looked to Virginia who still had a knot of tension etched into the lines of her face. "Virginia, get out of the house. Just go find something to focus your thoughts elsewhere."

"Yeah, this house is driving me insane. I can't fight these damn headaches." She rubbed at her head. "I'm going to the movies. Anyone want to go with me?" She looked pointedly at April.

April shook her head, partially because she didn't want any more lectures from her mother right now. She was still furious with her from earlier. But she also had work to do. "No thanks. I want to go through some more of those files today."

"I thought Beth was going to be working at the old office today?" James commented.

~ ☾ ~

"She is, but she gave me an extra key to the back door to use at my leisure. I just don't want to sit around here when I could be using the time to hunt down those documents." She quirked an eyebrow at him. "You interested in helping me with the tedious task?"

He seemed to ponder his options. "Reading, knitting, movies, or keeping my eye on a headstrong, beautiful woman by doing something tedious and mundane—I opt for the latter, just because I know she's bound to find some mischief to get into."

"Well, it didn't take long for him to figure you out, April," her mother said.

She was taken aback. It might have been the first kind words her mother had spoken regarding James. Was the infamous James Addison's charm beginning to work on the uptight Virginia Wilton-Branford? *That would be the day!*

***

Sitting on the floor surrounded by the various boxes and bundles of documentation pertaining to the history of Kings Mill was as monotonous as she'd thought. She did find some interesting articles and tid-bits of old information that might be of value to the society in general. Just nothing on James Addison, or Henry Samuel.

No, all the files were still too recent to help with her specific research. James wasn't having any better luck. She'd shown him how to gently handle the documents so the oils from their fingers didn't deteriorate the paper fibers. The violet colored latex gloves didn't put his masculinity in the best light though. He browsed through old scrap books and documents, sorting them by year/decade/century into piles on the lower row of file drawers bisecting the room.

"There you are. Your aunt said I could find you knee deep in history over here." Beth breezed in, removing her camel colored winter coat and hat. "Anything?" She nodded towards their work piles.

"Nothing of interest for me," April sighed. "But there are some interesting historically sound articles and letters. I started a pile for the Civil War period. They're mostly letters from soldiers when they were away at war. I found newsprint

~ ☾ ~

articles about some of the local battles and even a few recipes for 'Johnny Cake' and hard tack. But nothing about the mill."

"Well, there is a heck of a lot of Civil War history in these parts, as close as we are to Gettysburg and Antietam, not to mention various smaller battles around South Mountain. I'm thinking of dedicating at least a good portion of the exhibit to the era. But nothing on James Addison?"

"Nope." April shook her head.

Beth pulled over one of the brand new folding chairs and sat down heavily. "Sometimes I wonder if the man really existed."

"Oh, he did. Trust me," James piped up from his corner.

"Hello Jim. I didn't see you over there."

He waved at her and returned his interest to some black and white photos of stone-faced families.

"I'm sensing some negativity, Beth." April looked up from sorting through another loosely tied bundle of random letters. "Long day? Trouble with more contractors?"

"How about 'no James Addison'?"

"What?" April perked up. What did this mean? Was Beth trying to tell her he never even existed?

"It's the festivities. We have no re-enactor to play James Addison for the next few weeks. The man I had on retainer from last year called me today to inform me he's been offered a job out in Texas and won't be able to do the job. He leaves for Dallas this weekend."

"You had him on retainer and he's leaving? How crappy!"

"It's in his contract he has to pay back any wages he was offered if he couldn't honor his obligations. What I am worried about is I have tours, social teas, and of course the 'execution' of our local legend, and no guest of honor," she sighed heavily. "It kind of defeats the whole purpose of the event.

"This is a major highlight to Kings Mill's economy. The stores downtown are open for business, there is an influx of interest in the history, restaurants hold special events where James Addison makes special appearances—it's phenomenal the turnout. For the past few years since we put this event into place it's grown in stature and grandeur. We have some

~ ☾ ~

pretty influential people attending this year."

Including one Kenneth Miles, April thought to herself. But she wasn't allowed to announce anything for fear of too much paparazzi and reporters.

"It does sound rather entertaining. I think James Addison would have enjoyed himself at such an ado—taking tea with the local ladies, drinking ale at the taverns with his local business acquaintances, offering toasts to the tavern wenches..." James relayed knowingly as he rose from his cramped confines, stretched out his legs, and cracked his back with a twist or two of his torso. His voice trailed off though as Beth eyed him inquisitively.

"Did I say something wrong, Dr. Freelane?"

"No Jim, I think you said everything just right." Her eyebrow quirked mischievously as she looked at April. "Are you thinking what I'm thinking, *Dr. Branford*?"

April looked at Beth who was accenting her professional moniker for a reason. She followed Beth's interest back to James.

"Wouldn't he be ideal for the role?" Beth gushed. "He has the accent down pat, his manner and physique are perfect. I might have to have Ana let out some of the costumes though as the other guy was a bit thinner, not as muscular in build." She walked around James, inspecting him as James looked helplessly to April for direction.

"Actually, if you were to compare the portrait of James Addison we have on file with Jim, there is an uncanny resemblance."

April stood up from her position among the papers and folded her arms across her chest. "Are you saying Jim could play the part of James Addison?"

"That is exactly what I am saying!" Beth turned to Jim. "How about it? What do you think?"

"Umm...I'm...kind of at a loss..."

April stepped in. "What Jim is saying is he is without papers right now. He can't actually work in the states—he had his wallet stolen when he arrived. I've taken him under my wing until we can get things sorted out and new identification cards, visas and such taken care of."

~ ☾ ~

"...and I'm unsure how long I will be here truthfully,"
James added.

"It's a temporary position. Only until the seventeenth,"
Beth said. "As it is, your situation works out perfectly. I'm
going to have to do this out of pocket because until the other
guy's contract is voided out legally and financially, the
historical society doesn't have the funds or approval of the
board to pay another employee."

James looked to April, still unsure. She shrugged in a
positive way.

"I won't be able to offer benefits, and it will be strictly in
cash. Consider it a bit of spending money until you get your
wallet replaced."

James piped up. "How much for the position?"

When Beth gave them the numbers—a more than
generous amount for taking on an unknown for a two-week
stint—April wished she could play the part of James Addison.

But this would work out very nicely. She knew James was
having a difficult time dealing with his lack of funds and
living off of her. Though truthfully the man wasn't much of an
expense, she could claim him as a business write off—
historical research.

"So what does the job entail?" James asked as the deal was
struck.

"You'll wear period costumes we've designed from the
time period—something compatible with what a man of
James Addison's character would have worn. Attend three
social afternoon teas at the historic Kings Mill Inn, give two
tours a day, once in the morning and once in the late
afternoon, and then there is the final event, of course, the
dramatization of James Addison's execution."

April noticed James's body quiver involuntarily. "Nothing
is going to happen—it's just for pretend. You don't have to do
this, Jim, if you're not comfortable."

He nodded for her benefit, sharing the knowledge he
understood. "No. James Addison would have wanted to
support Kings Mill. He always did. I should honor the
tradition, in his name."

Beth's smile couldn't be blown off with a bazooka. She

~ ☾ ~

clasped her hands together tightly and did a very
unprofessional little dance of gratitude. The older woman
looked like a contestant on a game show winning an all
expense paid trip to Europe.

"Thank you, thank you, thank you! You have no idea how
much this means. This is going to save my butt! I owe you
guy's big time," she gushed and began to pace. "Okay, I need
to make arrangements with Ana for your fittings, see to the
events at the Inn..." She began ticking things off an imaginary
list in her head. "Wait! We need to go over your historical
information on Kings Mill from the colonial period. I want to
make sure you authenticate the tour with the history. Are you
available?"

April wanted to laugh. James could teach Beth about the
history of colonial Kings Mill. After all, he'd lived it. Tilting
her head in Beth's direction, she nodded to James. "Go ahead
and do what you need to start your 'job,' *James Addison.* I'm
just going to be here looking for your signature on some old
documents of yours," she teased.

*Oh, this was going to be an interesting couple of weeks
for Kings Mill!*

~ ☾ ~

Chapter Fourteen

"...All I am saying, Dottie, is April should let us know every detail she encounters."

Dinner was sitting heavy on her now that they were walking to the city park. She was actually going to do this. She was going to 'touch the tree' and see if it would transport her into the other realm. April had finally convinced her grandmother and great-aunt to listen to reason. The elm tree was the only way she had to connect with the past, to find the truth to James's execution.

With James heavily ensconced in his role of himself for Kings Mill's festivities, now was the perfect opportunity. He was out and about, enjoying an evening entertaining the guests of some of the older taverns he'd frequented back in 1774. She'd attended one to see him at work last night, the Old Town Tavern, in which he told the story of Millie...and the other maid.

He'd done an excellent job, she had to admit. The guests had found his tales and details of the past so realistic many of them had stopped eating and conversing to follow his every move. He hammed it up the more the audience responded. Being able to share his life with others, James glowed with happiness. He was a great story teller and stand-up comedian as he reflected on a bygone era. Not to mention he had every female eye on him in the traditional costume he'd been wearing when they'd first met.

April found herself just as immersed, until he spoke of the ménage. The other guests laughed at his humorous pride at having two women fighting over him. He preened and flaunted his charms—revealing the James Addison of the past, no doubt, and his great conquests.

As much as she'd found his telling of the stories

~ ☾ ~

fascinating, she'd been jealous as hell. How could she compete with the bawdy act he'd been famous for? Had it actually been true? Did he follow through? He never said. If it was, was he still into such things? When they got home, she took it upon herself to try to impart, in vivid detail, that he would no longer need another woman as long as he lived. Her face flamed at the memory of last night's escapade. She'd never made love against a wall before.

She turned her attention back on her aunt and grandmother who were arguing over her paranormal issues. This was not how she wanted this night to go. She had a limited window of time to get this done without James finding out. Her mother was staying home suffering another migraine and didn't want to be bothered.

It bothered April though. Why didn't her mother accept her gift and try to work with it—if not for the ghosts, then at least to relieve the damn headaches. Grandma Dottie was running out of her potions and herbs and they weren't going away.

"I am not saying anything to the contrary, Vickie. But she's not aware of what she's seeing. Her realm is different than ours. We can't see her ghosts, except for James, but he's a solid entity now." Dottie got side tracked but came back. "All we can do is *feel* the energy of our surroundings. Most of what we've encountered has been malevolent, from the house to the ruined remains. April is actually witnessing and being drawn into the past." She stopped walking and focused her attention on April.

Her aunt stopped too and was looking from Dottie to her, trying to clue in on why her sister stopped with sudden interest.

"What?" April looked from one mentor to the other. "What did I do now?"

"I'm wondering." Dottie turned to her sister. "Victoria, do you remember mother mentioning someone with a similar situation? Wasn't it Mother's friend Maggie? They ended up institutionalizing the poor soul. Maggie had the ability to see the past play out before her at certain times but could never interact."

~ ☾ ~

Great! Was she going to end up being institutionalized, too?

"This might be what's happening to April." Vickie nodded. "Then perhaps the key would be to find someone in the other realm able to 'see' you and interact with you."

"What then? Wouldn't it disrupt history? Think of the dire impact it would have," April added.

"You're right about disrupting history, dear. But there might be a way to document certain incidents for the history books without changing the past. That is what you want, just to find out the actual truth behind history's greatest mysteries," Dottie replied with a thoughtful look as they continued on to the park.

"Grams, someone from the other time period would have to be the one to document it."

"Or they would have to leave enough clues for the historians and archeologists to piece together the truth. You say Catherine Samuel is somehow trying to communicate with you? Would there be a way to get her to leave clues?" Aunt Vickie smiled deviously.

April thought about the chatelaine Catherine had tried to throw to her at the ruins. The ghost was trying to tell her something. She needed the chatelaine. "I think she already is."

***

The mood turned somber as the elm tree came into view. As much as April needed to do this, how would it affect her relationship with James? If he were to find out, how pissed would he be? Did the man have a temper? Other than his bluff and bluster over forbidding her to do this, he really didn't seem the type of person to harm another. But if she could find some clues, maybe talk with Catherine's ghost, if she was there tonight, then it would be worth it.

"Now, we will be here with you but try and stay in the past. Don't lose your connection. Listen to us if you can and follow our orders. We may or may not be able to sense what is going on," Aunt Vickie lectured.

"I know. I'm ready." She gave her aunt and grandmother a nervous smile. Now she understood what her mother dealt

~ ☾ ~

with. The uncertainty frightened her. If it weren't for James needing her help she might be running in the opposite direction, too.

Removing her glove she studied the tree. April turned to her family one more time. Aunt Vickie nodded, indicating they were ready as she and Grams joined hands and closed their eyes, preparing themselves for their own interactions. Placing her bare hand on the tree, April took a deep breath and held on.

A shock of pain took hold as her body was physically forced to turn and view what her ears couldn't hear. The image of Catherine Samuel flashed before her. The ghostly figure seemed momentarily indecisive and then stepped into her. April twitched with the woman's soul manifesting in her, taking over her physical form.

A strong scent of spring time lilac, even in the midst of winter's death surrounded her, became a part of her. April could hear and see everything happening around her! The sounds of the past came to life. April could hear the roar of a crowd, the vibrations of feet stomping as the people egged the prisoner forward to his ultimate demise. History was actually taking shape before her eyes.

Mobs of people crowded around them. Torches and bonfires in the middle of the town square and along the streets lit the night. A figure cloaked and on horseback, wearing black breeches and a white shirt caked with dirt was bound and brought under the outstretched branches of the tree. The hood obscured his identity but she could tell by the proud stance he could only be James. Even facing his death he sat tall, defying those who sentenced him on the block. They placed the noose over his hood and cinched it tightly to his throat. April gasped internally. Her physical host, Catherine, gave a startled scream.

A harsh voice whispered into her ear as she was held firmly in place. "Silence, wife! Look at him! See what you have done! It's because of you, whore, that the man sits and awaits his ultimate dishonor and death."

April could actually hear her assailant, his hot, fetid breath on her face. She knew the stench—from the day in her

~ ☾ ~

bedroom and again the other night. Her hand remained attached to the tree, and just like at the manor house, she couldn't move it. Henry Samuel was actually forcing her, holding her jaw steady, to watch the gruesome event about to take place.

The executioner whipped the horse on the hindquarters sending it galloping forward in frenzy, releasing James from his seat to dangle before the crowd. Now April's scream mixed with Catherine's, the two voices colliding and echoing in her head, calling out to James. She clenched her eyes tight. She didn't want to see any more.

The man's fingers bit into her jaw making her unable to do anything but face the action. She kept her eyes closed, knowing what was to come.

"Open your eyes, Witch! This is as much for your punishment as it is for his. Now perhaps you will learn not to defy me!" Henry seethed, shaking her.

What was he talking about? Had Catherine done something to sentence James to his death? *Talk to me, Catherine! Tell me something. You're using my body for a purpose—tell me why!*

All she knew was the force of being held against her wishes to watch something she never ever wanted to be a witness to, personal acquaintance or not. The whole act of this senseless execution was barbaric. She was angry now and struggled against Henry's hold on her.

Fight, damn it! Come on Catherine, fight this man! Don't let him see your weakness—don't let him take advantage of you.

"Let go of me!" April seethed around the pressure of his grip on her jaw.

It was her words but Catherine's voice. She even contained Catherine's fear but she refused to let it be a part of her. She fought not only Catherine's lack of fortitude, but the man she struggled against. Darkness clouded her vision, seeping around the edges of her sight. Fear and horror mixed with her anger and adrenaline. Was she going to faint?

Don't you dare let us faint, Catherine! Don't let him win. Stay with me. Focus on me, use my strength.

~ ☾ ~

If she could remove her hand she would have a greater ability to fight but she was attached to the tree, unable to let go. Fighting with what she could, April lifted her booted heel and slammed it into his shin. Her assailant immediately let go of her face as she brought her second boot up to get him in the knee cap but instead she felt a sharp sting to her face. She screamed.

No one could hear her. Muted screams and cries of horror emanating from the crowd of people watching the execution of James Addison drowned her out. She'd seen all she'd wanted and was remotely glad for the distraction as she fought for her life. Henry grabbed her by her blonde hair, wrenching her head up at a high angle with one hand and encircling her throat with his other meaty paw, slowly squeezing the blood flow to her brain.

"I'll make you pay! God help you, Catherine! *I'll make you pay!*"

She needed to get out of here! Henry was going to kill her. Where in the hell were her aunt and grandmother?

April felt her sanity slip a bit as oxygen seemed to leave her. Darkness surrounded her. Her body fell limp as a sharp kick to her ribs sent her into a spasm. Her grandmother called to her from somewhere in space and time as her aunt echoed, "Demon, be gone!"

On her back, finally separated from the tree at her aunt's single command, she swore James's angry face stared at her from a distance before she passed out on the cool, prickly lawn of Kings Mill City Park.

***

Having finished his night of revelry at this evening's hosting tavern, James strolled down the street toward home. He had to admit he felt more comfortable back in his old clothes. He was amazed at how willingly the patrons of Kings Mill accepted him in his role of their legend. The proprietors and customers alike greeted him as he walked the streets, day or night. He kept in character. Not that difficult considering who he was. It was nice to be himself and yet enjoy his new beginnings in a new era.

Beth Freelane thought he was perfect for the part. Of

~ ☾ ~

course he was perfect! No one could play himself better. He'd listened patiently over the past few days as she'd explained the details she knew of Kings Land/Kings Mill during the 1700's and what she'd found out about James Addison. April made sure he understood he had to go with it. To inject his own personal experiences might cause questions to arise, questions neither he nor she wanted to try to explain to Dr. Freelane. He tried hard to accept the older woman's ideas, even if he knew she was wrong. Besides, for the amount of money she was paying him, he would agree to her saying the sky was green. She was paying him more money then he'd ever dreamed of. It was by all means a king's ransom and then some.

He doffed his hat to a lady and her husband passing on the street. She twittered and gushed as he addressed them in character. It felt good to just be him again, even if people thought it was all an act. Perhaps he could continue to portray himself and have April join him as one of his 'lady friends' for the events.

He'd wanted to take her in his arms last night at the Old Town Tavern when he'd told the story of Millie and the tavern maid, just to reassure her. He'd noticed the challenging crook of her brow and would have apologized at the tavern but she'd left in a huff. He wasn't sure but he thought he'd sensed Millie's perfume, or maybe he'd only hoped to. For his own peace of mind, he wished her well but wanted to forget the past. He had April and hope for a bright future.

He'd chased after April, wanting to put things to right with her about his past indiscretions, but she'd had other plans. Upon entering their boudoir, she had literally attacked his person, stripped him of his clothing, and had her way with him up against the wall—letting him know in no uncertain terms, there would be no other women but her in his bed, or in his bedroom—as long as he lived. He smiled and greeted another passing couple. Oh, he could live very happily with those rules. As inventive and take charge as she was—he wouldn't need another!

He crossed the street, coming up on the park. His heart kicked up a notch, the tree loomed so foreboding, even

~ ☾ ~

though he'd seen it literally every day for hundreds of years. A small gathering near the base of the tree caught his attention. Someone seemed to have taken ill. He couldn't make out their features in the semi-darkened shadows. He raced towards them, his cloak flying behind him like a raven's wing, stopping short when two pairs of women's eyes cast a horrified look at him. His jaw tightened immediately as he saw the third woman lying unconscious across Grandma Dottie's lap. April's Aunt Vickie nudged her sister. Their guilt was all the proof he needed.

"Dottie, I think we are in trouble."

***

"I don't believe this!" James fumed, pacing in short strides in front of them. "I can't believe you would risk April's sanity and possibly her life for what—a peek into my past." He looked down at April's prone body. "But then I don't think it was your suggestion. Did April put you up to this?"

When neither woman responded immediately he already knew the answer. Removing his tricorne hat he threw it to the ground in barely controlled anger. Taking a deep, calming breath he smoothed back his hair, but his anger returned when he looked back down on the pale figure.

"I can't believe this!" He began to walk away but turned back on his heel. His colonial cape flew about him as he bore down on the women again. Aunt Vickie backed up a bit to avoid his possible attack. He walked straight over to April's prone figure, bent and lifted her into his arms as if she weighed nothing and walked towards the house.

~ ☾ ~

Chapter Fifteen

The women made him leave the room while they removed April's clothing and prepared her for bed. Pacing the hallway in agitation, James jumped when Virginia bounded out in a fit of fury to rival his own, nearly running into him. But it was her tears that had him taking her in his arms and comforting the proud woman.

Hearing Virginia's anguish, Dottie came out, exhausted, keeping her eyes averted from his condemning glower. After speaking softly to Virginia, she guided April's mother to her room, leaving him to deal with Aunt Vickie and an unconscious April.

Cautiously, he walked back into the room. Aunt Vickie had no emotion on her face. Reaching out for his hand and joining all three hands together, she closed her eyes and began to mumble strange words. Unsure what to do, James looked upon his weary angel and tried not to crush his hat in his free hand.

Vickie left shortly thereafter. He stayed by April's bedside, resting in the chair while she slept fitfully. She finally settled down a little after midnight, and he must've fallen asleep because he woke up sore from his neck lolling limply at his chest.

Agonizing over not attending the day's festivities, both Dottie and Vickie encouraged him to go. Beth was counting on him and today was a full day of activities. He had an early morning walking tour before his tea social event later on in the morning. He would return in between the tea and his afternoon tour to check in on her.

It was a little past twelve in the afternoon when he returned. He'd made a jovial excuse to his tea guests, explaining he had a young lady awaiting his presence and

~ ☾ ~

mustn't keep her waiting. They'd all blushed, called him a 'cad' and twittered the way women did, thanking him for attending the tea and hoping to see him soon.

He was still in his traditional clothing, never bothering to change with so much activity, when he returned. Virginia was sitting with April, who was still sleeping, much to their collective worries. James hoped it was just her natural body catching up on her lack of sleep over the past week since meeting up with him. Dottie shoed Virginia out of the room and gave him alone time with her.

The shades were still drawn. It was a beautiful day, sunny and pleasant for November. He walked over and pulled them up as he'd seen April do in the mornings when she'd remembered to lower them. The whole damn room smelled heavily of flowers. Scented gardenia oil helped in stabilizing emotions and objective distancing in a paranormal or psychic situation, according to Aunt Vickie, but it was so powerful it was sickening.

"James, is it really you?" April opened her eyes, blinking through the bright light shining into the room, and looked at him.

"Yes, my heart." He rushed to her side and took her hand, kissing it tenderly.

She looked bright and healthy as if waking up from nothing but a lovely dream. She closed her eyes and her expression changed with pain-filled emotion. Tears leaked from the tight creases at the corners.

"I thought I'd lost you. Henry was there and Catherine had merged into me—Henry tried to make us watch the execution. I wanted to die too when I saw you..."

"None of that talk." He scolded but felt like a bloody heel as tears continued to leak from beneath the twin fans of lashes lying against her cheeks. They ran down her face to pool against her pillow. He wiped them with his finger, smoothing them away, but they didn't stop.

"Why do women use bloody tears against us men? It's bad enough we feel helpless when dealing with a woman's emotions."

She sat up, her eyes flashed open, gleaming with more

~ ☾ ~

unshed tears and the nostrils of her pert nose flared. "I watched you die and couldn't do a damn thing about it. Don't tell me how I'm supposed to feel!"

"I recall a conversation in which I warned you not to go to the tree. What did I find upon walking back through the park last night? Hmm, would you care to tell me, April Branford?" James mocked with controlled anger. How dare she attack him with her tirade! "I found you unconscious, lying in your grandmother's lap. I didn't have to be born yesterday to know exactly what you'd done. Your aunt and grandmother were beside themselves with worry!"

April wiped at her face angrily in retaliation. "I needed to find out the truth, to find clues about your death. Remember, it's what I do. I just wanted to roam around and see if I could find something to go on about your death. I didn't expect Catherine to take over my body!"

"What do you mean Catherine took over your body?"

"As soon as I phased into the past, I was immediately met by Catherine. She merged into me, and I witnessed the scene through her eyes. Henry was there, too. He forced her and me to watch your death. He called her a whore and accused her of being the reason you were executed. Something tells me Henry thought the two of you were having an affair."

"Balderdash! What proof would he have had?" James paced the room trying to come to terms with what April was saying she'd witnessed. "Catherine just jumped into your body?"

"I think it's the only way she feels she can communicate with me. I don't know."

"Did Henry hurt you? Did he do this to you?" He indicated her prone position. "Or was it witnessing my execution?"

"I don't know. Maybe a little of both." Her voice was a soft whisper. "I never wanted to watch you hang, James. I only saw a bit. I couldn't watch all of it, even when Henry forced us to."

Good. He was glad to know she hadn't witnessed all of it. She might not be as mentally stable right now if she had.

April got up from the bed, throwing back the counterpane and kicking her legs over the side.

~ ☾ ~

"Where do you think you are going?" he demanded. She'd just recovered from a traumatic incident, and she thought she was going to just prance around?

"I have to go to the bathroom. Besides, it's afternoon. My deadline is dwindling and thanks to my lack of evidence, if I don't get something to appease Kenneth Miles, then I'm out of a job. I can't be lying around all day."

"You will use the facilities and get back in bed, or by God, I will put you there." If April wasn't going to behave rationally, he would make her.

"Whatever." She ignored him and walked to the bathroom door, waving him off as if he were a pesky fly.

When the toilet flushed and she came back into the bedroom, she began preparing for the day, reaching for a fresh change of clothes. She didn't say anything, but her casual acceptance of his fury and impatience was annoying.

"I don't think so." He grabbed her shirt from her hands and threw it behind him on the floor. "You *will* get back in this bed!" He pointed towards the bed.

"Don't tell me what to do, James Edward Addison!" she stormed right back. "I have things to do and you're in my way."

"I'm not playing games." He stood right in front of her, hands on his hips. He wasn't going to budge.

"Neither am I," April threw back, glaring up at him, her breath coming out in long exhales.

"This is your last warning, April Branford..."

"And what are you going to do if I don't?" She fumed as she tried to walk past him.

"You need to get back in that bed, or I will put you there."

"Really? I dare you." Her saucy smile mixed with a bit of anger delighted his sexual senses.

She was daring him to toss her on the bed? He felt his manhood spring to life as licks of fire danced in her eyes. She was a delightfully sassy lover beneath her cool, professional façade. The other night's love making against the wall would be but a memory to what he would do to keep her abed.

"Oh, you don't want to dare me, April love."

She smiled casually, her hand on her hip. "Why? Do you

~ ☾ ~

think you can scare me into submission with your threats? Bring it on, Old Man."

When she tried to walk around him to retrieve the shirt he'd tossed, James grabbed her against his chest in a quick move and gently but firmly shoved her down onto the big bed.

Bring it on, Old Man? He would show her with age came experience.

In their combined struggle for dominance they both managed to lose their clothing. Lifting April's shift, he balled it up and tossed it across the room. His costume came off in bits and pieces by a mixture of his hands and hers. Still, she struggled to get off the bed. Flipping her over he gave her bottom a swift swat.

April squealed and flipped over. James took advantage of her position to lay over her, forcing her down with his demanding, punishing kisses, until her body relaxed beneath his evident desire. His kisses gentled as her tongue dueled with his, taming his dominant side. Tussling and trying desperately to put raw, needy emotion into physical actions they somehow ended up sliding off of the bed onto the hardwood floor with half the bedding tangled around them.

April's hands untied the ribbon from his hair and grabbing a fistful she urged him to take the lead. He wanted to show her his experience. She wanted to know what James Addison was all about? Well, this was a new side to his old self. He nibbled kisses and bites down her body, taking time to explore and taste every morsel of delicate skin, leaving her panting and flushed.

Her breasts were so delicate and sensitive he couldn't help but lavish extended amounts of attention on them. Their nipples were ripe like sweet cherries. Her fingernails scratched into his shoulders in her response to his torturous suckling, making him groan as it sent instant fire to his manhood. He had her trapped against his solid form but who had trapped who?

Lifting her hips he continued his quick but thorough exploration of April's body. Her hips, the softness of her belly, the trimmed juncture of her luscious thighs. He tasted of her

~ ☾ ~

sweetness, making sure her body was primed for his assault—touching her warmth and setting her to squirm wildly in his hands.

Her flushed face and chest were a beautiful contrast against her pale perfection. Her green eyes stared up at him from beneath lowered lashes. She was his fantasy, his avenging angel and she held more than his life in her touch—she held his heart.

Burying himself into her warmth in one quick thrust, it was his turn to groan in pleasure. No woman fit him so perfectly. Her body arched off the floor into him as he raised her hips for a deeper penetration before they both moved in a rhythm no amount of time could erase from his memory. Her body tightened and released around him as her hands explored his chest. The sounds of her pants and excited whispers urged him on.

He'd forgotten this was supposed to be her punishment as the pleasure took over. The building of intensity, the soft warmth of her milking him caused a tide of delightful pain to mount. He was so close but wanted to bring her completion first. Giving her all he had exacerbated the situation but she joined in, her body trembling beneath him as he lost all control, clinging to her in the aftermath of feeling alive with her again.

***

April had showered and dressed, waiting for James to return home from his final walking-tour of the day. He wasn't scheduled to make any appearances tonight so she was excited to have him come back after their heated romp this afternoon.

His threat was well taken. The aggressive way he'd loved her excited her more than it frightened her. He'd stopped in his *assault* of demanding kisses to warn her never to go against his better judgment when it came to her well-being. He'd *driven* the point forcefully as he lifted her onto his body and counseled her on the ways to keep from angering him in the future.

They'd both been made to see the error of her ways when they'd fallen off the bed in a tangled mass of bedding and

~ ☾ ~

naked limbs. She'd ended up sated but anguished at his need to leave and attend to his afternoon tour group. Although, James did promise to reinforce her discipline later.

She'd gone downstairs, chipper and alive, offering her help to her Aunt Vickie and Grandma Dottie as they made dinner of ham, green beans, and au gratin potatoes. No one spoke much but the glances and knowing smiles she received from the two women said it all. She supposed they had been a bit loud in their earlier...fights.

When James walked through the front door, shortly after five, her heart gave a leap. It wasn't because of the fantastic sex—though her body flushed at the memory. It was the fact he was still alive, still here, still hers...for now.

They sat down to the family meal. James sat across from her. The women all exchanged knowing glances but said nothing.

"You slept quite a long time today, April dear," Grandma Dottie finally broke the tension by teasing her. "Last night's event must have really worn you out or was it the battle of wills you and James had earlier?" She looked to James. "I do hope you showed her a good 'what for' young man. She just doesn't listen to reason, I'm afraid. It'll take a special guiding hand to get her to understand."

James coughed slightly, bringing his linen napkin to his lips and taking a sip of his wine.

"Mother, I do believe we have a blushing ghost," her mother tried her hand at a joke. "So you are guilty of having sex with my daughter?"

"Mom, don't scare him away." April tried not to blush. Had they been too loud? Were the walls a bit thin?

James cleared his throat nervously.

"How are you feeling, April? We were so worried last night." Aunt Vickie came in from the kitchen, on the end of the current conversation and placed the bowl of green beans on the table.

April was thankful for the intrusion. Whether or not the woman overheard the conversation, she was good at changing the subject. "I don't know, it's all so hard to explain. It felt like a nightmare, only real. I couldn't wake

~ ☾ ~

up from it. I was unable to move my hand."

"Like in the manor ruins?" her mother added.

"Exactly. But I could feel everything. Catherine stepped into my body, used me for some reason. I don't know. Maybe to explain what had happened from her point of view, or maybe so I could hear what was going on. Henry Samuel kept forcing me to watch James's execution, saying all these horrible things to her. He definitely accused her of an affair with you, James."

"God as my witness, nothing happened. Catherine came out occasionally to the manor and dropped off scones and occasionally tended to someone who was sick or injured. She always brought along her personal maid as a chaperone."

"What about Henry's ill treatment? Did you notice anything about her when she did visit?" her mother asked. "I get the impression he might have been an abusive husband."

"In our day we didn't question a man's behavior within his own family. Unless we saw something personal, nothing was said. Women didn't speak ill of their husbands to others," James explained.

"I never saw any visible marks on the young woman. She seemed timid and rather quiet. But she loved to bake scones, pies, and biscuits. She would bring them out to us when she needed her ration of flour for the fortnight. Our enjoyment of her sweet baked goods always made her blush so prettily. She reminded me of Elsbeth. I would send a letter off to my sister every time Catherine came out to see us."

April still couldn't help but feel an immense sadness for the trials and tribulations Catherine must have gone through. The only times she witnessed her were during times of great duress and she knew she'd only gotten a taste so far. But if the man was as aggressive with his young wife as April witnessed first-hand, then she could understand the girl's fear of him. Was she still trapped within her fear as a ghost?

An idea formed inside her head. What if Hell was actually reliving the past horrors of your life when you died? Would a residual haunting be equivalent? James said he viewed his demise over and over again. Was Catherine's entity looped in the same hellish nightmare?

~ ☾ ~

"James, how often did you view your execution?" April asked.

"I am not sure. I've viewed it enough to know what to expect but still, I'm never allowed to interact with the images around me."

"What if Catherine were trapped in the same ordeal? Wouldn't she want some way out of it after all this time or would she be as accepting of it all as you are? She doesn't seem to be as strong, emotionally."

James paused, cutting into his ham slice. "You do have a good theory."

Aunt Vickie nodded in agreement. "From what you've encountered of her, April, I think she might be trying to seek you out because she senses your gift. She's our connection into the realm and possibly, as we talked of yesterday, set up our clues for us. She may know the secrets to James's death, why he was accused of treason. We need to work on contacting her. She's our 'seer' in the other realm."

"She's already 'seen' me. The first time I saw her was at the manor house. She acknowledged my presence in her residual time," April said. It all made sense now. Catherine saw her both times at the manor house and again in the bedroom. Catherine was trying to contact her!

"Then we already have the connection we need. We just have to remain in her realm long enough to interact and explain the truth," Dottie explained.

"Mother, are you suggesting April continue this? Didn't last night prove to you how this could affect her? It's bad enough coming to terms with our gifts, but this is cruel. You're asking your granddaughter to give up her sanity for something that happened two hundred years ago." Her mother turned to James. "No disrespect, James, but I love my daughter and will not risk her life, physically or emotionally for this crazy idea."

"I understand your concern, Virginia. But if I know your daughter, she won't rest until the job is done." James nodded slightly and gave April a wary smile.

Grandma smirked at her mother's deep agitation and turned to lightly punch her. "Wow, did he peg you, April."

~ ☾ ~

Still Virginia wasn't amused. "This is history. This isn't life and death, April."

April reached across the table to grab her mother's hand in hers, giving it a reassuring squeeze. She knew her mother didn't think they shared any commonality with their experiences. But this was important, and she wouldn't rest until she could make things right.

"History is one thing, but the issues surrounding James are real. His existence is at stake, along with his heritage. I've witnessed Catherine Samuel's grief and her trials are just as real to me now. Somehow I was meant to come to their aid. My whole life I've dreamed of nothing but helping solve the mysteries of the past. It's no less important to me now, Mom. In fact I think it's a part of who I am."

Turning to her grandmother, and nodding at Aunt Vickie, April took a deep breath. This was her time. This was the moment she knew she was made for. "Grams, Aunt Vickie, I'm ready to be taught everything I need to know to help my ghosts."

~ ☾ ~

Chapter Sixteen

James's smile couldn't be blown off by cannon fire. He was in his glory. The only thing that could have made him happier was to have Daniel back, running his mill while he cavorted around town greeting the tourists. His walking tours were well attended. The local proprietors greeted him as if he were a member of the ton, talking about the day's economic turns.

And his time with April was most appreciated. A man without his needs fulfilled for two centuries had a lot of catching up to do. She was a wealth of relief and great pleasure, always keeping his interest at peak, finding new and talented ways to charm him and make him delight in being alive—and nearly late for his first tour group of the day.

April had taken her time, attending to his cleanliness in such a thorough manner this morning, he'd felt the need to reciprocate. A ten minute shower had turned into a steamy, thirty-five minute sauna. They ended up washing, rinsing, and repeating many times over.

A group of thirty visitors were waiting patiently for him as he strolled up the sidewalk in front of the old historical site only a minute late. Most of them were elderly, on their way from traveling the New England states for the fall colors and making their way back to their homes in the southern colonies.

He hoped he could make the tour informative and educational, taking them a bit into his real life. Remembering young Tony from the ghost tours, he hoped he wouldn't become bored with a scripted routine. He wanted to interact and still maintain his true identity. James Addison was who they expected him to be...well, they would get the man, in the flesh.

He eagerly awaited the last few stragglers to catch up

~ ☾ ~

from taking photos of the home of Peter Hyman, the area's first attorney at law, and a prominent citizen who it turned out was a highly respected colonial patriot...the traitorous bastard! But James didn't care. He was James Addison, the legend, the man of the hour and the folks had eagerly questioned him about his loyalties and Kings Mill site in general. All questions he could answer without any problem.

"Are you aware of your impending doom this coming week?" a gentleman asked. He wasn't being rude. James knew the man figured he was only playing the part and had to know of the upcoming conclusion to Kings Mill's festive season.

"Harold!" His wife smacked him lightly on the arm. "Of course he doesn't know he's to be executed for treason! Don't spoil the timeline."

Without missing a beat, James stayed in character. "I'm to be executed? By whose rights? And treason?" James looked aghast. "That is unheard of! Unfathomable, my dear lady!" He stopped. Addressing her personally, but speaking also to the other guests, who'd been shocked at the man's audacity to ask such a question, he said, "I've been loyal to King and Country throughout the skirmishes those damnable Sons of Liberty have orchestrated. I would never stoop so low as to discredit my family's good name."

Another man spoke up. "I think James Addison was sentenced for his affair with the land commissioner's wife. Treason was just a convenient ruse."

"I can honestly say I have never touched Catherine Samuel. She's much too sweet. She reminds me of my dear sister, Elsbeth, back in Sunderbury. But she does bake some delicious scones. If you are ever invited to the Samuels for tea, make sure you try them. They are the best in the land." He turned his attention back to the other woman, taking her hand in his and placing a delicate buss of his lips across her gloved fingers. "Besides, I prefer my women to be a bit more mature, more experienced in the fine art of holding a man's interest."

A rumble of shocked laughter echoed around him. He

~ ☾ ~

turned to the woman's husband. "And sir, how long have you been wed to this delightful lady?"

"We recently celebrated forty years together," he stated rather proudly, taking the woman's hand James had just saluted with a brief, feigned kiss and giving him a curious stare.

James nodded, addressing the rest of the guests. "Forty years! Good Sir, I dare say your missus has *held your interest* with great care. I rest my case." He winked at the woman. "Well done, my lady! Well done."

The woman blushed, gushing and flirting casually with him the remainder of the tour. But he made a point to address each woman in the same fashion, never going too overboard with their husbands in attendance. He wanted to make sure the women experienced a part of the atmosphere of being courted by a gentleman of his time and standing. He'd noticed from observing life around him through the years, the art of being a true gentleman had died, along with most social graces. Perhaps their husbands could learn a bit along the way.

***

"If you don't stop looking at me like that I'm going to jump your bones, James Addison."

Sitting in the diner, just the two of them, April was about to have him for dessert. The looks James was sending her across the table when he thought she wasn't looking made her flush with desire.

"Jump my bones?"

"One in particular..."

"Well, I know there is no such 'bone' in there, but when I'm around you I definitely think otherwise."

He finished off his slice of pumpkin pie with provocative plays of his tongue, making damp heat collect deep inside of her. The cad! Wanting to pay for their meal and get him home before she actually pushed the dishes off the table and took him right there, she fished out her wallet. Why him? Why now? After two years her sex life with Jason had been timid at best. It had taken James Addison less than two weeks to turn her into a sex fiend.

~ ☾ ~

James was inventive. This morning's game of 'good clean fun' proved just how inventive he could be. Never had a removable, massaging shower head been so stimulating. But it wasn't all about her pleasure. April found her ability to explore her gift of touch went far beyond psychometry.

But then, she had learned the delicate technique of cleaning antiquities. She made sure every trace of dirt had been removed. This morning she'd used her knowledge on her very own two hundred seventy year old artifact. Between the two of them, James was nearly late for his first tour of the day. And she would have to leave Aunt Vickie a little extra money for the water bill.

"Put your money away. I want to pay for dinner tonight." He fished out a brand new twenty dollar bill from his leather wallet. "I've been receiving a good sum of tips from my tours. I never knew being me could be so lucrative."

April let him. The glow in his eyes at being able to pay for something as simple as dinner gave him confidence in being part of the human race again.

He held the door open for her and took her by the arm, escorting her down the street.

April laughed at the giddiness she noticed in James. He was alive in so many ways, not just physically. "You really are enjoying yourself."

"Of course. It gives me a chance to be me and still have time with the woman I've grown to love...plus a couple of coins to rub together in my pockets." He looked down at her and smiled. "What more could a man want?"

April had signed up for his last tour of the day, just to see him in action. There had only been a few random stragglers in the afternoon. Still, he'd given an Academy Award winning performance, although she knew he wouldn't qualify since he wasn't acting. She had been delighted when a man had commented on his authenticity and found him entertaining as well as informative. Seeing James's face light up from the enthusiasm warmed April's heart.

"So Grams and Mom went out to see a movie tonight and your Aunt has her book club?" James asked as they walked back to the house.

~ ☾ ~

"Yep, we have the house to ourselves." April turned to him with a saucy smile. "Whatever shall we do with all the time?"

"I saw a book in the parlor library I wanted to read, *Of Mice and Men*. I think I'll have a glass of port and read while you stitch a sampler."

"Like bloody hell you will." April tried for an English accent but judging by his laughter failed miserably. "Number one, I don't sew. Number two, I refuse to change who I am for anyone. And three, I bought these and intend to use them tonight." She handed him the shiny bag.

He peeked in and removed one box. "Ribbed for her pleasure?" He looked at the other. "Warming gel?" He turned the last box over and read the inscription. "What are they for?"

"I could tell you but I prefer to show you what they are for." She took his hand and removed the box, slipping into his arms as she laid a deep, wet kiss on him. His arms automatically came up around her, returning the ferocity of her kiss with his own.

"Are they animal skins used in preventing child birth?" His voice was a husky breath against her neck as he nuzzled her throat. "If they are...you can keep them, I would much prefer you rounded with my child. I've always been very careful but you're the first woman I've wanted to have a babe with."

April pulled away. Her womb quivered at the thought of carrying his baby. As sexy and wonderful as it sounded coming from him, she couldn't let it sway her. Too many uncertainties. For him to offer such hope in the midst of their crazy association, seemed like a far-fetched dream.

Was he even biologically able to be a father? Up until a few days ago, he was an energy mass. With no physical or medical history since then, she didn't know what he was. He had a heartbeat and blood, but they hadn't considered analyzing his chemical or biological make up.

Every day she feared waking up to find him gone and sending him to work only amplified her fears because he wasn't near her. Seeing him alive each night settled her nerves a bit. She'd wondered if he needed to remain near her 24/7 since she was the one who brought him to life, but he was still here.

~ ☾ ~

"James, we can't make promises. We don't know anything for certain. As much as I wish we could be together for the rest of our lives, have children, wake up to each other every morning, I'm afraid I don't know how long we have."

"No one knows how long they have, April. All I know is you are the reason behind everything in my life. I never believed in fate or knew of God and the afterlife, but I know now we were meant to be together. Is there any other explanation of why I was kept trapped in time for so long, to arrive in this era and have you to come along to 'see' me when no one else could? Is it any wonder you have the gift to bring me to life?"

"You've been talking with Aunt Vickie," she scolded playfully, but sobered once she noticed the hurt look on James's face. "I don't know. All I know is I want to take what we have, one day at a time and just enjoy each other. I want to make love to you and soak everything I feel with you into me and keep it for as long as I can. I don't want to think about tomorrow." April took hold of his hand, giving it a gentle, reassuring squeeze, trying to lighten the mood.

James grabbed her wrist and pulled her close to him. His eyes filled with promise. "I swear to you, my sweet lass—I will move Heaven and Hell to make you mine. If there is a merciful God, then we will be together, no matter what obstacles are placed in our way."

His lips nuzzled against the soft underside of her ear. All the moisture left her mouth and pooled deliciously into her nether regions. The intensity in his eyes showed her just how serious his claim on her was. Despite everything against them, James claiming her as his, only made her want him more.

They ran the rest of the way to the house, stopping long enough to catch quick kisses and love bites against a tree or a wall or anything solid to keep them upright. Prolonging the agony of their quiet night together had its advantages. This was foreplay at its finest.

When they reached their destination, breathless with laughter and physical exertion they were caught off guard by Dr. Beth Freelane standing on the sidewalk leading up to the house.

~ ☾ ~

"Dr. Freelane? Can I help you?" April asked the woman carrying a box with another crate beside her.

"Oh, Dr. Branford, I'm glad you're here," Beth said, placing the box down beside the crate and slowly walking away from the house, watching it as if it were alive and going to jump out at her. "I was hoping I might catch you home."

"What can I do for you?" April noticed Beth looking sheepishly toward James. He gave a little wave of his hand.

"Jim, I'm sorry—I almost didn't recognize you without your costume."

Smooth. The look on Beth's face showed she understood what was going on between her new employee and April was more than academic.

Beth blushed. "I didn't mean to intrude, I just wanted to stop by and give you some documents Allen from city hall brought over today."

Beth looked at the box she'd left by the door. "The custodial staff found these in the basement when they were cleaning out some of the old file boxes. I took a quick look and found something that might interest you. One of the files is labeled 1765-1775 and I know it would coincide with James Addison's time period. They might be the documents you're looking for. " She shrugged.

"Thank you. I really appreciate you bringing it to me," April replied excitedly. "This could very well be it!"

"I know you've had a rough time with your research. I'm sorry I haven't been much help with everything going on lately."

"It's understandable. You're one woman trying to handle it all. So again, thank you Dr. Freelane, I really appreciate this."

"Anytime. Oh, here's my cell phone number in case you need me while I'm away from work. Since you've brought our local legend to light again, I've gotten excited about restoring the ruins as we tried to do when we did the excavation back in the 80's. I wanted to see a restoration done but we didn't have the funding for it. I'm applying for grants and hope whatever you may find will shed some real light on our history. Well, I will let you two get back to your night. Enjoy." Beth turned to leave but stopped shortly and eyed the house warily before moving on.

~ ☾ ~

Chapter Seventeen

The file boxes ruined their original plans for a night of intimacy. April's mood shifted the moment Dr. Freelane left. She'd been looking for those files since before they'd met. This was her job. She had a chance to maybe find what she needed to appease Kenneth Miles and move on with her life. James couldn't help but feel the sense of excitement of possibly seeing the documents he'd signed over two hundred years ago himself. How odd would it be?

They'd been sitting on the parlor floor poring over the brittle papers for nearly an hour. She'd made a fire and opened a bottle of Aunt Vickie's wine. It was as close as they would get to a romantic evening.

James laughed. "I'll be damned!"

"What? Did you find something?" April looked up from her stack of files on her lap. She looked so adorable with a comfy pair of flannel pants and an over sized William and Mary t-shirt. A pair of latex gloves kept the oils from her fingers off the fragile parchment.

"Jonathan Turnbull, now there's a name I haven't heard in a long time." James shook his head, smiling. "Talk about a cad. He could charm a stone into clay, told some of the bawdiest jokes and could drink any man under the table. The tavern wenches loved him, but in reality, he only had eyes for his wife. As much as he fussed about her at the taverns, he loved her dearly. You could see it in his eyes."

If James could have found a man to emulate, it would have been Jonathan. He'd been a merchant who sailed out of Baltimore Harbor with a small fleet. But he wanted to settle down in Kings Mill for his wife's sake. When he was gone, he didn't like her staying alone in the house near the docks in Baltimore with all the unsavory characters. So he would bring

~ ☾ ~

her up to their townhouse in Kings Mill to be among friends.

"What about him?"

"He put in for a piece of land to settle and farm back in March of 1772. Not far from mine from the looks of it."

"So? What's so unusual?"

"Turnbull was a privateer. Had some ships that carried cargo in the triangle—molasses, rum, you name it the man could get it. Good man. Didn't think he would be settling as a farmer in Kings Mill." He stopped, his voice trailing a bit.

"He never made it back to settle. One night he was called away to tend to a crisis with one of his ships in Baltimore Harbor, and he never returned. His body was found along the old road leading to Baltimore, the victim of highway thieves. Left his sweet Marge a widow. "

"I take it you knew Marge well?" April's eyebrow rose knowingly.

"Not like you think," James scolded playfully. "Marge was a pip. Shortly before Jon's death, she badgered me to attend a social in his honor. I still remember the date, March twenty-sixth." He grinned, shaking his head. "She was persistent. Every time we met she would remind me of the date, insisting I had to be there. It was going to be the event of the decade."

He stopped. His thoughts turned inward trying to remember something.

"Jonathan signed for the land the third of March but he died before the end of the month."

"So?"

"This paper should have been signed by Henry Samuel and filed for audit."

"Maybe Jonathan didn't have the money for the land at the time?"

James shook his head. "Money is exchanged with the commissioner when the document is signed. See the stamp for payment received?" James pointed to the embossed, lightly faded stamp circling a number amount in British currency. "Henry would have approved it within days if not on the day, signed his name and filed each property. This paperwork should have already been signed by Henry but there is no signature."

~ ☾ ~

"There has to be some explanation." April moved over to where James had his pile. "Let me see."

James reached for another file. He opened it. They were all land grants purchased at various times through a decade. Kept separate, none had been filed under a specific year, like the others, and none had been signed by both parties. Not a single one had a counter signature from the commissioner but all had been bought and paid for by the signee.

The last one stopped James cold, his heart pounding as if he saw his life pass before him, again. There on the aged parchment stood his bold signature and a stamp for the five hundred pounds he had paid for the extension of land he'd purchased only a few weeks prior to his death. There was no counter signature. He quietly handed it to April. Their eyes met.

"Oh my God, James, this was never signed either. What's it all mean?" she gasped.

"It means this piece of property was never legally mine."

***

"Hello! We're back!" her mother called out as they entered the foyer. James waved at the women as they entered but went right back to the files, trying to concentrate again on the single piece of paper in his fingers.

"What are you two doing?" Dottie asked, removing her hat and coat and placing them on the coat rack. "Oh, dear! That's not very sexy, April. I would have hoped you would have more taste when it came to seducing a man. Flannels and t-shirts just don't do it."

"Grams, this is not the time," April sighed.

"What's going on?" her mother asked as she came into the room toting a big shopping bag.

April relayed their night of looking over the documents and their recent find. James stayed silent, reading and re-reading each document pertaining to the land grants. His brow furrowed in concentration as he intently studied the papers.

"These don't make any sense. This whole box contains deeds signed by the potential owners but never co-signed by Henry for the county records. Mine is in here too—the deed

~ ☾ ~

to my extended property I purchased shortly before my death."

"They were never counter-signed by Henry Samuel? Wasn't he the land commissioner for this area of the colony?" Dottie asked.

"Maybe he never got around to signing them." April's mother shrugged.

April reached across the small table they were seated around. "Let me see the deed for Jonathan Turnbull. Perhaps there was an extenuating circumstance as to why some were signed and filed but others weren't." She stopped talking momentarily as she gently rifled through the other documents laid before them. "I didn't realize Henry owned so much land."

"He owned a few pieces around, mostly out in the country at the time—not far from mine. He purchased a piece from an elderly couple just north east of the mill. They were in dire straits at the time, something about taxes owed according to Henry. He was able to purchase their land, though he leased it to them, to help with their tax burden."

"I see. How kind of him," she scoffed. "It's in this pile. He signed and dated the transfer of property on the day of the transaction," April said and searched for her mom, but she wasn't there.

"Where's mom?"

"She went upstairs to take a bath. We stopped at the specialty bath shop in the mall after seeing the movie. You know how she loves all kinds of bubble bath stuff and the porcelain tub in her room, she couldn't resist." Dottie leaned over and hugged April as she re-read a form. "Did you notice this?"

"What?"

James's interest peaked. Dottie nodded to Jonathan Turnbull's unsigned deed and then pointed to one of the deeds April held in her hand. A deed to land Henry Samuel had purchased. They had been in the same file. "Same parcel of land—at least according to description."

"It is. Henry Samuel purchased the parcel of land Jonathan Turnbull had purchased. Only his deed was dated

~ ☾ ~

the twenty-fourth of March," April noted in agreement.

"The twenty-fourth of March?" James slid over to look at the document they shared. "No. That's impossible."

"Read it for yourself right there. 'Land Purchased—24 March 1772.' Why would it be impossible? If Jonathan was already dead then—" Dottie shrugged indifferently.

"The land would have gone to his widow, or they would have had to wait to purchase after six months of abandonment, if the deed was signed properly," April finished.

James shook his head. "But no one knew Jonathan was dead. His body was found March twenty-fifth. The twenty-sixth was his birthday celebration and Marge had invited every merchant, well-to-do, and Loyalist around. She'd even invited the governor and Lord Calvert."

"Are you sure? Why would Henry purchase the land? He had to have known it was just purchased by Jonathan, and he was still alive."

"I don't think so. Jonathan left for Baltimore on the twenty-first. A group of us were in the tavern at the time when he received the summons one of his ships needed his immediate attention. I remember him saying he would have to make it a quick trip in order to be back before Marge's party."

"That would mean Henry knew Jonathan would not return to lay claim to having purchased the property," Dottie said a bit uncertain, as if trying to figure out the connection.

James looked back to the deed. "The land purchases were never counter-signed by Henry so it would have still been up for purchase. All Henry had to do was write up a new deed in his name and he would be the owner of Jonathan's land," he said, looking up fearfully at April. "It all makes horribly, perfect sense. But why would he have kept the original documents?"

"Maybe he was really terrible with his bookkeeping? Did he have someone to assist him?"

"Not that I remember. He maintained the office on his own. Still, he wouldn't have been hired for the position without a basic understanding of managing his books. This is

~ ☾ ~

blatant disregard for his job...or he knew exactly what he was doing," James sighed heavily.

"So what you are basically insinuating is Henry Samuel killed Jonathan Turnbull for his land?" April gasped.

***

Neither she nor James was in the right frame of mind to make love. Their earlier discoveries left them confused and exhausted, at least mentally. It was nearly midnight, and she couldn't focus anymore on the task at hand. After James had woken her up for the third time while she was bent over the old documents, he sent her off to bed and stayed below to lock the front door and check on Aunt Vickie as he did each night before retiring.

She reached the top of the stairs and stopped short. The door to Catherine Samuel's room was ajar. Had she secured it the last time she'd ventured in? She looked toward her mother and grandmother's rooms, but they'd retired hours ago and their lights were out.

Peeking into the dark room, she noticed movement on the bed. She sensed it more than saw it. A shadow of a figure sitting on the four-poster caught her attention. Taken aback, April was certain it was Catherine, but it was her mother's distinct voice. Did she have her hands free device activated? Was she talking to herself?

"Mom?" April whispered, stepping across the darkened threshold. The room was an icebox as if all heat had been sucked. April looked around, rubbing her arms and hugging herself.

"...Which is why we are here. Can you tell me more?"

Who was she talking to? Her mother sat eerily still in the center of the great bed, her eyes open but not seeing. It freaked her out. Her mother's brows drew down into a frown, blinking a couple of times as if to clear her vision. She moved subtly, as if trying to figure out where she was, and then sighed.

"You scared her away, April."

"Who?" A heavy lilac scent perfumed the air. "Were you talking with Catherine?" She'd never seen her mother actually converse with a ghost.

~ ☾ ~

"Yes. She seemed distraught, frightened...worried. Actually, I'm not sure which one was the most dominant emotion. She's the woman you encountered in your phasing, wasn't she?"

"Yes." April looked around the room nervously. She didn't know how much to say if the ghost of Catherine was still here. If this was a onetime residual she was trapped in, she wouldn't know about the other residual events yet. The sensitive nature of her death might be reason enough to make her panic. April didn't want to cause their ghost any undue distress. Her mother nodded in understanding.

"What are you doing here, Mom?"

"She called out to me just before I fell asleep," her mother said. "I thought it was you for a moment, but she asked for me specifically by name. You wouldn't have said my name."

April smiled at her mother's bravery. "And you came in to see what she wanted? That's not like you."

Her mother took her hand. "I know. But I think it's time to face my gift." She swallowed back emotion. "I only wanted a normal life for us, April. I didn't want to be odd or crazy—or to have my child have a stigma. It's why I fell in love with your father. He was so stable. If I could just have ignored my oddity, we would have been the perfect family. But when you were born I panicked. All I could think about was another Wilton female to endure the curse.

"I dreaded the day your gifts would be revealed. I never told your father until later when I couldn't control the voices. Working with him at the funeral home, the ghosts searched me out. So many ghosts, all wanting my attention." She agonized. "I thought your father would leave me because he would think I was crazy, but he left me because I couldn't control my gift. The ghosts frightened me because I let them, not because they were scary."

"Kind of like when I used to be afraid of Fritzi, our German shepherd. He was playful, but I thought he was trying to attack me," April said.

"Yes, but then he was your best friend and protector as you got older." Her mother smiled, sniffing back unshed tears. "I've been watching you face your gifts, the unknown

~ ☾ ~

situations not even Aunt Vickie or your grandmother can assist with, and I can't help but be proud of you and yet feel so ashamed of myself." Her mother tried to stifle a shuddering sob.

April sat down on the bed and embraced her mother warmly. This was a big step for her as they both learned how to accept and adapt to their gifts.

Her mother looked down at her hands knotted in her lap. "Tonight was my first acceptance. I took a chance when Catherine called out to me. She knew I would be able to hear her."

April nodded. "I think she's got an instinct. She knows we are the ones to set her free. I just don't know how." April bit her lip, thinking of the possibilities. Her eyes scanned the room, hoping to see their ghost sitting comfortably at her desk.

"She mentioned something about keys?" Her mother looked confused.

"Catherine carries around keys on her apron. I think she's trying to tell me something about them." April finally understood. Recognition hit her hard and she felt so stupid. "Of course! The chatelaine! Catherine is trying to get me to use her chatelaine. That is why she..." She stopped as James poked his head into the room. Biting her lip, she hoped she didn't say too much as she forgot how and when Catherine had tried to communicate with her.

"Ladies? Is everything all right?"

"Yes. We were just talking," her mom said as she gathered her heavy robe and maneuvered off the high mattress. "I should be getting back to bed and so should you. I understand tonight's information is not sitting right with you, James, but if I know my daughter, she'll figure it all out." She placed a motherly kiss to April's forehead and gave a quick peck to James's cheek. "Good night, you two."

James touched his scruffy cheek where April's mom had kissed him.

"She must like you, even if you are technically a ghost. She never gave a kiss to any of my other suitors...and she knew them longer."

~ ☾ ~

"Huzzah! Maybe she'll even dance with me at our wedding."

***

Dr. Branford,

I appreciate the update of your recent memo. Still, without documentation I am at a loss on my end of the bargaining table. The urgent need for any proof will greatly help in proving I have a stock in the property in question. My attorneys have been able to waylay a few various closing dates but I am losing time.

I urgently implore you to double your efforts in this matter as time is of the essence and I do not wish to lose this valuable piece of property by default. I am sure you will be able to accommodate my needs and I will do what I can to help with any financial, civil, or legal issues that might arise with the expedience of this project.

Best wishes,

Kenneth Miles

James and April stopped in the cafe for a scone, a cappuccino, and Earl Grey tea to go before she walked him to work. Now sitting at Aunt Vickie's dining room table she bit into her sweet scone, brushing crumbs off of her sweater and re-reading the email from Kenneth while she sipped her warm and frothy morning cappuccino.

What was so urgent about this project he was willing to send help in such an endeavor? And how much was he investing? He was taking this personally. This wasn't his typical business transaction he had his investors or associates deal with.

April promised herself she would make today count. After walking James to work, she'd felt a sense of urgency and couldn't wait to get into the thick of her true task. Today could be the day. She now had the documents she'd hoped for. Would she be lucky enough to find the exact paper to James's title on the land? If not, she still had the frustrating pieces of paper reporting Henry Samuel's lack of administrative accuracy. Whether the man was just inept at his job or had resorted to fraud, she couldn't tell without more research.

~ ☾ ~

She would send Kenneth copies of the documents they had questioned last night. With all of his knowledge in the world of real estate and finance, surely he might be able to come up with some solution. It would also give him the ability to see what she'd found and had been dealing with. It might not be the actual document he needed but it would show Kenneth she was on the right track. Taking photos of the papers with her phone camera, she sent them off to Kenneth immediately.

All of Henry Samuel's paperwork created a new mystery. If foul play was suspected in his schemes to purchase property out from under all these people, the cases would be difficult to prove. No one was alive anymore. Most of the property no longer existed, and if the land was still there and not a mini-mall or subdivision, she didn't have the ability or time to try to find out about it.

Still, it seemed more than coincidental to have the people with land Henry wanted to purchase fall on hard times or conveniently die. And when she'd concluded Henry Samuel had possibly killed Jonathan Turnbull for his property last night, James mentally shut down. Could the man have wanted everyone out of the way for his specific gain? Had he wanted James dead, too? What did Henry actually want?

April pored over all the documents again. She'd asked Aunt Vickie if she could set up her work at the large, formal dining room table. She was able to spread out all the paperwork and still have her laptop within easy access for surfing information. The book on the excavation site was opened to the picture of the chatelaine on one side of the page and the portrait of Henry Samuel on the other.

The more she looked at the beady-eyed 'fop,' as James liked to call him, the more ill at ease she felt. But she wanted to remind herself of who she was dealing with and also remind herself to contact Beth on the whereabouts of the chatelaine. Looking closely at the picture, she wondered was it the same one she'd seen Catherine wear? It was difficult to tell. She'd never gotten a good look at it when she'd encountered Catherine. She was still uncertain what the chatelaine had to do with anything important. It had unlocked the desk upstairs in the room where she'd seen the

~ ☽ ~

ghost. She'd been trying to hide something from Henry when he'd burst in on them. Was there something inside the piece of furniture that might solve the mystery? What mystery did the piece of furniture hold?

"How is the paper work going?" Aunt Vickie stepped into the dining room, wiping her hands on a kitchen towel. Her mother and grandmother had left to go out for awhile. Mom had decided it was time to try and work on her gift and Grandma Dottie thought a trip to the cemetery might be the best place to start, lots of spirits to try to sort through. Her mother had looked like a college quarterback at his first game—eager to get started but scared as hell to face the crowds.

"Fine. I just received an email from Ken Miles. He's anxious as ever—in his formal, diplomatic way."

"Why the scowl then? You seemed a bit more preoccupied than a simple email would allow. Something troubling you? "

April's brow twisted and she bit her lip. Indecision played over her thoughts, and she looked up towards the ceiling as if trying to see into the rooms above. "Do you have a minute, Aunt Vickie?"

Aunt Vickie raised her head. Her eyes widened, ready to scold. "April..."

She sighed. "It's not what you think. I just want to go check out the desk in the one room."

"The antique Chippendale secretary in Catherine's room?"

"Yeah. I know what you are thinking and no, I'm not going to touch it so I can phase into her time—if it was hers. But it must be if she'd been sitting at it during my encounter with her." April went to the coat tree and removed her leather gloves from her coat pocket and put them on. "See. I just want to check out its structure. I think Catherine might have been trying to hide something in it—away from 'you-know-who,'" she whispered.

"And you want me to go up there with you to keep 'you-know-who' at bay?"

April didn't like the knowing look her aunt was giving her. "No. Just be there for me—and maybe let me know if you sense anything—paranormal."

~ ☾ ~

They both looked up at the ceiling again. It was a stand-off between them and a ghost. Really? If it wasn't for the fact April had encountered Henry Samuel and all of his intentions she wouldn't be worried. Catherine didn't scare her. She liked the woman, even if she was a bit timid. And having witnessed first-hand her abuse from Henry, she sympathized with her.

Aunt Vickie sighed. "Well, I don't sense anything disruptive at the moment so I guess taking a quick trip up there wouldn't be a bad thing. But if I sense *anything* at all upon entering Catherine's room—we leave immediately."

"Fine. I agree. Unless it's Catherine—"

"Anything!" her aunt argued, raising her voice sternly. "Ghosts are unpredictable, April. They will do anything to get someone to listen."

~ ☾ ~

Chapter Eighteen

The desk was solid. No one made furniture like this anymore. A keyhole at the top and old rusty hinges at the bottom proved the desktop came down at one time. April had seen Catherine's ghost seated at it the other night.

April knocked with her gloved fist. It was difficult to get a feeling for a piece of furniture when you couldn't touch it. But it was better for her right now not to. God only knew what would happen if she dared to touch the desk! The top drawer didn't budge at all, only the bottom two drawers moved. Feeling around for a gap or anything unusual, April realized the top drawer wasn't a drawer at all. It was made to look identical to the others. It contained a keyhole the size of the one on the drop down leaf.

"The desk was in the house when I moved here. It's a beautiful piece of furniture. According to the records, it's fairly old and authentic to the colonial time period. I haven't been able to move it at all. I never felt the need to disturb it," Aunt Vickie said.

April tried to maneuver it away from the corner of the room but it was big and bulky. It would take a couple of strong men to manage it no doubt. She ran her gloved hand over it again. Was something in there? Did it contain some special clue to release Catherine from her continuous haunting? If she could help Catherine, she would. She didn't like to see anyone suffer. But without keys to the desk, there would be little hope of finding anything inside—and taking an axe to it would be her last resort.

The chatelaine had to contain the keys to unlock it.

***

For the rest of the morning and afternoon she focused on the documents. She believed in their earlier assessment of

~ ☾ ~

Henry Samuel being a killer. If he hadn't done the killing himself, he ordered the jobs done. There would be no use in trying for justice since the man was centuries gone but just knowing she abided in a killer's house brought a chill to her not even the hot tea she was drinking could ward off.

Aunt Vickie received a call from Mrs. Schmidt next door wanting to know if she could come over and stay with her while she was alone with the cable repair man. Her aunt was reluctant to leave, but April told her she would be fine. She wouldn't let James know though. He'd made it very clear she was not to be alone in the house. She promised if anything happened, she would get out of the house quickly.

The promise she'd made to him was weak, though. She'd given it but knew she would do whatever it took to handle the job at hand. And yes, if it meant dealing with a ghost or two or three, she would do so. She might enjoy his wrath again if it led to such delights like the other day. Defying him could be extremely sensual, nothing like 'hot, angry sex' once in awhile. And truthfully, thinking about it made her shift uncomfortably against the seam of her jeans as a tingling thrill warmed her.

She didn't have time for this right now. If she wanted to enjoy another *sexcapade* with James, she would have to get through this paper work. Or it would be another night like last night, trying to weed through musty old documents. She shook herself and focused on the task at hand. She wasn't being paid to be horny. She was being paid to locate a simple, historical document claiming James Addison owned the mill site. How difficult could it be? More difficult than she had imagined upon taking the job offer.

Settling in, she went over the various deeds. Between the file boxes of antique papers and her reference notes littering the table, she hoped her aunt didn't mind the mess. She liked to spread out when she worked. She wouldn't be a good 'office cubicle person.' She liked field studies and open roomed lectures on American History. In a few years she could see herself having the run of an actual historical site as a facility director. Some place like Jamestown, Virginia.

Carefully spreading out the county map from the mid-

~ ☾ ~

1700's they had found in the file box, April focused on the parcels of land Henry Samuel purchased over the years. The boundaries showing James's land and the creek running across it were in direct connection to land Henry owned or had purchased. The land belonging to the unsigned documentation. It was too coincidental not to notice.

Did Henry want the mill? What was so important about the surrounding land to make him want to commit murder? Had James been aware of Henry's motives? Perhaps the two had discussed the land's worth over a pint or two? She would have to ask James tonight.

A loud slam of a door startled her, making her drop the map. Catching her breath she called out, "Aunt Vickie?"

The noise came from the back of the house. April shook out her legs. She was used to sitting with one leg up under the other and it had fallen asleep. Hesitantly she walked into the kitchen and peered around the attached breeze way. No one was there. She could have sworn she'd heard the kitchen door slam. Checking it, April noted it was still locked.

She walked back into the dining room. The gentle tick-tock of the clock on the buffet seemed overly loud. A car passing on the street just outside startled her. Jumping at every little noise, her eyes rounded as she turned around, trying to survey every nook in the room. This was an old house with tons of creaks. Still, her reasoning didn't stop goose bumps from forming on her arms.

This was just great! She was such a wuss. If she was going to solve any paranormal mystery, then facing a few ghosts went along with the territory. Still, April picked up the iron fire poker from the hearth in the dining room. She'd dealt with Henry Samuel. She had every right to be scared.

Her scattered papers strewn over the table met her as she stood sideways in the entranceway between the butler's pantry and the dining room. The wind began to pick up outside as she looked out across the dining room and out the front window. The bare, Bradford pear trees along the backside of the courthouse swayed slightly. Perhaps that's what made the noise. The wind could have caused something to slam, making it sound like a door.

~ ☾ ~

A scuffling of feet overhead stopped her cold. *That wasn't the wind.* Her jaw tensed. Her eyes rose heavily to study the plaster and wood beamed ceiling above her. Leading with her poker, April walked to the bottom of the grand staircase. The landing above was empty, yet a feeling of dread settled in her chest. Her heartbeat quickened and her palms itched with sweat.

Another noise joined in, like heavy footfall running along the upper floorboards. Nope, definitely not the wind, and it sounded a helluva lot heavier than simple attic mice running amuck. Was it Catherine? Could she be in danger? April sidestepped up the first few steps, her poker at the ready. She must look pretty stupid. What could she do to protect herself against a ghost? A poker wasn't going to do anything. She could always knee him in the groin again. Neither one would really work but wielding the fire poker made her feel better.

She made it a few more steps when she thought a solid entity hurled itself down the stairs toward her. Squealing, April ducked back down the stairs. An icy breeze passed through her, catching her off guard. She tumbled down the last few stairs as the front door burst open.

***

"April! Sweetie, talk to me."

April opened her eyes to her mother hovering, patting her cheek in rapid succession. She moved stiffly until her mother's hand pressed on her chest.

"Don't move. You took a fall. Are you okay?"

Cautiously moving parts and pieces of her body she realized she was fine but would probably be sore later. Her lower back took the brunt of the bottom stair as she more or less slid the few steps down.

"He's dead," her grandmother said, slowly placing a bag of groceries at her feet.

With shaking hands, April rubbed her eyes. Her grandmother stood a few feet away, staring vacantly at a spot on the floor between the foyer entrance and the bottom of the stairs. April watched as her grandmother moved in a wide berth, avoiding the area at the base of the steps.

~ ☾ ~

"Broken neck by the looks of him," Dottie continued to explain what no one else could see.

"What are you talking about, Mother?" Virginia asked.

Grandma Dottie pointed to the empty floor she'd been walking around. "The man lying right here. It looks like he might have fallen down the stairs."

Grandma Dottie was viewing one of her ghosts. April couldn't see it though and neither could her mother.

"What happened? How did you fall down the stairs?"

April was about to reply to her mother when the outer door flew open on a burst of November wind. The gust was more than a breeze catching an unlatched door—it enveloped them in a squall, tossing her mother's hair about her face and rattling delicate knick-knacks on their shelves. The papers littering the table tossed about, like so many dry leaves in a wind storm.

Not having recovered from her tumble, April felt disoriented. Queasiness settled in her lower chest, her breathing became harsh and labored as if a large weight were pressing down on her. Was she having a heart attack? Gasping and struggling to breathe, she instinctively reached out for her mother's hand, but her mother was busy crying out and covering her ears.

"Be gone!" Grandma Dottie called out to the wind.

But the object remained firmly planted on April's chest.

Her grandmother began talking in tongues, reciting ritualistic incantations as she focused on the environment around them. "Be gone with you!" she called out again.

Finally, the force on her chest lessened, but April still wheezed as if she'd suffered an asthma attack. The heaviness in the atmosphere was a living, breathing entity.

"Virginia, get April out of here now!" Her grandmother ordered over the din of the wind still swirling around them.

It wasn't over yet. April sensed the pressure building again in the house, like a vacuum with all the air sucked out. Her mother grabbed her hand and dragged her out of the house and across the street. Shaking, they huddled against the naked Bradford pear tree.

Her mother disentangled herself and rose unsteadily to

~ ☾ ~

her feet. "I need to go get your Grandmother. Are you going to be okay?"

Shaking so violently her teeth rattled, April didn't know if she would be okay, but she nodded anyway, wanting her mother to bring her grandmother to safety. The afternoon was calm, no wind now. Even the slight traffic at the end of the intersecting street half a block away appeared normal.

Her mother didn't get far before her grandmother came out of the house, looking faint and weakened. April tried to step forward to go to them but her legs were so unstable she ended up clutching a 'No Parking' sign for support. She watched as the two women she loved the most embrace each other and hobble over to where she tried to stand on her own.

Her grandmother took a deep, cleansing breath before she tried to talk. "He's alive in his realm...and he's pissed. I suppose I would be too, having just witnessed my own death." She looked to the house as if she wanted to beat the entity messing with them with her fists, and then glared reproachfully at her.

April didn't want to comprehend what her grandmother was saying. But somehow she knew this was in direct connection to something she'd done. Her grandmother wasn't happy at all. What had she done though? Was it Henry or someone else causing all the commotion in the house? She didn't do anything!

"Who's dead, Mom?" her mother asked, looking from one to the other.

"Henry Samuel. He was the man who fell down the stairs. He died of a broken neck. But his residual spirit just witnessed his own death for the first time in two hundred and thirty-eight years and he is pissed! But he's even more angry over having been disturbed from his eternal rest." Her grandmother looked directly at her. "What did you do to wake his spirit, April Branford?"

***

"I didn't know I brought his spirit back to life! I was just taking a sketch of his tombstone and...wait! I felt a shock, like a charge of static electricity. James showed up about the same time as a ghost and I forgot all about it." She looked up

~ ☾ ~

in terror. "I didn't know I released his spirit by touching his tombstone." April stumbled over her words as her family and James sat in the round, secluded booth of a sports bar sharing an appetizer platter. "You're saying I released him into his own realm? How is it even possible?"

Her grandmother looked to Aunt Vickie. "You explain it, Vickie. You have more knowledge on the intricacies of live energy."

Aunt Vickie thought for a moment, swallowing her bite of chip and salsa and washing it down with a margarita. "Ghosts exist in a realm of their own time. Take James, for instance. He was in a specific space of time for two-hundred thirty-eight years where he couldn't interact with others. Don't ask me why. I don't think anyone knows. It might have something to do with exact times of death." She waved the thought away, trying to focus on the topic at hand.

"But when ghosts come into contact with high levels of live energy, they soak it up and use it to manifest, either into a higher level of consciousness and physical awareness or...possibly back to life." She motioned to James.

Up to this point, April wasn't aware of anything she'd done. Everything, touching the manor walls, taking etchings of tombstones, they were a part of what she'd always done in her research. But what Aunt Vickie told her made sense. How could she have known just a simple touch, something she'd done all of her life, would turn history upside down?

"I'm sorry. I didn't know I'd done anything wrong." April slumped smaller into the booth as she shredded her chicken finger into stringy bits. "But why now? What is so special about this point in time where I'm suddenly making ghosts come to life and phasing into history? I just don't understand."

"I, for one, am glad you didn't know what you were doing at the time," James piped up, giving her a reassuring smile. His hand rested warmly on her thigh, caressing and giving her his blessing.

Grandma Dottie glared warily at her. "Yes, well—we take the good with the bad. Unfortunately the bad is really bad since we don't understand the entity we're dealing with or the

~ ☾ ~

world they reside in. Because many don't have a social conscience any more, they play by their own rules."

Aunt Vickie nudged her sister. "Dottie, give the girl a break. We were given our entire life to understand our gifts. She's only had a week. I remember you playing tag with childhood ghosts when company came over. Mom would sigh and explain you had imaginary friends to people who questioned your behavior. You blamed them for small incidents, like breaking Mom's favorite vase."

"This is different! Henry doesn't give a damn about vases and playing practical jokes. He's angry. My guess is he did something he doesn't want the history books to know about and April is getting too close to the truth."

Her mother sighed heavily, shaking her head and wiping her face with her napkin. "This is why I had to slap your hands every time you went into a museum, April. You were compelled to touch objects from the past no matter what significance they had. Now do you understand why I was a basket case?"

Aunt Vickie cut into a mozzarella stick and dipped it in the marinara sauce. "Virginia, you had no more idea of her ability than she did. None of us knew what to expect from April," Aunt Vickie defended her against her mother. "Well, now we know. Unfortunately this whole situation is not good since none of us really know what we are dealing with."

April took a healthy sip of her margarita. It was going to take more than alcohol to calm her nerves. The three women had peppered her with questions since Aunt Vickie came home shortly after the incident and they were still at it. The questions had stopped briefly when they picked James up from the Historical Society, but he'd wanted to know what was going on when the silence in the car finally grew awkward. After filling him in, the questions started all over again.

Embarrassment and frustration ate through her gut. She hadn't done anything intentionally. All she was trying to do was her job. How was she to know her gift would get in the way—now of all times! But it was nothing she could control. Suddenly her life seemed to be going in a direction guided by

~ ☾ ~

something or someone else. Her episode with Henry's grave had led to finding out about James, which led her to his grave and bringing him to life. Would she change what she'd done?

She glanced over to see James biting into a jalapeno popper. He was trying to figure out how to bite off the string of melted cheese inside in a delicate manner. The hot, stringy mass broke off between his teeth and landed on his hand. Dropping the popper onto the plate, he tried to wash down the heat scorching his tongue and making his eyes water with his lager. April fought back a smile and lost. No, she wouldn't change a moment of time.

"It's a bit spicy," James whispered as he regained his ability to speak.

Grandma Dottie shook her head with mirth and continued on with their situation at hand. "When I saw the whole ghostly encounter today I was able to catch glimpses of what Henry was dealing with. He was frightened upon seeing his death take place. I watched him staring up at the top of the stairs from where he'd fallen with a look of fear. I think his entity is trying to comprehend his death, like James must have the first time you witnessed your death scene. He was content in his afterlife until he was forced back into a realm he doesn't understand. Now he's angry about not knowing how or why he died."

"So what does he want?" Aunt Vickie asked, sipping her margarita.

"Justice, whatever that means," Grandma Dottie replied.

James scoffed. His face flushed as his lips thinned out. "You tell the bloody bastard to bring it on! He wants justice? I'll give him a piece of my justice." James punctuated every phrase with his finger poking violently into the hard wood of the table. He looked around and lowered his voice.

"I don't think he knows you are here, James. It's probably better if he doesn't. Still, I got the feeling he didn't like seeing the paperwork spread out on the table either. He threw the tantrum and sent the energy vortex. I would have a care around him, April. He knows what you are up to. But he's not only angry about that, more, he wants revenge on whoever shoved him down the stairs," Grandma Dottie continued.

~ ☾ ~

"Could it have been an accident??" April asked. She sat back in the booth, trying to comprehend everything. "He could have tripped and fallen."

"No, from the look on his face, he was terrified when he looked up the stairs, as if seeing someone unexpectedly." Grandma Dottie reached across the table and took her hand. "You need to take it easy, April. I don't know what we are truly dealing with around Henry Samuel. You will not be left alone at all. I don't want you near his tombstone or anywhere else Henry might manifest from."

"I need to solve this case, Grams. Everything happened because of me. If I have to face Henry Samuel to get to the bottom of James's death and to find out the truth on his property then I will just get it over with. Henry will just have to deal. James is relying on me..."

James stopped her with an adamant shake of his head. "Not at the risk of your life or health. I won't let you do this unless you are positive you'll be safe."

"Your future is at stake. My future is at stake. I'm supposed to have something positive to report to Kenneth Miles." April threw her hands up in frustration.

"Kenneth Miles can go to the devil for all I care! If he's so damn rich, he can buy something else. No job is worth your life, April. We'll be fine as long as you promise to stay away from Henry. If he can have me killed, I'm afraid of what he may do to you."

Aunt Vickie held up her hand for calm. "There's no need for anything to be changed right now. April is right. The best thing is to continue solving this case. Otherwise if we walk away now, having brought forth all the spirits, we could leave a mess no one can handle. April, Virginia, you've both been in contact with Catherine, right?" she asked.

"I can only see her. I can't hear her," April commented with a bit of frustration.

Her mother piped up, sharing a smile with April. "But I can hear her. Between the two of us, we'll be able to communicate."

Her mother was willing to face her fear to help her? April couldn't help but feel as if a possible bond was forming

~ ☾ ~

between them after years of silent animosity. The one thing tearing them apart was now going to bring them closer together. Remembering her confession the other night made this moment extra special. The pause of shocked silence from her grandmother and aunt made sharing a smile with her mother really special. It was their secret.

"Really, Virginia? Are you ready to focus on communicating with a ghost?" her aunt asked.

"She did pretty well with her focus and separation today out at Lilac Grove." Grandma Dottie beamed proudly. "I think she can. If she's ready."

April knew it would be difficult for her mother and didn't want to put any undue stress on her. Her mom's offer of assistance really was a first step in acceptance. "Mom, I don't want you to do this if you're not comfortable. I can find another way. I can rent the electric voice phenomenon recorder over at the ghost tour shop. I can use it to communicate with Catherine."

"April, you wouldn't be able to get a clear understanding of what she's trying to say. You would have to ask direct yes or no questions for her to respond to. EVP recorders are good for finding out if there is an entity present, but we already know she's there. No, I recommend we communicate with Catherine directly."

"But if Henry is being an ass—he won't let us anywhere in the house again," James commented.

"Leave that to me," Aunt Vickie said finishing off a buffalo wing and wiping her fingers. "He wants to fight—I've been known to kick a few balls in my time. Ghost or no, he's never dealt with Victoria Snyder. I don't care if it was his house. It's mine now."

April noticed James squirming in the booth at the mention of having balls kicked. She could tell he didn't wish the injury on anyone, friend or foe. "It's all right, James. It's just a figure of speech. She's not going to kick him in the balls."

~ ☾ ~

Chapter Nineteen

James was thankful they weren't returning to the house tonight. Not with an insane ghost lurking. Vickie insisted on purchasing two suites at a local inn, making sure he and April had their own room. They had all spent the better part of an hour going over how they were going to try and make contact with Catherine and what they would do if Henry came along, too. Actually, James didn't want to let any of these women deal with Henry on their own, or collectively. He just didn't know how to stop them without getting kicked in the testicles himself if he tried to get in their way.

"I forgot," April gasped as she readied herself for the night.

James let her borrow his colonial shirt to wear for bed and it hung off of her, dwarfing her small, delicate frame in white muslin. She looked so damn cute. She'd untied her braid and her auburn hair cascaded around her like a flowing cape. James lost himself in viewing her sitting on her knees in the middle of the bed, looking so sensual. One creamy shoulder became exposed as the material slipped down, off of her arm.

"What's wrong?" He smiled, taking a cautious sip from the cola April retrieved from the nearby soda machine for him. He still wasn't quiet used to the fizzy concoction, but he liked the taste.

"I forgot I was going to stop in and see Beth about the chatelaine she found in the excavation. I think it might have been Catherine's." April tapped her finger against her lips. Her eyes took on a faraway look as if deep in thought.

"Chatelaine?" What the hell was a chatelaine? He didn't have a clue what she was talking about.

"They weren't called chatelaines in your time. A woman kept small instruments attached to a brooch or pinned on her

~ ☾ ~

ladies aprons. Usually keys to the house or pantries, sewing
needles..."

He didn't want to talk about keys, or ladies aprons, or
ghosts. Truthfully, he could care less. He placed his soda on
the side table and sat down next to her on the bed. Damn but
she was fetching in his shirt! He tugged at the criss-crossing
laces at the collar.

"You mean those keys Catherine had dangling from her
apron strings? I used to tease her and call her *Henry's
Keeper*. I should get a chatelaine for you because you hold the
key to my heart."

"You are a smooth talker, James Addison." April smiled
teasingly. She sat on her knees, the length of his shirt hiding
her thighs. "How many women have fallen for that line?"

"None so far."

April cocked a brow. "How many times have you used it?"

"In which lifetime?" James asked as he began stalking her
across the large bed on his hands and knees. He was feeling
animalistic tonight. They hadn't followed through with their
session last night but he was more than ready tonight. No
ghosts, no papers, nothing but her naked beneath him.

April backed up warily towards the pillows at his
approach, her green eyes wide with coyness. He was a fierce
wolf, stalking his mate. He growled, low in his throat.

"Both," she whispered on a gasp as he slid his hands up
under his shirt.

Dear God, she wasn't wearing any drawers! He groaned
inwardly.

"Once. Just now." James's mouth came down on hers as
his hands removed the linen from her body. This bed would
be their mating ground for the night.

***

Going back to Aunt Vickie's was their first item on the
morning agenda. The women felt more secure going into the
house with a man's presence, even though James couldn't do
much to help.

Vickie took it upon herself to cautiously check inside. After
what seemed like forever she emerged saying the coast was
clear. She placed a protective spell on the immediate area but

~ ☾ ~

couldn't promise how long it might last if Henry showed up again.

April gathered the notes and documents scattered about the main floor of the house. James grabbed a pair of latex gloves and tried to help her organize them into some order but he could tell she was still a bit on edge after yesterday.

"Did you find out anything more?" James asked, trying to get her to focus on her job.

Lowering her voice, April looked around. "Nothing much. I did notice a pattern though of the land Henry was buying up." She retrieved the wrinkled map still dangling half off the dining room table. "I wanted to ask if you might have known why he was so interested in purchasing all this land around your mill site."

"I'm not sure." He moved closer to where she had carefully spread it on the floor. "I was thinking yesterday about the deeds he purchased. I remember talking with him once, early on when I first came over to the colonies, about how valuable the land I purchased was. The water rights, fertile land near the base of the mountains." James sighed, holding his head as the truth hit him. "I may have bought it not realizing his intent. I didn't think anything about it. He made mention years later he'd been thinking about purchasing the land himself."

"Why hadn't he?"

James shrugged. "Any number of reasons I suppose. Maybe he didn't have enough collateral at the time. Henry Samuel wasn't from a wealthy English family. He worked his way up and was hoping for a seat in the House of Commons upon his return to England or a title. He—catered to everyone who could put a good word in for him. He'd tried to get in good with Lord Calvert, but he didn't care for Samuel. At one of his socials when I first came over from England, I remember his lordship mentioning how he just didn't trust the man."

James shook his head. "I don't know why I didn't see Henry for what he was when I was alive. Perhaps I was too trusting of a man. He gave me no need to doubt his abilities as a local official. We had many of the same peers. As the

~ ☾ ~

unrest broke out among the colonies, we Loyalists stuck together."

April laughed. "I keep forgetting you were 'one of them.'"

"Yes, well—there's always good and bad among both sides in a battle. I didn't want to stay neutral but I knew eventually I would have to either head back to England or take up a post as a commander in the British Army."

"What would you have done with your land?"

"Daniel was in line for over-seeing my properties. I'd already discussed the possibility of having to leave if the skirmish took a turn for the worse and wanted him to have the lands and manor house. He was a good man, like a younger brother to me. I miss him terribly at times.

"I remember taking Daniel out to the tavern one night. The man couldn't hold his ale. He was as sick as a mongrel dog. I took over in the mill the next morning and let him sleep. He may not have been able to drink worth a damn, but Daniel wouldn't have let anything happen to the mill if he could have helped it."

April studied James when he turned quiet. A sad, melancholy lingered over him.

"I think he was sweet on a girl in town. Maybe they settled down and had a long, happy life together," James said.

"I'm sure they did." Trying to look busy, April fought to hide her thoughts. A part of her somehow knew Daniel hadn't settled down with his girl.

But James saw through her. "You're thinking the man in the cellar with Catherine could have been Daniel. Aren't you? Don't think I haven't thought of the possibility. I guess I just don't want to accept it."

She squeezed his free hand. "I don't know any more than you do, James. I wouldn't wish it on anyone. All I hope for is that he is at peace wherever he is."

James nodded, and together they finished sorting and compiling the documents littering the room.

***

"April, it's time. Your grandmother thinks this is the best opportunity to try and get across to Catherine. We need to work fast. She's not sure how much longer she and Aunt

~ ☾ ~

Vickie can hold off Henry's ghost." Her mother walked into the room, trepidation in her stance.

"Mom, if you're not ready..."

"Honey, if I don't do this now, I never will. Am I scared? Hell yeah—but having seen what you can accomplish and knowing what you are going through is twice as difficult. I'm pretty sure I can handle listening to a couple of ghosts and try to sort through their chaotic thoughts."

April studied her mother. Somehow she wasn't the same up-tight, non-emotional woman she'd known all her life. With a chink in her protective armor now, she was willing to pick up a sword and do battle the best she could. April threw a subtle smile her way as her mother approached James. He stood and was ready to go with them upstairs.

"I want to apologize to you, James," her mother started sheepishly. "I've had a harsh relationship with ghosts in the past, always hating them for what they mean to me. Well, not so much hating—but fearing. Yes, I have a fear of ghosts and considering my association with them, whether or not I want it—well, I guess it's time to start realizing they are people too...or were...or whatever. Oh, hell." Sighing, her mother gave James a quick, unprofessional hug. "I'm rambling."

James returned the hug, a bit awkwardly. "Yes, well...I'm honored, Virginia. I will do whatever I can to not give you reason to doubt ghosts anymore—at least this one."

"I know." Her mother smiled weakly again and turned quickly away, adjusting the cuffs on her sleeves as if it was the most important thing she had to do.

April tried hard to suppress her grin. Her mother was trying to compose herself after such a show of emotion. Virginia Branford was not a woman to give in or surrender to anyone. And yet, here she was, trying to make past amends to a man who had been a ghost. Would wonders never cease?

"Whenever you are ready, April, but make it quick, your grandmother is upstairs getting antsy."

April watched her mother retreat up the stairs with her demeanor once again intact. Like the proverbial knight preparing for battle, her mother was trying to find the armor and weapons within herself, so she could forge into the

~ ☾ ~

unknown.

James reached for April's hand, pulling her close. They were at a moment of time where anything could happen. Parts of history could be revealed, his history. They could be moments closer to the truth. April had rehearsed in her head what she wanted to ask Catherine since early this morning. Now was the time to put all the questions to work and hopefully find the right answers.

"April, I meant what I said last night at supper. I don't want you to risk yourself for me. In reality I shouldn't even be here. My eternal rest isn't worth your safety and well-being, nothing is. You are so precious to me."

The sincerity in James's eyes told her if she walked away right now from everything, he wouldn't fault her one bit. But she couldn't. Not because she had anything to prove, and not because of her duty to Kenneth Miles or anyone, but because she knew this was where she was meant to be. Her gift had been finally revealed to her. Life had prepared her for this one moment in time. She leaned into him and kissed him soundly. "I need to do this," she said, tugging at the front of his shirt. "Let's go kick some ghostly ass!"

***

The atmosphere hung heavy with tension and the scent of eucalyptus and honeysuckle oils. Grandma Dottie, her mother, and Aunt Vickie all reeked of the scents, enhancing their psychometric powers and intuition for the task about to be performed. Two strong points needed in their endeavors if they were going to be successful in contacting Catherine.

The shades were drawn closed against the afternoon light. April didn't have to possess her aunt's psychic gifts to sense the spiritual energy around them. Her muscles bunched tightly beneath her long-sleeved t-shirt, as she waited for the unexpected to jump up and bite her in the ass.

Her grandmother sat quietly on the floor in the corner of Catherine's bedroom dressed in a loose caftan of vivid purples and pinks. Something reminiscent of the 60's and 70's. It looked comfortable enough for her to be able to maneuver in ritualistic movements. April's muscles loosened a fraction. She had the support and guidance of those she

~ ☾ ~

loved around her. She could do this.

Once again her mother sat in the middle of the high, four-poster bed, legs crossed and arms out, resting on her knees. She was taking the deep, cleansing breaths Aunt Vickie had taught her to use in preparing her mind and body for accepting and focusing on her phantasms.

Aunt Vickie waved her over. Taking a deep breath, April approached her aunt and held out her hands when she was motioned to do so. Aunt Vickie anointed her palms. Having 'the touch,' her palms were the high-energy contact, chakra points for her. They would be her tools. The strong combination of eucalyptus and honeysuckle *should* attract the dead! The slight tingling of the non-diluted oils bothered her, but she knew at a moment like this, the heavier the strength the better! At least she hoped. She pressed her hands together in a prayer-like stance, heating up the oils and focusing her chakras on the atmosphere.

April understood the intricacies of what she needed to do. She needed to be open to the live energy, not only her own but also the energy her ghost would manifest from. Still, she tried to grasp her own sense of power and accept it slowly without letting it overwhelm her. She hadn't been this involved in a situation since she'd presented her oral thesis to the history department. Hey, if she could face down four of the top history professors in the country and survive without puking, crying, or passing out, she could take on a ghost.

James's hands rested lightly on her shoulders, giving her additional support. His comfort and personal energy brought her strength. Praying what they were about to endure would help solve all their questions, April was ready to proceed.

"James," her aunt spoke softly from the floor, "I will need you to monitor all activity in real time. I'm not sure if you will be able to see or hear what we are going through, so keep in mind how we are being affected by what we witness. Especially April and Virginia—April more so since she's going to be viewing the past and possibly phasing into it. April, you let James know immediately if you are in danger, if you can."

April turned to James. She was about to discount the idea, but the dark look he gave her made her nod in response.

~ ☾ ~

James looked her deep in the eyes. "I want you out of there if Henry shows up. He's capable of anything."

The possibility of encountering a vengeful Henry Samuel at any moment of their séance hung between them. April gave him a subtle nod.

"Let us begin," Aunt Vickie chanted on an exhaled breath.

Finding an object of history for a conduit to her natural psychometry was easy. Catherine's writing desk was a piece of the woman's past. April could make immediate contact with it and prepared herself for the burning sensation to race through her. The shock always frightened her at first. Still, she held onto the desk, focusing her energy on it, to channel the past, as she did with various pieces of artifacts in her studies.

April picked up her mother's voice coming into play, bringing forth Catherine's gentle spirit, as she stayed focused on the desk's natural history. Soon, April felt the calming presence of the past before the atmosphere became charged with the exchange of energies. Her hand stuck to the desk, keeping her in the moment. The temperature around her suddenly dropped.

"Catherine, are you here?" her mother's voice asked softly, calling out to their host. It sounded muted though, as if coming from far away.

The powerful scent of lilac and a shimmer of unearthly light glowed beside the window and manifested into the familiar shape of the young woman. This time she was attired as the mistress of the house. Her hair coiffed perfectly and her wardrobe consisted of a day dress. She looked to April beseechingly.

"I'm here to help you. But I need answers," April said desperately as time was always an issue.

She didn't expect to hear anything from the woman, but her mother's voice echoed in the recesses of her mind, only moments after Catherine's mouth formed words and thoughts she wouldn't have been able to hear otherwise.

"He's in trouble and it is my fault. I need to go to him!" Her mother's frantic words echoed the thoughts and emotions of their ghost.

"Who is in trouble? Is it James? What did you do?"

~ ☾ ~

Catherine only looked confused and shook her head sadly. "No. I need to go to him. Henry locked me in, and I can't go to him."

"Who? Who can't you go to?"

"Daniel. Oh, my love! What have I done?" The ghost paced, frantically wringing her hands and toying with a mass of chains and keys attached to her apron. She turned on April, desperate and eager. "I must stop him. He'll kill Daniel like he killed Mr. Addison! It's my fault."

Daniel! Of course! It all made sense. James had told her Catherine used to come out to pick up her own milled flour and drop off scones. Then he would send Daniel to escort her back to town. Catherine was having an affair with Daniel, not James!

Catherine buried her face in her hands and wept. The sound was so familiar now. April wanted to comfort the woman but couldn't because of her connection to the desk.

"Catherine, help me," April pleaded with her ghostly friend. "Did James commit treason? Was he executed justly?"

"I did it. It was my fault. Henry thought...me...Mr. Addison."

"He thought you and Mr. Addison...what? That you had an affair?" She smiled knowingly at Catherine. "It wasn't James. It was Daniel you were in love with."

"My journal. It's all in my journal." Catherine came rushing toward her, grabbing for the chatelaine dangling from her waist. It held the key to unlock the desk! A journal. Of course, if Catherine kept a daily account of all activities, it would contain the information April needed.

Catherine raced towards the desk, eager to get to her journal inside, and her spiritual form merged with April's. An icy chill enveloped her body but she had little time to regain her own senses when a slam of the door caught her off guard. Henry Samuel stood in solid form before her. He grabbed her harshly, his beefy hand encasing her jaw with a vise-like force. This wasn't a ghostly presence. She was in his time, like at the tree.

"You were spying on me and Peter Hyman downstairs earlier! You think you can stop me?" His face grew closer, his

~ ☾ ~

eyes flared with beady hate. "I want that mill, Catherine! The land should've been mine. I was about to purchase the land when James Addison came and took it right out from under my nose. Years of working for mere pittance for the crown and then to have my future ripped from my grasp by some royal bastard! And now, I still can't possess it. According to Peter Hyman, Addison deeded his lands over to his foreman, Daniel Smith."

He let go of April's jaw and stepped away, studying Catherine. She should have taken the opportunity to let the others know Henry was here, and he had possible intentions to hurt her. But instead, she wanted to know what this scene might reveal.

"I'll have the land, Catherine, by God. If I have to go through every man standing in my way—I will have that land!" Spittle flew from his lips as he punctuated the threat with his anger.

"No! Leave Daniel alone. He's done nothing to you."

April didn't need her mother to translate. Every word was spoken through Catherine. Her heart pounded erratically with her heartbeat and Catherine's rush of adrenaline coursed through her. What was going on? This was about to get ugly. She was a participant in a historical time loop. She was no longer viewing the proceedings like at the manor ruins. She called out for help, but her voice died in a gasp as she took in the menacing form looming before her.

Henry turned his beady eyes back on her. Acknowledgement and understanding showed in their black depths. His chest rose and fell in great heaves beneath his over-extended waistcoat. Air rasped in and out of his inflated nostrils.

Oh shit, this wasn't going to be good!

The sharp sting of his hand crossed her face. April didn't even have time to flinch. He'd slapped Catherine and now they were on the floor, cowering in the corner between the desk and wall.

"You whore! On familiar terms with him are you?" He grabbed a fistful of Catherine's hair, pulling her up, right in front of his face. He shook her. "You weren't having an affair

~ ☾ ~

with Addison, you were fornicating with his foreman!"

April's feet fought for stability as she was dragged across the room. Every time she tried to get her footing she was knocked back down, her senses reeling. Henry Samuel could pack a punch with his beefy fists. She tried to call out for help, but her voice didn't carry outside of her inner thoughts. She was Catherine Samuel in this realm.

"I'll make you pay for your infidelities! We're going to pay a visit to your lover, my dear wife. He'll give me the mill or so help me God you're going to wish you'd never thought to play me for the fool!"

"Daniel will never give up the mill. He loves that mill as much as Mr. Addison did," Catherine spat out at her husband.

"Oh, he'll give it up all right. I'll kill the bastard for his adulterous nature. If I can't have it, I'll make damn sure no one ever will."

Catherine struggled and cried, begging and pleading for Henry's mercy. To leave Daniel alone. April was along for the ride, being pulled across the bedroom, fighting herself to get out of this realm. Her chest heaved from fear, adrenaline— fight or flight taking over. Was this the day Henry had killed his wife and Daniel in the cellar? Was it her punishment for being unfaithful? She had to break free of Catherine's spiritual hold on her so she could get back to her realm. If not, would she be subjected to the same gruesome death?

The rancid breath on her face was real, a mixture of alcohol and stale tobacco, his eyes blood shot and evil as his cheeks burned with fury and hatred. His burliness was not only fat but muscle too, as his strength kept her in check. She didn't have any leverage this time to knee him or do any damage to his shins. Internally, she fought Catherine's fear while trying to find her own strength to defend herself against the ghost-man.

Catherine and April pelted Henry with cries and curses as he grabbed them by the upper arm and forced them toward the door. April battled against Catherine's weakness as she fought to get away from Henry's hold on her. How could she still be in this realm? She was no longer attached to her

~ ☾ ~

conduit. She should be phasing back to the present now!

She struggled and kicked out with her feet as he pulled her closer to the door. A quick backhand to the face silenced her. April felt the sting, realizing how much force the man projected. This wasn't a ghostly form. This was a solid hit.

Oh hell, I'm not in Kansas anymore!

Before he could lead her out through the bedroom door, an outside disturbance caught her off guard. Her assailant stumbled backward as if attacked by an unseen force. April phased between the two worlds and thought she saw James shove the ghostly form of Henry before he drifted into mist.

Her aunt's voice commanded, "Be gone!" before she passed out.

~ ☾ ~

Chapter Twenty

Gasping for breath and shaking, April tried to relax. Her Aunt Vickie doused her brow and hands with a cloth soaked in gardenia essence to help her recover from the emotional shock and strain to her system. Her family and James surrounded her, providing comfort as she lay on the bed in Catherine's room, trembling.

"Calming breaths. Breathe in the essence, dear," her grandmother's voice soothed, as her fingers combed back her bangs from April's face. The washcloth was placed along the nape of her neck and jawline where she still felt the pressure from Henry's massive fingers.

"She's going to have bruises. Look at the red marks he left," her grandmother said.

"I'll kill you the next time you touch her, Henry!" James's voice echoed throughout the small room as he punched his fist through the air.

"Don't provoke him, James. This isn't the time," Aunt Vickie warned.

"I'm grateful to you James." Virginia breathed a sigh of relief and turned to April. "Between your grandmother's ability to see where Henry was and James's brute strength we were able to get Henry's entity to leave."

"Could you see me, Grams?" April asked warily.

"Not exactly. It's more like I could sense you. Catherine is using your physical essence to try to manifest. I'm not sure if I like that or not. I don't think she's doing it maliciously though."

"Maybe she's desperate and using me is the only way she can relay her actions." She thought for a moment. "It's not me Henry is hurting. It's Catherine."

Aunt Vickie had been remote and quiet. Assessing the area

~ ☾ ~

with her powerful senses she backed away silently from the group. "I don't like this. We need to get out of here. I fear there will be repercussions as soon as Henry builds up his strength again. Grab your purses, and let's head out."

It took them only moments to gather items they would need to leave safely. The house vibrated with energy. Static build up sparked the air, sending prickles of awareness throughout the atmosphere. Cold, icy fingers grabbed at them. April shuddered as the essence of her experience pummeled her nerves. James held her close while they waited in the foyer for the other three women. He looked around the room, eyeing every shadow with suspicion as if ready to do battle if Henry burst forth. She was afraid there would be very little Aunt Vickie and Grandma Dottie would be able to do to calm Henry the next time.

***

April had the truth now. James was not guilty of having an affair. But she didn't have any tangible proof. The evidence would be in the journal, if the journal still resided in the antique desk. And the chatelaine would open the desk. She needed to get to Beth and see if she still had it. April shivered again and took a sip of her latte, listening to James and her family discuss mundane things, probably trying to keep their thoughts off of the incident while her head filled with the known and unknown.

The chatelaine was the only thing that had survived the destruction and death when the fire had broken out. The thought saddened her to know nothing of Catherine's remains would ever be found to lay her soul to rest. Surely the fire and time had destroyed all evidence.

The chatelaine literally held the key to solving James's mystery. How would she explain to Beth Freelane why she needed the rare, expensive item? Would Beth find her a total freak if she told her about her penchant for psychometry? Or was the woman more open to the idea and abilities of the metaphysical sciences? Then what? Tell her a ghost needs it to unlock her desk?

Yeah, she'd really think you were mental then, April.

Her phone vibrated in her pocket, making her jump.

~ ☾ ~

Everyone stopped talking and looked at her as if perhaps she might have a possession going on. Lately, she wouldn't doubt anything happening to her. A collective sigh of relief roamed the table as she produced her small clam-shell phone. But the number on the screen really caused her heart to palpitate. It was Kenneth Miles.

"Excuse me," April stood up to leave. "I think I'll take this call outside."

From the corner of her eye, she watched her mother keep James at bay when he tried to follow her. It was probably for the best. She didn't want him to hear her failure and firing from her employer.

"Hello, Mr. Miles, what can I do for you?" She tried to sound pleasant as she meandered out of the café to the street side tables.

"I wanted to call and personally congratulate you on your evidence so far. I was excited to see the photo of the document you found. It sounds like you are on the right track."

April removed her phone from her ear and looked at it. Was this the same man? It was nice to hear a bit of praise from him and even the tenor of excitement about her findings was a nice change of pace. This was the first time he didn't sound like a gruff old man.

"I'm close, sir. I've found the document showing the deed to the land James purchased right before his death on the extension of the mill. But I haven't found the original deed. I'm still searching. I think we're on the right track. I may have information James had given over the property to his foreman. I think we may find the actual document in files held by a prominent lawyer at the time, a Peter Hyman."

"His foreman, Daniel Smith? James Addison spoke of him in his letters found along with his sister's journals from the time he was living in the colonies. I do have my people looking into the documents you said James might have sent over here to his attorneys in London. I'll let you know if they find anything."

"This is dandy! I was told you are the best. Putting my faith in you I haven't been disappointed. You've given me

~ ☾ ~

more than anyone else has been able to. When you do find the original document, please send me a photocopy, immediately."

"I understand your urgency in settling on the land..."

"This has gone further than just an interest in the land. Do you know the excitement of finding out about your past? Well of course you do, you're a historian. Anyway, I've taken a personal interest in this case and the history behind my great-great 'whatever' uncle. I've found rather interesting information on him here in England from his sister, Elsbeth, through her journals and letters from Great-Uncle James. The man sounds like a good fellow."

He is a 'good fellow.' She wished she could somehow share her news with Kenneth, to actually have them meet. April watched through the large plate glass window as James laughed and conversed with her family over tea and coffee.

"...Doctor?"

"I'm sorry. You were saying, Mr. Miles?"

"I was just thanking you for coming along so quickly in your endeavors. I'm quite impressed. Dr. Moreland was correct in suggesting you for this insurmountable task. I look forward to meeting with you soon, hopefully over a celebratory dinner?"

"Yes, of course. I would like that," she replied softly. Would she be able to introduce the two distant relatives when he arrived? What would Kenneth Miles think when she brought along his great-great-'whatever' uncle with her as a guest? She laughed at the bizarre situation.

"Dr. Branford, is everything all right?"

"I'm sorry, sir. I was just thinking about how I would be dining with the reclusive Kenneth Miles, and it has nothing to do with financial gain or politics," she lied, scrambling to figure out what was so funny.

"Yes. I suppose many would find it humorous. Please, no media or paparazzi. Keep it simple. I will see you within the week. There are some issues I'm still dealing with in London, but I plan on being in Maryland in time for the final day of the festivities. I think it's only appropriate I should be there to honor him in some fashion."

~ ☾ ~

"He would appreciate the effort, I'm sure." She couldn't wait to relay the information to James. What would he do with his 'nephew' when they met?

"Until then, Dr. Branford. Again, keep me constantly informed of any new developments."

The subtle click of disconnect wasn't so subtle to April's ears. It signified the lack of time she had left to work with. Things were moving fast in reality. She had less than a week to find one piece of paper lost for two hundred thirty-eight years.

***

James didn't have to be a mind reader to discern what weighed heavily on April's shoulders. The phone call was inevitable. She'd feared it since their meeting. He felt at fault for her lack of progress. Spending too much time on his mystery and not focusing on her original goal jeopardized her career. But when she relayed the actual oddity of the phone call he found himself grinning.

Not at Kenneth Miles in general but at the fact Elsbeth had kept her older brother's memory alive through her journals and letters from him. She'd been a woman-child when he'd left home, barely in corsets and with a will to match her fiery temper at times. At other times she'd been as sweet and docile as Catherine Samuel. But he never stopped loving his sweet sister. And it was good to know she had thought about him often.

"It'll be all right, April. I promise." James squeezed her hand gently, trying to reassure her.

"I'm fine," she sighed, tucking her hands deeper into her woolen coat. "I'll see if Beth has anything new for me to snoop out while you're giving tours. I might get lucky."

"Well, I for one can't wait to meet this Kenneth Miles. He's the financial king of England and to know he's a relative of yours, it should be interesting to see the two of you together." Aunt Vickie raised her brow. "Perhaps he'd be interested in a woman with some eclectic tastes?"

"Your niece is already spoken for. I will not share her. Not even with a distant relative. I'll be damned first!"

"James," Vickie patted his hand. "I wasn't referring to my

~ ☾ ~

niece. I was referring to me. I'm widowed, not dead. A man of his tastes, if he's anything like you but older, I can handle."

Blowing steam off of his fresh cup of tea, James snorted with disdain. "I'm very protective of my family and I will have to make sure the cad is worthy of your hand. Kenneth Miles claims to be a descendant of mine but I will still be the judge of the man's character. I will not have some jackal take advantage of your better nature." All four women stopped and stared at him curiously. And smiled, congratulating April on picking such a fine man to have brought to life and how he would fit in their family.

Had he just accepted this odd crew of women as his family? Aye, they were family to him, even before he spoke of bands and vows, and he would make sure no one dared to harm them, even a distant relative.

He couldn't let the tender moment last. It was not in his nature. "Yes well, we'll see. Besides, if he's anything like me, I would definitely be worried."

***

"You wanted to see me, Dr. Branford?"

Dr. Beth Freelane walked down the steps and approached April at the bottom of the landing of the Georgian townhouse. The historical house contained both the public domain, consisting of an information desk and a small selection of local history books, and the private residence of the curator for Kings Mill Historical Society. The place was still in disarray. Various boxes, totes, and crates of materials lined the narrow hallways and rooms, waiting to be moved into the new, modern facility. April wondered if any of these boxes might contain the document she was looking for.

After a few days of coming up with nothing more in the files at the house, it was time for drastic measures. She was running out of time. But how to approach Dr. Freelane and ask her for use of the chatelaine. The woman wouldn't understand. The professional appearance and demeanor Beth possessed was of a no nonsense business woman. She was what April aspired to be, practical and professional. How could she explain what she needed to do? If Dr. Freelane kicked her out for being a psycho would James's job be at stake?

~ ☾ ~

She needed the chatelaine though. It was the only way to solve the mystery. Maybe then she could focus all her time on finding the damn deed to his property. Hopefully, Henry signed at least that one. But either way, she would have the evidence. Kenneth Miles could decide what he would do from there. She couldn't change history, only see it.

"Good afternoon, Dr. Freelane." April greeted her with a wan smile. Reaching into her bag, she retrieved the book Dr. Freelane wrote about the excavation. Turning to the tagged page with the picture of the chatelaine she showed it to Beth. "You mentioned finding this article in the ruins on your original dig. I was wondering if you might still have it."

"Well, of course. Fully intact. Antique chatelaines are not easy to come by. I've had various offers over the years for the piece, but I've not been able to part with it." Beth tilted her head questioningly. "Would you care to see it? I have it upstairs in a private collection."

"I would love to!"

Following her upstairs, April's heart beat faster. This was it. She was going to hopefully view Catherine's chatelaine, but what else would she be able to do? She couldn't touch it. The temptation was great but she wouldn't let herself for the sake of not being sure what could happen, especially now. Touching artifacts and sensing the past was one thing, phasing in and out of time, would take some explaining.

How could she convince Beth to part with it? She didn't need it for long, just until she could match it up with the desk and see if Catherine's journal was still inside after all these years.

"Have a seat." Beth motioned to the chair in front of her desk, piled with unfiled paperwork. "Sorry for the mess, but until I can get into our new location I'm afraid my filing system has deteriorated."

She sat down at the desk and unlocked a large filing drawer next to her. Inside the drawer was a sturdy filing safe. April's palms tingled watching Beth unlock the safe. Beth retrieved a royal blue velvet bag. Opening the drawstring she carefully shook the contents onto her desk blotter. A small silver flur de lis held two small keys, one larger than the

~ ☾ ~

other, both daintily scrolled in detail. Beth smiled, her stare intense. "Go ahead, touch it."

The glow of knowledge in Beth's eyes worried her. This was an artifact. It shouldn't be touched without proper precautions. Did she know? How could she? "No. I can't. It's beautiful though." April's hand twitched as if it willed her to reach out, just once.

"Yes, you can, April," Dr. Freelane commanded with a reassuring smile. But her voice trembled slightly. The woman's eagerness for April to touch it electrified the room. "I've waited nearly three decades for someone to reveal who this chatelaine belonged to and why I'm so enamored with it that I'm unable to sell it for an offered price of $50,000."

April's heart thudded painfully in her chest. This woman knew of her gift. Fear and trepidation fought to escape. Her body quivered, wondering what Dr. Freelane would do or think. Was this a game? Some joke gone bad?

Dr. Freelane looked April directly in the eye. "Dr. Moreland told me you have the gift of psychometry and you could tell me what I needed to know. Touch it, please."

***

Did she hear right? April sat stunned, staring at Beth across her desk. She knew about her gift? Well, the woman hadn't discredited her or ridiculed her...yet.

"Bob Moreland told me he knew you had the sight when you were able to note information about the Jamestown dig. You two share a common interest. He has a bit of the ability, though not as strong from what he told me," Beth explained, eyeing her with warm appreciation. "It's not something people see every day. I understand it might not be a comfortable topic for you. Most people wouldn't comprehend, or they would judge or try to exploit your gift if it was revealed. I find psychometry fascinating!"

Beth sighed. "Bob tried to get some information from the chatelaine years ago, but he wasn't able to distinguish anything of significance. All he sensed was residual pain."

Well, of course! Residual pain was the prominent ordeal. The fire and trauma of what Catherine went through was nothing but pain.

~ ☾ ~

"You want me to actually touch it?" Could she without repercussions? "Really, I don't know if I should. Lately I think there is more to my gift than just 'touching' something to obtain knowledge."

Beth leaned forward, waiting for her to continue. "Such as?"

April hesitated. It was now or never. She would take what came. "I phase into the past," she whispered, bowing her head, waiting for the laughter or the gasp of shock. Perhaps it would be an immediate phone call to the psych ward at the local hospital.

Beth nodded in full agreement and understanding. "Live energy and residual energy converging. I've done some research on it, ever since my excavation at the mill site. Have you been out there?"

It was April's turn to be shocked. She wasn't being questioned or committed? She studied Beth warily. Did she have the gift? "I've been out to the site. I've been able to sense a piece of the past." She didn't want to reveal too much of the details. It was enough for someone of Beth's caliber to accept so much of her gift.

Beth steepled her fingers under her chin. "I sensed this overwhelming feeling of—I don't even know what it was. It was almost as if I were a part of the surroundings. I've never felt it anywhere else. Well, that's not true. There was a moment I had a connection when I toured one of the historical plantations down in St. Mary's county. But the mill site was definitely stronger."

She leaned across the desk. "What about you? What've you seen? Did you phase when you were out at the ruins?"

How much should she reveal? This was all so new and unbelievable. "I saw the fire." April would wait to say more. She wasn't ready to reveal more than the bare minimum.

"Would you be willing to touch the chatelaine and tell me its secrets?"

The curator was asking her for a favor? Should she, could she, ask for one in return? "I already know who it belongs to. The chatelaine belonged to Catherine Samuel."

Jumping up from her seat, Beth's eyes widened. "This is

~ ☾ ~

fantastic!" She sat back down, her brows knotted. "But how did the chatelaine end up at the mill site? Unless she *was* having an affair with James Addison and it ended up there!"

"No. She was having an affair with Daniel Smith, his foreman." April bit her lip at revealing too much. Damn! She felt the need to protect James's name but didn't want to blurt out the truth. Besides, she still didn't have the proof. Now she would have to explain seeing ghosts.

Beth came around the desk. Her eyes were critical and assessing, her stance slightly rigid. "How do you know? Why did you want to see the chatelaine?"

"I need to see if one of the keys fits in the lock of a desk at my aunt's house. I believe it belonged to Catherine Samuel. I think there is something in the desk we might be able to use to bring some interesting history to light."

Beth didn't ask any more. Her eyes traveled to her chatelaine. "Do I have your word nothing will happen to it in your care?"

"I promise," April breathed with relief. Beth was going to take a chance on her! "You can even come with me," she offered.

"No. I can't." Beth shook her head. "There is something about your Aunt's house I can't deal with. It took all my will power to bring over the boxes the other day and go up to the porch to ring the doorbell. I trust you." Beth placed the chatelaine back into its velvet bag and handed it to her. "Go now. I want to know if it works."

~ ☽ ~

Chapter Twenty-One

April worried about going back to the house. Was it safe after this morning's incident with Henry? She knew if James saw her head back he would forbid her to go, but she needed to see if the chatelaine would work.

Aunt Vickie's car was parked in the drive. She didn't want to go in the front door. She would see if her aunt was in her apartment in the back. The sooner she did this, the faster she could get on with her job of finding the information she needed. Besides, the journal could hold any number of clues helpful to her in locating the document.

"Aunt Vickie?" April called out as she knocked on her door.

Vickie pulled the curtain back to peek out, and then opened the door to usher her in. "How did it go with Beth?"

"Fine. She let me borrow the chatelaine," April gushed excitedly. Unable to contain her excitement, she hugged her aunt.

Her aunt held her at arm's length after their hug fest, studying her seriously. "I suppose you want to go try it?"

"Could we? Time is running out with Kenneth Miles coming in a few days. Anything I could send him before then would only be a plus."

"How did James take the news? I would have thought he would be with you." Aunt Vickie stopped talking to glare at her. "He doesn't know, does he?" Shaking her head, she started to walk back towards her small living room.

April bit her bottom lip and followed. "I didn't want to worry him. He's working, and I shouldn't have to get his permission. He knows I have a job to do."

Aunt Vickie turned on her, startling April. "Bullshit! You snuck in my back door so he wouldn't accidentally see you

~ ☾ ~

while giving tours." Aunt Vickie eyed her knowingly, tapping her foot. "And now I suppose you want me to try and hold off Henry's entity if he happens to be lurking about in his realm while you try out the key?"

She could feel embarrassment flush her cheeks. She was dealing with her aunt. Did she think she could pull one over on her? "You don't have to..."

Her aunt sighed. "No, I don't have to but if I don't, you'll go up there and be attacked. I'll be responsible for your death and your mother and grandmother will have my ass. Okay, let's get this over with."

***

Waving a smudge stick of white sage to ward off evil spirits and negative energies, Aunt Vickie led them up the stairs to Catherine's bedroom. The room was the same as when they left it earlier, except without the heavy feeling of evil. Bright sunlight soaked the room, revealing every shadowy nook and corner.

"All right, dear. Let's see what we find." Vickie motioned to the desk as she continued to wave the pungent smudge stick.

April removed the chatelaine from the pouch, letting it fall on the bed's coverlet. She was still hesitant to touch the antique accessory for fear of what would happen before she could use it in the lock. Her excitement suddenly turned to trepidation. The unknown effects of what this simple piece of jewelry could reveal hit her. Could she do this? She had to!

"You haven't touched it yet, have you?" her aunt asked. At the shake of her head her aunt picked up the large key and went to the desk. "Can't have you phasing without knowing where and when you'll be going," she harrumphed.

Chills traveled up April's arms. These were shivers of excited energy as she was about to find her buried treasures. Like Indiana Jones opening the Ark of the Covenant, she prayed it didn't do anything to harm her or her aunt.

Closing her eyes, April heard the small snick of the key turning in the lock for probably the first time in over two centuries. She took in the squeak of rusty hinges as the desktop came down with Aunt Vickie's guidance.

~ ☾ ~

"Well stop meditating and come take a look," her aunt said.

April jumped from the bed. The only things in the drop down alcove of the desk were an old piece of writing quill, a pewter inkwell of dried up ink, a small piece of ancient sealing wax, and a brass stamp engraved with the letter 'S'. Her heart dropped. They would be interesting items for the society, but not what she was looking for. No, there must be something she was missing.

Touching the desk, April was taking a risk of having her gift manifest but she let her hands roam over the piece of furniture quickly, searching around and under it. "There has to be a secret drawer or panel. What about the drawer with the lock? And the smaller key, it has to go to something."

"Let's give it a try."

She had her aunt unlock the drawer beneath the desktop and it popped out as if on a spring mechanism. But when she reached in to feel around in the back, it was empty. Disheartened, April was about to give up when her hand caught on a latch to a false compartment in the inside of the drawer. A small keyhole, slightly hidden from normal view caught her attention and excitement sluiced up her spine. A secret hiding area!

"Yes! I found it!"

Without thinking, April grabbed the chatelaine from the keyhole in the drawer so she could use it to unlock the secret compartment. She collapsed against the desk as wave after wave of nausea hit her. She closed her eyes to ward off the intense vertigo she was suffering.

When she opened her eyes she was in the room but her aunt was nowhere to be seen. The door opened and in walked Catherine. She was beautiful and glowing, her face animated as she tugged someone into the room along with her. She was giggling.

"Henry's gone for the weekend to Annapolis. Probably to see his mistress again."

"Are you sure about this? What about your maid?" A young man appeared, somewhere between his early to late twenties. A crop of reddish-blonde hair topped his head.

~ ☾ ~

"I sent her to see her family in Baltimore for the weekend. We at least have a few hours tonight." Catherine hugged the man and he returned the embrace.

"I've waited for this moment for so long," he said. "Each time I see you I can't help but remember how it used to be. I swear we will be together again soon. I won't let Henry have you when you've always been mine."

"Oh, Daniel. I just don't know how. I'm married to him now. It's all so unfair. I hate having to sneak around. If we're caught I don't know what will happen. But I want to be with you. Since your servitude with Mr. Addison is over and he's offered you land and a job, will you take it so we can still see each other or will you leave and head back to England?"

"I'm staying here until I can have you by my side. I'm building a house for us. Not going to be as fancy as what you're used to."

"I wasn't raised to be fancy, Daniel. I want you and a family." Catherine's voice became sad. "I lost our baby. They never even let me see her when they took her from me. I was so distraught when you left to go work for Mr. Addison. I thought we'd never see each other again. When Henry won me in the card game and brought me to Kings Mill, I never thought I would have to marry him. But it was my only chance of escaping the tobacco fields and to be close to you." She buried her face in his chest.

Daniel stroked her back with tender touches. He brought her face up so he could see it and kissed her troubled brow. "I know. I don't blame you, sweetheart. We will be together somehow, we just need to wait and the good Lord will let us know when it's our time."

April listened to the conversation and watched as they kissed. Did they not see her standing only a few feet away? Was she not in their realm? She tried clearing her throat, waving her hand—nothing seemed to attract their attention, except each other. She was a ghost in their time. Studying the couple, they seemed very much in love. She hoped to move on. Voyeurism was not something she was into. She turned away to give them a moment of privacy.

She glanced back one last time. Daniel seemed familiar

~ ☾ ~

and upon taking a closer look, she noticed the clothing and height. It was the same man from the cellar fire. The one she couldn't see. She knew the truth now. Henry had killed both Catherine and Daniel that day.

She needed to get back to her time. She called out to her aunt, hoping she could hear her and tell the spirits to 'be gone.' When nothing happened, April called out 'be gone' and felt herself whirling back through the cataclysmic cycle of time, closing her eyes as time spun around her, making her dizzy.

When she opened her eyes, her aunt stood over her waving a weathered black book tied with a piece of leather. "Welcome back."

"How long was I gone?"

"Long enough to have your mother and grandmother join us."

April looked up from the floor where she'd collapsed to see her mother and grandmother standing at the end of the bed. And boy did they look pissed!

***

"What part of 'don't come back here until its safe' do you not understand, April May Branford?" her mother scolded as the women converged in Aunt Vickie's living room.

"I wanted to see if the chatelaine worked in the desk. It does!" She looked at her aunt, still holding the aged book. Aunt Vickie had taken time to wrap it in a clean flour sack dishtowel to keep oils off of it until April could take a look. "Is that Catherine's journal?" she asked with wide-eyed awe.

"Don't change the subject," her grandmother added waggling a finger at her. "Your mother asked you a question. Did you not understand it's not safe for you to come here until we all made sure Henry was out of the house?"

"But Aunt Vickie was here—"

"And you'd risk her life against Henry Samuel to find out if a key works in a desk?" her grandmother asked.

April hadn't thought about her aunt, she'd wanted to get to the desk. "Sorry, Aunt Vickie, I guess I wasn't thinking clearly. I've been so focused on my research I've not thought things through."

"No you weren't thinking clearly, young lady!" her mother reiterated pacing the length of the room.

~ ☾ ~

"Would you two give her a break? No harm was done. The keys worked, she found the journal, a good time for all." Her aunt shrugged. "So what went on while you dozed?"

"Dozed?" April gave her a quizzical stare. "You mean I didn't phase?"

"No, you collapsed instantly against the wall when you touched the chatelaine. What happened?"

April quickly filled in her family on the lover's tryst.

"How tragic! Two lovers so close but forced worlds apart," Aunt Vickie said, sounding like a movie trailer.

"Yeah, it sounds like she bore a child out of wedlock after Daniel went to Kings Mill with James. I might research the ancestry of indentured servants in the colonies just to see what comes up. Some states and counties kept records of births and deaths of slaves and servants."

"Maybe she wrote about it in her journal," Vickie said, finally handing the towel wrapped book over to her. "Before you get involved with this ghost, don't you think it's time you went to get your other ghost?"

April looked at her watch. She'd forgotten about the time. "Crap! Yeah, I guess so." She grabbed her coat, tucked the journal into her purse, and made sure the chatelaine was carefully tucked into its pouch and secure in her purse. "What are we doing about a place to stay tonight?"

"We'll work on cleansing the area thoroughly while you take James out for dinner," Aunt Vickie said.

"Okay." April started to open the door but turned back at the last minute. "You won't tell James about this afternoon, will you?" She didn't want to get him all worked up. He would probably get angry with her. But then again, she'd enjoyed it the first time.

"No, dear. We won't tell him."

"Thanks Grams, I appreciate it." She could always count on her.

"We won't tell him," her grandmother restated. "You will."

***

April was eager to read Catherine's journal. She would start after dinner. Catherine would have the knowledge of what happened to put her husband in such a mood as to have

~ ☾ ~

someone executed publicly. The actual documentation of his death would provide the evidence for the history books and finally explain to James what happened. He would be able to move on.

Her heart fell. He would be able to move on. Would it be instant? Would he fade right before her eyes, never to exist again? She didn't expect to fall so hard for her subject. She'd known him for less than two weeks. How could she have fallen in love in such short time? Now she couldn't fathom how she would live without him.

Pulling up in front of the Historical Society she didn't see James waiting for her as he usually did if she was running late. Parking, she got out and put a quarter in the meter. Her over-active imagination played tricks on her. Was he already gone? Without her getting a chance to say good bye? With her heart palpitating and the worst-case scenario playing in her head, she raced up the steps and beat on the Victorian glass framed door.

After frantic, nerve wracking moments, James came to the door, still in costume but with an odd look of guilt and worry clouding his features. The lock tumbled with a hollow click and he opened the door.

"What's wrong?" April touched his face, running her hands over him to make sure he was really alive. His chest was solid as she frantically ran her hands down to feel the beating of his heart.

He didn't say a word, only led her into the empty front office. Beth Freelane was slumped against the wall, a wet paper towel on her forehead.

"Oh my God! What happened? She looks like she's seen a ghost." She bent down to check Beth's vitals. She was alive, just fainted.

"Well, she did, kind of." James said with a bit of chagrin and embarrassment.

April shook her head. *No, he couldn't have? Please, tell me you didn't tell her, James.*

"Who?"

James rubbed at the back of his neck and closed his eyes. "Me."

~ ☾ ~

Chapter Twenty-Two

"What do you mean, *you*?" April asked James and looked back down at Beth who was starting to come around. She knelt down to help the woman. "It's all right. I'm going to sit you up, Beth."

"I'll get her some water." James hurried to the water cooler in the hallway.

Beth groaned and struggled into a sitting position with help from April. "I'm fine. I just need..." She stopped mid-sentence as James came back with a plastic cup of water. She moaned, holding her head. "Please tell me it's a bad dream?"

April took the cup from his hand to give Beth.

James looked at the piece of parchment in his hand. Chagrined he ran his fingers through his already disheveled hair. If a man could look guilty, James's appearance spoke in volumes. He handed her the piece of paper.

April should have been ecstatic. The original deed to the mill site, signed by James, paid for and counter-signed by Henry Samuel on May 5, 1763 lay between her fingers. She now possessed the documents Kenneth Miles needed for his proof. But Beth's condition and the guilty look on James's face took away her joy of the moment. "What happened?"

Beth recovered enough to stand. Her eyes warily traveled between the two. "I've been searching through some of the boxes the staff brought over from the basement of City Hall. I came across a case of ledgers from Peter Hyman's historical files. I opened one of the files and this fell out. I realized it might be what you've been looking for so I came down stairs to share the news with Jim."

James sighed heavily. "I got a little excited at seeing my original deed after all these years."

Beth stopped and became pale again. Her lips trembled

~ ☾ ~

and she shook her head. "Please, April— tell me. This man really isn't James Addison...is he?" she whispered.

They sat Beth back down in the small settee in the hallway and explained the situation. "So you brought him to life by touching his grave? And you saw him as a ghost?" Beth asked, trying to comprehend. "All because of your psychometry and the live-energy between the two of you?"

April nodded slowly. "According to my Aunt Vickie, we've come to believe it's the only possibility."

Beth tentatively reached out and touched James's face. "But is he truly alive?"

"Yes, he is alive. To what extent, we don't know. We're just taking it one day at a time." April looked to James, her heart racing all over again at the thought of how close they were now to the truth being told and what it would mean for them.

April reached into her purse and retrieved the pouch with the chatelaine in it.

"Did it work? Does the key belong to the desk?" Beth asked excitedly and took the pouch.

April looked from Beth to James and nodded solemnly before retrieving the towel wrapped journal.

***

Beth invited them to stay for dinner and they retired upstairs to her apartments. James sat numbly, staring at the document he'd signed with Henry two hundred forty-eight years ago. His chest felt tight. The document would free April from her task, but he was unsure of what he felt looking at it. Unlike the other documents they'd found, this one proved he'd owned the land the mill had stood on. Beth would record the truth for Kings Mill history. But the mill and his house no longer existed. Only a piece of antiquated paper revealing the grandeur he'd once owned.

Beth went downstairs when the Chinese take-out they'd ordered was delivered. April told him of her incident with Catherine and Daniel when she'd made contact with the desk and journal. He wasn't happy with her going behind his back, doing something so dangerous. But she was here, with the evidence she'd been seeking. She sat on the sofa and carefully pored over the journal's later entries. The only clues of his

~ ☾ ~

time frame from someone who knew him.

Would the book reveal the reason behind his death? What then? He didn't want to lose April, but a part of him understood being in this time frame may have only been an accident.

Beth returned, set the table and arranged the food from the little folded boxes onto her good dinner plates.

"Listen to this," April said as she stood and came to sit next to him at Beth's small drop-leaf dining table, the journal in her hands. "*Friday, December 9, 1774—Henry locks me in my room every night. Ever since he made me watch poor Mr. Addison's execution, he's kept a close eye on me. He's afraid I will reveal the truth of what I know. But I'm too weak. I'm scared of what he could do to me. He's insane. I overheard him tell Mr. Hyman this afternoon, he planned to oust Daniel from the mill. Henry's always wanted the mill for himself. I never thought he'd resort to such a horrible crime in order to get it. I fear Daniel's life is at risk. I must let him know of Henry's plans. I am due to go to the mill tomorrow for grain. Perhaps we will have a moment to talk.*"

"It's her last entry in the book," April said sadly, looking into the rest of the blank book. She set the journal carefully out of the way. "When I witnessed the last ghost session with her and Henry, she must have just written this entry—before he took her to the mill."

James nodded solemnly. It would have been the day she and Daniel were killed in a senseless act of vengeance and greed. Having never seen beyond his own life disheartened him. He wished he'd known more of Daniel and Catherine's life and dreams. It wouldn't have made any difference. Knowing his friend's involvement with a married woman of Catherine's social status wouldn't have been well-looked upon. He couldn't have helped her, any more than she could've saved him from his execution.

He must put the past away. History couldn't be changed. April had read the last entry, now he wanted to find out about the day of his death.

"Did she have an entry in her journal for November 17th?"

~ ☾ ~

"Yes and no." April looked back and forth between Beth and James. He felt the uncertainty roll off her. This didn't bode well. Damn. The truth would either set him free or leave him to dwell in not knowing any more than they did now.

"Read the entry on my day of death," James ordered. He needed to know.

Wiping her hands on a napkin, April retrieved the book and gently flipped to the page. "Catherine didn't write on the night of your death, she wrote the following night. *Friday, November 18, 1774—I went to church this morning and prayed for James Addison to find peace in his final resting place. I will never forget the horror of last night when I learned the truth. Yesterday morning, Kings Mill buzzed with news of the traitor being held in the gaol. The name wasn't given to prevent family or friends from trying to break him free.*

I saw Daniel in town, frantically searching for James because he hadn't returned the previous night. A shipment of goods came in, and it wasn't like James not to sign for the parcels. I didn't think anything more about it until Henry dragged me to watch the execution across the street. So many people were shocked to hear Mr. Addison's name as the accused.

Henry forced me to watch. We stood on the outskirts of the crowds but within view of the tree and the horse with the man sitting atop, his head covered with a grain sack, his hands tied behind his back. Mr. Addison sat without fear, as if facing his maker with the pride of a man innocent. But I struggled. Henry said horrible things to me, gripping my face and accusing me of being James's lover. This would be my penance, to see an innocent man die a horrible death for my honor. I will live forever with the scene etched in my heart. Henry refused to listen to me as I cried, trying to explain James wasn't my lover, but he wouldn't hear it. I was weak. I needed to fight for the guiltless man and couldn't. This great shame I'll take with me to my grave. I only hope someday the truth will be told, and James Addison can rest knowing others are aware of his innocence."

~ ☾ ~

Beth shook her head as she wiped her lips. "My mind is overwhelmed. Kings Mill's history has exploded. This journal will bring out a whole new chapter to our legend, and a bit of truth. And it couldn't have happened at a better time, the anniversary of—" Beth stopped and gasped. "James, I'm sorry. I can't believe how insensitive I'm being. This Saturday night will be exactly two hundred thirty-eight years since your execution and now, I've hired you to portray yourself in the very role of your demise."

"I hired on knowing what you expected of me. I don't foresee a public display of an actual execution, so as long as it is pretend, I should be fine." James smiled wanly, trying to dispel some of Beth's angst. "Besides, it might be cathartic to relive the moment and know in my heart those who know me realize I'm innocent. I must say, no one will be able to play the part better than me."

"I'll have to agree there," Beth sighed with a bit of amusement and went to change the delicate subject. "Who's ready for their fortune cookie? I have a tradition. We have to interpret what our fortunes mean to us."

Unsure what a 'fortune cookie' was, James let April explain as he took a cellophane wrapped folded wafer from the small bowl Beth held out. Opening the package, he watched as April broke her cookie in half and pulled out a strip of paper. He did the same.

April smirked. "We'll let James go first since he's new to this."

"Very well." He took a deep breath. "It says, '*You will be wealthy above your monetary needs.*' Easy. I've seen what the power of wealth has done to some in my time. I think a man is truly wealthy when he considers the wealth of friends and family and the abundance of life around him."

"Spoken like a true gentleman, or a politician, not sure which," Beth laughed good-naturedly.

"All right, my dear Dr. Freelane, you are next if you are to be so bold," James chided.

"Mine says," she squinted to read it, retrieved her glasses, and chuckled, "well, so that is my problem!"

"What's it say?" April smiled.

~ ☾ ~

"It says, '*I will make a wonderful husband some day.*'"
Laughter and bawdy jabs were passed around the table.

"April, let's hear yours. You haven't even looked at it,"
Beth said as they settled down from her hysterical fortune.

"I always end up with weird ones that make absolutely no sense what-so-ever." She held up her small slip of paper and stared at it.

James began to worry. April's face paled and her hands shook slightly.

"Are you all right?" Beth leaned in, catching on to April's struggle. "What's it say?"

"It says—'*Believe in Fate.*'"

***

After dinner, April busied herself with her newfound evidence. She took pictures of the antique document and sent it immediately to Kenneth. She had to do something to keep reality in check. Her fortune was too coincidental. She wasn't sure if it angered her or frightened her. What was it about her and fate lately?

She emailed a copy of the photo along with texting him the message just to be sure he received it. It was two o'clock in the morning his time so she didn't expect an answer anytime soon. They talked briefly with Beth about the upcoming final day of the festivities. She wanted James to be active in town throughout the day, greeting visitors and guests, socializing with the merchants to get them to actively participate, too. April knew she wouldn't be able to do too much because Mr. Miles would be arriving sometime during the day. Her attention would be focused on him and trying to figure out a way to introduce him to James.

They arrived back at her aunt's late. Her mother and grandmother were already in bed and Aunt Vickie, engrossed in Jay Leno, couldn't be disturbed. *The Tonight Show* signaled her alone time. Besides, they wanted to sneak upstairs and enjoy celebrating the fact James was still here. After learning the truth about his death, he was still alive, flesh and blood.

"Come here," James said, holding out his arms for her. "What have you done to me? All I expected was to find out

~ ☾ ~

the truth about my death and move on. But you've given me a reason to want to live again," he whispered against her hair.

April snuggled into his chest, feeling the rapid staccato rhythm of his heart against her cheek. He pulled away from her just a bit to look down into her eyes. "Look at me."

Opening her eyes, she felt the heaviness of tears spill over onto her cheeks. She didn't want to cry. She was just so happy everything was over now. Trying for a smile, she was afraid it came out a bit wobbly.

"Do you believe in fate?"

"No," she spoke with finality, trying to pull out of his arms. *Please James, not you too—not now. I can't deal with this anymore.* He wouldn't let her go.

"Your aunt seems to think it has everything to do with how two people are aligned through time and space. You've listened to her talk about it. I believe, April! How can I not believe? Until you came along and were able to see me, hear me, and bring me to life, I was trapped in time, waiting for something to happen. Don't you understand? It's all so clear now. You were supposed to happen to me. Fate held me back, knowing it was just a matter of lining up our *time,* waiting for you and your wonderful gift to set me free."

"I don't know what I believe in, James." April sniffled back her tears, casting her eyes downward. "Things have been happening to me, around me, through me so much I just don't know. I've always believed we made our own decisions in life; each step, choosing or not choosing those open doors for us. It's all about what we do, not something as simple as 'fate.' There is no such thing."

"Then believe in this," he tilted her chin up, cupping her face in his hands. Holding her tenderly, she looked up at his face, "no matter what comes our way, I will love you forever, April Branford."

Kissing her mouth, he stopped her lips from trembling. Her hands settled on his chest, her hand lying tenderly over his pounding heart. James picked her up in his arms and settled her on the counterpane. Tonight, she would prove to him, with all of her heart, body and soul, she would never let him go. Fate be damned!

~ ☾ ~

***

James woke early Saturday morning. The day looked bright and sunny for a mid-November morning. He couldn't remember what kind of day it had been on the day of his execution. He never saw the outside. He'd been led from the dark, damp gaol out onto the streets with his head covered. He remembered a chill in the air but it could have been latent fear spreading through his soul, knowing what his fate would be once he'd been paraded in front of the crowds.

April's warm, naked body snuggling against him in exhaustion reminded him of where he was now. Wonderfully alive, sharing the present with a phenomenal woman who he knew to be his destiny. No other woman made him feel the internal pull of his heartstrings. If she'd been in his past, life might have been different for him. He thought about her residing in the manor house, bearing his children, working beside him through the day, loving him madly through the night.

He kissed her head. April gave a brief snort and rolled over to burrow down into the fluffy counterpane. James smiled and got up to prepare for his busy day. The schedule of his personal appearances for the festivities was overwhelming. A brief hour this morning would be all the free time he'd have.

Checking his colonial costume one last time for authenticity, he picked up his wallet and checked the bills he had tucked inside. It was enough for now. The small slip of paper fortune April had left behind at Beth's fell out. He bent and picked it up.

'*Believe in Fate.*' He did.

He'd picked up the fortune after April had wadded it up during their dinner. What did she have against fate?

Confronting her about her belief had been difficult but necessary. He wanted her to believe in something as great as what had happened between them. What other explanation could there be? Hopefully, someday she would see. And believe. He would find a way to make her believe, no matter what happened to them. Past, present or future, fate would bring them together. James tucked the piece of paper back into his wallet, blew his sleeping beauty a kiss across the

~ ☾ ~

room, and quietly walked out, closing the door behind him.

The household still slept. He would grab a bite at the café after he took care of his first private shopping trip in the modern world. With Christmas a month away, he needed to purchase the gift for April. He figured he'd be here to celebrate. Now that he was really alive, he wanted to start his plans for their future together. They would have a future. He knew it.

Things were looking up for him. After all of last night's reveals, Dr. Freelane had been excited about the changes his presence brought about. He'd received a bonus from Beth for what she considered hazardous duty for tonight's performance. She'd also offered him a part-time position providing tourism publicity as James Addison, along with a retainer fee to stay on as a historical reference to her research.

***

The tiny bell over the jeweler's door tinkled as he walked in. He'd been in the other day to look around.

"Ah, good morning, Mr. Addison." The jeweler smiled and bowed briefly at him.

"Good day, sir." He greeted with a flourish and doff of his tricorne hat. "I would like to see the ring I admired the other day." James peered down into the clear glass case filled with various rings.

"Yes, the princess cut emerald surrounded by diamonds." The man produced the ring, already nestled in a black velvet box.

James admired the simple yet elegant ring from every angle. The emerald glinted like April's eyes when they were full of passion. Like they had last night. She had been wild, trying to outdo herself with sensual fervor. He'd been enraptured and knew spending eternity with her would never be long enough. The sparkle of the gem made his breeches tighten in remembrance. The diamonds, small and simple but perfect in cut and clarity were his declaration of forever. The ad behind the store clerk stated, *diamonds are forever.* It proclaimed what he wanted with April. *Forever.*

"Is this the one?" the man asked politely.

~ ☾ ~

"Yes. I want to pay part now and the rest on your 'lay away' plan," James thought the idea of lay-away was perfect for his needs. Especially since he didn't know if he would be around come Christmas day. He only hoped he would be, but just in case.

Also, he didn't want to have the ring on him, tempting him to propose only to be rejected again. Hopefully by the time they celebrated he could convince April that fate meant for them to be together. Besides, the price was a little too expensive for his budget right now but with the pay he would be making, between now and then, he would have it paid off in time for Christmas.

"Very good, sir. Will this be credit?"

James paid in cash, the man wrote out a receipt for him, explaining he would have three months to pay the remainder and thanked him for his time. They talked about the day's activities leading up to the grand finale. James thanked the man, turned to leave, but stopped when he got to the door.

"One more thing," James said as he strode up to the counter again. "Do you have a piece of paper to leave a special note for my fiancée to go with the ring? I would like to capture my feelings on why I bought this ring for her today."

"Very romantic, Mr. Addison." The jeweler produced a small notepad and pen.

James smiled as he penned his thoughts for April to read on Christmas Eve when he intended to present her with the gift.

—The emerald represents the fiery passion in your eyes. The diamonds, one for every 'forever' I want to spend with you. The gold band represents how fate constantly circles to bring us together. Fate will always find us when our hearts lead the way. Merry Christmas, my love.

Yours for all time, J. A.

James opened his wallet, placed the small slip of paper fortune into the missive he'd just penned and folded the paper to fit inside the small ring box. Handing the box back to the salesman he doffed his hat again, wished him a good day's profit, and went out to greet his public. He couldn't wait for Christmas Eve.

~ ☾ ~

Chapter Twenty-Three

April rolled over, the sound of her cell phone ringing waking her up. Nine o'clock. She'd intended to sleep in until ten. She'd received an email from Kenneth shortly before going to bed. He'd been overjoyed at seeing the copy of James's deed and couldn't wait to tell her about his findings in London. His flight wouldn't be arriving until two o'clock her time. She had plenty of time.

Reaching for the phone she noted Dr. Moreland's name and number on the caller ID.

"Hello?" she greeted groggily.

"April, turn on the news!"

"What?" She rubbed her eyes and looked around. She didn't have a television up here. "Wait a minute, let me get my laptop. Why, what's going on?"

"I can't believe it...it's Kenneth..."

Oh great. "What's he bought now? Microsoft, our national debt...what?"

She waited for her laptop to boot as silence and deep sighs answered her. "Bob, what is it? Just tell me."

Her internet server page came up. The headline read, *Financial Mogul in Car Accident. Critical Condition.* "Oh my God! No." She scanned the article. Kenneth Miles had been on his way to Heathrow when the Bentley he was riding in was struck broadside by a truck. The official report didn't look promising. He'd been rushed to Ashford & St. Peters Hospital where he was listed in critical condition.

April surfed the net, looking at every news source available. All said the same thing, and the financial networks were already beginning to panic. They were wondering what his condition would mean for all of his investors. She didn't care about that. She was more concerned about the man.

~ ☾ ~

"Have you heard any word from his associates?" April asked Bob as they talked about the news.

"Nothing yet. They have my number, but I don't think we are high on their list of priorities right now. I'll let you know if I hear anything."

"Please do. I'll pass the word along here. With the event going on, I'm not sure Dr. Freelane has been keeping an eye on the news."

They said goodbye and hung up. April continued to check out all the news sites, but nothing more was revealed. She hoped he would be okay. Even though she hadn't met him face to face, they had been working closely together for the past couple of weeks. She sent a silent prayer for his recovery.

***

Sitting in the parlor of the historical society townhouse, April watched James prepare for his final performance of the day. She shared the news with him about Kenneth.

"I do hope he'll be all right. It would have been nice to meet him today, but perhaps it is better not to—until I can figure out how to introduce myself as his great-great-great uncle. For all I know, he might have me committed," James said with a wan smile.

The smile faltered and he weaved wearily on his feet. "Are you all right? You look pale," April asked, steadying him by reaching out and grabbing his arm. He pulled away abruptly out of her touch.

"I'm about to replay my execution," he said tersely adjusting the plain collar of the linen shirt, slightly dirty and mussed for authenticity. "What did you think, my love? That I would walk to this event carefree and easy?"

April hung her head. She wasn't thinking. "No."

James sighed and kneeled down in front of her. He touched her cheek, caressing a finger along her lips. "I'm sorry, lass. Forgive me. I guess I'm just nervous and a bit out of sorts."

She smiled weakly and turned her lips into his palm. His usual warmth was missing tonight. His hand felt cool and clammy. "You have every right to be, James. I should know. You don't have to do this. I never want you to have

~ ☾ ~

to face your nightmare again."

"I promised Dr. Freelane I would. It's my job, just as yours was to face your ghosts for me. This is something I need to do so I can move on."

April's heart clenched. Move on as in death? No. She wouldn't allow it. "—so we can move on with our life, together," she corrected.

His forced smile tried to reassure her, but something was wrong, she felt it like an ominous presence resting over them.

"Of course. That is what I meant."

She touched his face lovingly as if checking for fever. He looked tired, exhausted. "James, I think you might be coming down with something. You're not feeling well, are you?"

"Probably just tired." He tapped her nose playfully. "You kept me up for quite awhile last night."

"Yes, I did. You were 'up' for hours."

Laughing at the sexual innuendo helped to break the tension of the impending moment. The plodding clop of horses' hooves echoed outside on the cobbled streets. April went to the window and looked out. A black steed was being led to the curb.

"My ride's here." James tried to sound jovial as he stood. "How do I look?"

"Handsome and innocent," April said trying hard not to break down and cry for him. She would have never been able to know him centuries ago and bear witness to this event.

"Will you be there for me when this is all over with tonight?" he asked.

"James, I will always be there for you."

***

April stood with her family and Beth near the staging area of the execution. The crowds had been gathering in the city park for over an hour, waiting for the actual event. Many had dressed up in period costume, carrying old-fashioned tin lanterns. Bonfires and burning pitch pots illuminated the streets like a colonial village night. People huddled around them with their cups of cider and hot cocoas from local eateries staying open late to cash in on the mass of extra consumers. April felt a chill not associated with the night

~ ☾ ~

course through her as she watched James being led to his
execution just like two-hundred thirty-eight years ago.

Her mother hugged her shoulders as they huddled front
and center to see James's approach. She needed the strength.
After having witnessed the scene only the other day by
touching the tree, it seemed eerily familiar. She didn't know
what James could be feeling, but her heart ached anyway.

"He looks so formal," Beth whispered to her in awe.
"Remind me to give him a raise when we get the grant money.
He's doing a great job, considering what he must be going
through."

As all the players came onto the stage, April noted the
proud carriage Beth spoke of. James sat as she had
remembered in her ghostly vision just days ago. Drums
played a tattoo. Even though April didn't remember a
drummer being there, it added a dramatic touch. A priest
stepped forward and gave last rights to the victim, spouting
verse and lecture to fit the crime.

"Wait!" a breathless, feminine voice called out above the
hush of the crowd.

Murmurs of confusion and interest sparked the night.

"Stop!" the voice continued to cry out.

April looked to Beth to see what was going on. Beth
seemed just as baffled as everyone else.

A woman dressed in colonial attire ran forward, her
blonde hair askew as the heavy woolen hood of her cape
slipped to her shoulders. "He's innocent! You can't execute
him for any crime." Her voice, breathless and urgent rang out
through the crowd. "Henry Samuel accuses this man of
treason against the crown, but James Addison is an
upstanding citizen and honest merchant."

The crowds rumbling grew louder, people looked at each
other, perplexed. April turned to her mother, grandmother,
and aunt as they all tried to gauge the reaction of the crowd.

She looked just like Catherine Samuel! The girl
represented her ghostly heroine perfectly. April studied her
appearance. A flash of silver hung from the open folds of her
cloak and skirt. She even wore a reproduction of the
chatelaine. Wow! Talk about detail.

~ ☾ ~

"Well now, young lady, and who might you be?" The man playing the part of the executioner stepped forward, looking confused as if expecting someone to explain a change of script.

"I'm Henry's wife, Catherine Samuel, and I want you to let this man go!"

"Do you have proof of Mr. Addison's innocence?"

"The only proof I have is Mr. Addison's loyalty to his King and country. My husband is accusing this man without a trial so he can obtain his lands. Henry has been trying to acquire Mr. Addison's mill for some time."

There were murmurs among the attendees. The crowd seemed confused and excited by the turn of events. April knew this wasn't the normal program they were used to. Stepping closer to the staged area, she studied the young actress closely. Then the most amazing thing happened, Catherine's re-enactor stepped closer to her, as if seeking her out and began talking directly to her.

"The governor has suspicion of Henry cheating the good people of Kings Mill out of their property. Henry's ledgers show his lack of revenue and purchase of deeds from those who he's wronged. Some of the ledgers were destroyed, but the ones that remain show proof of my husband's deeds. The truth is in the numbers."

April's jaw trembled as the young girl held her stance. Her dialog finished with dramatic pause. Gasping, April finally realized the girl wasn't a re-enactor at all. This was the real Catherine Samuel standing before them. She'd somehow found a way from Henry's grasp tonight and was brave enough to tell the story to free James from dying yet again.

April nodded solemnly, letting Catherine know she understood what she was saying. Clapping her hands as if honoring an opera diva for her aria, April turned her attention onto the performance, playing along as if it were all part of the act. Others began to applaud along with her, until it was a standing ovation. She wasn't honoring her performance. She was honoring the woman's strength. Catherine stood proud, her head regal instead of bent in fear of reprisal. With hands firmly planted on her hips she

~ ☾ ~

awaited the executioner's next move.

But both April and Catherine paused as another voice broke out among the crowd. Costumed in common workman's clothing and a tattered leather tricorne, he hopped up effortlessly onto the stage next to Catherine.

April gasped. "Daniel."

Her grandmother turned to her and looked back to the stage in wonder.

"D...Daniel?" Beth asked, her voice shaking. She had finally picked up on what was going on.

"The lady is right! What say the villagers of Kings Mill? Should we let this man go? Let the colonists speak! This is your town, your fellow colonist being accused without a trial! Your voices need to be heard." The man began to chant, "Free him! Free him!"

A wide roar of 'aye' broke through the crowds. People chanted to let James go. The mob became excited as they got into character, adding their part to the festive scene, righting the wrongs of history through this simple adaptation. Catherine and Daniel stood on stage stomping their feet, rallying the crowds until the executioner shrugged and untied James.

Nearly in tears, April watched as Catherine and Daniel went to stand beside James. Catherine took the hood from his head and smiled at him. His dazed expression latched onto the two figures before him. A look of bewilderment and complete and utter astonishment highlighted his face. April fought back a sob. Her poor beloved ghost looked close to fainting.

"Is that the real Catherine up there?" Beth asked as the shock of what they had just witnessed actually registered.

"Oh yes, *that* is really Catherine." April grinned past the tears of joy. James was alive and receiving congratulations from the other actors on his part.

"And Daniel, too?" her mother added, trying to smile. But a tight grimace of pain creased her brow.

"Migraine," Aunt Vickie said as she nodded towards Virginia. "The ghosts of the past, there are so many here tonight. She can't concentrate."

~ ☾ ~

April looked around at the crowds and wondered how many of the people were modern citizens in costume, and how many were actual ghosts.

"I think I'll call it a night and try to sleep this one off." Her mother nodded slightly.

"Do you want us to go with you, Virginia?"

"No, Mom, you and Aunt Vickie go enjoy yourselves. I know you wanted to join in the fun at O'Toole's Pub. And you," she turned towards April, with a faint smile, "have fun with James as he celebrates his new life. He's waiting for you." Her mother gave her a hug. "I'm so proud of you, April."

April returned the hug, holding on for more moments than either one remembered in their past. "Thanks Mom, I'm proud of you, too."

Hugging her family and thanking them for all of their help, she made her way through the crowd towards James. Catherine and Daniel were gone. They must be among the citizens of Kings Mill, celebrating in their own way. Or they could have finally moved on, now that they were able to face their fears and speak up in truth.

***

April barely made it on stage before James wrapped her in his arms. She was his rock. His life giving energy. He was alive but the terror of facing the night, even a re-enactment of it had made him nauseous. The heavy fear of having no control again while he'd been tied on the back of the horse had hit him as if it were all really happening again.

It wasn't until he'd heard Catherine's voice coming out of the dark terror that he knew this time history wouldn't repeat itself. Still his body trembled. Seeing the ghosts of his past interacting with the present, he'd wanted to reach out and hold them but couldn't gather his wits in time before they left. Daniel had given him a small salute and Catherine had smiled warmly at him before they'd merged into the hundreds of people gathered for the event.

"James, you look like you're about to pass out. Sit down before you fall." April made him sit on one of the nearby benches. A few people passed by, congratulating him on a job well done. He'd nodded and thanked them, giving a brief

~ ☾ ~

wave. But his heart wasn't into the celebratory atmosphere right now.

"April, dear," he heard Aunt Vickie call out as the crowds dissipated, "Is James all right?"

James tried to put on a cheerful face for her family. But the dizziness left him feeling weak. He'd hoped to feel better after all of this. Now he was sure he might be coming down with something like April had said. "I'm fine."

"April will take care of you. We'll meet you at the pub. It might be a good idea for you to make the rounds with the town folk tonight."

Nodding, April waved them on. "Thanks. We'll check on Mom first. I'm sure James will want to tour the tavern to offer a toast to the town's people for their sense of justice tonight." April smiled at him. Her eyes misted with a sheen of tears.

James took her hand and kissed her palm. Feeling weak, his vision blurring, he didn't want to ruin April's night. He would buck up soon. Beth arrived with a couple of cups of coffee moments later as they sat alone, trying to regain their composure.

"You did good, kid." Beth handed him a cup. "You okay?"

Managing a brief nod he took a sip of the hot, bitter liquid. It wasn't his tea, but anything was welcomed right now.

James looked at Beth, he knew without her speaking the words what she wanted to know. She was still stunned by everything. "Yes, believe it or not, that was actually Catherine and my foreman Daniel Smith."

Beth stared at him as if he'd grown an extra head. "I couldn't believe it when April told me...but really, Catherine and Daniel—the lovers from the journal?" her voice trembled. "Oh dear God, now I've seen everything!"

"You're not going to faint again are you?" he asked.

Beth laughed nervously. "So you're saying what happened really wasn't part of the skit?" She blew out a breath. "Well, they did get the crowds to participate and put everyone in a festive mood. I think I'll keep it for next year's celebration."

A sudden chill enveloped them. James felt it go through him, literally. April backed away to check out the night sky.

~ ☾ ~

Tree branches twisted and crackled as the wind picked up. Standing up, his body felt light and weightless. James realized it was him. Something was happening to him.

No! Not now! He couldn't be phasing back into a ghost. He couldn't!

"What's going on? Are we in for a storm?" April asked, checking out her surroundings. Littered programs and random trash left on the grounds twirled in the strong breeze. The bonfires fluttered and sparked. People on the streets held onto one another, bracing against the sudden blast of air.

"How odd? The weather forecast wasn't calling for any heavy winds," Beth said.

"Fire! Hey—there's a fire over here!" someone yelled from a group of straggling visitors. Confusion and chaos ensued as people gathered at the backside of the county courthouse, just feet away. In the distance the blare of fire trucks could be heard, the sound growing louder.

They went to see what was going on. James tried to reach out to April, but he knew it wouldn't matter. He was afraid she wouldn't be able to feel it.

Now? After all I've been through? Now I'm moving on? I haven't had time to say good-bye to April!

The atmosphere around him sparked with electrical currents. April gave him a puzzling look as she reached for him but he stepped away. He didn't want to alarm her if he was phasing back into his former self.

His hands felt clammy and he stumbled. He shook his head and blinked a couple of times to clear his vision. Trying to blame it on the exhaustion and emotional turmoil from the day's activities, he focused on holding onto the present.

April tried to touch him again and he side-stepped. She dropped her hand, but her eyes misted over. He thought she knew or sensed the change, but she was trying to deny the truth as long as possible, like he was. "You're not all right, are you James?"

The smell of musky smoke hit him before they saw the red-orange licks of flame and gray billows as they rounded the back side of the courthouse.

"Oh God! April, your Aunt's house is on fire!" Beth gasped

~ ☾ ~

and stopped suddenly in shock at seeing the old colonial house ablaze. April ran past her at breakneck speed, straight for the house.

"No!" April screamed, racing up the steps of the burning house and straight into danger. "My Mom's inside!"

In his impetuousness, James couldn't stop his momentum and shimmered right through Beth on his way to save April from her foolishness. No one saw him run into the burning house.

~ ☾ ~

Chapter Twenty-Four

James's heart stopped when April raced into the burning house. As usual she didn't stop to think. Flames were already licking out the windows and roof like angry serpent tongues. James called out to her, but his voice sounded distant, even to him. He ran after her, a sense of weightlessness settling into him.

Plumes of smoke billowed in gusts as if the old house was alive and exhaling. The activity behind him was a mass of chaos, but he didn't catch any of it as he focused on reaching April. Fire had already settled into the parlor and flames were emerging from the butler's pantry. He should feel the heat. Why wasn't it affecting him? Popping glass and crackling wood caught his attention. One of her aunt's china hutches in the parlor blazed, the glass knick-knacks exploding. Thankfully, the stairs were still whole. He raced up them, only steps away from April.

He could hear her coughing and gasping for air. He had to get her out before the house caved in or she died of smoke inhalation. He reached her side but when he grabbed her arm, his hand went right through her.

Dear God! Not now, just a little more time?

The doorway to their room was in flames. Fire poured out as pieces of old timber and plaster walls fell. The blaze had already eaten through Catherine's room. He wasn't worried about the rooms. They needed to get her mother out. He knew April wouldn't leave without her. But he was afraid he was unable to help. He stood in front of April, between her and the door to her mother's room.

"April, get the hell out of here!"

"My mother's in there and I'm not leaving until she's safe!" She yelled back as squeals of blazing timbers echoed around

~ ☾ ~

them. The door was cool but locked. April beat on the door.
"Mom! Open up! Fire!"

"Move out of the way!"

James shouldered his way into the wooden door and his
body went straight through. He'd already phased. He heard
April scream his name. He knew this wouldn't end well but
he needed to get to Virginia before April died trying to save
her. Damn her for rushing head long into danger!

The room was strangely untouched by the fire. Virginia
crouched in the corner in satin pajamas, fighting against the
force field holding her in place. Henry Samuel stood there in
a ghostly form, holding Virginia around the throat, pressing
tightly against her windpipe, choking her. His other hand
wielded a flaming fire poker, and he waved it around as
James approached.

Henry's paranormal energies couldn't hold both forces. He
released April's mother. James watched her fall helplessly to
the floor as she struggled for breath. He reached for Virginia's
hand to help her up but realized she couldn't see him now he
had no solid form. But she would be able to hear him, if she
could focus.

Fire leapt from the poker Henry waved, trying to attack
him, catching the ends of the filmy window sheers. The
pristine room would be an inferno in seconds. James was
racing against time.

"Virginia," he said, hoping for a connection. "It's me
James. I need you to get April out of here. Tell her I love her
and I will find a way to be with her again. Now go!" James
said with flat finality.

Virginia nodded, her eyes widening with realization. Her
face clouded with anguish. James heard the wailing of more
sirens in the distance. She needed to get out.

"Go now, Virginia. Get April to safety."

The fire spread into the hallway. He could hear April
banging on the door, pleading and crying for him and her
mother as the flames leapt dangerously close.

James made sure Virginia got out and waited until he saw
her push April towards the stairs.

"Go April, I'm right behind you!" he heard Virginia yell

~ ☾ ~

over the sounds of screeching wood.

"James! Where is James?" April cried out, trying to fight her mother's manipulations.

"April go!" James shouted as his body was held back, snagged by some unknown force. The momentum of being pulled back turned him around. Henry's beefy face was mere inches from his own. James felt the force of Henry's fist strike across the jaw. Sprawling on the floor at the top of the stairs, he didn't have enough energy to right himself.

Fire fighters ran up the stairs, passed through his and Henry's souls on the way to Virginia's room. They were looking for him. He'd heard April's desperate cries as she'd called out his name while her mother had dragged her to safety. Not seeing anyone else in the rooms, the firefighters called 'all clear' and evacuated the house.

Heavy sprays of water flooded the remaining structure from the various hoses, but James paid no heed. It didn't matter.

"You blue-blooded bastard! I thought I had gotten rid of you once. Well now we are on equal ground. Welcome to Hell!" Henry spat out, yanking James up by his collar.

James feigned defeat until he was level with Henry. Pulling his fist back, he landed a right hook to Henry's nose, sending the older man reeling back. Yeah, they were on equal ground. It was Hell all right. Two ghosts fighting in a raging fire neither one felt.

Struggling to regain his footing, James weakened even further. Was this it? Was this him finally moving on? Why now! Why hadn't it happened sooner—or later? What piece of the puzzle was finally in place for him to leave this Earth completely? Henry ran at him and grabbed him around the middle, pinning him up against the burning wall behind them.

"Because of your lady-friend, my historical bearing in Kings Mill is going to be questioned. She made Catherine work against me. I wanted your mill and I would have had it, too. Now, I will be the laughing stock—" Henry stopped and looked to his left. His eyes rounded.

James looked, too. There, a few feet away was the image of

~ ☾ ~

Catherine. Her pristine figure stood straight and tall. With her shoulders back, she glared at Henry.

"Remember me, dear husband?"

"Catherine! It was you! You killed me!" Henry bellowed at the ghost.

"No. I would have if I had the same courage Dr. Branford showed me. No, it was your own fear of seeing my ghost that sent you tumbling down those stairs all those years ago. Don't go blaming anyone but yourself, Henry. You did this. It was because of you we've all been trapped for so long. Dr. Branford has shown me I can move past my fear of you to move on to a better life."

Henry let James go and stalked towards the figure of his wife. "I'll never let you move on. You belong to me, Catherine!"

Fear and uncertainty clouded Catherine's delicate face. James didn't want to see her fear anymore. She deserved to move on, too. Henry was such a bastard! James jumped the man from behind but sifted right through Henry's soul. Lying on the floor, covered with flames, he stared at his own vanishing form. He wasn't even able to see all of himself now.

But the distraction was all Catherine needed to move out of the way. Henry lurched forward, and screaming in agony, tumbled head first down the staircase, landing with a sickening thud at the base of the stairs in a hellish inferno.

"Catherine—" he found the last dregs of energy to stand up among the fire and burning embers, but there was nothing left of his form, only a sense of being.

"It's all right, James. Henry is where he needs to be now. I can move on. Thank April for me." She smiled.

It was becoming more difficult to see and function. The image of the fire was dying around him, being replaced by white, sterile walls and a bright light shining in his face. Catherine's image faded into the background. "I can't. I'm gone. I'll never see April again." His voice came out in a strangled sob.

He heard Catherine's faint, tinkling laughter. Why was she laughing at his peril?

"What? I thought you believed in fate? This isn't death,

~ ☾ ~

James...it's just the beginning of your new life."

Was she mocking him? Damn! His head hurt. Why did his head hurt? He shouldn't feel any pain. He was dead. Brightness surrounded him. Was this the light he was supposed to move into? Images faded into the light. He was no longer in the burning house. Had April and her mother gotten out safely? Where was Catherine? A figure moved towards him into the brightness surrounding them both. A man's figure—but it wasn't Henry. This man was taller, leaner. He walked with purpose as he approached and instead of going around James, walked right through him.

What the bloody hell?

His question went unanswered. He heard himself scream as he felt his chest explode from within. Electronic beeps echoed in his head, and then he heard a subtle thumping, like a heartbeat. A group of people with masks over their faces stood around him as the brilliant light faded to a glare of intense artificial light from lamps hanging above his head. One person stared down at him with wide-eyed wonder.

"Doctor, I have a pulse!"

***

Standing at the small pauper's grave stone, April gave her power one last chance. Kneeling with her hands flat on his tombstone, she focused on finding James's essence. But like every other day over the past few weeks, nothing happened. No matter what she did she couldn't bring James back to life. His spirit wasn't here. Her gift no longer worked. Throwing herself onto his stone she pressed her cheek against the cold, hard marble, letting her tears and anguish take over again.

What was wrong with her? Why couldn't she feel him anymore? Her heart constricted painfully. Why couldn't she have died in the fire, too? Where was all the live energy she'd had only weeks ago when she'd met him? The only time she felt any connection to the past was when she read Catherine's journal. But those memories brought on heartache all over again. She couldn't even find Catherine anymore. There were no more ghostly visions, no more haunted house, nothing to connect to.

The fire inspector had claimed faulty wiring as the cause of

~ ☾ ~

the fire. But she knew differently. It was the ghost of Henry
Samuel who'd started it. He'd been trying to get to Catherine
and kill her spirit. She'd angered him by revealing his secrets
at the festivities. Aunt Vickie was able to discern at least a
portion of information when she'd studied the remains from
the fire. She'd sensed Catherine was no longer there and
Henry was where he needed to be.

Thanksgiving had come and gone. Beth invited her entire
family over for dinner before April's mom went back home to
her condo in Rockville. Grandma Dottie invited Aunt Vickie
to stay with her in her riverfront home in Annapolis. April
was staying with Beth until she could figure out what to do
next. The Kings Mill historical society was going through
many changes, and Beth needed an extra hand, desperately.
There was so much left to do. Too much for one person to get
the new historical society opened by the first of the year. Beth
hired her on to help record information and make final
preparations.

Working at the Historical Society was the only thing
keeping April from feeling empty. The remaining ledgers
they'd found in the crates of historical documents belonged to
Henry Samuel. They were exactly as Catherine stated the
night of the festival—*the truth was in the numbers*, or lack
thereof, as the case ended up being. Henry's funds had
dwindled in games of chance and risky investing. The only
way he could have gotten the land was by stealing it, or doing
what he'd done to James and others over the years.

But some good came from her research. Catherine's
journal was a font of information. Catherine had given birth
to a child who'd lived. As Beth researched indentured files in
the southern counties of Maryland, she realized she may have
been a descendant of Catherine and Daniel's child. The
connection made perfect sense to Dr. Freelane, and she took
the knowledge as gospel.

Beth now had a new historical subject to research.
Catherine's plight as an indentured servant had inspired Dr.
Freelane to begin documenting the lives of early colonial
servants along the Chesapeake. April hoped to be able to shed
more light for her through the journal but there wasn't much

~ ℂ ~

to go on. Still, Beth hoped to one day have the opportunity to meet the ghost of Catherine Samuel personally. April didn't hold out much hope. She was sure all her ghosts had moved on.

April dried her tears on her already tear-soaked knit gloves wadded up in her hands. Kissing her fingers with trembling lips, she placed the tips to James's stone. Sighing, she knew it was a lost cause to try and hope for James to return to her. But hope was all she had. And lately, it was diminishing. Looking up she realized the sky had turned overcast while she was here. *Like my soul?* Now huge snowflakes the size of breadcrumbs began to fall. Reluctantly, she turned away and walked back to the office.

"It's about time you showed up!" Dr. Moreland greeted her as she walked into the Historical Society, shaking snow from her cap and coat before hanging them on the coat rack.

"Dr. Moreland," April replied with a brief smile.

"You do know we are on equal terms now. You can call me, Bob."

"Old habits." She shrugged. "It's good to see you. What brings you to Kings Mill?"

They'd spoken only briefly since he'd called her with the news of Kenneth Miles's accident. He'd called upon hearing from one of Mr. Miles's representatives that Kenneth would be postponing his trip until a later time. *Well, yeah.* The man had suffered severe head trauma and had been pronounced dead during an emergency operation. April didn't think he would be very active in such a short amount of time.

In the past few weeks, the news followed the medical reports of his miraculous return. Even the doctors were stunned at the rapid rate of his recovery, saying it was Kenneth's own determination moving him on. All April knew was she'd seen his stocks fish-flop due to the uncertainty of his health. The media reported the NYSE had his secretary and account reps on speed dial.

Dr. Moreland placed a finger to his lips. "I have some exciting news, but I wanted to wait for Beth before I announced it. She's coming down in a minute."

Beth walked down the stairs and made an entrance. And

~ ☾ ~

what an entrance she made. Her normal neutral business attire was replaced with a pair of casual, flowing black slacks, a deep teal silk blouse, and waterfall-style sweater. This accented the silver blonde crop of hair she'd styled recently into a short, pixie cut framing her long, narrow face beautifully. April raised her brow in amazed appreciation. The look Bob gave her and the slight blush Beth returned told April all she needed to know. Something was going on between the two. More than just a visit from a professional colleague was accounting for the 'new look.'

"So what's the news?" April asked, eager to find out why Bob was so excited about sharing news he'd waited this long to tell them. She could see by the way Beth was dressed they had plans for later. Dinner maybe? She felt bad for not knowing what was going on in Beth's life. She'd been so wrapped up with her own. Still, all she wanted to do was return to her desk and finish her work today, before she left for her small bedroom to face another night without James. She wasn't the best company lately. *Gee, I wonder why!*

"Sit down. This news is so big, you've got to be sitting to hear it," Robert Moreland gushed in excitement. He was not typically a gusher, so unless he'd found the Holy Grail, unearthed Atlantis, or located the Fountain of Youth there wouldn't be much for him to be excited about.

"Kings Mill Historical Society is getting a million dollar donation!"

She and Beth looked at the man as if he'd just grown another head and replied simultaneously, "Get outta town!" and "You're full of crap!"

"Nope." Bob reached into his breast pocket with a grin on his face and pulled out a folded piece of letterhead. "Guess who it's from?"

"Bill Gates? He would be one of the only ones who might be able to," April said with jaundiced surprise, getting an eye roll from Bob. "I give up, who?"

"None other than Kenneth Miles, and he's coming to present it himself next week."

"Miles is making his grand entrance back into society in Kings Mill, Maryland?" Beth gasped.

~ ☾ ~

"Read it for yourselves. I received this letter yesterday and called to confirm. I talked with his secretary this morning." Unfolding it, he handed it to Beth. "It's real."

"Oh my God! Oh my God!" Beth read the paper thoroughly, as color drained her cheeks. She gasped. "April, we have a million dollar grant to make plans for."

~ ☾ ~

Chapter Twenty-Five

James Addison stood in front of a full-length mirror, primped and prepared to meet the public for the first time since the accident. He smoothed back his short, dark hair, much shorter than he ever wore it, but a more professional style according to the latest in men's fashion.

It had all been a bit convoluted, coming out of a near death experience and awakening in a stranger's body. But then, he'd been without a body for a long time. It wasn't until he'd met April Branford that he'd felt whole again. His heart thudded excitedly in his chest. He would see her today. After nearly a month of recovery, he'd be with her again. It was the ability to see her that put him in the frame of mind to recover as quickly as he did.

"Your car is waiting, Mr. Miles."

"Thank you, Peter." He turned to his assistant Drew, who was taking a small lint brush to his suit coat still hanging on the hook. "Is everything in my briefcase?"

"Yes sir. I have the check and blueprints for the proposal to the site in there." Drew came around with his coat and carefully helped him into it, taking care of his healing body.

Some days the aches and pains from the injuries of the car accident slowed him down. He didn't want today to be one of those days.

"Good." James grabbed the classic, silver-tipped walking stick he'd purchased to replace the cane the hospital had provided. His leg was still not healed completely, but a few more months of physical therapy should suffice.

"You need to take it easy while here, sir," Drew commented. "The doctor didn't think you should've taken this trip."

"Are you judging my decisions, Drew?" He adjusted the

~ ☽ ~

collar on his coat and pulled at his sleeves to keep everything from bunching. "I need to be here. I owe it to Kings Mill and Dr. Branford for her research."

He did. Not as James Addison, but as Kenneth Miles. He owed more to April Branford than he could ever repay with his millions. It was still difficult at times to distinguish between who he was and who he had been. He was James Addison. All of his memories were of James Addison, from his time in the 1700's to his brief encounter with the present shared with April.

But a great part of him was still Kenneth Miles. It was as if he were both men in one body. It had taken him time to come to terms with what had happened. But he knew that fate had played her role. In a time when James Addison was due to finally move on, his descendant was scheduled to die. Perhaps it was meant to be—perhaps it was coincidence. But the timing of the souls merging into one man's body couldn't have been planned by anyone but fate. Weren't those the last words Catherine had said to him?

The limo awaited him outside the hotel. It was the same hotel he'd shared with April the night when Henry had angrily forced them out of the house. He swore they would share one of the suites again soon and continue where they'd left off.

They passed by Lilac Grove Cemetery on the way into downtown Kings Mill. It was Kenneth's first time here, but James felt as if it were only yesterday that he'd been walking the streets aimlessly, searching for the truth and someone to give a damn. He'd found it all in one woman. His heart quickened and he took a deep breath to calm the excitement coursing through him. It wouldn't be long now. The driver pulled up to the side of the courthouse and James looked out at the grounds.

A small group of reporters from Washington D.C. and Baltimore, along with CNN, Fox, CSPAN, and other national and international media were in attendance, their vans parked in various areas blocking the daily traffic. It was to be expected. This was Kenneth Miles's first appearance in public since the accident and a rare appearance in general. Whereas

~ ☾ ~

after centuries alone, James enjoyed greeting people, Kenneth abhorred the masses.

Peter opened the door for him, helping him out as Drew handled the crowds gathering at breakneck speed, wanting the first glimpse and exclusives. James buttoned his long wool overcoat around him. Peter held a black umbrella over his head as a light sifting of snow began to fall.

"I want to take a minute to check something out, Peter." James walked without a response from the man as he went in the opposite direction from the crowds of reporters.

Aunt Vickie's house had been behind the county building. He'd walked these streets the first night meeting April, taking her home. He turned the corner to see the skeletal remains of what had once been a historical, stately home. Now it was just a pile of rubble and memories with the woman he loved. A small yellow earthmover and bulldozer stood silent sentry around the taped off area. Charred support beams and brick chimneys were all that remained. "Sir?"

He looked at Peter. The man questioned him with the simple word. "I'm fine. Shall we proceed to the ceremony? I think there is a back way into this building where we can avoid much of the media. Notify Drew to meet us in there."

***

All week long Beth had run them ragged, and Dr. Moreland had finished up his end of term classes in Williamsburg early so he could help them. It was a good thing he did. By Tuesday, the day before Kenneth was to arrive, April didn't have the energy she needed to keep up with her normal workload, much less the extra push Beth put on her. It took her hours to fall asleep, and once she did, she found it difficult to wake up.

Mourning James was the culprit. How could she have fallen so hard and fast for a man? She hadn't felt this deflated and morose over her break up with Jason, and they had shared two years as a couple.

The morning of Kenneth's arrival, Kings Mill was teeming with activity. The phones hadn't stopped ringing as news of Kenneth Miles's arrival had leaked out to the public. Like members of the Secret Service, they could neither confirm

~ ☾ ~

nor deny anything about him coming to Kings Mill or the donation until the actual ceremony in the historical courthouse.

April splashed water on her face again to help wake her up. The small mirror in the bathroom of the old building didn't reveal her best self. She was supposed to represent the historical society. She'd played a big role in recent historical research. But she didn't feel presentable. Her wan cheeks wouldn't look good for the cameras. She tried to add a hint of pink lipstick to give them a fresh healthy glow but it only made her look washed out *and* pink. It was winter. She was in hibernation mode and moody. So it only figured her complexion would reflect dreariness.

"It's about time you came out," Beth scolded as she emerged from the bathroom. "Mr. Miles is in with the County Commissioners and Board of Directors right now. They'll call us in soon." She lowered her voice to a whisper. "Bob will be doing the introductions since he was the one to connect Kenneth with Kings Mill."

April only nodded. This was the man she was supposed to have shared a celebratory dinner with five weeks ago. Had it only been five weeks? Lately it felt like forever since the night. It was ironic how everything came together in a neat circle. Fate was funny.

No, she didn't believe in fate! She might believe in ghosts, but fate? How could she when nothing would bring James back to her. *Where was fate now, James?* She wanted to be angry and 'fate' was as good a scapegoat as any. She didn't believe, so what did it matter.

She yawned and tried to stifle the embarrassing gesture as media from Washington D.C./Baltimore and even some national news agencies were milling about in the narrow lobby of the two hundred fifty year old building.

"What is wrong with you lately? Well, besides the obvious. You're tired all the time and you look like death warmed over," Beth asked quietly from the side of her mouth.

"Gee. Thanks."

"Dr. Freelane, Dr. Branford, they're ready for you now. Please follow me." The publicity assistant escorted them to

~ ☾ ~

the side door to receive the large display check for the grant
and greet the man of the hour.

"How do I look?" Beth paused, taking a deep breath and
adjusting her new lime green suit.

"Well, you're not tired, and you don't look like death warmed
over," April mocked before she sighed impatiently. "You look
fine. Let's get this over with so I can go home and sleep."

They stepped into the room. April followed a few steps
behind. She smiled and walked in front of the reporters and
cameras. Beth came to an abrupt halt halfway across the floor
in front of the governor, mayor, aldermen, and county
officials sitting up on their dais. Hearing Dr. Freelane's gasp,
she was afraid her friend was going to faint.

Dr. Moreland was doing the honors of introducing the two
parties. April couldn't see around Beth so she stood where
she was. Bob announced her name as being an instrumental
part of the James Addison research project. Her heart
somersaulted at the mention of James's name.

Don't cry now, April.

Beth moved to the side. April pasted on her best fake smile
for the cameras as Kenneth Miles stepped forward. Her heart
literally stopped for a brief second as she looked up into
familiar steel gray eyes. He brought her hand to his lips and
brushed a kiss over her knuckles. "It's a pleasure to finally
make your acquaintance, Dr. Branford."

She swore the man standing before her was James.
Everything about him was James incarnate. Every minute
detail reminded her of James. Then—*everything* went black.

***

Her hand hurt. April tried to open her eyes but felt so
weak. Why did her hand hurt? She opened her eyes half-mast
and looked about. She was in a hospital room. Fresh flowers
in a vase sat beside the bed on a bed tray, a Mylar balloon
read *Get Well Soon*. She looked down at her left hand and
saw a tube connected to a needle in her hand and a bag of
saline IV solution on a computerized stand. A nurse was
checking the instrumentation and changing the bag.

"It's about time you woke up." A blurry face leaned over
her. "How are you feeling?"

~ ☾ ~

"Ask me again in the morning."

Confusion and disorientation warred within her as she tried to rouse herself from a lethargic fog. Her eyes came into focus. Dr. Moreland leaned over her, his smile warm and casual. Looking around she noticed the room was dark and still, except for the blinking lights from her IV monitor. The nurse smiled and said she'd be back to check on her in an hour.

Bob Moreland went to the window on the far side of the room and pulled back the heavy, institutional drape. Sunlight streamed in across him as he squinted at the blinding rays. "It is morning. Thursday morning to be exact."

April tried to sit up, panic setting in. "You're kidding?" *She'd missed a full day?*

Bob dropped the curtain, hurrying back to her side. "Easy! Easy now. Let's not pull out your IV."

"James, where's James?" She mumbled. "I saw him—"

"James who? I'm not sure what you're talking about, April." Bob shook his head.

James, she was thinking of James and wondering why she thought she'd seen him. Her mind was so focused on him, his smile, his eyes, but it wasn't him standing in the courthouse. Kenneth Miles, it had been Kenneth Miles she'd seen. Tears threatened to overwhelm her at the cruel irony. The man she'd feared meeting looked so much like her James. It wasn't fair!

She didn't care if they shared the same lineage. Kenneth Miles was supposed to be an old curmudgeon with a balding pate and an over-sized gut. That's what she'd expected—not a virile man in his mid-thirties who looked exactly like James.

She could have dealt with the image she created. The shock of meeting him and the stunning resemblance was too much for her. It was as if James was there again, and she'd seen a ghost. Now she wished it had been. She felt like hell and didn't want to think anything more about Kenneth Miles. He was not James Addison!

April lay back down, too weary to fight. "Why do I feel like crap? What is wrong with me? "

"You mean besides being exhausted, undernourished,

~ ☾ ~

slightly anemic, dehydrated, and pregnant? Why nothing at all."

Listing the ailments in her fog clouded brain, April didn't hit on what Bob had said, immediately. Did he say pregnant? She was pregnant.

"Pregnant? Really?" She closed her eyes and tried to process the news but succeeded in only having tears seep from under her lashes. "No. Impossible!"

"According to the doctor, about a month or so along." Bob quirked his brow, a small smile playing on his lips. "Who's the lucky father?"

April sighed, shaking her head in disbelief, letting the tears fall. She didn't give a damn anymore who saw her crying. "You wouldn't believe me if I told you." She didn't believe it, and she'd been there. Thinking about trying to explain James Addison's reincarnation to Bob right now seemed impossible. She didn't think she'd be able to tell him the whole story anyway. And how could she get him to believe she'd made love to a ghost?

She laughed at the idea. But the laughter wasn't cathartic. *Congratulations, James, your sperm is immortal.*

"Are you laughing or crying, April?" Dr. Moreland grabbed a handful of hospital issued, rough ply, tissue and handed them to her. "Are they happy tears or sad?"

Truthfully, she couldn't answer either one of those questions. She didn't know what she was doing. Whether she was happy or sad remained to be determined at a later date.

"April?" Bob smoothed a hand over her hair, trying to calm her. "Relax. You're hyperventilating. This isn't good. Come on, relax, and slow your breathing down." He tried to get her to breathe rhythmically. "Remember the techniques we went over when you studied metaphysics? Slow and easy," he said calmly.

She looked up at him with incredibility. She was pregnant with James's baby. And he wanted her to relax? "Screw metaphysics...and breathing. I'm going to puke!"

~ ☾ ~

Chapter Twenty-Six

The mill site was blanketed in white. Pristine snow
covered the fields. A rented sedan parked off the side of the
road just a few feet ahead told her someone else was here.

She wanted to be alone. This was the only place left
where she might have a connection with her ghosts. She
needed them to feel at peace. She laughed silently. Odd
thing to think—needing ghosts to make her happy. But she
didn't feel it. Not like she had. It was just an empty piece of
land now. Her thigh-high boots trudged through the crust
packed snow. The sound of the isolated crunch of her feet a
soothing balm as the open land stood before her. She
followed a set of deep foot prints, wondering who could be
out here. The footprints trailed down over the slope of the
ridge. When she topped the rise, the figure of a tall, broad
shouldered male stood in silhouette against the ridge-line.
Her heart flip-flopped in her chest. Her pace quickened,
fearing the apparition would disappear before her eyes. It
didn't. Dare she hope?

"James?" she called out. Was it really him? The figure, still
a good ways away, turned towards her. "James!" She
squealed with delight, tears clogging her throat. It was him!
She ran but came up short when he didn't return her fervor.
He gave her a strange, eager smile.

"Dr. Branford? I didn't realize you would be out here." The
man held out his hand in greeting. "I thought you might still
be recovering."

This wasn't James, but his look-alike. Her heart sank as
she tried desperately to recover her disappointment. She
wouldn't faint now. It would give Kenneth a complex for sure.
"Mr. Miles. I didn't expect you to still be in town."

"Well, I didn't have a chance to talk with you after you

~ ☾ ~

took ill. I do hope you're feeling better. Dr. Moreland said you'd been exhausted, working long hours to handle my case. I didn't expect you to wear yourself out physically."

He didn't know about her condition. She wasn't showing yet so no need to let on about her pregnancy. Besides, it was too complicated to explain. *Yeah, I'm also pregnant with your ancestor's baby.*

"I had some other family issues I had to deal with. I guess between it all, I didn't take care of myself."

"Ah yes, I heard about your aunt's house, I'm sorry. It must have been very taxing on you." He put his hands in the pockets of his leather jacket. "Since we will be working together, I will make sure it doesn't happen again. I can't have my historical research partner passing out on me during interviews while we are working to restore my...err...ancestor's home. You'll be assigned a personal secretary and assistant to run your errands while in my employ."

"You're restoring the old mill site?" April was taken aback, and then his offer stunned her. "You're hiring me to work for you?"

"Not for me, with me," he corrected. "I'm overseeing the construction process personally. It means a lot to me, and I was hoping we could work together."

"You'll have a full benefits package, a higher salary than what you could receive from the university you'd applied to. I had my people check into it."

He was a cocky, self-assured, presumptuous ass. She didn't care how much he looked like James. He wasn't James. As much as she'd enjoyed the later emails she'd received from him during her research, the man was a bit intimidating and high handed. *He's a billionaire! Of course he would have the traits of a monarch.* Did he assume she would jump at his offer? No matter how good it was?

"What makes you think I'll work for you, Mr. Miles?"

He smiled and his silver-gray eyes twinkled mischievously. *Damn your eyes, Kenneth Miles!* They reminded her so much of James's when he was up to no good.

"I was hoping we'd moved beyond formalities, Dr.

~ ☾ ~

Branford. I wish you would call me Kenneth. This is 2012 after all."

April looked up at him with a bit of shock. "What did you say?" It sounded so familiar. Like when she had told James the same thing during their romantic dinner.

"I said I wish you would call me Kenneth, or Ken. I thought with everything we've been through these past few months we might have moved on to something less formal."

"Everything we've been through?" She didn't want to encourage him to think a few emails exchanged in the name of business meant they had anything more than a professional connection. Calling each other by their given names would be disastrous to her well-being. Having him say her name in the same sexy English brogue as James had used would destroy her.

"I feel a connection to you through James. I don't know if I can explain it." He looked around the wastelands. "What do you see for the mill site? What's your vision?" he asked.

Was he testing her?

This was a safer topic. She could handle talking 'business' much easier than formalities.

"I want to see James's dream brought back to life. He loved the lands, the people who worked for him, the mill, and what it meant to the locals," she spoke softly, her throat constricted with painful emotion.

Kenneth nodded. "I feel James Addison would approve of your vision."

They spent most of the afternoon walking the land, scoping out the foundation of the house, the mill, even the location of Daniel's future home James was going to help him build, just down by the creek where an old willow tree grew.

Kenneth surprised her with an uncanny ability to know where things were. He didn't seem at all what she had expected. Not only did his physical presence shock her, but she'd assumed he would be gruff and demanding. Other than his earlier presumptuous offer, he seemed almost likable. For one of the world's top financial kings, he was surprisingly soft-spoken and quite intuitive.

~ ☾ ~

As they started back to their cars, April couldn't help but laugh.

"What's so humorous, Dr. Branford?"

"You've been reading too many of the letters James sent to his sister."

"Elsbeth's letters?" His brow quirked the same cocky way James's used to. "Why do you say that?"

"They must have detailed all the imagery to Kings Mill. You have an uncanny knack for knowing details about a place gone for so long." April's chin tilted in a challenge.

"Perhaps." He smiled at her. "Or perhaps I have a bit of James Addison in me."

***

James didn't want to disturb April. He'd already pissed her off earlier this afternoon at the mill site when he'd claimed to have a bit of James Addison in him. He hadn't meant to cause her distress. He'd only wanted her to question him on his knowledge about Kings Mill. He wanted to push her buttons to find out who he really was. She either couldn't see it, or didn't want to believe it. He could understand. It would be difficult to explain. But he assumed, she of all people, could grasp reincarnation.

She looked so peaceful, carefully arranging a small poinsettia plant near the block of marble. James approached her quietly, not wanting to disturb her and yet the urgency to be with her, to comfort her, tell her everything would be all right, ate at him.

She kissed her fingertips and placed them on the stone briefly before she stood. He reached out, gave into his impulse, and tugged on her braid. Startled, April gasped and turned to smack him. James reached out automatically, grabbing her arms to steady her.

"James!"

Yes, his mind screamed.

He smiled, trying to get her to smile in return. "I guess I do look like him a bit. His portrait is over my mantle in Sunderbury."

She'd called him James! She'd also called him by James's name as she'd run towards him at the mill site earlier this

~ ☾ ~

morning. She looked down at his hands, still gripping her upper arms. He slowly released her, backing up a few steps, to give her space.

"What are you doing here? Are you following me?" she asked, walking away hastily.

He thought momentarily and frowned. "Matter of fact, I am." He stopped abruptly. "Does that make me a stalker?" He shrugged and picked up his step again. April was walking backward, keeping him in her wary sights, her hands jammed in the pockets of her navy pea coat. This all seemed so familiar; so long ago, and yet only a short time, too.

"Yes. You are a stalker." She pointed out. "If you want me to work for you—"

Mildly hurt and confused he jogged up to her and stopped as she stopped. "Not for me, with me, remember?"

"Tomato...tomaut-o."

"How about dinner? Is it too much to ask? Most women jump at the chance for dinner with me."

"I'm not 'most women,'" April replied.

"No, you're not. You're like no other woman I've met, April Branford. I can't stop thinking about you."

She shied away from him like a fox being chased by hounds.

"Dinner? I promise I won't ask for more than what you are willing to give. Let me prove to you we would be good together, professionally," he added for her benefit. He smiled his most charming smile, trying to get her to loosen up, until he saw her eyes cloud with grief.

"I don't want to go to dinner with you. It's not you, Mr. Miles, it's me. I've been through a rough relationship lately and everything you do just reminds me of him. I don't want to be hurt again."

"I would never hurt you, April," James said softly.

Her name rolled off his tongue like when he'd said it to her in the past. Her eyes glittered with some unspoken emotion. *Come on, damn it! Remember me, April. Give me something to go on, to start the conversation...to give you some clue.*

"He never thought he would either. But he did."

"Maybe he didn't do it intentionally." He shrugged

~ ☾ ~

casually and played his trump card. "We can't control fate. It works in mysterious ways."

Her jaw tightened visibly. *That's it baby, fight me! Tell me how much fate hurts us.* If eyes could shoot fire, he would be burned alive with the glare she stabbed him with.

"Please tell me you don't believe in fate."

"I used to think I controlled everything around me. My destiny was based on what I did, who I associated with. My daily routine was scheduled down to a fine time-line someone typed up for me every week. Until my accident."

"What happened then?"

He took her face in his hands. "An angel saw me and made me real. She woke me from death's door after being in limbo for so long, and I felt like I'd been given a second chance at living a real life. I was given a second chance to be human again, to share it with someone special. Fate knows where we are supposed to be." He wasn't describing the accident in London, he was describing the night they'd met on the ghost tour.

Seeing April's eyes mist over and drop tears down her flushed cheeks broke his heart. She angrily wiped them away with the back of her hands.

"You're wrong! Fate doesn't exist. You're here because of your interest in your past, I'm here because you hired me, and tomorrow I can leave and start over somewhere else, because it's my choice!"

She turned and walked away from him. He would give her space. He didn't have any other choice. She only saw him as Kenneth Miles, even with the subtle hints. What did he have to do to make her see him for who he really was?

***

"What did you do to April?"

Upon walking into the new building for the future visitor center/historical society, James wasn't prepared to be blasted by Dr. Freelane. Very few people had ever cornered him and those who had ended up regretting it. But that was the old him. He knew Beth for what she was, a friend to April and him, but still feeling her way around Kenneth.

He was taken aback, not sure what to say.

~ ☾ ~

"It's bad enough you look like her former boyfriend who died less than a month ago. But now you waltz into her life and do something to hurt her?" Beth crossed her arms over her chest and leaned into the doorway. "What did you say to her?"

"I talked to her about my job offer." He figured it was mostly true and a safe enough topic.

"And she turned you down?" Beth stood up again and sighed. "I'm sorry, Mr. Miles, she's not been well lately. Christmas is in a few days. She lost someone very special to her. And now that she's pregnant with his baby, she's probably an emotional wreck."

At first, James didn't comprehend Beth's full lament over April's situation. The woman let slip April's condition like a nanny sneaking medicine into a dish of pudding. Or it could be his brain, still slow from his accident. But when he finally understood, his heart raced with frantic joy.

"What did you say?"

"Which part?"

"She's pregnant?"

"Um...yeah."

He didn't wait around for Beth to say anything more but ran out the door, sans coat, sans walking stick, hoping to catch April on her way home. They both had some things to explain.

***

April didn't notice the influx of people in the coffee shop. She couldn't believe she'd over-reacted like she had. Kenneth Miles must think her a fruitcake. He was trying to be nice, offering her a job, a simple dinner he'd promised her over a month ago, and she'd jumped down his throat about something as asinine as believing in fate. He didn't understand her situation in the past few weeks, and how fate had screwed her royally. Fate had messed her up so badly her gift wasn't even working.

Taking a sip of her decaf latte with skim milk, she pondered leaving earlier than tomorrow morning to go to Annapolis for Christmas dinner with her family.

"Your usual, sir?"

~ ☾ ~

"Yes, Earl Grey, please."

The sound of the rich English tenor and the distinct order of Earl Grey had April nearly choking on her froth. He sounded so much like James when they used to order their daily cup.

April's breathing accelerated. She needed to get away. No matter how closely he resembled James in looks or speech, Kenneth Miles wasn't James, her James. The sooner she got away from him the better. There wasn't a part of him that didn't remind her of James, and she hated the man, knowing it would never be the same. She'd never experience the feelings she'd had for a few short weeks, ever again.

Afraid of confronting the man and not being able to control her emotions in public, she quietly gathered her things and tried to slip out unseen. She almost made it to the door when her name rang out through the coffee shop. Damn him! She would keep walking, quickly, pretending she hadn't heard him.

But the pounding of feet behind her made her increase her step to nearly a run.

"April May Branford, you can't run from me—it's my baby, too!"

***

April stopped dead in her tracks. James couldn't help but smile. He hadn't intended to blurt it out like he had, but it saved his leg the agony of running down the street after her. He would have, too. He didn't notice the odd looks he was getting from last minute Christmas shoppers trudging up the sidewalk with their bags of gifts. He didn't care.

"What did you say?" April turned to face him, two store fronts down from where he stood, catching his breath.

"I'm not sure. What did I say?" he asked.

"You're an ass, Kenneth."

"So I've been told a time or two." He approached her. Her eyes widened in fear. She was scared of him and he wondered if it was because she'd started to piece things together, or if it was Kenneth's bravado. She was going to run. He needed to do something. "Do you believe in fate, April Branford?"

"Go to hell," she seethed under her breath, her chest

~ ☾ ~

heaving as tears coursed down her cheeks.

"Do you believe in fate?" he asked again. "November 18th, 4:10 a.m. London time I was pronounced dead from severe internal injuries I'd sustained in an auto accident." She was shaking, her eyes wide in disbelief as he knew she understood what he was going to say. "And then I woke up on an operating table. The last thing I remembered wasn't being in London on my way to the airport, it was fighting off a ghost in a burning house."

"No." She shook her head as she tried to deny what he was implying. Not wanting to hear anymore.

He continued on. He needed her to believe. "When I gained conscious thought, I had various recollections of a life as Kenneth Miles, but it was surreal as if it really wasn't my life. My solid memories were of you, your family, and a past I knew hundreds of years ago. My life as Kenneth was still there but only as hazy memories.

"When I saw the paperwork on Kings Mill, everything rushed back to me. I knew I had to return, not for finding my past or retaining the historical sanctity of the mill site, but to be with you. I felt it April. I more than felt it, I knew it! Everything finally made sense to me." He pleaded for her to understand what he was feeling inside. "Fate has brought us together!"

"You're mad!" She spit out as her eyes filled with more tears.

Yes. He was mad as a Hatter but he needed to prove to her he was right. He was James Addison inside the shell of Kenneth Miles. He searched his memories of their time together, frantic to make her see who he really was inside.

"Catherine's ghost saved me during the public event," James said quietly, his smile eager to see her belief, but she continued to shake her head. "You wore my colonial shirt and nothing else while we stayed at the inn. Your grandmother taught you how to dress a cucumber when you were sixteen, I danced a jig for you our first night together at the old elm tree to see if you could actually see me." He ticked off the moments, each one as fresh in his mind as the day it happened.

~ ☾ ~

She shook her head backing away. Her hand went to her trembling lips trying to deny everything. James searched for a sign, something to bring her around, to make her believe in fate, in him.

He found a sign, literally, the jewelry store sign down the street! His last hope to prove to her fate had somehow brought them together. He grabbed her by the wrist and dragged her down the block and into the store, all the while taking a few beatings from her and a couple of odd stares. He even heard someone say to call 911. It would all be worth it if he could get April to believe.

The bell over-head tinkled as he opened the door.

"Hello. Can I help you?" The clerk who'd waited on him in November said, staring at the struggling woman with a curious glance.

"Do you remember me coming in and putting a down payment on a ring?" James asked. "I was playing the character James Addison."

"Yes, it was..." The clerk tried to remember.

"Saturday, November 17th a little after nine in the morning."

The man snapped his fingers, his eyes lighting up. "Yes. I had just opened for the day."

James took out his money clip and placed several hundred dollar bills on the counter. "I wish to finish purchasing the ring." While he waited for the clerk to bring him the small box and envelope, April's struggles ceased, but he still held her by her wrist for fear of her running.

She looked pale, her eyes closed, and her head shook from side to side as she whispered, "This isn't happening. Don't do this to me, please."

It tore at his heart but this would be his only chance to make her see the truth. Hopefully she could put aside her disbelief and find her faith in something magical again.

"Here you go, Mr. Addison."

James smiled at the man's slip of the tongue and took the box, thanking him for holding on to it for him. He was about to open it and get down on his knee when he remembered something important.

~ ☾ ~

He handed the black velvet box to April. "Open it. Inside you will find a ring, an emerald, princess cut stone, surrounded by diamonds."

Releasing her hands he stood back, giving April room. He prayed she wouldn't bolt. Her hands trembled as she opened the hinged box.

"I was going to give it to you on Christmas Eve."

Tears flowed faster down her cheeks as she stared at the ring inside. He ached to enfold her in his arms, kiss her senseless, and ask her to believe in him, if not fate. James didn't want to scare her by moving too fast. He needed her to come to her own understanding.

She opened the note next, and a tiny piece of paper fluttered down to land on the ground.

James read, verbatim, inflecting the emotion and love he'd felt when he'd written the missive over a month ago.

"The emerald represents the fiery passion in your eyes. The diamonds, one for every 'forever' I want to spend with you. The gold band represents how fate constantly circles to bring us together. Fate will always find us when our hearts lead the way. Merry Christmas, my love. Yours for all time, J.A." He bent down and picked up the other small piece of paper, the fortune he'd kept from her fortune cookie. He held up the ends of it for her to read. "April May Branford, do you believe in fate?"

She stared at him for a long moment, tears streaming down her cheeks. She could only nod. Her hand tentatively reached out and touched his chest. His heart beat erratically, hoping she'd make the connection.

"It really is you, James," she finally choked out.

"April May Branford, will you marry me?"

The crowd outside that had gathered to watch the scene unfold waited with baited breath as they watched Kenneth Miles drop to one knee and present the ring to her. But it was James Addison who was staring up at the most beautiful woman in the world, his angel, his savior, his special gift fate had saved for him for two hundred thirty-eight years after his death.

April nodded again and wrapped herself around him,

~ ☾ ~

sending him sprawling on the old hardwood floor of the store. She was crying and laughing. He was unsure where one emotion ended and the other began and he didn't give a damn. She was in his arms, and for once in his crazy existence, he knew this time was forever.

~ ☾ ~

Epilogue

Eleven months later

April held their three month old daughter, Catherine Danielle, in her arms as she watched her husband perform for the crowds. From the front porch of their colonial manor, James greeted the very first guests to King's Mill Historical Gristmill and Manor.

KJM Enterprises had hired nothing but the best to build the site. The rebirth of the legend had been overseen by the only person who could do it justice, the man who'd built it nearly two-hundred and fifty years ago. Nothing was overlooked. It was identical, right down to the grindstone in the grist mill.

Jostling little Catherine in her arms, April listened with heart palpitating pride to her husband's performance. James was the man before her. She knew without a doubt. Everything they shared were moments of their first few weeks together, personified in a body so intricately different but the same in so many ways. It was the heart and soul of the man she loved.

"...Enjoy your day today here at Kings Mill and make sure you frequent our taverns and pubs in town. And gentlemen, give my best to Millie Taylor down at Old Town Tavern..." A series of laughs came from the crowd. April stepped forward and put her hand on her hip, giving her husband a reproachful glare.

"Better yet, give *your* best to Millie. I'm saving my best for my own special ladies," he corrected, giving April and their bundle a gentle, loving embrace.

The crowd cheered and laughed as James doffed his tricorne with a gentlemanly flourish. April curtsied daintily and waved.

~ ☾ ~

The departing guests made their way around the grounds to view the mill in operation, take in the fields being readied for the winter season, and enjoy a sense of simpler days.

"You did a fine job, my love," April said as she kissed her husband and tugged at the tail of hair hanging just past his shoulders. He'd grown his hair out again for her. "Are you ready to go out and give our respects to our friends?"

"Yes. I think we should introduce them to their name sake." April swaddled their daughter close to her as James took her arm in his.

They walked over to the willow tree down by the creek. They'd exhumed the remains of James Addison from the pauper's grave. His remains were now buried in the land he'd loved so much. A proper stone monument honored the body and his past. His grave overlooked the lands and the small cabin they built in remembrance of their friends.

It was part of the land James had given to Daniel upon the end of his servitude. It was now their home, literally. The two-room cabin he and Daniel had designed back in the day would be used as an exhibit as things were added to the site.

A marbled plaque lay in a vegetable and herb garden commemorating the spot, dedicating it to Daniel and Catherine Smith. Without remains to bury, James and April hoped the small cabin would be a symbol of a new beginning for them, after all these years.

April reached down to touch the chatelaine, her direct connection to Catherine. She'd realized her powers hadn't left her when Beth gave her the token, pinning it to her gown as a bridal gift right before her wedding. She'd felt Catherine's presence as she'd held the silver trinket and keys. There was a sense of peace and contentment from the previous owner.

"Do you think they approve? I wanted to make it as close to the design Daniel had for a home. I know Catherine was used to a bit more splendor."

"They love it, just as it is." April fought hard to hold back tears as she watched the young couple wave from their front porch, their arms around each other.

She reached for Catherine Danielle's chubby little fist. "Wave Catherine, wave at them."

~ ☾ ~

"Are they there?" James asked in delighted shock.

"Right there on the porch," her voice broke, and the tears flowed freely, dropping onto the baby's bunting. April readjusted her precious bundle, turning the baby to see her first ghosts. Baby Catherine cooed and smiled as if she actually saw them, a happy spit bubble forming on her little bow of a mouth. April waved at the couple as the ghost of Catherine covered her heart with her hand and waved back to them. Daniel beamed and touched his floppy tricorne in salute to James.

"Daniel is saluting you."

"Is he still wearing that damn ragged looking hat?" James joked. She noted the emotional catch in his throat as he waved back.

"Yep." April laughed, trying hard to keep her emotions from showing. She jostled their daughter happily. A bright light emanating from the small cabin door stopped her. Her heart thudded warily against her chest, knowing what it meant. Daniel and Catherine waved happily once more before turning to enter their new home.

"I do believe fate has finally brought them home where they belong," April sighed in contentment, turning her face into James's side, hiding the sudden spring of tears.

James captured her face between his roughened palms, wiping away the moisture as it fell freely down her cheeks. "Fate only led you to us. It was you who helped us all to move on. You brought them peace after all these years so they could be together. And you gave me the chance to believe by bringing me to life."

She felt the stirring of heat and warmth in her heart heading to warm other places in her body as James kissed her soundly, tenderly, stealing her breath.

Reaching up she caressed his face. "You made me believe by coming back to me when I had no reason to believe in anything anymore." She believed now. He was real. She could touch him, be with him for the rest of their lives, because he made her finally *Believe in Fate.*

~ ☽ ~

ACKNOWLEDGMENTS

There are so many people I wish to thank for helping me on my journey. For the record, no one should travel alone.

For my mom, who always believed in me and took the pencil out of my fingers at night. To all my brothers and sisters and other family members who've been there to support my dreams and cheer me on.

To my friend Betty Ludwig for listening to the idea for Wanted: One Ghost as I scribbled the plot onto a legal pad at our bagel cafe. To Rob Carusone, who 'gave' April the gift of psychometry. To Lisa Sullivan, thank you for being my very first critique partner. Hugs to my Maryland Romance Writer's critique group, *all of you,* who saw the first few chapters, made comments and gave suggestions to put this book together. Thank you to Christi Barth and Amy Villalba for your beta reads. To Eliza Knight for her "Edit Your Book in a Month" class. To the talented romantic suspense author and good friend, Gail Barrett who's been a fount of guidance and support over the past year, I hope to plot like you someday. To my writing angels: Mindy Klasky, Susan Andrews, and Laura Thomson who tutored me on pitches and kept me from passing out when I did them.

To all my friends at Maryland Romance Writers, Washington Romance Writers, RomVets, and Waterworld Mermaids, your continued support and guidance will always be needed. Romance writers are each other's best friends and are always willing to share.

The great people at Crescent Moon Press; thanks for taking a chance on me and my story. To my editor, Judy Roth, who has been so patient and easy to work with, you are the best! I've had a blast, let's do it again.

I wish to thank my daughters, Sarah and Jen, for their creative spirit and for keeping me in stitches with their entertaining dialogue. You are my inspirations! To my in-laws, Cat and Jim, for giving me my own hero, Bill. Your continued love and support are what have kept me going for twenty-plus years. Thank you. I love you.

To my readers, thank you for reading my story. I would like to mention, this is a work of fiction. Any and all mistakes in reference to history or metaphysics are strictly my own doing.

LONI LYNNE

As an author of paranormal/fantasy Loni Lynne believes fate determines her life as well as the lives of her characters. She's managed to live an eclectic life, experiencing various cultures in different parts of the country. From the Midwest to the East Coast, she's been fascinated by the people she's met and the history of each area. She began using some of these experiences as backdrops for her early, penciled stories.

After graduating high school, Loni served in the United States Navy at the US Naval Academy. Upon the end of her tour, she married her Army husband and spent four years stationed in Hawaii.

Returning to the mainland they settled in western Maryland to raise their two daughters. In between volunteering for various organizations and carpooling, Loni constantly jotted down ideas for plots, characters, and turned them into short stories for herself.

One fateful day her husband had seen enough. He noticed the desire in her eyes and the piles of printer paper in the office. It was time for action. Loni's husband bought her a laptop, a portable hard drive, a new printer, a membership to Romance Writers of America, and gave her a challenge; have a book ready to be published by her next birthday. She accepted that challenge and this work is the result of fate leading her on this journey.

Visit Loni at:

http://www.lonilynne.com

CPSIA information can be obtained at www.ICGtesting.com
Printed in the USA
BVOW05s0414100214

344386BV00001B/4/P